D0934746

Mistress
of the
GAME

By Sherrie Walker

This is a work of fiction. The authors have invented the characters. Any resemblance to actual persons, living or dead, is purely coincidental.

Compilation and Introduction copyright © 2008 by
Triple Crown Publications
PO Box 6888
Columbus, Ohio 43205

ISBN-13: 978-0-7394-9813-2

Author: Sherrie Walker
Photography, Cover Design/Graphics:
  www.TreagenPhotography.com
Typesetting: Holscher Type and Design
Associate Editor: Maxine Thompson, Rhonda Crowder
Editor-in-Chief: Mia McPherson
Consulting: Vickie M. Stringer

Printed in the United States of America

acknowledgements

FIRST AND FOREMOST, I thank and give God all the praise and the glory for blessing me with this gift of writing. I know that through him, all things are possible. I also, humbly, thank Mo'Nique, the funniest comedian ever, for believing in me. I love you Mo'Nique. My thanks to Sherry McCovey for your perseverance in helping me to see this deal through. Thanks goes to a special group of friends in, "The Club," Ashanti Pettijohn, Sabrina Flowers, Tina Stewart, Sandy Watkins and my helper, Leslie Thrasher—thank you. I especially and warmly thank my two mothers, Mrs. Erma "Dee Dee" Walker-Hairston and Mrs. Ruth Barnes. Your unconditional love, wisdom and guidance have made me the woman that I am today. You are the ladies in my life. I love and adore you! Thanks and much love goes to my sisters and brothers, Herbie (his adoring wife Yolanda), Gregory (his loving wife Marie), Rayshawn, Alicia, and Jean Walker (husband Calvin Stearnes), Reginald Green, LaShawn and Nicholas Austin. A most special thank you to Margaret Ford-Taylor for your unyielding friendship, support and expertise. Special thanks is given to, Uncle George Nixon, Sonia Thompkins, DeShuna Robinson,

Marla Taylor, Christy Washington, Janice Doakes, Kathy Nichols, Glenda Williams, and Martha Roth for their individual support. I extend many thanks and much appreciation to Cleveland's very own Rhonda Crowder, for your untiring editorial work, passion and commitment. An editor extraordinaire you are. Maxine Thompson, it's been my pleasure making your acquaintance, you are awesome! Vicky Stringer, thank you for this opportunity and for adding me to the TCP family. For this I am grateful. Thank you to Mia McPherson for your guidance and kindness. To my very "Best, Dearest Friend and Partner", *Kecia Green*, thanks for being such a creative force behind this splendid work. You had a vision and a desire to pursue your dreams, and in doing so, your dreams are being fulfilled. May God's grace and mercy guide and protect you always.

Love, Sherrie!!

Finally, I thank my fans. Without you, there would be no success. I love you all and, with your continued support, I look forward to creating good, inspirational reading material for you for many years to come.

one

(1994)

"SEARCH THE ENTIRE HOUSE!" a strange voice barked so loudly that Que and his thirteen-year-old sister LaKiesha heard it upstairs where they stood in Que's bedroom, frozen in fear. "Tear this mothafucka up!"

"Find the money, dope and kids."

Just seconds earlier, Que had been awakened by the blast of the front door being kicked in and his mother's piercing screams. In a flash, he'd darted to LaKiesha's room, woke her up and yanked her out of the bed. Rushing, he led her back into his bedroom. Even though he was only fifteen years old, he knew that the men who had barged into his house were not there for a social gathering with his father, Marcus Hayes. Although his father tried to hide it from them, Que knew he sold drugs.

Looking down at LaKiesha, he knew he had to think fast. He grabbed her hand, barreled over toward the wall, then pounded a button behind the bookshelf. Suddenly a doorway opened, leading to the panic room Que's father had drawn into the blueprints before building the five-bedroom Shaker Heights home. Que snatched LaKiesha inside and punched another button.

Sherrie Walker

The door closed behind them, sealing them off into a hidden room.

"What's this?" LaKiesha said, sounding amazed. "This looks like a space ship."

Que looked down at his sister and felt his heart jerk. He put his arms around her shivering shoulders as she gawked around the room. He walked over to the console and, heart in his throat, turned on a monitor that allowed him to see and hear what was occurring downstairs. Que punched the button to the screen, which had a TV monitor of the entire house. He zoomed in on the living room and looked on as the scene unfolded.

"I gave you all my money, man," Marcus said in a steady voice. His face twitched though. "Let my wife go. She don't have shit to do with this. And my kids ain't here, so you're wasting ya time."

Que watched his father Marcus closely. He could sense his father was worried about them by the way Marcus kept stealing glances at the stairs. Even though Marcus had drilled him about what to do in case of a situation such as this one, Que could see the fear on his father's face each time he furtively glanced toward the staircase.

The burglar referred to as Canine stalked over to Marcus and looked down at him kneeling on the floor. He smiled in a smirk which looked more like a grimace. Without warning, he hauled off and hit Marcus across the head with the butt of his gun. Mrs. Hayes screamed while trying to break free to reach Marcus.

"Dawg, shut that bitch up before she alerts the neighbors," *Canine commanded.*

His partner, Rock, leaned over and pulled her back by the hair then licked the side of her face. He grabbed her breast and

Sherrie Walker

squeezed as she tried to scoot away, then yanked her back by her fine, shoulder-length hair. She cried out from the pain. He then hit her across the face with his gun. She crumpled to the floor. Marcus sat up, looking at Canine with murder in his eyes.

"Do you know who I am?" Marcus asked.

Canine didn't answer.

"Whatever you're getting paid, I can double it," Marcus tried to negotiate. "I can set you up nicely. The shit you came up in here for is peanuts compared to what I can pay you. Let my wife go and I will take you to get the money, man."

Canine looked at his partner, and for a few moments, Marcus looked hopeful. Marcus knew there were very few people who had the heart to try their hand by breaking into his house. He had a strong idea as to who may have sponsored the hit.

"You don't want to do this," Marcus pleaded.

Que watched his mother leap toward his father and he jumped back from the monitor, wanting to go help them.

"Please don't hurt us. Please!" Pearl cried, watching Canine walk closer to Marcus.

Canine looked at Marcus, then slowly pointed the gun at his head. "In fact, I do," he said, coldly. Canine squeezed the trigger and bullets lunged from the nickel-plated nine millimeter, crashing through Marcus' temple. He was dead before his body hit the floor.

When his body slumped, a loud thud resounded throughout the room. Pearl screamed and lunged for Canine. Canine's sidekick yanked Pearl back by her hair and she screamed again as the pain seared through her body. He came down across the side of her face with his gun, knocking her hard onto the floor. As Que watched, he felt anger swell inside of him as he ached to run to his mother's aide.

Meantime, Que jumped back from the monitor and

hugged LaKiesha to his chest. She was shaking, tears cascading down her cheeks. He held her for a few minutes, then he knelt down to speak to her. He grabbed her face and brought it up to his so she could look him in the eyes. "Kiesh, we're going to be all right. I promise. I won't let anything happen to you."

Que looked back at the monitor and watched as the men tore up their house looking for drugs and money.

"We're gonna search the house thoroughly. We're not leaving empty-handed." Canine threw the couch pillows on the floor and, finding nothing, then looked under it.

"Do you think the kids are here?" Canine's sidekick questioned.

"They're supposed to be. That's what da boss said. He should know better than anyone," Canine replied.

LaKiesha started to cry again and Que held her tightly. "I wonder who da boss is. How does he know Daddy?" Que whispered. "Shh, don't cry, LaKiesha. We're going to be ok."

Feeling helpless, Que watched the monitor as the men searched the house from room to room. Both men, going their separate ways, left the room. They left his mother lying motionless on the living room floor. She appeared to be unconscious or dead. Que didn't know which. With tear filled eyes, Que stared hard at the screen, looking for any sign of life from his mother.

At that moment, Que noticed his mother's hand twitch. His breath was caught in his throat as he watched her slowly lift her head and attempt to look around the room. He watched Canine descend the steps going into the basement as his sidekick tore the kitchen apart.

"Get up, Mama," Que mumbled as he watched her slowly sit up, holding the wound on the side of her face.

Sherrie Walker

"Come on, move." Que willed his mother to hurry up before Canine and Rock came back into the living room.

Pearl started to slowly rise up. Que ran closer toward the monitor, wishing he could warn her as Rock was walking back to the living room. Pearl must have heard something, because she lay back down, pretending she was still unconscious. Rock walked over to her and watched her for a few seconds before turning to run up the stairs.

Que let out a gush of air after holding his breath in fear. After sensing the coast was clear, Pearl sat up, apparently trying to detect the whereabouts of the intruders. On shaky limbs, she managed to stand and creep into the kitchen. From the sink she removed a long butcher knife and started for the stairs.

Que was so caught up in what was going on that he never noticed LaKiesha walk up beside him. She started viewing the scene as well.

"What is Mommy doing, Que?" Que turned to LaKiesha as if in a trance. He looked back toward the monitor, trying to think of something fast that would help his mother. He looked at the other screens, trying to locate the two intruders. At this point, Rock was in his parents room, tearing up the closet and Canine was still in the basement pulling up the carpet looking for a hidden safe.

Que and LaKiesha continued watching the screen as their mother crept up the staircase with her back against the wall. Pearl reached the top of the stairs and peeked around the corner looking for the men. As Que watched, he wished there was something he could do. Filled with dread, Que and LaKiesha looked on as their mother stepped into the hallway. Meantime, Canine's partner

Sherrie Walker

started for the door.

Que hit the screen as if she could hear his cry. "Look out, Mama!" Que screamed. It was obvious Pearl heard the robber coming because she ducked into the bathroom just as he stepped into the hallway. He stood there looking down the hallway with his head cocked sideways as if he was listening intensely for any type sound. Hearing nothing, he continued his mission and moseyed into the master bedroom.

LaKiesha started squirming again.

"We have to be real quiet, Kiesh. We gotta wait until these terrible men leave."

"I'm … I'm scared, Que. I want Mommy!" LaKiesha screamed hysterically. Que quickly covered her mouth but didn't cup the noise in time because Rock stopped looking through a closet and spun around. He quickly walked out of the master bedroom and to the top of the stairs.

"Canine!" the sidekick yelled.

Canine appeared at the bottom of the staircase and hollered up. "Yo' Rock … Rock … you find something?"

"Nall! But I could've sworn I heard a child's voice."

"Search under the beds, behind dressers and everywhere. If those kids are here we're going to find them," he ordered. "I'm going back down into the basement."

"What do I do with them when or if I find them?"

"Smoke 'em."

"With pleasure."

"Hey, Rock, make it painful," Canine ordered. Rock smiled and stepped into Que's room.

Que and LaKiesha heard the man come into the bedroom. LaKiesha started to tremble, but Que held her tightly. Holding their breath, both children huddled

Sherrie Walker

closely together. Their fear was palpable. They heard Rock as he entered Que's bedroom, throwing things around. Que didn't realize just how long he had been holding his breath until he released it. His heart was pounding so rapidly in his chest that he wondered if Rock could hear it through the wall. Trying to soothe LaKiesha, Que rubbed her back. Suddenly, everything fell quiet outside the hidden room.

Que was sweating and praying. He felt perspiration trickling down his face. It rolled onto the top of LaKiesha's head.

Que's mind began playing tricks on him as he imagined the man outlining the indentation of the panic room door with his finger, tracing the slight imperfection on the wall which marked the sliding door. He was sure he had found the secret hideaway. As they looked at one another, they recognized that they were thinking the same thing and were overwhelmed with paranoia. In all the years LaKiesha had been coming in and out of Que's room, she had never noticed it. She hoped the man didn't either.

Canine's sidekick sat on the bed after searching the room. He appeared exhausted, frustrated and pissed off. He hadn't found anything to come up on. He picked up a boot off the floor and tossed it against the wall.

BANG!

LaKiesha screamed. Que covered her mouth again and glanced at the screen in time to see his mother exiting her hiding spot in the bathroom. She was inching her way closer to the bedroom. Que scanned the other screens to locate Canine. He was no longer in the basement. In fact, he was walking up the basement stairs.

Canine's partner looked and listened as he got off the

Sherrie Walker

bed and walked toward the bookshelves. He put his ear up to the wall. After a few seconds, he ran his hand along the surface until he discovered an indentation. He followed it, then smiled and stepped back. Slowly, he brought up his gun.

Without warning, Mrs. Hayes eased up behind him with a butcher knife in her hand. She shoved the blade into his back, twisting and turning it before pulling it out. When he slowly turned to face her, a surprised expression on his face, she looked him dead in the eyes, then plunged the knife into his heart. He made growling sounds as he fell to the floor clutching his chest.

"That's for my husband, YOU STANKIN' BASTARD."

While she bent down to extract the knife from his chest, Canine entered the bedroom, ready to release the bullets in his gun.

"Don't even think about it, *Pearly* Pearl," he said as she also reached for his partner's pistol. "I wouldn't advise it. You'll never make it, baby girl." Canine moved in closer and motioned her toward him.

"Now, this can be quick and painless or painfully torturous. I'll leave that up to your *pretty-ass*, Pearl. Tell me where the dope, money and dem brats are, and you won't feel a thing."

Pearl peered into his deep, dark brown eyes. "GO TO HELL."

"Have it your way." He backslapped her and knocked her to the floor. From there, the screaming seemed endless.

Hovering behind the sliding safety door, Que had no choice but to listen to the sick, fleshy sounds of his mother's tortured death. With each resounding blow, his vow

Sherrie Walker

strengthened. He would find Canine and whoever else was responsible and kill them all. He now knew and would always remember Canine's face and voice. As Que held LaKiesha in his arms he heard her whisper, "Please God, stop my mother's suffering and crying."

After two excruciating hours, they finally heard gunshots.

At that moment, they became orphans. In a daze, Que hugged LaKiesha, sensing that she would never be the same. He was left with the sounds of their mother's cries and screams ringing in his ears. There was no one left in his life but LaKiesha.

Sherrie Walker

two

ELISE OPENED HER EYES and looked over at her little sister's mattress, noticing it was empty. *Did Simone go to the bathroom?* she wondered. She glanced at the clock on the dresser and saw that it read 4:30 a.m. The flickering lamppost in front on their house caused her to look out the window toward it. Giving Simone's absence the benefit of the doubt, Elise lay in bed, staring out the window while listening for the pitter-patter of Simone's feet. Simone knew Elise didn't like her using the bathroom by herself. It was too dangerous for a seven-year-old girl to wander around their house in the middle of the night alone. Elise was extremely protective of Simone.

They lived on 89th and Hough Avenue in a big old, run-down, roach-infested dwelling that, at one time, was a baby mansion, but that had definitely seen its better days. Nonetheless, the landlord, Mr. Lee, rented out all nine rooms, thus forcing more than a dozen people to share one bathroom.

They only saw Mr. Lee once a month when he came to collect the rent. Mostly drug addicts, alcoholics and societal rejects called the place home, so it was more like a crack house. Elise's mother Agnes and her current hus-

Sherrie Walker

band—husband number three— qualified as all of the above. Elise's mother told her this house was all they could afford on her social security check.

Although she was only thirteen, Elise was very mature for her age and knew differently. She was aware that her mother had vices. She also knew her mother couldn't afford a better place for the three of them to live because of her heavy drinking and constant crack smoking. The one time Elise voiced her opinion on their living conditions, her mother smacked her so hard on the mouth that she bit her bottom lip. Needless to say, she kept her comments to herself from that moment forward.

Agnes, who now sometimes resembled a walking zombie, was once built like a stallion with chiseled facial features and beautiful, thick, shoulder-length hair. She had been quite attractive before she started drinking and drugging. Unfortunately, over the recent years, the men used her like a punching bag whenever they couldn't have their way, and that didn't make matters any better. But it hadn't always been that way. Her mother hadn't been strung out when she was married to Elise's father.

Then, their lifestyle had been one to be envied and admired. Because Elise's dad was a construction worker and earned good money, they lived in a nice single-family house on Columbia Avenue off Martin Luther King, Jr. Drive. At the time, Elise had her own bedroom with a nice, mother-of-pearl-colored canopy bed, pretty clothes and plenty of toys. Unfortunately, her father went to work one day and never returned. At the young age of thirty-five, he suffered a massive heart attack and died. At the time, Agnes was six weeks pregnant with Simone.

From the moment they pulled out of the cemetery gates, Agnes took her husband's death hard. She

Sherrie Walker

remained depressed throughout the rest of her pregnancy. After Simone was born, things took a turn for the worse.

Agnes started drinking every day and leaving Elise with the responsibility of taking care of the baby. Mr. Green had left a large insurance policy, but Elise's mother spent it so quickly it seemed as if she'd received nothing. A man would pick her up and she would disappear for days. Elise believed that it was during the disappearances that her mother started using drugs.

After watching her mother deteriorate before her eyes, Elise promised herself that she would never use drugs or rely on a man for anything. Instead, she would always be independent. Elise was barely going to school, so with nothing to do during the day, besides take care of Simone, she watched television and read books. She loved to read.

For a few months, the girls actually moved out and lived with their aunt, a loving and caring woman who provided a home for Elise and Simone. Elise was happy and seemed to regain some normalcy in her life. Living at her aunt's house allowed her to go play outside with other children, eat properly and attend school regularly. But, just when she started to develop an ounce of hope, things took a turn for the worse again. Her aunt had a stroke and had to be placed in a nursing home. At that point in her life, Elise gave up on God.

What type of God would allow these things to happen? Elise wondered as they returned to the chaotic turmoil of her mother's environment. Nothing had changed ... only the date.

Shortly after returning to the crack house, Elise's mother had brought home her latest husband, Walter.

Sherrie Walker

Elise immediately disliked him. He was the *ugliest* man she'd ever seen and when her mother proudly announced her marriage to "it," Elise stood disgusted, her mouth hanging open. Walter immediately took a liking to Simone, which didn't sit well with Elise. There was something strange about the way he watched Simone as she played and how he was always trying to get her to sit on his lap.

Elise was taught about men who liked doing perverted things to little girls at school, and his actions fit the description—he had "pedophile" written all over his face. Therefore, Elise never left Simone alone with him. Whenever he called for Simone, Elise would follow and that really pissed him off.

He would get drunk and tell all kinds of stories about people he killed in Vietnam while waving his gun around. No one believed anything he said but Elise's mother. Even Elise doubted his so called "gangsta" stories. She was convinced that he was nothing but a lying sack of dog shit.

Elise looked at the clock again and it read 4:35. She pulled the covers back and slipped on a shoe. She couldn't find her other shoe, and stopped looking when she heard a scream and jumped with a start.

"Nooooooooo!" Simone squealed. Her cry came from a distance.

Elise bolted through her bedroom door, ran down the hallway and burst into the bathroom with so much intensity that the door smashed into the wall, releasing a puff of dust as the doorknob connected with the plaster. The old alcoholic man who lived down the hall was sitting on the toilet with his pants down around his ankles, reading a "*Hustler*" magazine. His legs were spread as far as they

Sherrie Walker

could open and his penis was throttled in one hand. Elise was so embarrassed that she mumbled apologies. He smiled, showing his three rotten teeth. Elise slammed the door and stumbled back to the hallway. She heard another cry and realized the sound had come from the living room.

"Nooo, Lise … Lise …"

Elise rushed into the room and it took a few seconds for the sight to register. Even after it did, she could hardly believe it. Simone was lying on the floor naked. Walter was crouched on his knees, attempting to force his penis inside her mouth. Elise snapped and reached toward the table, picked up his gun and pointed it at his back. In a drunkard's sleep, her mother was lying on the couch just an arm's reach away, yet was oblivious to what her husband was trying to do to her child.

"You will *never* hurt my sister again, " she growled through clenched teeth. Elise pulled the trigger.

PAP, PAP, PAP, PAP, PAP, PAP

Blood splattered over the walls, the furniture, the floor, Elise and Simone. The gun blasts startled Agnes awake. She screamed as she watched Walter fall backwards and slump to the floor, while Elise stood, holding her huband's gun in her hand. Simone ran up to Elise sobbing wildly.

Stunned, Elise realized she had killed a man. Her mother, still screaming, scurried to her man's side and cradled his head in her arms. "Walter," she cried over and over, while rocking him back and forth.

Simone pulled on Elise's pajamas. "Lise … Lise …"

Elise gazed down at Simone and realized that she had failed to protect her little sister. She knelt down and scooped her up in her arms, smothering her with kisses

Sherrie Walker

as they both cried and held each other. "Simone, Simone are you all right. Are you all right? I am so sorry … I am so sorry you were alone. Please forgive me. I love you. I love you and I promise I will always take care of you and love you. Nothing like this will ever happen to you again. You're my very special bay sister and I'm going to see to you always being protected and loved." They were still clinging to each other when the police arrived nearly twenty minutes later, even though the station was less than five minutes away.

Detective Johnson took one look around the room and knew what the situation was. He'd seen it one too many times. He walked over to Elise and knelt down in front of her as she held on tightly to Simone.

"My name is Detective Johnson. Can you tell me what happened, young lady?" Detective Johnson gently inquired.

Elise looked the officer in his eyes, never blinking and replied. "He tried to hurt—molest—my little sister." Simone wrapped her little arms around Elise's neck and buried her head in the fold of Elise's neck.

Detective Johnson looked at Walter's dead body and then at Agnes, who was sitting next to Walter, crying hysterically. Detective Johnson walked over to Agnes to try to get some information for her. "Ma'am, I'll need to ask you a few questions." Agnes looked up at him. Johnson studied Agnes eyes and in them he saw a broken woman. "I can imagine this may be hard for you, but if you'll just cooperate and bear with me a little longer I'll try to expedite this procedure the best I can. Can you tell me what happened here?"

"She killed my husband," Agnes, whose eyes were bloodshot red, blurted out. "That's what happened. That little demon child killed my husband and I want her to go to jail. Get her out of my house, NOW!" Elise heard the words her mother screamed and couldn't believe what she was hearing.

Once again Detective Johnson proceeded with his questioning. "Ma'am, I realize this has been a traumatic ordeal for you and your family, but it's important that we get to the bottom of this. Was he," Johnson pointed to Walter, "hurting and or molesting your daughter?"

"No! Walter would never hurt Simone. He loved her as if she was his own. I want her arrested for killing my Walter." Agnes continued to weep.

Johnson looked at Elise and Simone sympathetically. He turned back to Agnes. "Ma'am, we will be forced to put your daughter in the juvenile detention center if..."

Agnes cut him off and started ranting and raving. At the same time, she rushed Elise and tried to physically attack her. The police intervened and restrained Agnes.

"We are going to have to remove you and your sister from the home," Johnson explained to Elise. He went on to tell her that she would have to be placed in the detention center and why. He assured her though that once a prosecutor and Judge was assigned to her case, he would personally speak with them on her behalf.

The officers escorted them into separate police cars. Walter's body was removed from the scene, Elise was taken to the juvenile detention center for booking, her mother to the Fifth District, and Simone to University Hospital for a rape kit. Simone had held onto Elise's leg and wouldn't let go when they reached the curb and the cars that awaited them.

"Nooooooo ... I go wit' Lise ... noooo ..." Simone cried.

Sherrie Walker

Elise's effort to be strong was weakened. She knelt down and cupped Simone's little face in her hands. "Boo Boo, don't cry. I'll come for you. I promise. I'll come back to get you." Elise fought back the tears. "Please don't cry, Simone. I love you. You remember that Lise loves you, baby."

The police officer picked Simone up and she fought, kicked and cried. While Elise was being placed in the vehicle, her tears began to flow uncontrollably. Simone was in the backseat of one car while Elise was driven off in another. Feeling as if her heart had been ripped out and stepped on, Elise knew that from that moment on, at the age of thirteen, she was about to enter young adulthood *fast*.

As she was driven to her fate, she glanced down and noticed her foot. She gazed up, then back at the house and wondered, *Where's my other shoe?*

Sherrie Walker

three

"HELP ME ... PLEASE ... someone help me. My mother, my father ..." Aparis cried while wandering aimlessly up her driveway. As she watched the orange, yellow and red flames illuminate the night sky, the heat from the blaze felt as if it was frying the hairs on her body. Sweat mixed with tears rolled down her smudged face and with each moment that passed, she grew wearier and wearier. The smoke was so thick in the air that she fell to the ground, holding her breath, hoping not to choke to death.

As she lay there in her backyard, she wanted to get up, to keep going—especially knowing that safety was only a few feet away. She wanted to move, she was daring her body to obey her mind. Just when she felt as if she was emotionally paralyzed and physically drained, an inner strength took over and gave her the boost she needed. Slowly, she started to crawl toward the front of her house. The gravel lying underneath her was scraping her belly as she dragged herself forward. She ignored the throbbing in her abdomen.

Painstakingly, she got up on her knees, wobbled, then stood on her feet. As she staggered toward the front, she turned and looked back. From a distance she saw an

Sherrie Walker

army of ghosts carrying burning crosses. Dumbfounded, she froze in her tracks. Next thing she knew, she heard a loud BOOM! as her house exploded into a ball of fire. Shattered glass flew everywhere with pieces landing in her hair and all around her. She felt a stinging sensation on her face and reached up. She felt something wet; she knew her face was bleeding.

In a trance, she steadily moved toward the street only to notice a few neighbors standing around while others were scrambled in all directions away from her house.

She stopped and looked at the people but no one budged. As she glanced at them, the hatred they harbored became as real as the fiery inferno behind her.

At the tender age of thirteen, Aparis was introduced to a cold, cruel world. How did the night end like this when it had started off as a bright, sunny day?

~ ~ ~

Earlier that day, Aparis had awakened and anxiously dressed so she could meet her parents in the great room.

This was a Saturday, which meant family day for the Nixons. Because she was an only child, and pretty much got whatever she wanted, she always chose a movie and a restaurant on family day. In her father's opinion, Aparis was a Black American Princess in the making. Her father Robert was an attorney, whose brilliant reputation in his craft placed him in high demand. In fact, he was the first African American to partner with a prestigious law firm in the heart of downtown Cleveland. Being the excellent criminal defense attorney that he was, he didn't come cheap.

Standing 6 feet, 5 inches, with a 215-pound muscular physique, her father was handsome. He had a golden complexion with light hazel eyes and thick, wavy hair.

Aparis' mother, Alicia, mixed with Indian and African American blood, was extremely attractive as well. Her silky hair hung slightly past her shoulders, and against her olive skin, but her most striking features were her set of deep brown eyes and high cheek bones. Their genes combined nicely with the results revolving around their very beautiful daughter.

Although Aparis' father was successful, he never forgot his roots and was known for representing people who couldn't afford to retain a private attorney. For instance, he learned that a longtime faithful church member's son had been arrested for a robbery. His mother said he didn't commit the crime and was being railroaded into pleading guilty. The young man had no prior record and a full scholarship to college, but his parents couldn't afford an attorney, so Aparis' father took the case pro bono. He'd proved it was a case of mistaken identity and all charges were dropped. The mother, one of those proud sisters, insisted on paying Mr. Nixon, so they worked out a deal in which she cleaned their house a couple of days a week for six months to pay off the debt.

The saddest times for Aparis were when her parents argued about living in a predominately white community. In fact, they were the third African American family to move into the outer ring suburb, but the other two families moved out after a month of receiving death threats. The Nixons weren't exempt from the terrorizing. They received several threats and even came home to broken windows and racial slurs written on the aluminum siding of their home. Aparis never saw the writings because her father wouldn't allow her on that side of the house until it was repainted. Her mother wanted to move to a suburb on the eastside, but her father was stubborn and was-

Sherrie Walker

n't hearing it. Aparis would hear him scream. Hearing them argue made her sad and she wondered if they would get a divorce.

"NO ONE IS GOING TO RUN ME OUT OF MY HOME. NO ONE!" her father would sometimes yell, so loudly that it felt like his words rattled the house.

He would then apologize and explain that he was a hard-working, tax-paying citizen who was free to live wherever he chose. He would go on to say that he liked the neighborhood because he received more land for his money and wasn't about to allow anyone to impede upon what he was trying to build for his family.

On her street, Aparis didn't have any friends and wasn't allowed outside in the yard after dark. She attended a private school and loved it, but all of her more personal playmates lived off St. Clair, in the Glenville neighborhood where her father grew up. Her father reminded her that it was the home of Superman—one of her favorite comic book heroes. She loved spending time with her friends in the "hood" because they were laid back and fun. She would sometimes go to sleepovers at a friend's house or host one herself, but on most occasions, she entertained herself or played with her poodle, Gatsby.

For the family day activity, Aparis chose to watch the movie *"Forrest Gump,"* and to have dinner at Pier W, her absolute favorite restaurant. She loved their seafood platter, which included calamari and fried jumbo shrimp. As she looked up toward the kitchen, she saw the server approaching with their entrees. After the servers placed everyone's plate on the table, Aparis and her parents bowed their heads as Mr. Nixon said grace. He believed in praying before doing anything.

Sherrie Walker

After dinner Aparis stared out across Lake Erie while her father settled the check. With a full stomach and an absorbing day under her belt, she couldn't wait to kick back in the car for the short ride home and dream about her future, which had been mapped out just prior to her entering pre-school. She was clear on what she wanted to do and become in life.

"So how's your science project coming along, honey?" her father asked as he peeked through the rearview mirror at his growing daughter with prideful eyes.

"I'm not sure, Daddy," she responded, looking out the window at the beautiful tree lawns along Lake Boulevard. "I'm still learning CAD so it's taking me a little longer than I expected when I initially took on this challenge."

"You're a straight A student, you'll ace it, I'm sure," he declared.

"Don't let it stress you, Paris," her mother added. "If it becomes too much, let your teacher know that you may need a tutor before it's too late to get help."

"She doesn't need a tutor when she has a brilliant father," he boasted.

Alicia playfully hit him on the shoulder. He maintained control and cut a smile at his wife.

"Uh huh, she'll mess around and fail, 'cause if my memory serves me correctly, you barely passed science class, *Robert*. Child, don't fool with your daddy." Her mother laughed.

Aparis laughed also, but in her mind she was thinking, *I will do my best. Anything to please my parents. I love pleasing them and getting their praises.*

After entering the house, Aparis made a beeline to the entertainment room and played video games. Her father

Sherrie Walker

went into his study and began reviewing notes in preparation for his trial, which was to begin on Monday. It was a high-profile case involving a white woman who was carjacked. Although she fully cooperated and turned over all of her possessions, the culprit shot her anyway. Apparently, she was the wife of one of Cleveland's most beloved white businessmen.

Nevertheless, Robert believed the district attorney didn't have enough substantial evidence to convict his client, Mr. Dobb, who had priors, but continuously professed his innocence. Aparis' father sensed that Mr. Dobb did not commit the robbery but was the perfect patsy. His criminal record was long as a Conrail pulling commercial cars.

Robert was to argue his case before Judge Stearnes, one of the meanest on the bench. The Stearnes family had Cleveland's criminal justice system on lock down. Most of the males in the family were either state or federal judges. Knowing that cold justice would rule harshly, Mr. Nixon advised clients who sincerely professed their innocence to take it to the jury box. He was confident he could win over the hearts of twelve citizens as opposed to one born of class and privilege, never knowing anything less.

Robert retired to his study and Aparis took Gatsby outside to pee. She referred to him as her guard dog, although she knew that he was anything but a protector. Gatsby barked like crazy if someone walked past the house. He would climb in the chair in front of the big picture window, woofing his little head off. But the minute someone placed a foot on the foyer floor, he would run for cover. Mr. Nixon bought the adorable, white miniature poodle featuring one big black eye, for Aparis' second birthday and she fell in love with him on sight.

She took him outside and watched as he ran toward his favorite tree in the back yard. He heard something in the bushes and ran back to Aparis whimpering. She laughed.

"Some watch dog you are, Gatsby." She looked in the direction he ran from and didn't see anything. "Silly little scary dog. Nothing's over there but a squirrel."

Gatsby continued to snivel, and Aparis shook her head as they went back into the house. She flounced back into her father's study and kissed him goodnight, then headed upstairs to take a quick shower before going to bed. As she prepared to put another Saturday to bed, Aparis' mother entered her room to say goodnight.

"I love you, Paris, baby. You'll always be Mommy's little girl."

"I love you, too."

"Sleep with the angels," she said.

"You, too, Mama. Night night."

"Goodnight," her mother replied after she turned out the lights and padded down the hallway. Aparis noticed that she forgot to close the door but was too tired to get up and do it herself. She didn't want to call her back, so instead, she began to say her prayers and fell fast asleep before she could say *Amen*.

At approximately 4:00 am Gatsby's barking startled Aparis, but she couldn't seem to focus her eyes. She jackknifed up in the bed and looked around, but it was pitch black and she was disoriented. Suddenly, she smelled smoke. She jumped out of the bed, then stumbled into the hallway. Blinded, she realized the smoke seemed thicker in the hallway, causing her to cough and gag. She managed to find her way into her parents' bedroom. She

Sherrie Walker

couldn't make out the shape under the comforter but it looked like it was just one person, so she continued to approach.

"Mama ... Daddy ... something's burning!" she screamed as she approached the figure. Her mother's silhouette became apparent. "Mama, get up, get up." Aparis shook her awake, but she was disorientated as well. "Wake up, Mama. I smell smoke." She continued shaking her. "Ma!"

Her mother finally woke up out of her smoke-induced slumber. "Where's Daddy? Oh, my God! Robert! Where's Robert?" she questioned, frantically looking around the room. "Come on, baby."

She leapt up and grabbed Aparis' hand. Together, they ran out the bedroom door and toward the stairs, but a raging blaze was crawling up the staircase, so she pulled Aparis back in the direction of her bedroom to exit the house from the second floor deck, which had stairs leading into the backyard. They coughed and tried to catch their breath as they reached ground level.

"I wonder why the smoke detectors didn't go off?" said Aparis. "Where's Daddy and Gatsby, Mama?"

Her mother looked back toward the house and could hear Gatsby barking. "Stay right here," her mother commanded. "Do not come back into the house, Paris. No matter what! You hear me?"

Aparis nodded her head as her mother kissed her sweaty forehead then turned and ran to a window. She peered through it and saw her husband on the floor of his study with Gatsby barking and running in circles. Alicia quickly found a brick and smashed it into her kitchen door window to gain entry into her home.

Trembling, crying and full of fear, Aparis stood and

stared at the many windows on the back of the house as red, orange and yellow flames illuminated the rooms. Several minutes passed. Panic consumed Aparis and as her fear increased she began to pray like she never prayed before. "Dear God, please let my mom and dad be ok and Gatsby, too. Please, God."

In a trance, she steadily moved toward the street only to see some neighbors standing around, while others scrambled in all directions away from her house.

"Help me ... please ... someone help me ... my mother, my father ..." Aparis cried, wandering aimlessly. She stopped and looked at the people, but no one budged to help. As she glanced at them, the hatred they harbored became as real as the fiery inferno behind her. It became evident as she peered into the windows of their souls.

Then, Aparis slowly turned toward her house and the hatred slapped her in the face one more time. She saw what her father had tried to hide. Written in red paint across her father's silver Mercedes were the words she knew were responsible for their home going up in flames, for causing her parents' death. They were words she would never forget: DEATH TO ALL NIGGERS.

Sherrie Walker

four

St. Agnes' Orphanage was situated in the Tremont area of Cleveland. The gracious two-story Victorian house was built in the late 1800s and provided 4800 square feet of living space to include 3 and a half baths, a basement and an attic. On the exterior, St. Agnes had an ominous, Gothic appearance. Composed of gray bricks and cathedral shaded windows, it looked sinister. The reconstruction of the five bedrooms that were combined into two dormitories was the only modification the interior appeared to have received.

The girls slept in very close quarters. Every girl had her own dresser but shared one of the two large closets.

They all shared the living quarters of the foyer, the large living room, the common area where they watched TV or played board games, the spacious kitchen and dining room. The staff had their own offices and rooms where they slept if they worked the night shift.

St. Agnes provided shelter for 20 young girls, 10 to a dorm, who were orphans or children who had been removed from troubled homes.

The name on the sign in front of the edifice read "St. Agnes' Orphanage," but the residents referred to it as

"St. Agnes' Prison for the criminally insane." The "criminal" referred to the staff, while the "insane" referred to the blossoming girls who endured emotionally damaging torture as a result of being wards of the State.

Aside from food and shelter, they were provided bare necessities and half the time, Mr. Harden, the abusive assistant director, didn't want to give the girls that. He relished in seeing the young girls suffer, which stemmed from his evil, sick, sadistic nature. And Mr. Tool, the resident manager, wasn't any better.

Nine months prior to Elise's arrival at St. Agnes, she had been remanded to the juvenile detention center, pending indictment for the murder of her stepfather, Walter. As her case moved toward a grand jury hearing, Detective Johnson, who took a personal interest in the case, kept true to his word to help Elise. He pleaded the fact that she had been pushed to do the unthinkable, criminalized by a crime of passion, induced from the will to save her younger sister whom Walter was molesting. Simone had been sexually assaulted and the hospital records proved it.

Detective Johnson knew he had the power to help Elise, and did so. Johnson used his influence and clout to persuade the prosecutor, his wife's uncle, to dismiss the case. All charges were dismissed against Elise, but her joy was shattered when Detective Johnson informed her that she would not return home because her mother was charged with child endangerment and was declared unfit, which caused her to lose custody of her children. Agnes was sentenced to probation with stipulations.

If she wanted to reestablish custody, her mother had to admit herself into an in-patient drug rehabilitation facility, successfully complete the program, and attend

Sherrie Walker

counseling sessions at Cocaine Anonymous meetings and parenting programs. The court order, in turn, made Elise a ward of the state. She remained in the Cuyahoga County Juvenile Detention Center until further placement. Shortly after the court hearing, a bed became available at St. Agnes' and Elise was placed in the group home. There she met LaKiesha who was her bunkie. They immediately bonded and became the best of friends.

Very few people wanted to take on the challenge of one teenager, let alone two. Therefore, LaKiesha and Que were immediately separated upon entering the foster care system. Even though they hadn't seen one another since their separation, they talked regularly because on Saturday mornings between 9 and 10 a.m., LaKiesha's assignment was to clean Father Boris' office. During this time, she was alone and was able to make and receive phone calls from Que. Their code was, if he called during this time and she wasn't alone she, of course, wouldn't be able to answer the phone, and if someone else answered, of course, he knew to hang up.

On one beautiful, sunny, summer Saturday morning as she was tending to her chore and dusting Father Boris' bookshelves, the phone rang and she immediately snatched it up. Before speaking, LaKiesha listened cautiously for a voice.

"Hello … hello," Que said.

"Hey, Que. What's up, bro'?"

"You got it baby girl. Listen, I called to let you know I'm 'bout to dip the fuck up out this spot."

"What! What you mean you 'bout to dip? Dip where? Where are you going?" LaKiesha began to panic.

"Calm down, baby girl," Que cut her off. "I got you.

But, I got to bounce from this spot *now*. It's full of drama and the so-called people who run it got issues fo' real. Kiesh, they barely feeding me, let alone putting clothes on my back, despite the hefty checks they receive for allowing me and six other kids to live under their roof. I'll be better off on my own."

"What. It's like that? You never told me all that, Que!"

"Baby girl, that ain't the half of it. Truthfully, all they gave us was an address and a house to be in, because it surely ain't no home. Then to top it off, the state wanted the foster parents to perform major home repairs to the inside and outside of this old raggedy nasty ass motha-fucka!

"All winter was spent cleaning out the basement and painting the interior. But, now it's done got warm out-side, they want us to fix the roof and paint the house. When they said they wanted us to lay cement in their driveway that was the straw that broke the camel's back. That's when I decided enough was enough. These moth-erfuckas straight crazy fo' real tho! They reaping all the benefits, and we ain't seeing a dime, not jack! Yet we're being worked like the runaway slaves that got caught.

"Fuck that, I'm out. The state no longer has to be overburdened with me. I'd rather fend for myself than be subjected to this version of modern day slavery. I got enough of our Dad instilled in me to make it. He taught me well how to be an independent and responsible man. Now, it's time for me to exercise all that he taught me. I didn't need you worrying about me with what you going through over there so that's why I thought to call and fill you in on what my mind is made up to do."

"Where are you going? How will you take care of yourself? Well … well, how will I talk …"

Sherrie Walker

"Listen, you got a pen. Write this address down."

"Hold up," said LaKiesha, as she scanned Father Boris' desk. She didn't see any writing tools so she opened the top drawer then shuffled her hand through the clips, staples, pieces of paper, business cards and sets of keys and other miscellaneous items scattered around before finding a pen. Then, she removed a sheet of paper from the legal pad that was neatly placed on top of the director's desk. "Go ahead."

"Eighteen-fifty-five East 55th, Apartment D. Here, take this number, too." Que paused.

"Ok."

"Three-nine-one-one-nine-sixty-four. That's my dude Trey's number. Soon as I get straight I'll have my own. Sis, I got plans, I'm 'bout to put some shit down out here so I can raise us up fo' real. You just hold on a little longer, but soon as you can, get at me, ok."

"Ok, I will. In fact, I'll call you at that number, and two weeks from today I'm going to try and come see you."

"Aight. Look, I'm outta of here before they get back. Mr. Foster Father will try to be on some strong-arm shit and I don't want no unnecessary static. I love you, Kiesh."

"I love you, too." LaKiesha ran back to the room to tell Elise about her phone conversation.

After Que hung up, he grabbed his one bag with all his worldly possessions in it, marched out the house and didn't give looking back a second thought.

He hooked up with Trey, his childhood friend. Trey told Que about a spot "down the way" where he could rest his head and make a little money. Que knew the spot he was referring to and wasn't comfortable with the

Sherrie Walker

thought of resting on a grungy sofa in a strange apartment with unfamiliar, ghostly-looking people constantly walking past or standing over him. Instead, he convinced Trey to contribute half on an old house where they could temporarily reside and step off operations.

~ ~ ~

Que wanted LaKiesha to come "down the way" to the King Kennedy Projects where he started his workday, even though he was on no one's payroll. So for two weeks La Kiesha planned, prepared and waited for this Saturday to roll around. Finally the day arrived.

Even though the brother and sister spoke regularly, LaKiesha could barely contain herself. The very thought of seeing her brother was a happy and long awaited moment. Standing next to Elise, she anxiously jumped from foot to foot as they waited for the bus.

When the Regional Transit Authority's number 14 pulled up, LaKiesha and Elise hopped on, found a seat and chatted all the way to the location where Que hung out. LaKiesha talked about Que to Elise quite often, so the chitter-chatter about Que was something that she was already immune to.

"Elise, I'm soooo excited."

"Ooowee, like I can't tell." Elise smiled.

"Can you believe I'm about to see Que? I did tell you he said he's going to get enough money and raise me up out of St. Agnes', didn't I? Gurl, I'll be so glad when that time comes. I can't wait to be out that bitch. And you're coming with me when I leave."

"Uh huh. Yeah, you told me, gurl. But, LaKiesha, Que won't be able to afford to take care of all three of us. I'm savvy enough to make my own money, and I will. So don't worry about me."

Sherrie Walker

LaKiesha jumped up and pulled the string, alerting the driver that she wanted off at the next stop. "We're here, Elise. Let's go, baby."

~ ~ ~

They exited the bus at 55th and Woodland and waited to meet Que at the Jesse Owens Post Office. In the meantime, Elise listened, providing several nods and automatic utterances as LaKiesha rattled on and on until the moment when she finally saw the fine, dark-brown brother she had been talking about. *Damn! Mr. Goodbar. I feel like chocolate tonight!* He most definitely had the power to attract and was unquestionably easy on the eyes. Seeing him made Elise think, *All that talking LaKiesha's being doing about her brother, the heffa didn't tell me he put the capital F in fine. Ump, ump, umph!*

Que looked like chocolate thunder. He had the smoothest, prettiest cocoa brown complexion she had ever seen. Although he had on an oversized white T-shirt and baggy Sean John jeans, she could tell he had a well developed muscular body underneath his clothing. With more waves than a sea's shore, Que's hair was gorgeous, but his most striking feature was displayed when he beamed his beautiful smile, offset by the dimples that deepened when he spoke. His swagger was a sexy stride; his slightly bowed legs swayed as he approached the girls. Once he spotted LaKiesha, Que hollered out her name. "LaKiesha … Kiesha."

She immediately recognized him and took off running in the direction of her big brother's voice. She shot into his arms in a playful manner and gave him the biggest hug she could muster. "Oh, my God, Que … Que, it's you. I've been living for this moment. I am sooooooooooo happy!"

Sherrie Walker

"Me, too, sis." He lifted her perfect petite frame and spun her around, like they were caught up in a whirlwind.

Meantime, Elise watched them embrace and closed her eyes for a moment and fantasized. *Umph! What a pleasing vision for my sore eyes. If he ain't a sexy treat I don't know what is. Whoa, whoa, whoa!*

"Que, this is my friend, Elise, the one I told you about," LaKiesha said,—collecting herself. "Elise, meet Que."

Que spoke but Elise was stuck, unable to put two syllables together, let alone a sentence. Elise, who sensed he was waiting to hear her say something, was so mesmerized that she couldn't get passed a silent *duh*.

"What's up, slim?" Que spoke, staring into Elise's eyes. "My sister told me good shit 'bout you. Thanks for looking out for my blood, fo' real."

Elise didn't respond. She simply smiled as she stood there, still stuck on stupid, because she had instantly fallen in love with her best friend's brother. *Ok, let me do the math. He's seventeen and I'm fifteen. Oh, well, so what. I like it that he's older. Gives me more reason to live by Aaliyah's motto, "Age ain't nothing but a number."*

Que, LaKiesha and Elise hung out by the Boys and Girls Club on Bundy Avenue, then trudged through various sections of King Kennedy, which was broken into sections by color. When they reached the section called "The Blues," Que made several business transactions while the girls sat on a bench watching little children play with anything and everything but toys.

To her right, Elise noticed a couple kids with pop cans on the heels of their sneakers, making a click-clacking sound while their feet went through motions as if they

Sherrie Walker

were tap dancing. On her far left, she turned to watch two children playing on a makeshift seesaw made out of a giant barrel with a long piece of wood in the middle that they rocked back and forth on, steadily at that. Her front view was of a small group of boys playing basketball while using a milk crate as a basketball hoop. Elise looked around at the run down tenements. Some of the buildings looked like they were or should've been condemned. The windows were broken out in many of the apartments. Empty beer and wine bottles, syringes and crack vials were strewn everywhere. "This shit is crazy." Elise commented as she shook her head, looking around.

"My sentiments exactly," LaKiesha agreed.

Once Que was done, he joined them on the bench and counted his money. He handed LaKiesha several dollars and told her to put 'em in her pocket.

"Like I said, Sis, soon as I'm up, I'm gone get you outta that place," Que told LaKiesha as they stood to walk toward the old, small shopping center called The Plaza to grab something to eat from the Muslim restaurant. They set at one of the six round tables in the restaurant and Que ordered them each a Fish Boy sandwich, two pieces of cat fish topped with cole slaw, French fries, and BBQ sauce on a wheat bun, with a cold beverage and a thick, rich slice of bean pie for dessert.

"Yeah, Kiesh, like I was saying earlier. I got some people who gon' help me get a condo so you'll be able to come stay with me. That's why I'm grindin', so we'll have somewhere decent to stay."

LaKiesha looked bewildered. Elise looked puzzled as well, but with interest. Elise perked up, leaned in closer to the table with both hands on her chin, listened intensely and clung to his every word. The thought of making fast money appealed to her. To capitalize off of it doubled the appeal.

"Do you feel bad selling drugs to these people, Que?" LaKiesha asked.

"Not a little bit! I got to eat, too. Nah, let me back that up … on the fo' real, I do have a conscience, but right 'bout now, I can't let my conscience get in the way of my come up. Hell, I'm not trying to live like this for the rest of my life. I'm gon' rise up out this shit. I'm a baller. I gots to stay down fo mine. With da' roll I'm on, it won't be much longer either. And you can come, too, slim." He looked at Elise and exuded gratitude.

"Why can't I come stay with you now?" LaKiesha asked.

"'Cause I ain't gone have you staying just anywhere, especially not in no damn crack house, Kiesha. Rollers could run up in there at any unannounced moment. Just on a whim. Then what, you be jacked up. Nawl, that ain't gon' happen," he explained. "Men are supposed to grind it out. So be patient, let me be that man and grind this out for us, ok."

Que paid the check and they left the restaurant. LaKiesha and Elise followed Que, as he left King Kennedy to make his way toward Central Avenue. The average person would have walked north along East 55th Street, but Que was headed in the opposite direction. However, there was a method to his madness. They crossed East 55th to enter the Outhwaite Projects, the second public housing unit to be built in the county. With his final destination being his central location, a stash house on a side street between Central Avenue and Cedar Road, he made several transactions before leading the girls toward the Carver Park units, then zigzagging through a few back streets and alleyways.

It was hard for Que to walk for several minutes straight without being stopped by a customer. "Hey, cuz, you straight? Let me holla at ya." Que and dude stepped to the side as he served the fiening customer.

As he turned to catch up with LaKiesha and Elise who continued walking while he satisfied his customer another guy trotting up the street as if he was about to miss his ride, hollered out, "Yo, yo, yo ... hey, cuz ... hold up. you got that thang."

"Yeah, hurry up though dude, I'm 'bout to roll out." Que stopped in his tracks and once again took care of his business.

"See how business is booming fo' me. In a few months I'm gone have these jets sewed up and on lock down. If they're looking for a quick fix or 'a beam up to Scotty,' I'm gon' meet their demand with a nice supply. I'm going to do it bigger than Nino Brown, Cleveland style. Watch what I tell y'all."

Elise watched, studied and quickly developed a deep infatuation for Que's business mind. At a young age, she recognized that he was on top of his game, in addition to hearing others refer to him as "master rock" along their trail. She was intrigued and incredibly interested in becoming part of his world.

Once they reached the house, Que pulled out his cell phone to call a cab, and while waiting for the taxi, Elise spoke. "What time is it?" she inquired.

"Damn, slim, I was wondering if you could put a sentence together."

"Actually, I can put two or three together. I just choose to listen and observe before speaking."

"I can respect dat. It's about 5:30. So, what's up with

Sherrie Walker

you? Can I get in yo' business for a sec? I hear you hold yo' own down real swell. How is it that you coming up?"

"I'm into retail sort'a speak." Elise smiled. "They make 'em, I take 'em. I hit my licks boosting. Feel me?"

"Oh, yeah. Mm hmm … Interesting! Well dig, depending on what you get, and if you're interested, I got some customers who might want to cop what you snatch off yo' moves," Que continued.

"I feel you. That'll work."

The cab pulled up and Que approached the window to pay the driver then directed him to take the girls to their destination.

"Kiesh, we're not going to be victimized by living disastrous. I'm on a mission and it's to bring us … you and I … up and out this shit. You just be easy and let me work my hand."

"I love you, Que. Be good, ok? Or better yet, if you can't be good, at least be careful." She smiled.

He hugged his sister, opened the cab door, said goodbye to Elise, then watched them pull off.

During the ride back, LaKiesha wasn't the only one rattling on about Que. They both bounced Que compliments like Venus and Serena in a warm-up match. But like Serena, Elise served hers with more style and finesse than her sisterly opponent.

As she unwrapped a piece of gum and put it into her mouth Elise asked, "Kiesha, do you believe in love at first sight?

"Not really."

"Gurlll, well, I do and I am," she said, " I just met and fell in love with your brother." For the umpteenth time, she popped her gum. In between a pop she caught herself when she remembered her father saying it was unla-

Sherrie Walker

dylike to chew gum in that manner, especially in public. To be sure she didn't pop it any more, she put it in the ashtray. "He's going to be my husband," Elise continued as she watched LaKiesha laugh it off, until LaKiesha saw that Elise was not joking.

"Are you serious?"

"Is that a trick question? Yeah, I'm serious. Watch what I tell you. That fantasy is going to be my reality. I love him already. He's going to be mine."

"Well, shit, we're sisters anyway. So I can roll with that."

Sherrie Walker

five

"DID YOU CALL APARIS to see if it was cool that we come over?" Elise asked.

"Yeah, she said it's OK. Aunt Garnett has already left for work."

Elise directed the driver on how to get to Aparis' aunt's house. Aunt Garnett used to be a nurse at St. Agnes, but now worked twelve hour shifts at The Cleveland Clinic hospital. She was fired from the orphanage for reporting abuse, as well as filing a lawsuit for sexual harassment. She worked at the orphanage for eight years and had the chance to work with and help LaKiesha and Elise for the last year and a half of her employment there.

Aunt Garnett was the first person LaKiesha and Elise encountered when they entered St. Agnes'. The sweet, attentive, compassionate, childless woman took an imme-diate liking to both Elise and LaKiesha. Shortly after their meeting, she taught them about feminine hygiene and their menstrual cycles, which started simultaneously. She took time to get to know them; she was their comfort zone and they opened up to her. Their stories reminded her of Aparis. They were all young girls surviving this

Sherrie Walker

great big world without their parents due to tragic deaths.

Elise, LaKiesha and the other children at the orphanage loved Aunt Garnett. She was the only one who really cared and showed compassion when the girls would tell her about the abuse taking place in the orphanage. She listened to the different girls who lived in the group home because they all had intense stories to tell, especially when the plot was driven by the same characters she worked for every day—the very same men who sometimes gawked and made lewd remarks that were embarrassing even to her grown ears. When she would tell the director, Father Boris, what some girls mentioned to her, he brushed it off as hearsay.

When Aparis' parents died, Aunt Garnett immediately assumed custody, then adopted her, because there was no way she would allow her only sister's child to grow up in the foster care system.

Aunt Garnett was a short, hefty, boisterous woman with a round, pleasant face and a good sense of humor. When she smiled, it appeared as if there was a twinkle in her eyes. Her salt-and-pepper hair was medium-length, and she spoke her mind to whomever she was addressing. Sometimes she was liked for this gesture; sometimes she wasn't. She did a lot of fussing which led people who didn't know her to believe she was mean. However, she was really tender-hearted, soft as a marshmallow and most times, her bark was worse than her bite. Aunt Garnett was dedicated to helping others, especially children who were victims of circumstances stemming from some adult's negative choices, which was why she took the job at St. Agnes'. Her spirit was compassionate and she had a desire to provide the less fortunate with hope and a meaningful life. And a friend.

Aparis was just thirteen when Aunt Garnett adopted her and even as a youth she exuded independence, maturity, direction and drive, despite the fact that she lived a sheltered life when her parents were alive. Aparis was blessed with beauty and brains. She was a straight A student and felt a B was not an option. She wanted to finish school and attend college to become a computer engineer. She was quiet and spent the majority of her time reading. Anything related to computers and technology interested her. If she wasn't reading she was exploring, familiarizing and teaching herself about the technology of computers and stereos and how they worked. She loved and welcomed the challenge of figuring things out. Aparis loved pastel colors and was a stylish dresser, took pride and detail when selecting her clothes, and possessed a serious fetish for shoes. Aunt Garnett would tell LaKiesha and Elise about Aparis all the time and they looked forward to meeting her.

When Aunt Garnett she was fired a year and a half after Elise and LaKiesha arrived, she slipped her phone number and address to Elise before her departure. Aunt Garnett wished she could take them home with her, but knew she couldn't without cutting a lot of red tape. "Call if y'all need anything," she whispered in Elise's ear before leaving the home.

Two weeks later, Elise and LaKiesha had dinner with Aunt Garnett and Aparis, who instantly bonded with the girls. From that point on, Aunt Garnett's home was open to Elise and LaKiesha whenever they wanted to eat, bathe, rest, hang out, or simply get away from St. Agnes'.

Unbeknownst to her, Aunt Garnett gave the girls what they needed in order to maintain hope during

Sherrie Walker

moments of despair. Elise and LaKiesha would spend a lot time at Aunt Garnett's because it felt good to be in a comfortable environment once again. Plus, they preferred hanging out with Aparis as opposed to being cooped up at Agnes'.

They spent a lot of time in Aparis' bedroom. It held a warm and cozy atmosphere and became their sanctuary and meeting place. The walls were painted in soft pastel hues. Aparis' bedroom was full of all the latest games, videos and electronic gadgets on one wall that she bought with her monthly allowance, and a computer and stereo system on the opposite wall with a poster size picture of 2Pac and TLC.

Her bed was a four poster, white canopy frame, accessorized with tie-back drapes that matched perfectly with the décor. Her bedroom window had a view of the backyard and pond at the end of the yard. Her carpet was so plush that when you walked on it your feet automatically sank into its cushion.

They would lay across Aparis' bed and talk for hours about their dreams, goals, likes and dislikes. Although they were confronted with tragic situations at a young age, they were strong in their own right, yet their ambitions in life were different as night and day. Elise was the rebel, the thinker of the three. She didn't wait for things to happen, she created her happenings. She was savvy and always thinking of ways sneak out of the orphanage and make money. She mastered ways to manipulate and trick the staff. The desire to go to college wasn't in her. Yet, her desire was to become an entrepreneur — to organize and manage enterprises at that. And she was a romanticist. She definitely wanted love, marriage and a baby in her life. She had an undying passion for reading and would pick a good book over a good movie any day.

LaKiesha was intelligent, excellent in math and wanted to attend college for financing as soon as she finished high school. They would meet at Aunt Garnett's house and discuss their future plans. They clicked from day one and it was like they had always been together.

They were hurting emotionally over the loss of their loved ones, yet knew they had to get on with their lives. They all wanted the finer things in life, wanted an education, successful careers, families. Elise found Aparis to be extremely intelligent and enjoyed her collection of books. Aparis enjoyed going to school, wasn't into drugs, had ambition to attend college, was obsessed with fashion and had the wardrobe to prove it. They all were fashion divas and had the bodies to wear whatever. Aparis always made them feel welcome to anything she had.

In a short time, they developed a bond that was unbreakable, which they referred to as "three the hard way."

Aunt Garnett's house was also a great place for Elise to stash her stolen clothes since no one lived there but her and Aparis. There were enough clothes already there to open a flea market, so Elise's clothes fit in unnoticed.

LaKiesha and Elise went to see Que almost every day after school. They would come in, change clothes, complete their chores and leave out. Elise was able to step up her boosting game from merely clothing herself to servicing others, so she got her first taste of entrepreneurship. Que would get the young honeys and his dudes who hung out around the Jets to buy her merchandise.

Elise tried to give Que some clothes, but he would always pay for what he got. She tried everything she could think of to be more than a friend to him, but he'd

Sherrie Walker

always laugh and reason that she was too young and was like a little sister.

At fifteen Elise knew who she wanted and was determined to have him. She kept trying to find cracks that would allow her to slip into the chambers of his heart. She made absolutely sure her appearance was always pretty and eye-catching. But Que didn't bend, not unless one of his boys approached Elise or LaKiesha. Then he would have a stone-cold fit, running whomever it was out of their faces.

For four-and-a-half months LaKiesha and Elise traveled to Que's stumping grounds. They excitedly thought about and looked forward to the day they would leave the orphanage and never return. Seeing Que operate within his element gave them hope, but on this particular day as they approached Que's spot, they noticed the windows were boarded. The one on the door had a red dot on it while yellow and black police tape streamed across the front porch. Both girls stood speechless, trying to figure out what was going on as Que's best friend, Trey, walked up.

"Trey, what's up?" Elise watched him approach.

"Police ran up in there last night," he explained. They caught my boy wit' dope and a hotty."

LaKiesha appeared puzzled. "What's a hotty?"

"A gun."

"My brother is in jail?"

"Yeah. Shit ain't looking good, yo. I'm on my way to 22nd right now to see what's up, but y'all know shit's different in da juvie system."

"Damn," Elise commented sadly as LaKiesha began crying.

"Why? Just … when things were looking up … getting right, Elise," LaKiesha continued to sob.

"Come on, Kiesh. We better head back."

Trey wrote his number down and handed it to Elise.

"If y'all need anything just let me know. I got you. Call me in the middle of the week and I'll let y'all know what's up wit' my nigga." Trey reached in his pocket and handed them several folded bills. "Be up, catch a cab."

"Thanks, but we straight. We'll call you Friday." Elise hugged LaKiesha as they walked away with broken hearts and shattered dreams.

At that point, Elise started stealing more and more so she could secure an apartment for herself and LaKiesha. She was determined to stack enough money to get them out of the orphanage because the conditions were becoming utterly ridiculous. The mental, physical and sexual abuse and screams at night were driving Elise crazy. It was like they were helpless and no one would listen to or believe them.

Mr. Harden was becoming more sadistic with his punishments by locking the girls up in the isolation room for hours or sometimes a day or two. There was mention of locks being put on the dormitory doors, which was definitely a fire hazard. For supper last week, the crust of the bread had mold on it; the bologna between the bread smelled spoiled, and the pea soup was cold.

Elise was at her wits end and knew they had to get out of there soon. She knew that getting someone to rent an apartment for her wouldn't be a problem. Having enough money was her main concern, so she hustled with a vengeance, stealing men's suits and fencing them. On a good day she swung five to ten suits and earned nice money fencing them to an old pimp-turned-fence named Pretty Ricky. Why they called him pretty was

Sherrie Walker

beyond her logical mind because in her eyes, he was anything but. He would pop game and tell her old pimp stories while reviewing the merchandise. But she wasn't trying to hear that antiquated garbage.

"Pimpin' ain't dead," he often chimed.

Whatever, Elise would think. His ability to purchase her goods at her price was all that mattered to her, so she could save and move.

"I'm going back! I ain't done pimping, pimping is hard work. I'm just taking a break. But once I stable up with a couple two, three tenders, I'm gon' be back in action," Pretty Ricky declared. "Watch!"

Please. Elise couldn't begin to imagine any prostitute who would give this simp her hard-earned money.

six

THREE MONTHS AFTER QUE was arrested, he was given a four-year sentence. LaKiesha cried herself sick when Elise told her. They kept in touch with Trey the whole time and he informed them of everything when it came to Que. Almost on a daily basis, LaKiesha and Elise wrote letters to him. Elise would tell him she loved him and was waiting for him. He would ignore her promises and would respond with everything but what she wanted to hear. Elise ended each letter with, *One day we'll be one.*

Because Que was seventeen with previous convictions for possession of drugs and would be turning eighteen in a matter of weeks, and now with two F1 felonies, drug trafficking and possession of a firearm, the judge sentenced him as an adult. After Que went to jail, LaKiesha didn't leave the orphanage as often with Elise anymore. She slipped into a state of depression and would just mope around after school, writing Que, doing her homework or reading.

Elise would make her go out sometimes, but rather than press her, she would leave her alone most of the time. She hated seeing LaKiesha in that state and tried

Sherrie Walker

to do whatever she could to make her happy.

Six months after Que was sent away, Trey caught a possession of drugs case and was incarcerated and sent to the same joint as Que. Trey would send greetings to the girls in Que's letters and wrote Elise a few times, but she didn't bother to respond. Instead, she would just tell Que to tell him that she said, "What's up."

~ ~ ~

The majority of the girls in the orphanage liked and admired Elise and LaKiesha, except Selena Gonzalez. A sloppy, evil, fat Puerto Rican girl, she just could not stand Elise. Her dislike was rooted in a jealousy as green as artificial grass. There was no love lost between the two until Selena told Mr. Harden about Elise sneaking out every night, which led up to the Linda Blair incident.

One night Elise slipped back into the basement window of St. Agnes' and changed into her pajamas. She made her way back to the room and opened the door, knocking Mr. Harden, the midget master, on his ass. The girls gave him that nickname because he was short with a huge head. It took him a minute, but he managed to pick himself up. He stood with his legs spread apart and his hands placed on his hips. Everyone except Selena, who stood next to Mr. Harden, was afraid to move.

"Busted!" Mr. Harden screamed with an evil leer on his lips.

"Busted what ... busted who? I was in the bathroom."

"For six hours?"

"I had diarrhea," replied Elise with a straight face, while the girls in the background giggled. LaKiesha sat on her bed a nervous wreck.

"She wasn't in the bathroom, Mr. Harden," Selena

Sherrie Walker

exclaimed as she looked at Elise with a snide, sneaky grin. "I checked the bathroom three times. You've been sneaking out for the last six months, Elise."

Elise mean-mugged Selena, giving her that "I'm going to get you bitch" look.

"Thought I wouldn't find out, huh?" Mr. Harden asked.

"With snitches like Selena over there, I guess you might hear anything." Elise looked at LaKiesha who stood on the sidelines looking as if she could shit her pants any moment. Elise had to take her eyes off LaKiesha. Otherwise, she was going to bust out laughing. *LaKiesha is so damn scary.*

"I want you to report to the isolation room, young lady." Mr. Harden turned around and walked toward the door, then stared at Elise as an evil smile crept up to the corners of his mouth. "In ten minutes—be there."

Unspeakable, haunting things occurred in the isolation room. The isolation room was a small, dreary, mildew-smelling room in the corner of the basement. The ceiling was cracking and when it rained outside, it leaked. At night you could hear mice running across the floor. A dim light bulb inside gave off shadows, frightening most little girls.

Gawking at Elise like she was dead already, the other females stood quietly once he exited the room. Plenty of beatings and abuse took place in there and it was said that some people had been left in the room for days at a time, coming out a nervous wreck and jumping at every little noise and movement. Elise walked over to face Selena and spoke to her barely above a whisper.

"Selena, payback's a bitch and you will get yours. But, first things first," Elise unleashed a verbal threat as

Sherrie Walker

she walked over to her bed, gathering items and placing them in a bag. She took her hair down and shook it loose, which left it wild looking.

LaKiesha approached her. "Elise, he's going to beat you. You have to leave here and go to Aparis' house."

"I ain't scared of no Harpo. You told Harpo to beat me," replied Elise, imitating Sofia in *"The Color Purple,"* while pointing her finger at Selena as if it was a gun. Elise cracked up laughing at LaKiesha, who stood at her side, nearly in tears.

"This ain't funny, Elise. You have to run, please."

"I ain't leaving you here, LaKiesha. When I leave, you leave, and we're not financially strapped yet. I'll be ok. I have something for Mr. Harden." Elise continued gathering her items and finally walked to the door with LaKiesha in tow.

"What are you going to do, Elise?"

"Scare the shit out of the midget. Watch, I'll be back," Elise said, imitating Arnold Schwarzenegger. Elise smiled and went out the door. She hurried down the hallway, turned left and went down three cement steps into the basement. She walked past all the doors then stopped at the last door on the left and entered the isolation room. *Good, he's not here yet.* She set her plan in motion.

"Do you think he'll hurt her?" one of the girls asked.

"He's going to skin her alive," Selena answered, smiling.

"Elise is going to beat your ass, Selena," another girl warned.

"She won't be beating no one's ass once Mr. Harden is finished with her. Say goodbye to your friend, LaKiesha. She won't be sitting pretty no mo'."

Sherrie Walker

"You fat, ugly, garlic-bean-and-rice-eating bitch," LaKiesha spat. "Elise will get out of this like she does everything else. Trust and believe!" Just as the words left LaKiesha's mouth there was a scream so loud and piercing it caused everyone to freeze.

"You hear that?" asked someone.

"Yeah, I heard it," answered LaKiesha as she ran to the door and swung it open to peer down the hallway.

The rest of the girls piled behind LaKiesha and tried to see what was going on. Mr. Harden, screaming, ran past them with the front of his shirt covered with green gook. Frantically, he attempted to brush it off as he ran and screamed. He passed them and never looked their way.

"Oh shit. What the hell was that about?" LaKiesha whispered as they looked in the direction Mr. Harden had run. The girls didn't see Elise as she came up the hallway because they were so absorbed in what was going on. She jumped in front of them and they all screamed and took off running back into the room. Elise's eyes appeared to be protruding, her hair was wild and green bile covered the front of her gown. LaKiesha ran into the room and slid under her bed, leaving her feet sticking out from underneath. Elise walked in and saw them, seized the moment as well as LaKiesha's ankles, and fell on the floor laughing hysterically at LaKiesha's squeal.

"I don't believe y'all," she laughed while removing the eyeballs and wiping the cosmetic bile off her face. "Y'all a bunch of chickens. You should've seen Mr. Harden though. I scared the shit out of him. I don't think he'll be bothering us anymore."

LaKiesha scooted out from under the bed and hit

Sherrie Walker

Elise in the arm.

"You play too damn much. Where did you get that stuff? What did you do to Mr. Harden?"

"Girl, I steal all kinds of shit. I picked this up at the costume shop for the hell of it. And it worked, too. I scared the bejesus out of Mr. Harden."

LaKiesha was tickled. "I would have paid to see that."

Elise held up a tiny camera and smiled.

"How much?"

"Oh, hell nah."

Elise smiled and looked at Selena as she sat on her bed with a disappointed look smeared across her face.

"So you wanna tell, huh, Selena?" Elise challenged.

Selena mustered all the fake courage she could to bluff Elise. "I'm not scared of you, Elise."

"You don't have to be scared, but you betta be aware."

~ ~ ~

A week later, LaKiesha and Elise were lying around playing cards when a package arrived for Selena. She ran into the room with a beautiful box of chocolates, showing off the package as she danced around the room.

"Who sent it?" one of the girls asked.

"One of my secret admirers," Selena lied. She had no idea who sent the chocolate-covered confections, but she made sure to walk past Elise and LaKiesha so they could see her delights.

"Isn't this pretty?" Selena bragged.

"It's aaight," Elise replied. "You going to share your goodies with us?"

Selena made a face and walked back to her bed.

Sherrie Walker

"Why should I?" she asked while stuffing her mouth. "I only share with my friends, and I don't have no friends in here. I came by myself and I'm leaving by myself. Fo' real, I don't like no one up in here."

"You are so selfish," Elise replied.

"Whatever." Selena sat on her bed and ripped into the box as Elise sashayed over to the door carrying a chain she had stolen just for that moment. She wrapped it around the door handle, removed a lock from her front pocket, and attached it to the links of the chain, pulled tightly on it one last time while smiling mischievously, secured the lock then tucked the key in her bra. Everyone watched her except Selena, who was so engrossed in her candies that she wasn't paying any attention to what was going on outside of her box. When Elise strolled back over to the bed and plopped down, LaKiesha observed her suspiciously since she had developed a knack for determining when Elise was up to something.

"Why da' hell you chaining us up in this piece?" LaKiesha asked. Elise didn't answer, but she maintained a sly smile on her face as she watched Selena gorge herself.

"Just wait and find out. Go on, shuffle and deal the cards. Just let me cut this time ok … you always seem to conveniently forget."

Elise and LaKiesha continued to play cards. It almost made Elise sick to watch Selena gobble up the candy. *She's just an overindulgent pig.*

Suddenly, Selena grabbed her stomach and doubled over. She tried to stand but the cramps knocked her back over. She lay in her bed writhing. "Oh my … I … I think … I … I was poisoned. Someone … help me …"

Sherrie Walker

All the girls sat up in their beds to observe Selena.

"Help … please … .help …" She jerked off the side of bed then walked toward the door holding her stomach only to realize there was a chain on it and it was locked. She spun around and her eyes landed on Elise. "Open … the door."

Elise stood up and began feeling in her bra, looking around, down at the floor and underneath the bed. "Damn. I seem to have misplaced the key."

Selena screamed and doubled over further. "Pleeeeeassse …"

LaKiesha looked at Elise with pleading eyes while Elise merely rolled hers and smiled at Selena.

"You said you didn't have any friends, right? So who do you think is going to help you?"

Just as soon as the words escaped Elise's mouth, there was a loud rippling sound as Selena released. Her bowel movement ran like water down her legs. She let out another loud sound and fell against the wall and slowly slid to the floor, stinking and crying as Elise laughed.

"Please … I … have … to get to the bathroom. Please," Selena cried.

"Elise, please let her go. That's enough," LaKiesha pleaded until Elise looked at her and stopped laughing.

"You a big old wuss." Elise sneered and rolled her eyes at LaKiesha as she walked over to door and unlocked it. "Get on my nerves sometimes."

Leaving a trail of funk behind, Selena took off running down the hallway. She turned to face LaKiesha and the rest of the girls in the room. "See what happens to snitches? Let that be a lesson."

Elise walked over to the bed then lay across it. She

Sherrie Walker

picked up the Puzo classic she had been reading and flipped to her book mark, having become intrigued by Michael and Kay's story, but her mind kept drifting as she tried to read. She saw visions of Simone, remembering the last day they were together and the promise she had made. Elise lived to fulfill her promise. She awoke and went to bed with the desire to find Simone. *I must and I will,* she thought then closed her eyes and envisioned a happy reunion.

Sherrie Walker

seven

THREE WEEKS LATER, on a Saturday night, Elise was sneaking back into the orphanage. She climbed through the window, went to the bathroom and changed into her pajamas, then made her way through the basement and up to the room, undetected. Immediately, she knew something was wrong when she stepped inside the dorm. LaKiesha and Selena were hugging each other crying and the other girls were huddled together as well.

"What's wrong?" Elise questioned. LaKiesha ran over to her crying.

"Mr. Tool took Tabby to the isolation room because she wet the bed. We tried to stop him, but he knocked Selena down and threatened me."

Elise looked at Selena and saw the ugly bruise on the side of her face. Elise and Selena had their differences but after the chocolate incident, they buried the hatchet and now maintained a cordial disposition toward one another.

Elise knew how much Selena loved Tabby, who had just arrived at St. Agnes'. She took an instant liking to the cute little girl when she was placed into their dormitory. Selena named herself in charge of feeding and bathing

Sherrie Walker

the three year old. She spoiled Tabby. In fact, everyone did.

As a result of suffering from malnutrition, Tabby was under-developed for her age and weak. But she managed to follow Selena around most of the day. She had even started calling her "Mommy." Apparently, Tabby was found sitting alone in a car at the Lake, and no one could find her mother. Some suspected her mother may have jumped in the lake and left the baby behind. Elise looked at Selena and saw a sad puppy with green eyes.

Mr. Tool was known to be a sick, twisted pedophile that got off on raping very young girls. Up until Tabby arrived, everyone in their room was a teenager.

"How long have they been gone?"

"About fifteen minutes," LaKiesha responded. "What are we going to do?" LaKiesha, standing next to Selena, tried to figure it out.

Elise dashed over to her bed, reached underneath it in a swift swoop, and removed an aluminum baseball bat that she hit against her the palm of her hand to test its strength. All the while, she bit her bottom lip as she controlled her rage. She spun around on her heels, then started for the door with the bat in her hand. Selena trotted and caught up with her, grabbing the mop out of a bucket of water. She removed the handle from its head and held the stick up like a cavalier on a mission.

"I'm going with you."

They stood, staring at each other, until Elise nodded her head. Together they stalked toward the door heading downstairs to the basement, to the last door on the left where the isolation room was located.

"Wait, I'm coming, too." LaKiesha reached down, grabbed her pillow off the bed and removed it from its

Sherrie Walker

case. Elise and Selena gave each other a perplexed look as if to say, *What the hell is she is going to do with a pillowcase?*

LaKiesha walked over to a small, old, rusty cabinet against the wall where supplies were kept. She opened it and proceeded to fill the pillowcase with bars of state soap. After it was about a quarter full, she marched toward the door with them and they all left out, making their way to the isolation room. They walked silently. When they arrived at the door, Selena turned the knob and pushed, but it was locked. She signaled for them to step back and she kicked it open with the first attempt.

They rushed into the room and everyone stopped in their tracks. They saw Tabby tied to the bed and Mr. Tool lying beside her naked, with a video camera pointed in their direction. He looked up at the girls and scrambled to find his clothes as Tabby lay naked, scared and crying. Instead of seeing Tabby, Elise saw Simone. Her little sister who she hadn't seen since the system separated them over two years ago.

She thought about Simone and the last time she saw her and her heart began to ache. Having no idea where Simone was, Elise vowed to find her once she left the orphanage. Flashing back to the infamous night when she walked into the living room and saw her stepfather raping her little sister, she stood before Mr. Tool, trembling with rage and anger.

Selena let out a scream that shattered Elise's thoughts and snapped her back into what was occurring at that moment. LaKiesha jetted over to the bed and untied and covered Tabby as Selena ran over to the bed and started hitting Mr. Tool with the stick. As Mr. Tool tried to wiggle into his pants he fell to the floor and tried to cover his body. Selena continued to hit him over and over while

LaKiesha secured the entrance and Tabby. Elise swung the bat, striking her target, which knocked the air out of Mr. Tool. He attempted to crawl toward the door but Elise cracked him over the head with the piece of aluminum. She was beat him like an area rug hanging over a clothesline and Selena joined in, swinging the mop stick. Mr. Tool's body slumped against the wall, limp and nearly lifeless. The crunching sounds were like music to Elise's ears as she clobbered the bones in his legs.

"Stop. You're killing him!" LaKiesha screamed. She ran over to them with a crying Tabby in her arms and grabbed Elise's arm before she could swing the bat again. Elise and Selena stopped and looked at Tabby who was scared and crying uncontrollably. They slowly brought down their weapons and looked down at Mr. Tool who lay in his blood.

"Let's go, we have Tabby."

Tabby reached for Selena, who slowly took her from LaKiesha and smothered her with kisses as they both began to cry.

"Let's get her back to the dorm," Selena said.

Everyone headed for the door and Selena kicked Mr. Tool one last time before walking past him. "Hold up," Elise replied as she ran toward the video camera and removed the tape. She held it up for them to see. "This is our insurance."

They left the room, returned to the dorm and gathered around Tabby. Selena examined her body. A bruise was on the side of her face and her wrists and ankles were red and swollen, but there was no sign of blood between her legs.

"I don't think he had time to do anything," Selena said.

Sherrie Walker

"We interrupted him before he got started," LaKiesha added.

"Thank God," Elise responded.

"He won't be raping anyone else for a long time. I tried to beat him all across his pathetic-ass dick, I don't know how many times," Selena interjected as she gave Tabby a piece of candy. They sat around the room talking and planning for a long time after everyone turned in for the night. Elise left to take care of some business and to prepare for what was coming next.

~ ~ ~

Two days later, Father Boris, the director, summoned Selena, Elise and LaKiesha to his office. As he sat in his large leather chair awaiting their arrival, confusion yet sympathy was written all over his face as he looked at Mr. Tool in his bandages and casts.

"I can't understand why you don't want me to call the police, Mr. Tool. These young ladies committed an assault and should be arrested for what they've done to you."

Mr. Tool lowered his head, feigning repentance, playing on Father Boris' sympathy. When he lifted his head there were tears in his eyes.

"Father Boris, I agree, they should be locked up. But, these young girls are lost and their souls are in jeopardy as it is. We have to pray for them and try to help them, Father. That's the whole purpose for St. Agnes, is it not?"

As Father Boris looked at Mr. Tool with a newfound respect, there was a knock at the door.

"Come in," instructed Father Boris.

When Selena, LaKiesha and Elise entered, they saw Mr. Tool bandaged with one cast on his arm and another on his left leg. He tried to look pitiful and innocent,

Sherrie Walker

which pissed the girls off more since they knew he was not the victim he portrayed. Elise smiled angelically as she watched Mr. Tool. A nun sat next to Mr. Tool and fussed over him, making sure he was comfortable. She had discovered him moaning in the isolation room the morning after the beating and had called for an ambulance. Every now and then she would cut evil looks in the girls' direction.

"Have a seat," Father Boris offered.

"We choose to remain standing," Elise responded.

"It's been brought to my attention that you young ladies are responsible for Mr. Tool's injuries."

"True," Selena answered.

"My only regret is that we didn't finish his sorry ass off," Elise added. The nun clutched her chest and Father Boris cleared his throat.

"Well, then, you leave me no choice but to call the police. You girls have committed a crime and that will not be tolerated. And, Ms. Green, with your record, this won't look good at all."

"I'll take my chances. In fact, I invite you to call the police. I would love to tell them about what goes on behind St. Agnes' closed doors at night. Better yet, I'll contact *The Call and Post*. I'm confident they won't turn a deaf ear. The media will expose him and as we know that the public doesn't take kindly to child molestation."

"What nonsense are you speaking? Molestation. What do you mean? Nothing like that happens here. You think the police will believe such a far fetched lie?"

"They will once they see this tape." Elise took the VHS out of her inside jacket pocket and held it up. "We know you aren't aware of the nighttime activities that go on here, Father. This is why we are giving you three

Sherrie Walker

things that you must do to ensure the safety of these children. We're tired of the bullshit and we're willing to go as far as we deem necessary with this."

"Mr. Tool was disciplining Tabby Wright. You had no reason to do what you did."

"Is that right? Well, do allow me to show you how your staff disciplines the children here, Father." Elise walked over to the TV/VCR combo and turned it on while putting in the tape. While the tape was being programmed to play, she watched Mr. Tool as he shifted in his seat several times with a worried look on his face. Elise loved watching him squirm.

The screen was blue for a few seconds, and then the show began. Mr. Tool walked into the isolation room with Tabby in his arms, then threw her on the bed and aggressively removed her nightgown and panties. With one hand, he held her flat on the bed as he tied her feet and wrists to the post. He removed his clothes and stood there massaging his irregularly small penis while smiling. The nun vomited in the midst of making an unsuccessful attempt to run out of the room. Father Boris looked away from the television screen.

"Turn it off. Please!" Mr. Tool's eyes were big as cereal bowls as he nervously gazed from the director to Elise. No one spoke until Elise turned the TV off and placed herself in front of Father Boris. All three girls stared at Mr. Tool who shamefully dropped his head and eyes to the floor.

"I didn't know!"

"We know you didn't, Father." As Elise watched him, it seemed as if he aged ten years before her eyes and shrunk down into the large chair. "We have to come to an agreement, Father. I know you don't want this to leak to the press. It would not be good. There are more copies of this tape safely tucked away."

"What do you want?" Father Boris asked dejectedly.

"First, the removal of Mr. Tool and Mr. Harden."

Father Boris snapped his head up and looked at Elise, appalled. He pointed to the television. "Is he ... is Mr. Harden doing ...?"

Elise's voice remained chilly. "Not rape, but he's extremely abusive to the children here. For no reason are these monsters to be given a recommendation. None whatsoever. Second, LaKiesha and I will be leaving this place in a couple days. But we'll continue going to school until we graduate next year. However, we don't want to be reported as having absconded or AWOLed. So, fix the paperwork. Whatever you have to do, do it. Just make it happen."

"Where will you go? How will you live? If something happens to you I will be held responsible."

"Nothing will happen to us, I promise. Third, allow Selena to take care of Tabby, and if it can't be arranged, make the arrangements for Tabby to leave with her."

"I cannot promise that one because if her mother returns looking for her, I have to give accountability. However, I will allow her to take care of her with no interference until we see what happens with her mother."

"You need to make more rounds, Father Boris, be more attentive and know what's going on in your house," LaKiesha said. "Listen to the kids around here—all of them ain't bad. They'll tell you what's wrong if you just take the time to listen."

"After this, young lady, I will be more diligent. This will never happen again. I assure you."

"That's fair enough. We'll send you the rest of the

Sherrie Walker

tapes after we leave. It will probably be around the end of the week."

"How will I know I'll have *all* the copies?"

"You won't," replied Elise. What you have is my word. If you keep your end of the bargain, we'll keep ours. Don't worry about that sack of shit sitting next to you. If he opens his mouth about anything, this tape will wind up in the hands of some people we know, and he'll wish he was dead by the time they get through with him. Take it or leave it."

Father Boris was silent for a second. He stood, then extended his hand to Elise. They shook hands. "I feel sorry for your enemies, young lady," the director uttered. He looked down at Mr. Tool. "I resent the thought of letting a scumbag like Mr. Tool get away, but it seems necessary if the school is to remain open."

LaKiesha and Selena walked out of the door. As Elise reached the door she turned and smiled at Father Boris. "Who said he got away?"

eight

TWO AND A HALF weeks later, after Elise and LaKiesha exposed Mr. Harden and Mr. Tool, everything seemed to fall into place. Elise and LaKiesha collected their belongings, left the orphanage in a taxi and headed straight for Aunt Garnett's since they were sure she would allow them to stay at her house until they made other arrangements.

The house was located on Shakespeare Parkway, off of Martin Luther King, Jr. Drive. It was an elegantly decorated brick house with five bedrooms and two-and-a-half bathrooms nestled in the heart of Cleveland near the Rockefeller Cultural Gardens. It featured a huge finished basement and third floor, as well as a spacious backyard and redwood deck with a beautifully manicured garden. Elise loved the house because it reminded her of the one she'd lived in before her mother became overwhelmed with addiction.

As Elise and LaKiesha rode in the back of the taxi, Elise peered out of the window looking up into the gray sky and suddenly felt a sense of impending doom. As the taxi driver sped along Martin Luther King Drive her mouth became dry and she felt like she was suffocating

Sherrie Walker

for no apparent reason. Her mood became black as she sat back and closed her eyes trying to figure out why her attitude had suddenly taken a dive. It was LaKiesha's grip on her arm and gasp as they got closer to Aunt Garnett's that made her eyes pop open with apprehension.

There were two police cars in the driveway. As the driver was coming to a stop, Elise put a twenty dollar bill in the tray, asked the driver to set their luggage on the porch, and jumped out of the car and took off running toward the house. They bounded up the steps onto the porch as two officers were leaving. Aparis was standing in the doorway with her housecoat, slippers and rollers in her hair, crying.

"Aparis, what's wrong?" LaKiesha asked. "What's going on?"

"My ... Aunt Garnett is ... dead," Aparis sobbed.

"Oh my God! What! What do you mean she's dead? What happened? How?" The questions flooded from Elise's mouth.

LaKiesha immediately embraced Aparis. Aunt Garnett had been her second mother. She was the only person the Nixons had trusted to continue to nurture their princess, as well as properly manage Aparis' trust fund and execute the wishes they had blueprinted for her. Aunt Garnett's legal guardianship had been set in place to assure Aparis remained on course rather than cursed.

They walked into the house and sat on the couch with LaKiesha on one side of Aparis and Elise on the other. Aparis tried to explain the incident to her two friends as the officers had explained it to her upon their arrival. "Aunt Garnett," she said between sobs, "was on her way home and was driving too close to an eighteen-wheeler. It jackknifed and slammed her car into the wall at Dead Man's Curve. She was killed on impact. About three other cars were involved … her car was totaled … they had to pry her body out." Aparis continued to cry hysterically and her friends tried to console her.

"What are we going to do, Elise?" Aparis cried. "We're sixteen, high school juniors. If the Department of Family and Children Services get wind of me not having legal guardianship they are going to take custody of me. Aunt Garnett was the only person I had left. Why…"

"Listen, Aparis this is very emotional and tragic for us all. But, try not to fall apart. Give me time to think and I'm going to come up with a plan to keep us together. I promise! We are not going to be split up."

LaKiesha started pacing back and forth while at the same time twisting a strand of her hair. "Do you have something in mind, Elise?"

Elise sat in deep thought for a few minutes before responding. She looked at Aparis. "Yeah, I was thinking … you do know to make contact with your Uncle Wayne, don't you?"

Aparis blew her nose. "You talking about under-cover-dope-smoking Uncle Wayne? Aunt Garnett's step-brother?"

"Yeah, under-cover-dope-smoking Uncle Wayne," Elise reiterated. "He may like to take a little hit here and there, but right about now we can use him and he's about the only one that I'm convinced will come through for you. He's nonchalant, always willing to help someone, and doesn't ask a thousand questions. And, when there's money involved he's twice as nonchalant and willing to help. So my thought is, if he's not on one of his binges,

Sherrie Walker

perhaps you can proposition him with a nice piece of change to fake taking custody of you. Meaning, he'll go to The Department of Family and Children Services before they come to you and claim his interest in wanting to establish and provide you with legal guardianship. Despite his little vices, he manages to keep a steady job. So, that's a plus. He can prove employment. He can also state that you, he and Aunt Garnett lived in the house together. So you and him both would be comfortable with the arrangement. All you have to do is give him the script, he'll follow it. He's been around enough to know your ability to take care of yourself. He knows you're mature and smart enough to survive without adult supervision.

"On a couple of our visits, I heard him comment to Aunt Garnett on how mature, independent and responsible you are. He'll be all for it, I betcha! He can kill two birds with one stone. Attend Auntie Garnett's funeral and assist you in a matter that can easily be resolved with his kind assistance."

"Ok, but I can't do it just this second. I need a little time to get myself together and ingest all that's happening. First thing tomorrow, I'll call and see if I can connect with him. In fact, I won't stop until I do. Besides, I was going to have to make contact with him anyway to inform him of Aunt Garnett's passing."

Aparis attempted to stand, before she could complete her effort, Elise gently pulled her back down. "LaKiesha, stop pacing and com'ere." Elise took both their hands. "We're going to get through this and I promise I won't let anything split us up. I'll die before I let that happen. Do y'all trust me?" Elise looked at Aparis who nodded her head and smiled weakly.

Sherrie Walker

Elise turned to LaKiesha. "I trust you with my life, Elise," LaKiesha sincerely replied.

"Three the hard way is going to stay down for theirs. Now give me some." Elise brought her fist up and placed it in the middle. Aparis connected with her fist and LaKiesha completed the circle. "Three the hard way."

"Three the hard way," echoed Aparis and LaKiesha.

~ ~ ~

It has been said that the greatest misfortune can bring to life unforeseen rewards, and such was the case with the untimely death of beloved Aunt Garnett. Her death eased the burden of securing one of man's most basic needs—that of shelter—for Elise and LaKiesha as they remained at Aunt Garnett's, helping Aparis cope with burying another close family member. They helped her make funeral arrangements and took care of the majority of the process. Aparis had family scattered all over but aside from Uncle Wayne and a handful of local relatives, they weren't close at all. Therefore, Aunt Garnett's funeral was small and intimate as there were only a few in attendance.

Aunt Garnett had left the house for Aparis. Fortunately, the mortgage was paid off, along with the house insurance and taxes for the next five years. Thanks to the forged paperwork provided by Father Boris, all the legal difficulties the girls anticipated as minors living alone in the house seemed to disappear.

After appearing in court three times and children's services inspecting the house that Uncle Wayne claimed to live in with Aparis, he was awarded permanent custody of Aparis. The arrangement was sealed with Uncle Wayne being nicely compensated.

Aside from the emotional affects of Aunt Garnett's

Sherrie Walker

death, the girls were fine living on their own and their friendship soared to another level. Not to arouse suspicion or draw attention to themselves, they stayed in school, attended diligently and achieved excellent grades. No matter what, Aparis was determined to attend college and graduate Summa Cum Laude. Aunt Garnett tried to talk her into becoming an attorney like her father, and for a while she considered it, heck for that matter for a brief instance she entertained the thought of becoming a fashion designer on the strength of her love for clothes. That truly was a passing thought. Her fascination and love for computers and her desire to design computer software superseded their wants and any other brief thought she may have possessed. Therefore, with all due respect and love for her loved ones, she chose to follow her dreams and pursue the career of her choice. It was a must, for it was *her* passion. Besides, they would approve of her choice because it was a good one.

Of all of Aunt Garnett's things, Elise most liked the vast selection of books, which kept her occupied. She loved to read and didn't have to leave the house to do so. She read everything from Shakespeare to Stephen King to Alex Haley.

She realized that she had dreams and goals and that the best way to achieve them was through self-study. *Why pay someone to do what I can do myself? I'm a self-starter. I'm a go getter, and as I know what I want that's what I shall get. Even the library is free*, she thought in the midst of brainstorming. *LaKiesha and Aparis have plans to attend college, but I have other plans. If my plans work, as I'm confident they will, we'll all be rich in the near future.* Elise's train of thought was interrupted by a phone call. She answered and Selena was on the other end.

"Hello," Selena said. "What's up, Mommy? I need you to pick me up down the street from the orphanage ... at the little candy store."

"What's up?" Elise questioned.

"I wanna cop some gear from you."

"All right. I'll be there in twenty minutes." Elise hung up the phone, grabbed her coat and keys and left.

Sherrie Walker

nine

APARIS WAS CROUCHED on her knees in the back of her computer, hooking up some cords that ran from her stereo speakers. Ever since she was young she'd had a natural knack for knowing how to fix practically any type of electronics. She became fascinated with video games and computers when she was five years old. She had often sat back and observed her father work on them. She always asked questions about everything he was doing and he always explained. At seven, she had mastered every level of "Bonk's Adventure" and was playing challenging video games such as "Wing Commander" with her father. Aparis was almost as good as he was.

But Aparis wasn't happy with just knowing how to play. She wanted to know how they worked. She had a vast collection of games and electronics. She even had science kits that taught her how to build things electronically. Her father had always told her there was a need for African-American women in science, technology, engineering and math.

"Look at Mae Jemison," he would say as he plugged thoughts into her brain.

Her mother had been a good artist and would sit

around the house drawing and painting. She had been commissioned to create portraits for several politicians and judges. Her father would always joke around and say Aparis inherited her creative ability from her mother, since he couldn't draw anything more than stick figures.

But Aunt Garnett's demise took its emotional toll on Aparis. The first few weeks, she was shattered. Aparis drooped around the house, crying, seemingly disinterested in life. She didn't want to eat, get out the bed, attend school, read, touch the computer or bathe. Elise had to make her bathe and talk her into attending school.

Slowly, with the love and support of Elise and LaKiesha, Aparis began returning to her old self. She began grooming herself, feeling enthusiastic about attending school, reading, and piddling with her computer and sound system. Through it all, Elise and LaKiesha were there for here. It sealed their bond and their friendship soared to another level.

After Aparis connected the wires to the back of the computer, she walked to the stereo, turned it on and listened as the music blasted through the computer's speakers. She chuckled. "I'm back, and … I'm the shit, baby," she proclaimed while dancing around.

She sat down behind the computer and stared at the screen. She pulled up Case Western Reserve's website and clicked on the link to the school's College of Engineering. Although her major had changed, her desire to attend college was what her parents and Aunt Garnett had wanted, and she wanted it as well. Plus, she imagined finding her dream man on campus, someone who would be smart and handsome like her father. She reasoned they would have kids and a wonderful life like

Sherrie Walker

hers before that tragic night struck. Aparis still couldn't understand how people could be so cruel.

LaKiesha sauntered into the room, rapping along with the same 2Pac song coming from Aparis' computer and jarred Aparis from her thoughts.

"What you doing? Working on that damn computer again?"

"I am the bomb, baby. I hooked my stereo up to my computer so my system is the shitsnip. Listen to this." Aparis turned the volume up and 2Pac's *"Hail Mary"* came through the computer loud and clear. Then she walked over to the stereo and put in a tape and pressed play. Marvin Gaye's voice also came through the computer's speakers, but after a second or two, there was a popping noise then no sound at all. LaKiesha looked in the back of the computer, at the stereo then toward Aparis.

"You're the bomb all right. You blew up the damn speakers. I don't know why your ass keep thinking that you're a computer queen. Always around here blowing shit up." LaKiesha burst out laughing, but Aparis was salty.

"Forget you. I can fix this for real." Aparis stepped behind the computer and began to redistribute the wires in the back as LaKiesha lay across Aparis' bed watching.

LaKiesha closed her eyes after a few moments and snapped them back open as *"What's Going On"* blared out of the speakers. She thought of her mother, who was a huge Marvin Gaye fan, and saw her singing his song. But even as she enjoyed the memory, that haunting image crept back into her mind. That image, along with the screams, haunted her nearly every day of her life. There were times she woke up from nightmares, soaking wet,

Sherrie Walker

especially when she had the recurring dream in which her mother lay with her eyes wide open in a pool of blood. Her mother, who was once so beautiful and lively, was dead, a bullet hole in the center of her forehead. Her dress, ripped into rags, was at the end of the bed and her legs sprawled wide open. Once she and Que made their way down the steps, they'd seen their father in a pool of blood as well, but instead of throwing up as she did then, she would wake up covered in sweat and heaving. This was the image she couldn't shake.

She thought about how her life had been shattered into a million pieces as she reached for the deck of cards sitting on Aparis' nightstand. She remembered how her father used to come home from his business meetings and give her large stacks of money to count. By ten, she could look at a stack of money and just about equate the amount. She was excellent in math, she could calculate large numbers in her head and easily solve equations. She shuffled the cards and dealt a hand of Solitaire.

Her eyes filled with tears as she thought back to the day before the men had barged in. She was helping her mother make dinner and forgot about the biscuits in the oven. By the time she realized they were still baking, they were burnt. Que walked into the kitchen, picked one up and bit into it. LaKiesha stood there watching, feeling bad because she felt responsible for ruining the biscuits. She expected Que to spit it out and run for a glass of water, but instead, he just looked at her and smiled good-naturedly.

"BBQ biscuits, creative, sis," he responded as he walked out of the kitchen, still nibbling on the scorched bread. That was only one of the small reasons LaKiesha loved her brother so much. He would go that extra mile

Sherrie Walker

to appease her. He always knew what to say and do to make her feel better. Que was always very protective of her and defended LaKiesha right, wrong or correct. The other kids used to tease her, calling her bookworm and nerd because she sometimes broke the grading curve, but Que always put them in check. *Don't mess around and get a beat down,* he would threaten. LaKiesha smiled, reminiscing back to happier days.

"What the hell you smiling about, looking all crazy and shit?" Aparis said, snapping LaKiesha away from her most precious memory. "Get up off my bed."

"Que and my parents. I miss them so much, Aparis." LaKiesha gathered the cards and placed them back on the nightstand.

Aparis sat down next to her and looked away, thinking about her own parents. "I know. I miss my parents, too. I dream about them all the time."

"I know, and I wish the dreams would stop. I keep dreaming about … about death." LaKiesha's sadness was heard clearly in her voice. Aparis wrapped her arms around LaKiesha and she laid her head against Aparis' shoulder.

"Why did this have to happen to us, Aparis?"

"I don't know. I don't think we'll ever know."

"I've lost everyone that I've ever loved. My parents, Aunt Garnett, Gatsby and all for what? They say God works in mysterious ways. I say He's just plan ole mysterious, period. What kind of God would allow these things to happen in the first place? They say that God is love and He disciplines his children. What the hell did we do to deserve this?" Aparis questioned as Elise stood in the doorway, looking on, watching her two morose-looking friends.

Sherrie Walker

"What do we do from here, LaKiesha?"

"We create our own destiny," Elise answered. Her sudden voice and appearance scared both her friends. Both women jumped with a start.

"Why in the hell do you always have to creep around and shit?" Aparis laughed.

"Creeping is in my blood. Now listen up! I've come up with a plan to get us some money."

"I ain't going in no damn store boosting shit. I'll get busted before I get the stuff in my girdle."

"Calm down, LaKiesha. I'm not talking about boosting. Gurl, this is bigger than some ole boosting dollars."

"What are you talking about then?" Aparis' curiosity was piqued.

"I'm talking about over ninety thousand in cash," Elise whispered, watching their faces as her announcement slowly registered.

"Ninety thousand … dollars? As in cold hard cash?" Aparis stuttered.

"Correct … as in fast cash."

"Who the hell do we have to kill for that kind of money?" LaKiesha jokingly questioned, but Elise didn't smile.

"While you playin', Mr. Tool." Elise crossed her arms. LaKiesha's and Aparis' mouths opened as they looked at each other, then at Elise to see if she was serious, but she had not flinched.

"Are you fucking serious, Elise!" Aparis yelled.

"Is fat meat greasy?" Elise moved and sat in front of the computer and began playing a game of solitaire as she waited on LaKiesha and Aparis to respond.

LaKiesha rose from the bed and started nervously pacing back and forth.

Sherrie Walker

"Where the hell did Mr. Tool get ninety thousand from?" Aparis asked.

"He inherited it from his uncle who passed away a few months ago. The beautiful part is that he keeps it at home because he don't believe in banks."

"How in the hell do you know all of this?" LaKiesha questioned. She never stopped her pacing.

Elise watched Aparis as she began twitching her mouth to grip and bite down into the inside of her jaw. A sign indicating that she was nervous and worried.

"Selena was running her mouth. She called me to buy some clothes, but, in the process, she started telling me that she overheard Sister Pernell telling Father Boris that Mr. Tool came into ninety thousand dollars."

"And just how we gone rob him? We don't even know where he live," Aparis said. She looked confused.

Elise went into her pocket, pulled out a piece of paper and waved it in the air.

"We're going to his house. He was listed and easy to find in the phone book. He lives about twenty minutes from the orphanage. His house sits way back off the road and it's perfect. I already checked it out," Elise explained.

"Oh, my goodness." LaKiesha stopped pacing and stared at Elise as if she saw a foreign object attached to her friend's body. "You can't be serious? How could you even think about doing something like that? Even if … and I am speaking hypothetically, mind you … even if we did rob him, why do we have to kill him?"

"Two reasons. One, he knows who we are and he would tell the police. Plus, he's a child-molesting, sick-ass pedophile."

"So we're playing God now. We determine who

deserves to die, is that it?" LaKiesha demanded, sounding disgusted at the very idea.

"It's not about playing God, it's about getting paid." Elise burst out laughing. "Girl, we ain't got to and ain't gonna kill that old man. All we gone do is go in there and get the money. Kiesh, just think, with that kind of dough you would be able to go to college with no problem."

"We're fucking sixteen years old talking about robbing somebody, Elise! You're talking about almost a hundred grand!" LaKiesha screamed. "We shouldn't even have these kinds of thoughts."

"Girl, I committed murder at thirteen. Do I regret it? Hell no. I would do it all over again if I had to. My sister ... my little sister was being molested, and I feel as if I let it happen. Me! I should've been more protective and maybe it wouldn't have happened. As far as I'm concerned, he deserves it before he rapes another three-year-old. He has money now, which gives him access to more children."

"He was a sick-ass bastard," Aparis murmured. "Aunt Garnett used to cut him up every day, talking about how she always caught him staring at the girls and even saw him masturbating in his parked car one morning. I don't put nothing past him, or any of them–peckerwoods for that matter. They killed my parents for no reason. No reason!"

Elise stared at Aparis and then turned to LaKiesha. "Your parents wanted you to go to college, LaKiesha. This is your chance to do that and to help Que. He needs us right now. Now, we didn't ask for none of this shit to happen, but it did. So what are we going to do about it? We have the chance to come up." Elise paused, then slowed down. "I want to find my little sister and this

Sherrie Walker

money is going to help me do just that. We can't sit around here crying about, 'Why did this happen?' or 'Whoa, Why me?' We got to show the damn world that we are not beaten. Hell, nah, we're coming out fighting and it starts now, today." Elise looked at Aparis and could see that she was struggling, but listening.

"How are we going to rob him?" Aparis asked.

"At gunpoint."

"We don't even own a damn gun, Elise," Aparis argued.

"I put an order in for untraceable guns with one of my niggas down the way. I can pick them up in two days. Once we're done we will dispose of it."

"What about a car?" LaKiesha asked. "We can't drive ours."

"My boy works at The Ritz as a valet. He knows the regulars' schedules so we'll have use of a vehicle for several hours."

LaKiesha appeared sick then dropped down onto the bed, holding her stomach. Aparis looked almost as sick as LaKiesha.

"Listen, we'll go by his house and check things out to make sure that it is what it is. Then, we'll get familiar with his routine. We'll plan this week and execute the week after next." Elise got up and walked over to the bed and sat down next to Aparis and LaKiesha, who had finally stopped pacing. She grabbed both their hands. "Look, I'll understand if you two really don't want to do this, and I won't be mad. I just thought I'd put y'all down on this come up. But, with or without you, I'm doing it. I have to find my sister and I need this money."

Neither LaKiesha nor Aparis responded for a few minutes, as each was lost within her own thoughts.

Sherrie Walker

Aparis slowly brought her fist up, placing it between Elise and LaKiesha. For a moment, the other two girls paused. Then, finally, slowly Elise extended her arm in the same manner. LaKiesha looked at both fists for a few seconds before she slowly raised hers and placed it between the two, making it a complete circle.

"Three the hard way," Elise announced.

"Three the hard way," they echoed in unison.

~ ~ ~

"You ready to die, pervert?" Elise asked as she pointed the gun at Mr. Tool who lay in his bed looking befuddled as he gawked at the three masked girls standing before him with pointed guns.

The girls had spent two weeks following Mr. Tool and putting the finishing touches on their plan. And now, here he was, trembling before them. "What do you want?" He scanned their faces, then nervously licked his lips. "I don't have any money."

Elise reached down and hit him with the butt of her gun. He fought to stay conscious, but a wave of dizziness engulfed him. Aparis began to search the closet and LaKiesha looked in the drawers.

"Wrong thing to say, Mr. Tool. We know you got some money. So, where is it? All we want is money, so if you tell us, we won't kill you," Elise said.

Mr. Tool tried to sit up but was knocked back down when the gun connected with his jaw. He spit out the blood that formed in his mouth and he began to whimper.

"Please ... please ... oh, God ... why are you doing this?"

"Think about all the little girls you hurt, raped, beat and tortured!" Elise screamed.

Sherrie Walker

Mr. Tool looked surprised. Surprised to think that the ones who exposed him and knew about his history of molesting young girls, was now in his home, in his bedroom in the wee hours of the night, to rob him and possibly shot him. *Oh my God, I'm a dead man.*

Unveiling her mask, not caring that he recognized her, Elise said, "You thought we forgot, huh? I told you, you wouldn't get away. Now, you are going to tell us where the money is at, because I'm not gonna ask you again." Elise paused.

"Where's it at?" Elise interrogated.

"Please … don't … it's over there under the floor-boards. There's over ninety-six thousand. Take it …please …don't hurt me."

"LaKiesha, Aparis, go see if this nasty little red moth-afucka is lying," Elise ordered.

They walked across the floor, tapping on various boards and searching for a crack. After several minutes of searching, LaKiesha and Aparis hadn't found anything. Aparis held up her arms and shrugged.

Elise looked down at Mr. Tool and felt nothing short of hatred for him.

"WHERE'S THE FUCKING MONEY?" Elise yelled. She pointed the gun straight at his forehead.

"Pull the …the chair … back … please … under the chair. I promise it's under there. Pull the chair back and move the rug."

LaKiesha scooted the chair over and Aparis moved the rug. LaKiesha noticed a couple loose boards sticking up, and she reached down to pry up the plank. When the board gave, it revealed stacks of money with wrappers still attached. She picked up a stack and held it up so Elise could see it. She smiled. "Ta dah." LaKiesha

Sherrie Walker

grabbed the duffel bag and they filled it.

"Please, you have the money. Just go … please …" Mr. Tool begged as he lay in excruciating pain.

"I'm sure those little girls begged you to spare them. Did you?" Elise asked, although she wasn't expecting an answer. She basked in the fear revealed by his eyes. Elise had dreamt about this day.

Aparis walked over to the bed and glared at him, thinking about how he treated the foster children, as well as her aunt. Additionally, she thought about the prejudiced white people who had killed her parents. In her opinion, Mr. Tool was just as bad because he was a child molester. The longer she stared at him the angrier she became.

"You sick son of a bitch," Aparis hissed.

Elise slowly aimed her gun. Suddenly Mr. Tool's eyes grew round. He begin gasping for air, clutched his heart with both hands, then passed out. His body slumped to the floor with a dull thud.

Aparis grabbed his wrist and checked for a pulse. When she felt none, she leaned over his face. "He's dead," she pronounced, sounding shocked.

LaKiesha started to panic shaking her head no as she backed up into a corner with her hands covering her mouth.

"No! You said wasn't nobody going to get hurt Elise. Oh my God, no," cried LaKiesha.

"Shit, I didn't lie. We didn't hurt nobody. His ass keeled over.

"Is he dead for real?" echoed LaKiesha as she stood back looking at Mr. Tool in a state of shock.

For a moment no one moved, then Elise moved in closer and double checked his pulse. "Well! I'll be

Sherrie Walker

damned. Yep, his ass *is* dead as a crushed roach. I feel cheated. I didn't get to get my funky off." She laughed, almost maniacally. "His ass done double our work. Now we gone have to wrap him up and roll out."

Aparis exploded. "You have a twisted sense of humor, Elise. This shit ain't fucking funny. We're going to jail for the rest of our lives. We may as well say fuck college and anything else we planned to do with our lives. We're fucked!"

"Both of y'all calm the fuck down. Listen, the main thang is not to panic. We gone get rid of this old mothafucka's body and act like this shit never happened. Now let's find something to roll his ass up in and drag him to the van."

"And then what?"

"Then we'll ride him to this spot I know and dump his body."

"Dump him."

"Yeah, dump him. Dump him just like the turd he was." Elise found humor in her statement and chuckled.

"My goodness Elise, do you have to say all that? Where will we dump the body?" Aparis questioned, sounding like she really didn't want a reply.

Elise nodded her head up and down. "LaKiesha, remember when Que took us to that old condemned factory that used to dispose of waste and showed us those wells without bottoms?" Elise asked. LaKiesha slowly nodded as she realized her mouth was too dry to form words and where Elise was going. "We'll dump him there."

"LaKiesha, finish bagging up the money. Aparis, you help me wrap him in this blanket. And we'll drag him to the back door. The van is parked right by the door so we won't have that far to drag him." Aparis continued to stand there looking down at Mr. Tool. Elise had to stand between her and Mr. Tool and snap her into the moment. "Aparis, come on, baby. We have to move so we can get out of here. Remember, it was scum like him that killed your parents. So, snap out of it and get a grip." Aparis looked at Elise and began to move. LaKiesha grabbed the money.

After he was securely wrapped, Elise grabbed him by his feet and labored strenuously to drag him across the floor. *Phew, I'm glad his home is ranch style, otherwise a set of steps could'a been torture.* Aparis flinched and froze up again. LaKiesha looked up from her mission. "Come on Aparis, get a grip. Don't start tripping again. I can't do this by myself," coaxed Elise. Aparis began to help Elise drag Mr. Tool through the house to the back door. After LaKiesha tossed the money in the van, they partnered up and struggled with the dead weight of Mr. Tool as they pushed his body into the van. Out of breath, tired and sweating, they leaned against the van to catch their breath.

Elise drove the van and eventually pulled behind an abandoned building. Then she backed up to a well and climbed out. Before unlocking the cargo door, she surveyed the surroundings. LaKiesha and Aparis helped hoist the body from the van. Struggling, but managing, they got to the mouth of the well. In one heave, they dropped and deposited Mr. Tool's corpse. They listened, but didn't hear him hit the bottom.

Elise turned to look at LaKiesha and then Aparis. Fear was written all over their faces. "Listen to me." Elise said with intensity. "We are going to be all right. According to Que, bodies have been dropped here and

Sherrie Walker

never discovered by law enforcement. No one is going to find his body." Aparis wanted to believe Elise, but her heart was beating fast from just the thought of what they did and perhaps getting caught and going to jail for the rest of their lives. She looked down into the well, straining to hear Mr. Tool's body hit and with a nervousness in her voice asked, "How do you know we won't get caught, Elise?

"Truthfully, there is no definite guarantee. But, what I do know is, only the three of us know about this. I know I'll never tell anyone. Will you?" Elise watched Aparis as she awaited her response.

Aparis looked away from the well and directly into Elise eyes. "No."

Elise and Aparis looked at LaKiesha. "Never."

"This will be one that we'll take to our graves," Elise said as she held her fist up.

LaKiesha and Aparis connected their fist with hers. "Three the hard way."

The girls climbed back into the van and Elise drove downtown and met the valet. She gave him the keys and an envelope, then climbed into a cab with LaKiesha and Aparis. Elise leaned back in the seat. She closed her eyes, then quickly drifted into a fretful sleep.

Sherrie Walker

ten

IT WAS A HOT MUGGY day in the middle of July as Elise waddled out of Dillard's at Beachwood Place looking like she was nine months pregnant. She played the part to a T, with all the proper mannerisms—stopping to grab her back every few steps and constantly sipping on a bottle of water. She wobbled to her Honda Civic and scanned the parking lot before sliding behind the wheel. Elise pulled out onto Cedar Road and turned right to access the freeway and head toward home with a trunk full of Ralph Lauren men's suits, calculating the money she would savor from that one lick.

It had been a year since the demise of Mr. Tool and everything was going smoothly for the girls. LaKiesha and Aparis were registered into college, with Aparis studying computer engineering at Case Western Reserve University and LaKiesha studying finance at David N. Myers University. Elise decided not to go to college, staying true to her independent notions and regimen of self-study. She'd read every wealth creation and self-help book she could find when she wasn't stealing.

She had started back boosting because her portion of the money from Mr. Tool was dwindling since she'd paid

Sherrie Walker

an investigator to find Simone after learning that she had run away from her last assigned foster home. Simone's caseworker had no idea of her whereabouts and the investigator came up with nothing. Elise tried to save money but learned that the cost of living was expensive and $32,000 was chicken feed.

She told herself that the boosting was temporary, merely a stepping stone. She was working to develop a business model and plan that would put her in the driver's seat of her own destiny.

There was another reason Elise kept motivated – after two and a half years, Que's out date was bumped up and he was getting out on early release next month, for good behavior and applying himself toward successfully completing every early release program the system had to offer.

Elise was just as excited as LaKiesha. The day before he was to arrive, they both ran around getting things together. Being on their own they had developed and mastered cooking skills that allowed them to throw straight down in the kitchen, and some fine cooks they turned out to be. They could cook anything from gourmet to soul food meals. Que loved soul food, so Elise planned to cook a huge dinner, fit for a king, with a menu consisting of "slap-yo'-Momma" fried chicken and fish, ribs off the grill, a mix of fresh greens, macaroni and cheese, stuffing, yams, potato salad, a fresh garden salad, a French apple crème cheese pie, a punch bowl cake, and a gooey sweet potato pie for dessert.

Elise popped the trunk and pulled out the groceries and hefty bags of clothes she had boosted, include a fresh pair of Wheat Timberlands and Air Maxes, a few pair of Polo, Nautica and Levi's jeans, shirts and T-shirts, Polo

Sherrie Walker

underwear, an abundance of socks and men's toiletries and a bottle of Gucci cologne to make sure Que was on point. LaKiesha pulled in the driveway behind Elise.

"Damn!' exclaimed LaKiesha. You robbed their ass good, didn't you?" She started looking through the merchandise. "What you get us?" Elise swatted her hand and started handing LaKiesha bags.

"Come on, help me carry these bags inside so I can get out of this girdle. Girl, it's killing me."

Aparis was sitting at the table doing her calculus homework when Elise and LaKiesha entered the dining room

"Y'all just missed Que's call," Aparis said.

LaKiesha dropped the bags. "What? When? What did he say?"

"He said to be there at eight o' clock sharp in the morning, because he don't want to be down a minute longer that he has to."

"What else did he say?" Elise set her bags down.

"That's pretty much it."

"Did he ask about me?" Elise questioned.

LaKiesha and Aparis laughed. "Yes, Elise, he said to tell you what's up and he'll see you tomorrow, too." Elise puckered her lips, start popping her fingers and doing a dance motion as if to say, *that's what I'm talking about. It's on now*, while Aparis and LaKiesha went through each piece of clothing oohing and aahing.

"Come on, LaKiesha, we have to start cooking. Aparis, fire up the damn grill, my man's coming home." They laughed again.

~ ~ ~

The next morning, Que exited the Grafton Correctional Institution like a prize-winning horse, hur-

Sherrie Walker

rying to reach the car. As he approached the car wearing a sleeveless white wife-beater and the state's khaki pants, Elise felt incredibly aroused as her eyes filled with lust and her mouth began to water. She thought to herself, *damn, he's finer and sexier then ever and desirable as fuck. Look at that muscular body, it's tantalizing, buffed and sculptured like a piece of serious artwork. Hmph ... ain't nothing changed but the date. The penitentiary preserved him well.* His hair was cut short with waves that spiraled. Elise continued to stare and rape him with her eyes as LaKiesha jumped out the car and raced into Que's arms as his muscles flexed when he lifted and spun her around with ease. He put LaKiesha down and stood back flashing that pearly white gorgeous smile of his.

"Damn, sis, look at you. You gonna make me have to cap some niggahs the way you've filled out and shit." He turned her around. She went through modeling gestures as she spun around in her loose-fitting mini dress over a pair knee-length leggings and Fendi sandals. "Just look at you, girl." LaKiesha smiled and hugged Que tightly as Elise stepped out of the car. He did a double-take. His mouth dropped as a newfound passion stirred inside of him. She had on a spaghetti-strapped, tight-fitting black tank top that laid nicely across her perky breasts and flat stomach, a tight pair of jeans that hugged her perfect little plump butt and curvaceous hips and were snatched just right around her defined waistline and a signature pair of Coach sandals. He felt a throb in his heart and an instant bulge in his pants.

"What's up, Que? Welcome home. It's good seeing you." She stepped forward, gently touched his face and embraced him.

"Yo', you got it baby girl. It's good to be seen," he said

Sherrie Walker

as he gently pulled her into him, returning the exchange. "Looks like life has been treating you well. Now with that being said, let's get the fuck up out of this spot. I've had enough of being on these grounds. Feel me." He held the door open for LaKiesha and Elise, closed it and climbed in the back seat. Elise drove as LaKiesha and Que kicked it non-stop all the way to Aparis' house.

Once they arrived, Aparis met them at the door wearing a pair of white denim capris, a bright multi-colored midriff top that tied around her neck, large silver hoop earrings and a pair of Nine West flip flop sandals.

"Man, you girls look great."

"I wanted to come with Kiesh and Elise to pick you up, but they insisted that I stay and keep the pots burning and everything intact until y'all got back."

In a brotherly gesture, Que put his arms around her shoulders. "If your staying back meant me walking into this warm atmosphere combined with a wonderful aroma of food, I'm glad you did." He smiled. "Y'all got it going on up in here ... up in here."

They feasted on the meal that was prepared special for Que, chopped it up in good conversation, showered him with multiple presents, listened to the sounds of Jay-Z, Usher, SWV, TLC, Master P, L.L. Cool J and a host of other hot artists blast through the speakers of the stereo system. As the night wound down, they simply chilled.

Que stole glances at Elise throughout the evening as she strolled throughout the house doing thus-and-so with those curvaceous hips of hers moving in suave slow motions.

At seventeen, with a 36-24-36 frame, Elise had a body that had men and some women turning their heads. At 5

Sherrie Walker

feet, 6 inches and 130 pounds, with long, thick hair hanging down to the center of her back, exotic almond shaped bedroom eyes, high cheekbones, full perfect-shaped lips and a blemish free caramel complexion, she was gorgeous.

After everyone had settled in for the night, Que tossed and turned with an ache in his lions, thinking about Elise. He knew he couldn't spend another night in that house, not without having her. The temptation and desire was too great.

eleven

AFTER BREAKFAST THE NEXT morning, Que put on his new gear and hit the streets. He borrowed LaKiesha's Honda Accord and set out to start his grind. During his incarceration, he hustled as if he was on the streets – everything was two for one or more. He didn't have any vices; he wasn't a smoker therefore he managed to save enough money so that upon his release, he was able to cop a couple ounces of cocaine and flip it. He hustled long and hard.

He rented a studio apartment, but took care of his business on the block. The streets became his second home. Some days he didn't change clothes or sleep. And when he did buy clothes, he still bought the majority of his clothes from Elise no matter how hard she tried to give them to him. His driven force was generated by his desire to "catch up and come up." He checked in on the girls every day, but he never spent the night. He knew he couldn't be around Elise and not succumb to temptation.

On the other hand, Elise had her own agenda. She was determined to show him that she wasn't a little girl anymore. But he dodged every flirtatious gesture she

Sherrie Walker

tossed at him, causing her to start doubting her appeal. She decided to try another tactic, which included cooking for Que, running his errands and cleaning his itty-bitty-ass apartment. She was determined to have him.

Shortly after Que was home, Trey returned from prison as well. Que and Trey immediately picked up right where they left off. For the two of them, it was on and popping like microwave popcorn. It was no surprise when Que and Trey started staking some serious claims, coming up and eliminating major players from the game. Together they had coped a spot and traffic was flowing through it like a revolving door.

When Elise would stop over to their spot, many of Que's opponents expressed interest in her, so she knew she had physical appeal. For whatever the reason, Que continued to front and masquerade his lie by showing her no interest. She couldn't understand why she wasn't appealing to Que, or what kind of macho hard-to-get game he was playing.

After three months of chasing Que to no avail, Elise decided to stop—just quit— no more going over to his place, no more cooking or running errands for him. And every time he came around, she made like Houdini and got ghost.

One day, Elise pulled up to the house and Trey's car was in the driveway. As she stepped out of hers, he approached her smiling.

"What's up wit' you, beautiful?" Trey stood 6 feet, 195 pounds, with skin as sweet and smooth as a chocolate candy bar. He had sparkling white teeth and kept fresh braids in his medium-length hair. Trey was indeed handsome.

"Just getting in from work."

Sherrie Walker

Trey laughed and helped Elise carry the pile of bags in her hands. "Girl! Give me that." He took them all as she proceeded into the house. "You better leave them people's shit alone, Elise." She propped the door open for him as he entered the house.

"They're insured, so this little bit of stuff ain't hurting nothing. I bet it don't even put a hell'va indent in their inventory. Far as I'm concerned, they should give it to me for coming. For real tho. Look, you got yo' hustle, so don't knock me for mine."

Trey threw his hands up in the air to signal submission.

"Whoa, whoa, baby girl. Ease up. I ain't knocking nothin'. I just know what the consequences of crime can entail and I don't wanna to see nothin' happen to you." Trey took a moment to regard Elise. "Hey, I got tickets to the Jay-Z concert. My date stood me up and I don't want to waste 'em. I ain't down wit' kickin it wit' just anybody. So…You wanna go wit' me?"

"Why me? Why not Aparis or LaKiesha?"

"Why not you? When was the last time you went out, Elise? All you do is hustle and stay cooped up in this house reading. You need to get out more. LaKiesha and Aparis are always going out. They're out now, ain't they?"

"Nigga, you don't see or hear them do you? So you know they're out. And, for your information, I enjoy staying in the house reading." Elise knew she was being unfair to Trey. He was only trying to be a gentlemen. And truth be told, she'd grown weary from chasing after Que so hard. She considered Trey's offer.

Trey watched her closely before she responded. He removed the tickets from his back pocket and placed

Sherrie Walker

them on the table. "Look, I'm just trying to get your mind off of other things. Trying to get you out of the house and show you a good time. Stay in the house and wallow in issues if you want to …" He struggled to find the words. "Nevermind, I'm out."

Trey walked toward the door and Elise stopped him before he could exit.

"Trey!" He turned to face her. "How 'bout a play?"

"A play?" He looked confused, but Elise did not.

"Yes, a play. I've wanted to see '*Black Nativity*' for some time. If I call now the tickets can be prepaid for, placed in will call, and waiting for us to pick them up at the box office. How about us doing that? You want to go?" Elise stood with her hands on her hips awaiting his reply. Trey couldn't help but smile. He welcomed the opportunity – especially if it meant being with Elise.

"A play it is. I've never been to a play, but I try anything at least once, before I turn my nose up at it. So we'll do the play," answered Trey.

"Good. Pick me up at seven. Curtain is at eight." Looking at her watch, Elise said, "LaKiesha and Aparis will be coming in shortly. If you don't want the concert tickets to go to waste, you can leave 'em for Kiesh and Aparis and I guarantee you they'll put them to use. I can see them asses now taking a quick shower, tossing that hair this way and that, throwing them bodies into something skimpy, sliding into a pair of 4 inch heels, primping to the last stroke of their lipstick, and being in their designated seats before the curtain goes up."

Trey agreed and left with a smile. Elise sat down on the couch to think about what had just transpired. She had been stuck on Que for so long that she never considered platonically or intimately dating anyone else.

Sherrie Walker

Maybe it's time I move on. I've been saving myself for a man who doesn't want me. Hell, I ain't suffering from a severe case of need reduction. Quite the contrary, I do want and I do need. So, fuck it . . . She ran to her room to find something to wear.

Since the Karamu House was a small theatre company, Elise figured she didn't have to think too hard about what to wear, especially given that it was a keep-it-simple kind of night. She selected a cute DKNY jogging suit. She wanted to be comfortable while viewing her first production of Langston Hughes' *"Black Nativity."* She'd wanted to see the play ever since she found one of Aunt Garnett's old playbills while going through an old trunk in the attic.

The show was amazing. Hearing the nativity story told from a Black perspective, as well as the gospel-styled Christmas carols, was enchanting to Elise's ears, but it was the opening scene that stayed in her mind. The curtain rose to reveal complete darkness except for barefoot singers, whose white robes shone with the light of the candles they were carrying. While watching, Elise felt a light breeze blowing against her face. She asked Trey if he felt anything, but he didn't answer, just looked straight ahead. She asked again.

"Probably the ghost of Langston Hughes," he chuckled softly, then shushed her.

After the play, they went to The Lancer for something to eat. It was still early for their crowd but the regulars were perched at the bar, filling up on spirits.

"What you want?" Trey asked Elise, whose eyes skimmed the menu.

"Frog legs."

"Why you want frog legs?" Trey had an amused

Sherrie Walker

smirk on his face.

"I just do. What's wrong with frog legs? I like frog legs. Didn't you ask what did I want? she said, setting the menu down.

"Yeah, I did." Trey waved his hand to attract the waiter to the table. "Let me get a frog leg and a catfish dinner."

After eating, Trey drove to Lakefront Park and pulled in the lot beside The Inner City Yacht Club. They sat and talked. Elise learned that Trey also liked to read and that they enjoyed a lot of the same books. She would never have guessed Trey was a bookworm. During his childhood he'd indulged in reading great African American authors and to escape the reality of prison during his incarceration, he read. He read Malcolm X, *The Color Purple*, Donald Goines, *The Willie Lynch Letter* and many others.

After their first date, they spent a lot of time together. They grew closer as they discovered other similar interests. They were both sports buffs, and spent hours talking about games, players and great moments in sports history. When Trey had just a little bit of business to conduct, Elise would ride with him. And keeping it real, Elise enjoyed hanging out with Trey, but no matter how much she tried, she just couldn't take it to the next level, even though he never actually made any sexual advances. *Maybe I'm not ready for a relationship*, she thought.

Regardless, it had been over a month and she was comfortable being around Trey and enjoyed their time together. With Que always hanging around, though, it seemed unlikely that things could stay so smooth.

One day, Trey and Elise were sitting on the porch

drinking beer and kicking it about the Celtics and Lakers game when Que pulled into the driveway. When Que got out of the car, Trey and Que exchanged a closed fist, hand-to-hand pound while Elise spoke to Que nonchalantly.

"You want another beer, Trey?" Elise asked. He looked at the bottle and saw that it was almost empty.

"Yeah! Hook it up. Thanks," he replied.

Elise turned to go into the house, but Que stopped her. "Oh, you ain't gon' offer me one? I can't have one?"

Elise rolled her eyes and sucked her teeth, "Nigga, you know where the fridge is." She allowed the wrought iron security door to close loudly as she entered the house.

She grabbed two beers and popped the tops, throwing the caps into the trash. When she stepped back out, Trey and his car were gone.

"Where's Trey?"

"Somebody hit him up. He had to go handle some business. Said he'd holla at you later. Can I get that beer?" Elise looked down at the beers and reluctantly handed him one as he watched her intensely for a few seconds before speaking.

"So you sleeping with Trey or what?"

Elise looked at Que like he was 14 karat crazy, like no he didn't just ask me that like that. With her hands placed on her hips, head thrown back and lips curled, and standing on the ball of her feet Elise said, "Nigga, say what ... you got me bent and twisted. First of all, where do you get the nerve to ask me who I'm sleeping with? Like it's your business. Ain't none of your business who I'm sleeping with. You ain't my man to ask me jack. Furthermore, what I look like to you, some kind of situ-

Sherrie Walker

ational   do-what's-convenient-for-the-moment-type skank? I don't spread myself thin by becoming involved in meaningless freak affairs. I'm selective and can be. Whoever I have a sexual relationship with, it won't be just sex that we'll have … we'll make love. And that man, will be my man. It will not be someone who I consider myself to be mere friends with. And that's the only existence between Trey and I … we're just friends."

"Damn, baby, don't be so fierce. Lighten up on the mood. Lose the attitude. I was asking because … I was just saying…"

Elise looked Que up and down then locked on his eyes. "You were just saying what? You weren't and ain't saying shit, Que. Not a damn thing. Have you lost your rabid-ass mind? I'd be wrong if I commenced to slapping the taste out your mouth for asking me some none-of-your-business shit like that, now wouldn't I?"

Que threw his hands up and backed up a few steps. "Why you got to talk crazy and get all hostile? Why you got to get all defensive, ma?"

"Defensive your ass." Elise snapped her manicured fingers in his face. "I don't have to defend anything to you."

"Can I ask you this question with out you verbally attacking and threatening me?"

"It depends, what is it."

"Are you feeling dude in a special way? He ain't said it, but I know he's seeking an intimate relationship. He don't want to just have a meaningless freak affair with you as you so bluntly phrase it. He wants you to be his girl. Does your feelings…does your interest match?"

"WHY?" Elise fired.

"'Cause, I want to know … THAT'S WHY," he shot

Sherrie Walker

101

back.

"It's none of your business who I'm feeling, Que. Where the hell is this coming from anyway?"

"From my heart, that's where."

"What? Stop. Let's rewind this. What did you just say?"

"I said … from my heart."

"Why the sudden interest? Why the sudden admission?" Elise inquired.

"It's not sudden. These pent-up emotions and the desire to have you has occupied a space in my heart and mind for a very long time. I just didn't know how to release them. I wasn't sure if I should.

"I've never felt this way about a woman and there was a part of me that wouldn't give into my feelings. So dig, I didn't know what to do. When it comes to getting money, selling dope, popping a nigga, I'm the man. But when it came to pursuing a romantic relationship with you, I froze up and ran. That's what I did Elise, I ran."

He continued, "For a long time I was in denial, and thought it best I keep my distance. That was the fiction that I used while trying to get on with my life and pocket my feelings for you," he explained. "I thought it would go away. But it ain't gon' nowhere. Then I was finding myself fucked up when I heard you would be with Trey at the spots, and y'all was out all over town, going to plays and concerts, and hanging out at the Lancer's." Que sighed and continued. "With that nudge I knew it was time to come on with the come."

Elise was in la-la land, though she listened closely. She studied Que as he talked and was at a loss for words.

"Que, don't toy with me. Matters of the heart and matters of the pocket are deep. I don't play when it

Sherrie Walker

comes to either. If you're playing some type of game, I suggest you cease it now. Que? You knew I was attracted to you before you went away, while you were away and when you came home. I waited on you your entire bid. I told you how I felt in all my letters and tried to show you when you came home, but all you did was shit on me. Now that you think me and Trey is kicking it, you wanna run your waterhead ass over here with this true confession bullshit."

"Waterhead?" Que looked astonished. "Look, I've always felt you, Elise. I recognized you being down with me on my bid and we weren't even together. Now that's real gansta shit, fo' real. I recognized your maturity and sincerity, felt your loyalty and was convinced that if I wanted a real woman, you were the one. But, because of your age I was skeptical and let mixed feelings cloud my judgment. I just thought you were too young."

"Que, you're only two years older than me, dang!"

"Yeah, I know. Listen, while my nerves are up will you let me finish without interrupting." He swallowed hard and began to articulate. "You don't know how hard it was for me to not push up on you, especially the first night I came home. I struggled like a mothafucka. That's why I didn't spend another night in this house. I never wanted you to feel like I was taking advantage of you. But I wanted you—badly. Keepin' it real , you was all I could think about. Man, I remember the first time I saw you, I thought you was a hotty. I was open then... and open big time, but was afraid to give into my emotions. Elise, I don't want to disappoint my future and I feel you and I can have a future together. You appeal to me mentally and emotionally. Girl, you are indeed a quintessential diva in your own right, featuring all the right qualities to hold a nigga like me down. You're savvy and mentally aggressive. Your mind is powerful. You're smart, you're a thinker, a planner, a calculator, a navigator. You don't wait for things to happen, you create your happenings. I love that in you.

"You possess a unique charm. Physically, well, some things just go with out saying. But for the sake of acknowledgement...you're   definitely   all   that! Emotionally, you're willing to give and receive love, especially to the right person. Elise, I know I've been an idiot...but if it's not too late, I want to be that person. Would you consider giving yo' nigga here a chance to ... uhm ... show his loving side ... and be my woman?"

"Que..." she looked into his eyes and brought both her hands to her mouth.

"Before you answer, another thing that was unforgettable and I tend to reflect back on is the time when you told me in one of your letters that you were saving yourself for me. That spinned my top fo' real. Now if that's true..."

"Niggah! What you mean if it's true?" Elise snapped, rearing back on one leg, head swiveling on neck, pointing her finger in his face as if it was a pistol.

"Whoa. Don't go getting fierce again. Before you go ziggedy boom can I finish? What I was trying to say is, if that's true *I* would really feel pumped and special. Without causing any offense how am I supposed to know you saved yourself for me?"

"Oh, I can prove it."

"How, Elise? A woman can and will tell a man *anything*. So, please, tell me how you can prove it."

"And how would you make sense of it all if I did?" Elise retorted, letting the words slide across her lips,

Sherrie Walker

then biting the bottom one and leaving Que stuck for one brief moment.

"If you can prove it then that makes us soulmates," he replied.

Elise smiled and took Que by the hand, leading him upstairs into her bedroom. She was so glad she hadn't followed her second mind earlier that morning and had instead taken more time than usual to clean her room. Que pulled away and sat on the bed. He was impressed by the reading selection on her nightstand. He picked up her copy of Mario Puzo's novel, *The Godfather.*

"Hell, nah. *The Godfather*. What you know about the Corleones, girl?"

"I came across it in the orphanage, so I've read that several times. Now I just pick it up to study different scenes and characters."

"So, who's your favorite character?"

"I think Kay was interesting." Elise smiled.

"Gotta love Kay." Que placed the book back on the nightstand. "Puzo was brilliant. That was the first thing I read while I was down. 'Cause it wasn't shit else to do, I used to read all kind of stuff while I was in the joint. But, back to you. How you gone prove this to me, girl?"

She took Que's hand and licked his finger. She batted her eyes as he steadily watched her every move. She placed her lips on top of his full set, puckered and pushed inward.

"Hold up, Elise!" Everything seem to stop. "You don't have to have sex with me to prove that you love me."

"See, that's why I called you waterhead, waterhead." She laughed. "Can't you read between the lines?"

"Now you the one playing games. Just give it to me.

Whatever the proof is." He had a look on his face like he had won.

"That's what I'm trying to do. I was going to show you, but instead I'll tell you." She paused. "I'm a virgin," she announced, nonchalantly shrugging her shoulders.

Que's mouth dropped like loose change.

"Pick up your lip," she said. "Are you surprised?"

"Baby, I'm surprised, thrilled and happy as a lesbian in a coochie camp."

"So what do we do now?" Elise asked .

"We make this shit happen. From this day forward it's me and you. I want you to be my girl. You cool with that?" he asked.

"How would you discover your best love if I wasn't cool with it. Yes, hell yes, I'm cool with it! Que, some people know they are meant to be together. We were destined to be together. I knew I was meant to be with you from the moment I first laid eyes on you. I have been waiting on you all these years. Those emotions you tried to hide, I'm going to bring out of you and make you love it in the process. Yes, I'll be your girl. Boy, don't play."

"That's all I needed to hear."

Elise quickly turned and thrust her body upon Que. He fell back onto the bed with her on top of him, kissing him as if she was an actress in an overly dramatic stage production.

Que gently turned the tide so that he was in the more dominant position, then stared in her eyes and chuckled with the biggest grin on his face.

"What's so funny?" Elise asked, apparently frustrated.

"Slow down, baby," Que whispered in her ear then

Sherrie Walker

kissed the lobe before stroking his tongue behind it. "There's no need to rush. We're going to take this nice and slow."

Restless with anticipation, Elise squirmed.

"Relax." Que's voice was soft and low. "And trust me."

Que's hands began to slip under Elise's blouse to caress her body as his tongue explored her mouth. She could feel her nipples harden from his touch.

"Uhmm … awww." She released a whispery, long sigh.

Slowly undressing Elise, Que removed her blouse and began placing supple, wet kisses on her neck and shoulders as he unclasped her black lacey bra and slide it off her shoulders, down her arms onto the floor. Her small, perfectly shaped, firm breasts were just enough to satisfy the heated desire of his mouth. He soothingly nibbled on one while he rolled the nipple of her other breast between his fingers.

Elise closed her eyes as she began to feel his mouth giving her pleasures that she had only read, thought and dreamt about. He began sucking on her other nipple and Elise could feel a warmth and wetness build between her legs. Que unzipped and lowered her pants placing kisses down her legs and between her thighs before moving away from her. They both stood and she stepped out her jeans.

Que's breath got caught in his throat as she stood before him in a black lacey thong that accented her baby soft skin. He stood before Elise as she removed his shirt and began kissing his hard stomach. As the passion between them increased, so did Que's breathing. Simultaneously, Elise pulled his jeans and boxers down,

Sherrie Walker

revealing his large and long penis that caused her to twitch at the sight. Que looked down at himself, then up at Elise and smiled with delight.

She had a somewhat welcoming yet frightening look on her face.

"I won't hurt you, baby, I promise. Can I taste you ... can I satisfy my imagination ... I want to taste every part of you."

Her mouth didn't respond, but her body said yes. He reached out for her then pressed her body against his before he gently laid her across the bed, removing her thong with his teeth and mouth, and exploring every curve and inch of her luscious body. Where he touched her with his hands, he followed up with his tongue until he was licking and kissing between her creamy smooth warm thighs. He parted the lips of her vagina with his tongue and began to slowly and softly lick her clitoris.

"Ooo, Que. Ssss. She hissed as she arched her back. "Ssss...ooo."

Then all of a sudden, his lengthy tongue gently penetrated her fiery furnace.

"Que ... oooh, Que ... ssss." Elise tried to voice her emotions, but her body began to tingle and move on its own, causing her to relinquish her language capacities.

Que stopped, allowing Elise's first orgasm to take its course. As her body trembled in ecstasy he started to kiss his way back up her body and across her breasts to her lips. They kissed and Elise reached past his leg to stroke his manhood.

"I want you to have your way with me. I want to feel you inside me ... I need you to make love me," Elise breathed passionately.

"Are you sure you're ready, Elise?"

Sherrie Walker

She looked into his eyes and nodded her head while bringing his mouth down to hers. Que positioned himself over her as the passion between them remained electric. He massaged the outside and center of her vagina with his penis before slowly, gently attempting to enter her. The tightness made it apparent that she was a virgin. As the head of his penis tore the hymen, he felt the warmth of her blood greet his penis.

"Ooooh, Que … awwww!" Elise cried out from the intense pain. Que, still on top, embraced her, stopped his movement, then brought her close to his chest.

"It's ok baby. It's ok. I'll stop."

"No, don't stop … please don't."

Que eased himself a little deeper into her wet, shallow pond, a little bit at a time. When he was halfway in, he stopped and started kissing her with so much passion Elise forgot about the pain as her crying transitioned into moaning.

"Uhmm … aaaah … ohh, yes baby, go deeper inside. I want all of you. Give it all to me," she continued while he kissed and caressed her.

Eventually, Elise began to meet Que's thrust and their rhythmic connection was that of a couple soaring on a rollercoaster of passion and emotions. Elise's body began to spasm as she clung tightly and softly spoke into Que's ear.

"Baby, I love the passion between us. I never want this feeling to end … will you always give it to me this way … will you always give it to me when I want it … I love it … I love you."

"Whatever, however, whenever you want it, it's yours," Que whispered in her ear, rising her to a higher and higher plateau. "I'm yours. I'll satisfy your every

Sherrie Walker

desire." He was now stroking her with a full thrust and she was meeting his demand when they exploded as one in ecstasy.

"Oooh....yes...yes...yes!"

They simultaneously screeched. Feeling drained and sedated, Que rolled off Elise and held her tightly.

"I will never doubt you again, Elise."

Sherrie Walker

twelve

AFTER THAT DAY, Que and Elise were inseparable. When he moved, she moved and vice versa. He saw that Elise's business mind was deeper than a Texas oil well and that she had an insatiable hunger for street knowledge, so he gave her the game. He instructed her on how to purchase, weigh, cook and cut both cocaine and heroin.

They discussed, and Que demonstrated the manufacturing process of the business—how much money she should bring back, depending on the size and quality of both products. But most importantly, he concluded each lesson with one message: "Trust no one in the game but me and ya girls. Dat's it. If a nigga catch you slipping one time, you gon' come up short or dead."

Elise immediately stepped in, taking charge and exercising her skills. Elise would sit in one of Que's spots serving and learning to master the game. Of course, she pulled LaKiesha and Aparis in so they could make some fast cash. It didn't take much persuasion – anything that make sense out of their dwindling cents they were game to try. LaKiesha was in charge of counting the money, pick-ups and payday. Aparis was in charge of the cell phone operation and distribution in which she would make sure all the soldiers had new cell phones every week and would dispose of the old ones.

Everybody was getting paid. Que was respecting Elise's knowledge and game even more when she stepped up to the plate.

In return, she taught him how to read body language and other forms of non-verbal communication because she believed actions spoke louder than words. Most of the time, anyway. Que took her to the majority of his business meetings so she could see exactly how situations played out. Once the meeting was over, he would ask her questions about one person or another to see how she felt about them, and she always kept her observations gutter real.

He saw just how observant she was the very first time he took her to sit in on a meeting with the top soldiers on his squad. The meeting was held on 67th and Hough in a small white nondescript building that served as a candy store front that the crew used as a weekly meeting spot and to move large quantities of cocaine. It was clean and had three rows with one of those old fashioned ice cream freezers that extended the length of the check out counter. The small back room held a long table that sat in the middle of the floor and took up most of the room. An old computer sat in the corner on top of a desk with an old leather chair. The computer was used to order candy, chips and other small items that the store sold. There were a total of fourteen chairs that surrounded the table, six on the left and six on the right and a chair at the head of each end.

In attendance were Trey, Cali and Dre. Cali and Dre were brothers-in-law. Elise thought the two together was a comical sight. They made the oddest pair, and one was

Sherrie Walker

never seen without the other.

Cali was soft spoken and stood 6 feet, 3 inches, and was 240 pounds of solid muscle. Dre on the other hand stood a mere 5 feet, 4 inches and weighed 158 pounds. He was mild-mannered and hardly ever said more than a few words when she was around. Nevertheless, Elise got the distinct impression that he was no joke and that one would rather run through a Muslim camp with a pork chop then to fuck with him. Elise always got good vibes from Cali and Dre.

Then there was Spoon. Elise watched and studied him like she was studying for a calculus exam, and didn't like him off the rip.

Que pulled out her chair so she could sit next to him. "Everybody, I want y'all to meet my wifey, Elise. She's going to be sitting in on a lot of the meetings from here on out."

"What? What the fuck is this, yo? Since when did our women start coming to our sets?" Spoon challenged.

Que turned to Spoon with an icy stare. "Excuse you! Today, and since I said so, niggah. And, I'm going to suggest that you put your mouth and attitude in check, dude." Spoon smiled condescendingly and turned away from Que's stare. "This one will be coming anytime I choose to bring her, or anytime she chooses to come. You gotta problem wit' it?"

"Nah, dawg, my bad. You call the shots. I'm tight … whatever you say, boss." Que felt and heard his sarcasm, but made a mental note to get with Spoon at a later date and proceeded to continue with the meeting. After an hour of discussion, the meeting ended and Que and Elise headed out. On the ride home Que asked her what she thought about the meeting.

Sherrie Walker

Elise took a moment examining her opinion before she answered. "For the most part, the meeting went fine. But I have some issues with Spoon. Baby, I sense everyone's loyalty and dedication except his. Call it a woman's intuition, or a gift, but my gut tells me he ain't right. He has an appetite for destruction and given the opportunity he will set out to satisfy it."

"That nigga might get a little simple at times, but he ain't crazy. He ain't crazy enough to try me, baby."

"Nah, he don't want to try you, he want to be you! And if it meant crossing you, he would. It's all stemming from his admiration and envy of you. He wants to be you so badly he can taste it."

Que looked at Elise for a few moments, astonished. "Damn, you feel it's like that...you analyzed him like that?"

"Yeah. The whole time you were speaking he kept clenching his jaws and wouldn't look at you when you spoke. It's like he resents you having the power to dictate and call the shots. I don't feel him a little bit. Baby, all shut eye ain't sleep. He ain't sleep at all, he's just laying for the right moment. He's replaceable. Let his ass go. Can't you get rid of him?"

As they were stopped at the light, Que rubbed the side of Elise's face. "Baby, I'll stay on top of Spoon. I'll pay closer attention to him and his moves. But I can't just put the nigga out the crew. Up until this point, he's been right. Never short and always on point with the product. But since you feel this strongly about him, if he ever pull one stupid move, his ass is history."

Elise turned to look at Que and thought, *I love this man so damn much.*

"Baby, I'm serious. Use the information I gave you

Sherrie Walker

and stay aware and be cautious of him at all times."

"Our feelings match, because I'm serious, too. Trust me baby, I'm on this and I will be cautious."

They rode the rest of the way home talking about business and the progress they were making.

Elise told Que that she dug what he had going on, but she wanted to know what he planned to do with it. He was perplexed by the question, so Elise broke it down for him. "You getting all this money, and for what? What would happen in three years or even in six months?"

Elise started schooling Que on investing. She shared with him her plans to open a computer store. She showed him figures and stats, proving that computers were lucrative. Once Que saw her business plan, he agreed that he would follow her lead. Their goal was to have businesses up and running within a year, close down their drug business and go strictly legit. Elise would be in charge of finding the properties, space and negotiating costs. Que would supply the money.

They hustled with a vengeance, and were making money hand over fist. They saved their money and on a daily basis were getting closer to their mark.

After several months of grinding, Elise started looking at different properties. Que told Elise about some cats that were trying to get on in Akron and had been at him about a meeting. After several persistent phone calls, Que set up a meeting place at one of his boys' empty apartment buildings in Akron. The apartment building was one of the spots they used to move weight and hold important meetings. Que set it up for the following week.

Elise rode with Que to the meeting and discussed what was about to go down. She didn't feel good about the whole set-up, but agreed to at least meet with the young cat and feel the situation out. Trey and Cali were already at the spot as they pulled up to the apartment building. The building was six stories high with three exits. It was a red brick building and some of the windows were missing. There were four cars in the parking lot. Trey and Cali rode together parking their car near an exit door. The other car belonged to Tango, the look out man who covered the roof.

The third car had to be G-Grip's, and Que's car made the forth. He and Elise got out and checked out the surroundings. "You sure about this, baby? How do you know we're not walking into a set-up?"

"Because, remember I told you this is my boy's spot. It may seem as if we're out here naked. But, trust and believe, we're not! Eyes are everywhere." Que grabbed Elise's arm and lead her toward the back of the building and through a large, metal, rusty door. Once inside Elise covered her nose as the smell of urine, beer and decay assaulted her nose.

Que lead the way up two flights of old, raggedy stairs until they reached the second floor. He opened the door allowing them to enter into the hallway. As they proceeded down the hallway, Elise noticed there were beer bottles everywhere. Some of the apartments didn't have doors attached as they made their way to the last door on the left-hand side.

Que and Elise stepped into the old apartment. Trey was sitting down at a long, brown table conversing with G-Grip. Another dude, Tony, stood by the window looking out. Tony made eye contact with Elise and she tried to read his eyes but he shifted away quickly. Que and Trey nodded.

"Que, this is G-Grip. Standing over there is Tony."

Sherrie Walker

Tony and G, this is my hip bone, Que." Trey turned to look at Elise. "And this is Elise. Like metal drawn to a magnet, Elise immediately picked up bad vibes.

Elise watched G-Grip closely. He was so light that his complexion seemed to illuminate the room. He had small, beady eyes, a medium-sized afro and long side-burns. He had the largest set of pink lips that Elise had ever seen. What bothered her about G-Grip was how he kept shifting in his chair and how he chain smoked. The room was so smoky it put one in the mind of an after-hour joint.

His partner, Tony, at 5 feet 8 inches with a solid build, was a nice looking young guy with curly locks pulled back into a ponytail. He had thick eyebrows and long eyelashes with neatly trimmed side burns. But Elise peeped something about Tony, too. Throughout the whole discussion, he didn't look at G-Grip at all. Instead, he looked straight ahead or out the window. There was something nagging about his demeanor that kept Elise on guard. It wasn't necessarily him, but the whole set-up, period.

Trey looked at G-Grip for several seconds as he lit his seventh cigarette. "So, G, where did you say you heard 'bout me?" G-Grip smiled as he stubbed his cigarette out on the floor. "Shoot, who ain't heard 'bout you, playa. I'm ready to take care of business and get this money, nai mean?" G-Grip looked toward Tony who stared out the window. Elise watched in silence. G-Grip shifted in his chair a few more times and began to cough. Que tried another approach. "How long you been slinging?"

G-Grip went into another coughing fit before he replied. "Shit, probably as long as yo lil' ass been talking, son." G-Grip tried to laugh but it was more like a choking sound as he coughed.

G-Grip just looked plain shady to Elise. Every time Que or Trey asked him a question, he got a twitch in his eye. It was barely noticeable, but Elise recognized it right off. It became more apparent when they asked him where he was from and how long he had been in the game.

"Que, can I speak to you in the hallway for a second?" Elise asked, deciding that G-Grip was getting too antsy.

"Yo, son, we gonna do business or what?" asked G-Grip, glancing over at Elise.

"I feel you, dawg," Que replied. "Hold up, this won't take but a second. Trey, count the money and I'll be right back." Que and Elise walked out of the door.

"That nigga ain't right, baby," Elise spat.

"Why you say that, Boo?"

"Every time you ask the nigga a question he gets this twitch in his right eye. That tells me he's nervous about something. Que." She shook her head. "He ain't right."

Que looked at Elise for a few seconds and then kissed her softly. "Take the keys and go home. I'll be there shortly."

"Nigga, are you crazy?" Elise said. "This ain't no movie where you send the broad home. I leave, you leave. You stay, I stay." Elise glared defiantly at Que, her hands punched on her hips.

"It may get ugly."

"I've seen ugly before," she continued.

"Where's the Gat?"

Elise opened her purse and showed Que her gun.

"Put it on you," Que instructed.

Elise nodded, took it out of her purse and put it in the small of her back.

Sherrie Walker

"Just sit like you were and don't say a word or do anything unless I tell you to," Que commanded.

"Ok."

They walked back into the room as Trey was zipping up the bag of money.

"We ready to take care of business now?" G-Grip asked.

"It's all good, son," Que said as he slightly nodded his head to Trey when they made eye contact. "Trey, give 'em the good stuff."

Trey opened his suitcase and pulled out two nine millimeter pistols and pointed them at G-Grip as well as Tony.

"Let's try this again," said Que, as he walked over and frisked the men before taking their guns. "Now, where did you say you heard about me and who sent you?"

"I told you … niggas are talking about you, son," G-Grip replied. "Word gets around when you moving them thangs. What's the problem?"

"I think you lying, dawg, and you're not going to leave here walking if I don't get the truth," Que asserted. He pulled out his cell phone and dialed a number while keeping his 9 mm pointed at G-Grip. "Come up here. We got a little situation going on up here. Come on up."

"Look, we'll just take our business elsewhere. If you ain't trying to get this money, we out," G-Grip said as he got up and headed toward the door. Before he went three steps, Trey shot him in the leg and he fell to the floor screaming and holding his wounded limb.

Cali marched in and stood next to Elise with a gun in each hand.

Que walked over to G-Grip and stepped on his bleeding leg. He screamed like a woman in labor.

"Dude, what's the problem? What's this 'bout? You're makin' some kind of ... big mistake ... a ...a ...mistake. Please, let's talk!"

Trey walked over to Tony and put the gun to the back of his head. "You want to walk out of here or be carried out in a body bag?"

Tony closed his eyes tightly and an image of his fifteen-year-old sister came to mind. His sister was all he had left in this world. It was breaking his heart knowing that Canine had control of her mind to the point that he had had her strung out on crack and selling her body. Tony tried doing everything to get her away from Canine. But nothing seemed to work.

Reluctantly, he joined Canine's crew slinging rocks to be closer to his sister. The longer he worked for Canine, the more he despised him. If only he could figure out a way to 187 Canine.

"Depends."

"Depends on what?" Que asked.

Tony opened his eyes, looked up at Que and asked, "Will you help me, if I help you?" He looked frightened and began to sweat under the pressure and glare of Trey.

"You better shut up, nigga!" G-Grip yelled.

"Check it out. This fake, wanna-be John Gotti sent us to get at you, man. But I don't give a damn about dude. This here ... it's strictly business, for real," Tony explained. "I got a personal beef with the lame and been wanting to see someone murk the nigga. It's gone get done one way or the other."

"What's your beef, young blood?" Que inquired.

"He got my fifteen-year-old sister strung out on crack and got her out on the track, making money for his grimy ass. No matter what I do or say, she won't listen. She's all I got, dawg, and I'd die for her. But she won't listen to me, so I got to get in where I fit in, nai'mean?"

"You're a dead man," G-Grip pronounced.

"I'll give you five grand and help you get your sister if you lead me to this cat," Que proposed.

"It's on," Tony responded.

"What's this nigga's name?" Trey asked.

"He go by Canine."

Que froze, and for a few seconds, he couldn't breathe. It felt like someone knocked the air out of him. He couldn't hear anyone in the room talking as his mind flashed back to the day when Canine and Rock barged into his home, and in cold blood, killed his parents. Que had made a promise to his dead parents, LaKiesha, and himself that he would find and kill Canine. For years, he tried to locate him but couldn't. While doing time, Que learned bits and pieces about him, but no one could pinpoint his exact location.

Que walked over to the window and stared at the cars traveling along Exchange Street for a few minutes. The room was quiet.

"Where this nigga at?" Que asked.

"Right here in Akron, but he outta Cincinnati. So he kind of roams everywhere," Tony sang like a studio gangster.

"You just signed your death certificate," G-Grip said.

"So did you!" Trey walked over to G-Grip, paused, then knelt down to his eye level. He brought the gun up slowly, all the time maintaining eye contact and looking G in the eyes. He placed the tip of the gun against his temple. Trey looked up at Tony who began to shuffle from one foot to the other.

Sherrie Walker

Without looking at G-Grip, Trey fired the gun and blood splattered across his face and mouth. He slowly stood and wiped his face with his sleeve. Trey looked down at G-Grip's body and fired two more times. PAP...PAP.... Each bullet ripped his head open until it looked like a busted melon with blood oozing from the gunshot holes. "We gon' actually trust this little nigga, just like that. You trust him, Que?" Trey asked as he looked to Tony.

Que gazed at Elise. She nodded. The room fell silent for a while.

"His beef was personal, Trey. But, if he's lying, we'll bury his ass too," she said with confidence and a smile.

"You lucky my girl feel you. I trust her judgment. So, since she said you're in, it's on. You ready to put in some work?" Que asked.

"I was born ready," Tony responded. "I want to raise my sister up out of that hell hole first and foremost. You help me get my sister and you don't owe me shit for real. She's fifteen, dawg, all the family I got, nai'mean. Nothing in this life is mo' important to me then my fam first, and my music second. After I get this money it's all about my music and making that green so I can take care of mine.

"What, you a rapper, Youngblood?" Cali asked.

"Yeah, I got my own thang going. I'm the best thang out since L.L. *'Rock the Bells'*, and I'm badder," Tony responded.

"Hell nawl," Trey and Que said together and laughed.

"But I'm fo' real, I'm the truth baby. Just let me create. And y'all a see."

"So we do this shit fo' real," Tony replied with so

Sherrie Walker

much conviction that you couldn't help but believe him.

Que finally `spoke up. "You in,` youngblood. But remember a picture show beats a thousand words. So just know that all eyes will be on you."

"I'm cool with dat."

"Tango," Que ordered, "y'all can get this mess cleaned up, then meet me at the spot so we can determine how to pull this thorn out of my side. Let's go, baby. Trey, take Tony with you and we'll meet you at our spot on 67th and Hough. Have everyone there in an hour." Que and Elise left the spot.

Walking to the car, Que was in deep in thought.

"Baby, what is it?" Elise asked, but Que just continued to walk to the car after they got in. He sat behind the wheel but didn't turn the ignition.

"Que!" Elise raised her voice. "Talk to me. Please!"

"I been looking for this fool since I was a kid."

"Who? Canine?" Elise asked, then quickly realized Canine was the same person who had killed Que's parents. She knew how badly Que wanted him dead, but she also knew Que couldn't act on anger because it would impair his ability to reason. He'd taught her that philosophy.

"Baby, listen to me." She turned Que's head so she could look directly in his eyes. "I'm with you on this to the bitter end, and I'll smoke the fool for you if you want me to, but you have to think this out and don't let anger cloud your judgment. I know you want him bad. I do, too. He hurt you, and what hurts you, hurts me. However, I will not let you run into a set-up.

"First, we got to make sure Tony is on the up and up. Then, we'll act only after we strategize. Now, we still have time before Canine knows that we are on to him, but we

Sherrie Walker

need to come up with our plan and execute it ASAP. We won't do some bootleg drive-by only to shoot up everybody but Canine.

"Let's go to the spot, posse up and see which way we gonna hit this nigga. I need you to stay focused, baby. Let go of the anger, for now, and let's do this. You feel me, bae?" She reached for his hand, pulled him in close to her, and gave him a kiss.

Que looked at Elise, and then he took her in his arms and kissed her passionately. He stopped and stared in her eyes. "I love you, girl. You complete me."

"And I love you. I've loved you from day one. So, let's do this!" She removed her cell phone from her purse. Que pulled off as Elise made calls. For Elise, this moment sealed their relationship. She now knew that she could die for Que Hayes.

They arrived at the storefront location on 67th and Hough and assembled with the others. Que stood at the head and Elise, LaKiesha, Aparis, Trey, Tony, Cali, Dre and Spoon sat around the table.

Que glanced over his most trusted soldiers. He locked eyes with Trey. Trey was Que's best friend and his top lieutenant—they went far back as an old man's receding hairline and were like brothers. As Trey looked at Que, he knew what his partner was going through. He's shared in his pain and was ready to go find this nigga Canine.

Que trusted Trey with his life and there were no secrets between them, they never argued, and they always split the profits down the middle. Then, there was California, who everybody called Cali. His family moved from Compton to Cleveland into the King Kennedy projects when he was twelve. That had been a big change for

Sherrie Walker

Cali.

Six months after moving to Cleveland, his father left his mother for a younger woman. It was a struggle for Cali's mother to take care of six children alone, so he started selling crack to help take care of his family. He was muscular, worked out religiously, ate healthy foods and was always getting on Que and Trey about the junk food they consumed. He didn't smoke, drink or do drugs, and reminded everyone in the crew that their body was their temple.

Cali's brother-in-law, Dre, was notorious and known to take a nigga's life faster than the blink of an eye. Cali could never recall a time when Dre was afraid of anything.

Spoon talked shit and let his mouth overload his ass. Plus, he thought he was God's gift to women. Despite his character defects, he was thorough and took care of business. Que was confident that his crew could get the job done.

Que started the meeting. "I appreciate y'all dropping what you were doing to rush over here. This is indeed important," he began. "I know some of you are wondering who youngblood is. He's going to be joining us since he brings to the table some very valuable information."

Everyone looked at Tony then back at Que.

Que cleared his throat. "Since hitting the game and coming up, I have always been motivated to reach the top because of my O.G. He was true to the game and didn't deserve to die the way he did. My mom didn't deserve what happened to her, either. So, I say all this to say, for a long time I've been in the dark, but finally I know where the man is who murdered my people."

"Well, what we waiting on? Let's smoke da fool, yo!"

Sherrie Walker

Dre said.

"We will, as soon as Tony gives us the particulars," Que replied.

"Here's what we got to do," Tony started. He talked for over an hour and by the time he finished everyone knew what needed to be done.

"Let's do this," Que commanded. Everyone got up and started to file out then jumped in their cars. "Kiesha, let me holla at you, baby girl."

"What's up?"

"You down wit' this?" Que asked as his hands cupped her arms. "You don't have to do this. I can handle it," he continued.

"Please, Que, they were my parents, too. How you gonna play me?"

"I just want to know if you feeling what we 'bout to do. Anything can go wrong." LaKiesha drew her gun, pulled back and loaded the chamber.

"Let's go," she stated firmly.

LaKiesha, Aparis and Elise jumped in the car together and everyone pulled off.

"I appreciate y'all for this one," LaKiesha said.

"Girl, please! We fam. We all we got," Elise responded.

"All for one and one for all," Aparis chanted.

"Three the hard way," they sang in unison.

Sherrie Walker

thirteen

AN HOUR LATER, Elise, LaKiesha and Aparis arrived at a crack house on the Westside of Akron off Copley Road. They cut the car off, sat for a second and watched the flow of traffic walking up and in and out of the crack house. LaKiesha thought back to the day Canine and his partner barged into their home killing their parents and changing their lives forever. She rolled the window down and looked towards the sky. *The moon and stars are so pretty and out of place in this cold, uncaring world.* She sniffed the night air.

"Do y'all smell that?" LaKiesha asked.

"What? You smell something? Aparis asked.

"Uh, uh…"LaKiesha turned to look at Aparis, pulled her 9 mm out and attached the silencer to it. "I smell death in the air tonight."

They got out the car and went up to the door and rang the bell. Moe, standing 6 feet tall, black as midnight with a rock hard muscled frame, sporting a pronounced Black Dragon and Black Panther tattoo on each of his forearms and a Gangsta skull on the side of his neck, answered the door with a Glock in his hand. He looked Aparis up and down and slowly licked his thick lips.

Sherrie Walker

"What can I do for you, lovely?"

"I'm looking for G-Grip. I'm supposed to meet him here at twelve, but I'm a little early," Aparis replied.

"G ain't here, but maybe I uhm … can help you."

Aparis seductively licked her lips, running her tongue across them and biting gently on them while looking at the man. "Maybe you can, maybe you can't," she cooed.

"Come on, sweets, we ain't got time for this. We came for business," Elise interrupted. LaKiesha stood to the side of the door.

The man looked at Elise and, if looks could kill, she would have died on the spot.

"I can't help it if G ain't here. What you want me to do?" Aparis continued, running her hand up and down his sleeveless arm. "Really, he can do the job."

"I … I can. I got whatever you need."

"Well …" Aparis said, like she was undecided.

"I ain't got all day!" Elise retorted, standing to the side of LaKiesha.

"We want two ounces, big Daddy. We 'bout to have a little party and maybe, if you're nice, I will invite you," Aparis cooed persuasively.

He stood back, let them in and drooled all over himself as he watched Aparis sashay into the house. She opened her jacket to expose her cleavage.

"Where you from, slim? I ain't ever seen you around the way?" he asked.

"Bowling Green University, big daddy. Just here for a little party, trying to have some fun."

Elise looked around the house while they stood in the living room with its dingy curtains. The spot-stained living room walls were a pale beige that clashed with the old, ugly, green couch that had the audacity to have two

Sherrie Walker

matching chairs. Then the tannish-brown carpet, if it was safe to call it that, was so worn it resembled lawn carpet. The black hole in the center of a wall, where a fireplace obviously once was, had the residue of everything but burnt wood in it. It look like it was a gigantic ashtray that cigarette butts and chicken bones were disposed in. There was a 15" television that sat on top of an outdated floor model television in the far left corner of the room. Both were on, yet serving two different purposes, one was for audio, the other for visual.

The room reeked of a foul, musty smell that tickled her nose when she inhaled. Stepping further into the living room, she noticed the wooden staircase and a door to the left of her, which was closed. Elise walked slowly toward it while Aparis talked to Moe. As she got closer, Killa, a 5 foot, 6 inch scrawny, bumpy faced, nappy ponytail wearing mustard-colored man came through the door, talking on his cell phone. He looked at Elise, Aparis and LaKiesha, then abruptly ended his call.

"Who dis?" he asked.

"Can I use your restroom?" LaKiesha danced like she would relieve herself any moment. Moe pointed to the half bathroom right next to the kitchen to indicate its location on the first floor.

"These fine women are trying to have a little fun. They here to see Grip, but I got dis," Moe replied. He walked over to Aparis and began to whisper in her ear. She giggled while Killa approached Elise.

"What's up wit' you, yo?" he asked.

"Two ounces. That's what's up," she said.

"Two ounces? How I know you ain't po po?" he asked, touching her hair.

Elise smacked his hand away. "I'm not. Ask G, he

Sherrie Walker

knows us."

"Where you know Grip from?" Killa asked. "We haven't seen Grip in a minute."

"From back in the day. We went to Butchel together. Now, can we get served or are we gonna play twenty questions, nigga?" Elise snapped.

"Oh, you flighty, huh? I like 'em wit' fire." He rubbed her face and this time Elise thumped his hand like she was thumping a bug.

"I can give you two ounces, baby girl. But, you got to do something for me in return." He started to massage his manhood as he looked Elise up and down.

"So, it's like that, huh?" Elise raised her eyebrow.

"Most definitely! You down or what?"

"I think I can handle it," she asserted.

Elise walked up on the man and seductively pushed him onto the couch, then began to dance in front of him. She shimmied around him to the back of the sofa and rubbed his head, so of course he didn't see her pull out a nine millimeter with an attached silencer. She put it to the back of his dome and pulled the trigger. He flopped over the couch. His friend stared at the limp body but, before he could react, LaKiesha had her gun pointed at his head and Aparis was removing his gun from his hand.

"What? Dis a stick up? You know who you fuckin' wit'?"

"This ain't no robbery, trick. How many more in here?" LaKiesha questioned.

"I ain't telling you shit. You got to kill me."

"No problem," LaKiesha responded, then shot him in the foot. Aparis covered his mouth to silence his scream. LaKiesha put the muzzle of the gun to his head. "Before you release another sound, I will put a bullet in your

Sherrie Walker

brain. Understand?" He nodded his head. "Now, I'm going to ask you one more time. How many are left in the house?" she demanded. He held up two fingers.

"Where?" Elise asked. He pointed upstairs.

"Is Canine upstairs?" LaKiesha inquired. She aimed the gun at his crotch. His eyes got as big as saucers and signified as much. He nodded his head up and down really fast. "Plea ... please don't shoot ... please," he begged.

"Where is he?" LaKiesha probed.

"In the bedroom ... with some broad."

"Thank you," she said. "Now was that so hard?" Without delay, LaKiesha shot him in the back of the head.

Elise walked over to the door and opened it. She dialed a number on her cell phone. "Front door." She closed her phone and posted up with LaKiesha and Aparis as Que and Trey entered. "He's upstairs in the bedroom with a broad," Elise informed the men.

Que scanned the room and saw the dead bodies. He smiled, then immediately put his game face back on.

"Y'all aight?"

The girls nodded as Tony, California, Dre and Spoon stormed the front doorway. After realizing the entrance was clear, they started looking into the rooms. Que took off up the staircase and Trey and the girls followed.

Que stopped at the first door that was closed and listened. He could hear moaning inside the room. He pointed to the door, then stepped back and kicked it open. When Que burst through, Canine jumped up from the coupling and the girl screamed. Tony had to look away as tears formed in his eyes when he glimpsed into the room and recognized his fifteen-year-old sister,

Sherrie Walker

Tiffany, as the one lying there naked. Que took one look at Tony and knew that that was his sister. "Get your sister and take her out of here, Tony." Without hesitation, Tony's sister jumped off the bed covering her naked body with the sheet and darted from the room. Tony ran after her.

Canine reached toward the dresser drawer and Que shot him in the hand.

"Ah, mothafucka!" Canine automatically grabbed his hand and examined the hole in his palm. "Nigga, are you crazy?" he yelped in pain.

"I've been told that a time or two," Que retorted.

LaKiesha walked over to the bed and looked down at Canine. She hacked up all the mucus she could generate then spit the glob in his eye. Everyone else stood and watched.

"What the hell y'all want? Y'all want money? Take it, but y'all lil' mothafuckas don't know who y'all fuckin' wit'," Canine growled.

LaKiesha slammed the butt of her gun across the lower half of his face. Canine spit out blood and a couple of teeth.

"BITCH! What the hell? What do you want?" In the face, Canine almost looked like Nino Brown after he received the beat down by Scotty Appleton.

"Retribution," Que demanded.

"Payback? Payback for what? Who da fuck is you?"

"Six years ago, nigga … Shaker Heights … Marcus and *Pearly* Pearl, remember dem, nigga?" Que pronounced each word distinctively.

The light of recognition registered in Canine's eyes and he started sweating.

"Uh! Look here, young-blood …that wasn't personal.

Sherrie Walker

That was business. I was hired ... wasn't my idea," Canine explained.

"Then whose idea was it?" Que interrogated. Canine looked around the room at everyone. Aparis and LaKiesha looked puzzled. Tony was yelling before he entered the room. Canine lunged for him.

"You ... you set me up ..."

"You fucked my sister one time too many. You won't fuck her no mo', you maggot!" Tony exclaimed.

LaKiesha cracked Canine in the head with the butt of her gun again and he fell to the floor. Tony walked over to him and looked down. Canine was out cold. Tony picked up the ice pitcher, removed the bottle of Moët then dumped the contents on Canine. He awoke, startled. Tony kicked Canine in his ribs and he curled into a ball on the floor. "Dis for my sista." He continued to kick him until Que pulled him off.

"That's enough, T. Don't kill him yet," Que commanded.

"Come on. We got work to do." Trey directed the crew. "We going to clean up and see what all we can find. You all right, Que?" he asked.

"Yeah. Elise and LaKiesha, take the basement. Tony, take your sister somewhere safe then call me in an hour. Trey, you and Dre dispose of the bodies downstairs. Aparis, wipe down. Spoon and Cali, we'll take care of this."

Everyone dispersed to take on their assignment. "Let's get him on the bed and tie him up," Que ordered. They lifted Canine and threw him on the bed. California ripped the sheets and began to tie Canine up. "Turn him on his stomach."

"Please, don't kill me ... I'll give you dope, I'll pay you

money ... big money ... whatever you want," cried Canine. He scrambled on the bed but California gutted him one good time.

"You sent your boys to rob me," Que said. "You know I don't want your money, fool. What I want is information. Give me that, and we good. Otherwise, you know what time it is."

"I don't know who hired us. I never met the cat. Please, you gotta believe me," Canine pleaded.

"Gag him," Que commanded. He walked toward the door and grabbed a broom that was leaning against the wall then marched back over to the bed. He took the end of the stick and pointed it right at Canine's rectum.

Canine trembled and thrashed around. Que rammed it into his anus. Canine tried to scream, but the rag muffled the sound. Que pulled the broomstick out, waited for a few minutes, then snatched the gag out his mouth.

"Let's try this again. Who hired you?" For several seconds, Canine couldn't put words together. Que stood at attention with the broom to the floor in front of Canine. The two men stared into each other's eyes.

Hesitantly, Canine spoke. "He ... he ... went by the name Ghost."

"Ghost?" Que pointed the end of the handle to the tip of Canine's nose and pushed upward. "Nigga, come better than that. I need a name, address and description, something better than some fuckin' Ghost."

"We met at this spot ... King's bar. He knew your old man."

"How do you know that?"

Before he could speak, Canine passed out from the pain. Que stuck the rag back into his mouth, then rammed the handle back into his butt, pulling it in and

Sherrie Walker

out with a rapid motion. He then shoved it in as far as it could go. Canine's eyes popped open and almost out their sockets, as tears rolled down his face. He urinated and defecated simultaneously all over the bed. The smell was so nauseating that Que heaved but quickly regained his composure.

"This is how my mother felt when you violated her in every way imaginable," Que spoke in a calm, yet sinister tone. "One more time! What's the mothafucka's name? And how do you know he knew my family?" Que snatched the gag out of his mouth.

"Oh, my God ... please ... please ... stop ... I..." Que slapped Canine and saliva and blood flew from his mouth.

"Answer my questions, niggah, and it will stop."

"He knew everything about your family, even the lay-out of the house. He was close with your father. Whoever he was ... he knew your people. He paid cash and said whatever we found was ours to keep. It wasn't a robbery, like I said before, it ..." he groaned, "it was a hit."

Que stood still in deep thought for a few minutes. There weren't that many people his father had been close to. J. Dobb was a long time friend, business partner of Trey's father. He and Marcus had grown up and put in work together just like Que and Trey. Marcus had trusted J. Dobb like a brother. *We called him Uncle JD,* Que remembered. Six months after his parents were killed, Uncle JD had been arrested and sentenced to fifteen to life.

Then there was Smoky, another one of his father's partners. He'd taken Marcus' death hard and gotten out the game. Red, my father's brother, wasn't in the game and wanted my dad to get out. He tried to adopt us but the state wouldn't give him custody 'cause he had an extensive criminal record. Who could this nigga be talking about?

"Please … let me go. I got two kids, dawg."

"Funny, that's the same thing my father said before you killed him." Que pulled out a switchblade, clicked it open, snatched Canine's head back and slit his throat from ear to ear. Bright red blood splattered all over the bed, floor and Que.

The smell of feces and blood polluted the air. "Let's get this mess cleaned up and bounce," Que ordered.

Sherrie Walker

fourteen

ON SEPTEMBER 24, 2000, Elise stood with her mouth open at the entrance of one of Cleveland's hottest night clubs, the Metropolis, as she realized on this cool night LaKiesha, Aparis and Que had surprised her with a party on her nineteenth birthday. They had tricked her good, making her think she was merely going out clubbing it. She was thrilled, happy and speechless to think that they went all out for her birthday.

The birthday girl looked stunning in an Armani gown as she wore the perfect Spiral up-do with a bit of color. Elise stood still and glanced around at everyone. *For once in my life I've been caught totally off guard*. Players and hustlers from all walks of life were in attendance. They were dressed to the nines in their Armani, Versace, Escada, Michael Kors suits, minks, gator shoes and their bodies reeked of expensive perfume. Young, old, black, Ricans and a few whites were present. The music added the right touch. DJ Bim had the music pumping. She considered him the best DJ in town, so he was picked especially for the gig. Her favorite song by Biggie Smalls just so happened to be playing. "I love it when you call me Big Poppa. I love it when you call me Big Poppa, the show stopper," Elise sang as she stood, scanning the room.

Several faces were familiar to Elise, while a few were unrecognizable, but she smiled and graciously spoke to each and everyone of her guests. Cameras were flashing everywhere. Everyone wanted to take turns getting individual and group pictures with her.

"Girl, yo' mouth still open. You can close it any moment now. Yeah, we know we got you good," Aparis said.

The white, green, ivory and platinum colored balloons, confetti and other decorations personalized the occasion very well. Ice pitchers of Cristal, placed at select tables in the VIP section, added the perfect touch. All kinds of people were walking up to Elise and pinning money on her.

"I don't believe this," Elise said. "Did you and LaKiesha do this?"

"Nah, girl, you know my money is funny. Every dime I got goes toward tuition and books," said LaKiesha as she made eye contact with a cutie pie who resembled Usher standing at the bar. Absently, she flashed a dimpled smile.

Aparis looked at Elise. "I can't hang out too late 'cause I have finals Monday morning. Gots to get an A+. I'm still at the top of my class and those white boys hatin' for real," Aparis bragged. She spotted Tony walking through the door. He was killing them in his impeccable tailored orange and black, raw silk Valentino suit, accessorized by a pair of black Mauri gators and a form-fitting black shirt that gripped his abdomen, making Aparis want to gobble him up and savor the seed. Her conversation abruptly stopped. Elise watched Aparis, who smiled mischievously.

Sherrie Walker

"Why you trying to front like you ain't sweating that nigga? We know you are, Aparis."

"Girl, what you talking about? I ain't on him." Aparis tossed her head, feigning innocence.

"Miss us with that bullshit, Aparis. Your mouth dropped wide open as soon as you saw him walk through that door," LaKiesha added.

"Oh, y'all on that. Sound like some hating going on for real," Aparis responded.

Elise grinned as Que walked toward her. *Que! Mr. sexy. My man is FINE! Eat your heart out, biddies,* Elise thought as she watched him approach. He had on a cream-colored Armani suit with matching Italian leather shoes. His hair was cut low, with waves so deep they made you seasick. Elise thought he had the sexiest eyes and a body that made her feel like she was in heaven. *Que went all out for my birthday. He is so special.*

It had been a good year for everyone. Elise moved in with Que and business was booming. They were looking to shut down their drug operation by the beginning of next year at the rate they were going. LaKiesha and Aparis were in college. For the first time in a long time, Elise was happy. Que hired two of the best private investigators to track down Simone and she felt very hopeful that she would find her this time. There wasn't a day that went by that Elise didn't think about Simone and yearned for them to be reunited. She looked around at everyone at her party and had to smile. Que never gave her any idea that he was throwing a party for her.

Elise's party was off the chain with the best liquor flowing, plenty food for her guests and DJ Bim rocking her name every five minutes. There was even a huge cake carved to resemble her face. And just as she thought

Sherrie Walker

everything was absolutely perfect, Bone Thugs-N-Harmony made a special appearance and performed *"Foe tha Love of Money."*

Elise was overwhelmed when she realized how much she was loved. Que knew she adored the group and had arranged for them to appear since he knew them from around the way.

My man is the best, Elise thought becoming emotional as she wiped tears that flowed slowly down her cheeks. *I am so loved ... I am so blessed to receive such overpowering, intoxicating love as I have been showered with on my special day. Everyone I love is in this room except Simone.* Elise was overcome with a sudden sense of sadness, but was snapped out of it when Que crept beside her kissing her on the cheek.

The last few weeks had been hectic, Elise knew, as Que was engrossed with finding Ghost. She couldn't figure out how he had time to plan a party.

In truth, Que had become so obsessed with finding Ghost, Elise thought he had forgotten about her birthday, let alone had taken the time to plan a surprise party. Over the past week, he'd visited J. Dobb, trying to get information.

The bar where Canine said he had met Ghost was torn down, so Que went through a lot to track down the owner and question him. He remembered some guy who went by the street name Ghost, but it had been so long ago that he couldn't give a description. Que had his soldiers on the street putting in work, finding out info about Ghost, and finally, it paid off. He'd received a phone call just the day before about someone having valuable information.

Que quickly relaxed and started showing signs of his

Sherrie Walker

old self. In the midst of all the drama, he took time to put together what would become one of the most talked about affairs of the year. *My baby spared no expense*. Elise thought back to the night before last when she and Que made love. Just as he was about to enter her he stopped and looked deeply into her eyes. Elise blushed from the intensity of his stare.

"What? Why are you looking at me like that Que?" He kissed her lips softly.

"Because I want you to have my shorty Elise. Are you ready for that?"

Elise paused and looked deeply into his eyes as her heart melted with just the thought of having Que's baby. Yet, she knew that there were things that prohibited her from taking it to the next level.

"Que, yes I will have babies. I will have babies with you, but…" Elise bit down on her bottom lip and looked away. Que gently turned her face around to face him.

"What's wrong baby. You know we can talk about any-thing."

"Baby I realize we're only using the game as a step-ping stone. Using it to gain capitalize financially towards building our own company. But, until we're are out of the dope game baby, I don't want to have a baby. Anything can happen and I wouldn't want our child to grow up in the system. Once I know that we're done, we're going to have babies. By this time next year we'll be ready." Que leaned on both his elbows and stared at Elise with so much adoration and love in his eyes. Her body tingled with a warm sensation as she reminisced about that amazing night with Que.

It was about 2:30 a.m. when LaKiesha pulled Elise over to the table to begin opening her gifts. She was opening the last gift when Que walked over with his hand behind his back. In one swift motion, he presented the small, blue velvet box. Elise's heart started beating fast as she stared at it. She looked up at him and he had a mischievous smile on his face. She opened it to view the prettiest ring she had ever seen. It was a beautiful 8 carat marquise-cut diamond and platinum ring.

Que dropped to his knee, took it out of the box, and held it in front of her. "Will you marry me? Will you be my wife?" he asked. Tears slowly rolled down Elise's face. She was speechless, though everyone stared and awaited her answer.

"Yes, I'll be your wife," she said. Que picked her up and kissed her so passionately that she felt like she had died and gone to heaven with Que by her side. To them, it seemed as if no one else was in the room. Everyone clapped and cheered.

"Congratulations!" their friends called out in unison.

Que pulled away from the passionate kiss and held Elise's face between his hands, looking deeply into her eyes. "I've never felt so complete and happy in my entire life. You're my ride or die chick. Baby, I love you so hard until it hurts sometimes. Baby you've strengthened me in love and labor and in turn I pledge my life and love to you. I want to share and fulfill my hopes, my plans and my dreams with you. I want you to be my wife and have my kids and I want at least ten. All boys." Que smiled.

With tears flowing down her cheeks, Elise stared at her man and knew that he was her one and only love for life. Wiping a tear from her eye, she responded, "Everyone has a soft spot, baby, and you're mine. I want to be your wife, baby and give you babies. I don't know about no ten, but I might be able to manage six. Three

Sherrie Walker

Boys and three girls. How's that for a compromise? I have always been about you. Even when you tortured me, playing hard to get," she kidded. "I love you so damn much, boy."

Que didn't answer. He just pulled her in his arms and kissed her softly on her lips, nose and eyes. Elise began to feel a tingling sensation down below.

"We can start working on baby number one tonight," Elise suggested seductively. Que snuggled her butt in the palm of his hand while pressing her body close to his.

"Now that sounds like a plan ma." Elise gently stroked Que's face before pulling away. "We better stop now before we find ourselves sneaking away to satisfy our love jones and celebrating our engagement," Elise teased.

~ ~ ~

The party continued until 4:00 a.m. Aparis, LaKiesha, Trey, Spoon, Que and Elise were among the last to exit the building. LaKiesha gave Elise a hug. "I'll see y'all tomorrow. I got a little somethin' somethin' waiting for me at The Ritz," LaKiesha said.

"Girl, there you go with that. When are you going to find one good man and settle down?" Elise asked her dear friend and soon to be sister-in-law.

"When it's time, baby girl. Until then you can say I'm on a little test drive," LaKiesha replied. "You just worry about taking good care of my brother, sis. I'm out."

"Be careful and use protection," Aparis emphasized.

"Always." LaKiesha walked over to Que and hugged him. "Congratulations, big brother. You got a good one."

"I know," he replied with a smile. "She reminds me of Mom so much. Let me walk you to your car."

"That won't be necessary. He got me." She pointed to

a handsome guy standing at the door.

"You know that clown?"

"Yeah, I know him. Why he got to be a clown?"

"He could be a clown or a serial killer for all you know. How long have you know him, LaKiesha?"

"Long enough to know what I want from him. Which isn't love, marriage, or a baby carriage. Hell, I ain't trying to ride off in the sunset with ole boy. He's a booty call Que. That's it and that's all! I'll see you later."

She waved and strolled away. As LaKiesha walked toward Swan, whom she'd met on the dance floor and after a few drinks and dances she decided he would be her one night stand ... tonight. She grabbed Swan's hand and guided him out the door.

"You rolling with me, Que?" Spoon asked.

"Hell no! What I look like hanging with some stiff legs and it's my boo's birthday ... I'm getting ready to chill with Elise. I'll catch y'all on the 2-4, but hit me up if it's an emergency. Other than that, don't bother me!"

"I wanted to holla at you on the business tip, for real," Spoon continued.

"Holla at Trey. He can take care of it. I'm out." Que walked over to Elise. "You ready to roll, bae?"

"Yes, baby," Elise replied. "But I want to walk Aparis to her car."

"Let's roll."

Que and Elise walked Aparis to her Lexus GS 300. Aparis hugged Elise. "I'm so happy for you, Elise. You deserve all of this."

"Thank you, Aparis," Elise held out her fist and Aparis extended hers, then they pounded fists. "Three the hard way?"

"Three the hard way."

Sherrie Walker

"I love you, girl," said Elise.

"I love you, too," Aparis responded.

Aparis got in her car, locked the doors and pulled off. Que and Elise stood still for a minute, just looking at each other and enjoying the crisp morning breeze that blew off Lake Erie. He pulled her close to him and kissed her slowly. When he pulled away, he said, "You're my soulmate and to spend the rest of my life with you is my sole desire."

Elise touched his face. "You are so gorgeous, Que. You're also my soulmate, Boo. I knew the first day I laid eyes on you that you would be my husband. I loved you from the gate." They kissed again. "Now, let's get out of here before we start something in the parking lot."

They got in the car and Que pulled off. Elise slid over and began nibbling on his earlobe and licking his neck. Her hands started to roam all over his body, then she slid one downward to feel his manhood. It was hard through his pants and Que let out a moan that excited Elise even more. She unzipped his pants, pulled out his magic number and stroked it as she licked his ear and neck.

"Girl, you drive … me … crazy."

Elise eased down and licked the head of his penis. Then she took the whole thing in her mouth and ran her lips up and down the shaft. She heard Que moaning and increased her speed. She felt the car stop and figured they were at a traffic light. She seized the moment and sucked faster. Que looked around to make sure no one could see what was going on. He saw a car approaching on the left, but the windows of the car was tinted and he couldn't see inside. He thought about stopping Elise, but it was feeling so damn good, he couldn't.

He closed his eyes and was enjoying the feeling when

Sherrie Walker

he noticed movement out of his peripheral. He looked to his left and saw a shotgun pointed his direction. Que's eyes widened. "What the fuck…" He held Elise's head down as he tried to reach for his gun under his seat, but was too late as a bullet tore into his brain, splattering blood everywhere. Elise smelled the metallic smell and heard the sounds of tires burning rubber as she struggled to disentangle herself from Que's arm and body that slumped over from the impact of the shot.

After maneuvering his arm, she slowly sat up pushing Que's body back against his seat. Elise stared at Que for several seconds and had to fight the urge to vomit. Half his face was blown away and his eyes were wide open.

Her lips started trembling as her eyes filled with tears. The smell of blood and burnt tires filled the car making her stomach wrench with each breath she took. Elise started to rock back and forth as a scream slowly worked its way up from deep within her soul. She let out a piercing cry that shattered the stillness of the night and cried wrenching sobs which sounded like a wounded animal.

That's exactly the way the police found her twenty minutes later. In shock, she was hugging her body, rocking back and forth while crying. In one moment, the happiest day in her life turned into a nightmare and shattered her whole world.

Sherrie Walker

fifteen

IT TOOK EVERYTHING in Elise to keep moving. She had to make the arrangements for Que's funeral and at times it felt like she couldn't go on. LaKiesha was so devastated and just as depressed. Together they leaned on each other for support. But it was Aparis who was the source of strength that held them together. She made all the phone calls and funeral arrangements, to include the selection of his coffin, his gravesite, his five page obituary, on down to where the repast would be held.

Que was well loved and respected and there was a large show of people that attended his funeral to prove it. Boyd's funeral home was filled to its capacity. Chrysanthemums and lilies surrounded Que's casket and podium.

The arrangement was beautiful. Que had to have a closed casket because no matter how hard the mortician tried, he couldn't restore Que's face. Elise and LaKiesha wanted Que to be remembered exactly how he looked in life. There was a large, handsome picture of him on top of his casket that captured his innocence. It was Elise's favorite picture.

The minister delivered a powerful Home Going sermon that stroked many souls. Elise and LaKiesha broke down during remarks and had to be helped off the podium and back to their seats. Trey's remarks about Que were so powerful that there wasn't a dry eye in the house. Trey, LaKiesha, Aparis, Cali and Elise rode in the family limousine to the cemetery. The ride was silent, depressing and painful.

Elise stared out into the beautiful sunny day, which didn't match her mood at all. As she watched the scenery in passing, she reflected back to the time shared with Que. She remembered how she chased him for a long time and after a while she finally gave up and then he revealed his true feelings for her. She remembered the late night talks they used to have, the secrets they shared. The plans they made and the love they shared. He would always be her first and only true love. Que gave her the best years of her life. Those precious memories were forever etched on her heart.

As they pulled into the cemetery, Elise wiped her tears and made a silent promise to Que. *I'll never love another man the way that I loved you, baby. You will always have my heart, Que.*

After they lowered Que's casket into the ground, everyone left to give LaKiesha, Elise and Aparis time alone. They held hands in silence as they stood looking down at Que's casket. Elise broke the silence.

"Nothing and I mean nothing, is more important than finding who is responsible for this. The only thing I ask is that I be the one to bury this motherfucka. Me!" LaKiesha said with so much pain in her voice. "This Ghost is responsible for taking my whole family from me. I have to do this. This is my personal mission.

"I understand, Kiesh. You know I've begun tracing

Sherrie Walker

everyone's cell phone transactions the night of Que's murder," Aparis said.

"Anything yet?"

"Not yet, but I'm not done. Y'all know that if it's anything to be found, I will find it. We may not have been brother and sister, but Que was just as much my family as he was y'alls. I won't sleep until I find something."

Elise voice cracked, "I … miss him … so much. How will I go on?"

"Like we always do Elise, together!" said LaKiesha as she brought her fist up. Elise brought hers up and Aparis completed the circle. "Three the hard way." They said in unison.

"Let me have a minute alone, will you?" asked Elise.

"Sure." LaKiesha and Aparis hugged her as they strolled away.

LaKiesha allowed her rose to fall free from her hands onto Que's casket. "I love you, brother." She held a hankie up to her eyes as the tears flooded her face as she turned and walked away.

Aparis approached the grave site and put her rose on top the casket. "We got you, boo. Sleep with the angels."

After LaKiesha and Aparis walked away, Elise approached the casket and knelt before it, kissed her single red rose, brought it close to her heart and gently placed it upon Que's casket. "My baby, my special baby. I won't stop until I find out who did this and bury them face down. I will do all that we talked about. I will exercise our plans and continue pursuing our dreams and goals.

"And I'm going to do it strong with you in mind and heart. In a year or so we are going to go legit. I won't let you down and I'm going to keep our dreams alive. I will

Sherrie Walker

always love you, Que.

"When you died, you took my heart with you, daddy. I love you. May your soul rest in peace." As Elise stood over Que's casket, before she could walk away, a tear rolled down her cheek onto his casket. She turned and walked away and thought, *Hell hath no fury like a woman scorned.*

Sherrie Walker

sixteen

As ELISE CLIMBED INTO her Toyota Camry to head to the meeting place on 67th and Hough, she sat back and closed her eyes before starting the car. She reflected on all the information she'd learned since Que's death. The betrayer was amongst the crew. To her, the ultimate sin was when someone close to you betrayed you. She made a promise to Que and was determined to keep it. She would avenge his death no matter what.

For six months, she planned on how she would seek revenge. Not a day passed that she didn't think about Que, how much she missed and loved him. She still found herself grieving over him and crying at times. Every room she walked through in their condo reminded her of him and the beautiful times they shared there. She still hadn't been able to bag up all of Que's clothes and belongings to get rid of them. She felt like once she did that, she would lose what little piece of him was left in their home. At times she felt like getting out of the game but the thought would leave as fast as it came. She would complete what they started.

Elise started her car and pulled out into the flow of traffic. She felt for her 9 mm and smiled. *Yeah, it's time for*

a reckoning.

It had been six months since they buried Que and this was the first meeting they had held since his death. Elise called everyone and told them to meet her at the spot at six sharp. Christmas was in three days and there were some things she wanted to discuss with the crew.

After Que's death, Trey stepped up to the plate and ran the operations but for him it just wasn't the same. He loved and missed Que so much that at times he wanted to just get out the game. Plus, with Que's death they didn't have the connect. Que's connect did not want to do business with anyone other than Que. As much as Que tried to bring Trey into the folds with him, his connect wouldn't allow it. Elise and Trey stayed in contact on a daily basis and he kept her informed on the operations and the situation they were faced with when it came to a connect. This meeting was vital to the survival of the crew.

Elise, LaKiesha and Aparis entered the room and everyone sat still as all eyes were on them. Elise was stunning, wearing a black leather pant outfit with matching black riding boots, a leather Kangol turned to the back, driving gloves and a pair of Chanel sunglasses. LaKiesha wore a velour Rocawear jogging suit, Timberlands, leather gloves and a black bandana. Aparis had on a chic multi-colored BCBG pant suit, solid-colored shoes and a pair of BCBG sunglasses. LaKiesha and Aparis sat as Elise remained standing.

"What the hell are we doing? Are we going to let some broad dictate to us what to do? I don't care if she was Que's woman. She don't tell me what to do," Spoon complained. "That's why that nigga got caught up in the first place, listening to a bitch."

Sherrie Walker

Trey stood, walked over to Spoon and punched him in the face. Everyone heard the crunch as Trey's fist connected with Spoon's nose. Undoubtedly, it was broken.

"Don't you ever, ever disrespect Elise again," Trey growled between clenched teeth. "Next time, I'll put a bullet in that shallow-ass brain of yours. Now, we're all here because Que respected her and her mind. If my nigga trusted her, I trust her."

Spoon grabbed his nose and held his head back trying to stop the blood flow.

"Thanks, Trey. Que had mad respect for you as well. He trusted you like a brother."

Everyone acknowledged the girls with a nod of the head, except Spoon. He didn't say a word. Instead, he held his nose. "I brought you all here today for two reasons. I want the business to continue, and I will oversee things. But we have to grow, we have to get bigger," Elise explained.

"What about Que's connects?" Tony asked.

"Trey and I are meeting with them this week, and if things go according to plan, we'll soon have the cheapest, best quality dope in the state. Our birds will fly for fifteen."

"Fifteen? You must be smoking yourself," Spoon said, applying tissue to his bloody nose. "In order to sell a brick for fifteen we would have to get it for at least—"

"Seventy-five hundred," Elise finished.

"And who is giving keys for seventy-five?" he continued.

"That's none of your business. Just as long as we get the product, that's all that matters." Elise turned away from Spoon. "Now, Trey will be the first lieutenant, Cali will be the second, and Dre will be the third. LaKiesha

Sherrie Walker

will take over all bookkeeping, banking and financing matters, which Que used to handle.

"Now, y'all may not know this, but Que and I had discussed going legit, at length. We even had plans laid out. Starting real soon, we gone wash this money. Within the next few months, we're going to buy a string of computer stores and sell hardware as well as software. Aparis is also currently looking into designing and developing software. That's where the money is today. In addition, we're going to work on opening a studio and record company to snatch up a lot of the raw, local talent. Tony will be our first."

"Are you serious?" Tony's eyes lit up.

"Yes, we are serious. No more nickel-and-diming. We are going to do what Puff Daddy, 50 and the rest of these rappers and music executives are doing. Invest, transform and get rich," LaKiesha answered.

Everyone looked around for a few seconds, allowing themselves to absorb Elise's announcements. Trey walked over to Elise and hugged her. "I see why Que loved you so much, baby girl. We can do this. I'm in."

"Good, because I need you on this," Elise responded.

"Fuck this bullshit," Spoon spat venomously. "We supposed to be drug dealers and we sitting up here listening to this corny-ass bullshit. How the fuck we gone convert without the Feds being on our ass like a scab on a sore? This shit ain't gone happen. We either gone lock this shit down gansta style or we not. Que wouldn't agree with this bullshit."

"Unfortunately he's not here to speak for himself, and you don't know what me and my man discussed about the future. Que was for this one hundred percent. See, unlike you, Que didn't think with his dick and defi-

Sherrie Walker

nitely didn't have tunnel vision. He had plans, plans that your simple ass could never comprehend. Your dreams and visions go no further than a pair of new tennis shoes and rims for that piece of shit contraption you call a car. " Elise looked him dead in the eyes. The tension weighed heavily on the crew.

Cali looked around the room. Spoon had challenged Elise's authority. Cali stood up and turned to Elise. "I'm in," he said, shaking Elise's hand.

"You said it was two things you wanted to discuss. What's the other?" he asked.

Elise walked around the table. "Yes, there is another matter we must address. Everyone knows that when Que was killed, a part of me died with him. I swore to him that I would avenge his death. We have a feeling that Ghost was involved. However, we also have a Judas in our camp. Someone told him when Que was leaving the party and gave him our destination. Because they were strapped with this information, the assassin was lying in wait for us. Someone set it up, someone in this camp."

Elise gave everyone time to absorb her words while she watched and waited.

"Does anyone want to be man enough to admit it?" Elise asked.

Silence filled the room.

"I didn't think so," LaKiesha spoke.

"Tony, were you loyal to Que?" Elise questioned.

"My sister Tiffany is off the street because of Que. Hell yeah, I was loyal!" Tony responded.

"Ssspt, yeah right," Spoon scoffed.

"You calling me a liar, Spoon?"

"What if I am? You came from the other side, dawg. Just like that, you jumped ship. Where was your loyalty then? You set your own nigga up, so why not do Que too?" Tony struck out toward him from across the table, but Trey interceded before Tony connected with Spoon. "That nigga is lying, yo," Spoon continued.

Tony looked into Elise's eyes. "I had mad respect for Que, Elise. He knew why I did what I did. My sister is free now. He was good to me. I would've never crossed him like that," Tony pleaded.

"Never?" Elise thought about it. *Tony's been down with the crew for a little over a year now. I've never had reason to doubt his loyalty.* She pulled out her nine millimeter with the silencer and pointed it at Tony for a second before she swung around and shot Spoon between the eyes. His body remained in an upright position for a few seconds before her toppling over with his head hitting the table, making a loud banging sound. Trey, Cali, Dre and Tony looked around at one another confused.

Elise turned to look at Tony. "I believe you."

"That nigga was in bed with Ghost all along. He set Que up. We traced his cell phone calls the night of Que's murder and bingo—he made three strange calls, one before we left the club at 3:59, one when Que and I got in the car, and another at 4:30, after Que was killed. It was a Jersey number and I got an address, Cali. I want you and Tony to take a trip up there. See what y'all can find. It's listed under Jackie Merritt. Just see what's up."

"Ghost had our parents killed eight years ago. And now Que is dead. I want him. Don't do *anything* with the information but report it to us," LaKiesha instructed.

"Let's call the crew to get this mess cleaned up," Elise said as she pointed to Spoon's body. "Trey, we have a plane to catch on Wednesday at 8:30. You have a couple days to take care of your business and tie up your loose

Sherrie Walker

ends, so I'll see you then," Elise commanded.

"It's on," Trey replied.

"Cali and Dre will hold things down until we return. LaKiesha and Aparis will know how to reach us in case of an emergency. I'll see y'all when I return. Until then, everyone be safe." Elise stood to leave and waited by the door while Aparis finished her conversation with Tony. Without saying anything else, LaKiesha and Elise left the meeting.

Dre walked over to Spoon's corpse and spoke as he stood looking down over him. "Damn, who would've ever thought? You fucked up, nigga."

"I'll say one thing ... I'd never want to be on her bad side," Tony remarked.

"I'd have to agree with you there, youngblood," California said.

~ ~ ~

On Wednesday, Elise and Trey met at Cleveland Hopkins International Airport to board a plane headed to Orlando, Florida. They arrived early to make it through the checkpoints and to the gate on time. As they walked through the terminal, Elise noticed a sign that read, "President's Club."

"What's that?" she asked.

"That's where CEOs and other big movers and shakers hang out before or after their flights. It's private," Trey explained.

Elise stared at the signage and wondered. After a short while, people seated in the first ten rows were called to board, so they pulled out their passes and proceeded to board the plane.

"How did you pull this off, Elise?" Trey asked once they settled into their seats. "Que tried several times to get me to meet his connects but they never wanted to see no one but him."

"It wasn't me. It was the money. Que was getting anywhere from twenty to thirty keys every other week, right? Well, I told them I would get forty to fifty every week, especially if they came down on the price."

"Wow! Can we move that kind of weight?" Trey asked.

"At fifteen, we won't be able to keep it. I want Northeast Ohio on lock so that within a year, I'll have some millions in the coffers."

"Moving that kind of weight is going to bring major players and the Feds at us. You know that, right?"

"The Feds already want us ... one key or fifty, it's still jail time. I'd rather go big if I gotta go. But I don't plan on going nowhere. Most dealers get popped because they get greedy. They don't know how to get in and get out. I don't want to be looking over my shoulder the rest of my life, worried about whether or not my phone is tapped, or if my life is going to be interrupted. So we're going to establish a legit foundation as soon as possible." Elise changed the subject. "How are you coming along with that other assignment I put you on?"

"So far, the trail has grown cold. The last place Simone was known to be won't give any information as to where she was placed. I'm sending this white boy, Roger, in to investigate. He's good and he looks the part. I should be hearing from him soon."

"I have to find her, Trey. She's all the family I have. Simone was seven the last time I saw her, and it's been eight years. I wonder if we will ever be reunited. I wonder if she would remember me, Trey," Elise sadly responded.

"We are going to find her. Don't worry about that. If

no one else can find her, this white boy can. She'll remember you, too. You seem to leave an everlasting impression on everyone you meet." Trey smiled, trying to lighten her mood. He knew how baldy she wanted to find Simone and he was doing everything possible to help her. He was pretty confident that Roger would find Simone. The white boy was the best in his profession.

"I miss Que and Simone so much. It's times like these that he would make me feel like I had nothing to worry about." Elise sighed heavily.

"Hey." Trey turned her face around so she could look at him. "I may not be Que, but I am going to help you find your sister and anything else you want. You can trust me. Believe dat."

"He used to always say that you were the brother he never had. I miss him so much, Trey. My heart is so heavy." Trey hugged Elise and she laid her head on his shoulder.

"I miss him, too, Elise. I'm here for you. Get a little rest, because our livelihood depends on the outcome of this meeting." Trey sat back and looked out the window.

Elise closed her eyes and tried to rest. Trey stared off into the atmosphere at the mesmerizing sky and clouds, then turned his head back toward Elise.

"I'm going to protect you, Elise. I would die for you," he whispered.

seventeen

THE FLIGHT WAS SMOOTH and quick. Elise nodded off for about a half an hour then sat up when she heard the flight attendant's instructions for landing.

They exited the plane and the airport then took a taxi into the city. "It is beautiful. Just how I imagined it," Elise said while examining the landscape.

"I spoke with a travel agent and found a lot of places that we can visit while passing time. Not too far from the hotel, either," Trey said.

"We have about four hours to burn. Let's get checked in at the hotel, shower and hook back up," Elise suggested.

"Sounds like a plan to me."

The cab pulled up to the Clazzi hotel, and the building was breathtaking. The hotel stood twenty-five stories high, and the entire structure was made of mirrors. The entranceway had the prettiest chandeliers hanging from its ceiling and the walkway had red, plush carpet that lead from the sidewalk to the doorway.

Two uniformed bellboys immediately grabbed their luggage when they stepped out of the cab. The sun was beaming and blinding as Elise walked toward the main

Sherrie Walker

entrance, and shaded her eyes with her sunglasses.

Once they stepped inside, Elise could do nothing but stand and absorb the richly designed hotel lobby. There was a white grand piano in the center of the lobby playing elegantly as the guests lounged and went about their business. There were some of the most beautiful paintings adorning the walls. The lobby smelled like citrus fruits as Elise closed her eyes and inhaled the pleasant scent.

"I've only seen something like this on TV. It's flawless."

"Nothing but the best for the best," Trey responded. He checked in and received their key cards then handed one to Elise. "Do you want me to walk you to your room?"

"No, I'll be OK. I'll meet you back down here in forty-five minutes," she replied.

"It's on. I'm two doors down from you if need me. Room 2014."

Elise walked away, taking in every inch of the hotel. Trey had booked Presidential suites for both of them. Elise's room had a kitchen, Jacuzzi, sauna and a balcony overlooking the city. *Trey definitely has taste,* she thought. Roses were on every table in Elise's suite and a box of Godiva chocolate-covered cherries was on the pillow. A bottle of Cristal chilled next to the bed. "Man, he thought of everything."

She picked up one of the roses and smelled it. Smiling, Elise sat on the bed and reached for a piece of chocolate. She opened the box, removed a piece and was about to eat it when she suddenly laughed, remembering her last encounter with a box of chocolates. She thought back to Selena and the box of chocolates she'd laced with

Sherrie Walker

Ex-Lax. She ate the confection and several other pieces then reclined on the bed to think, knowing that by the end of the day, her life would be forever changed.

The bellhop delivered her suitcase and she tipped him fifty dollars. After he left, Elise immediately stripped out of her clothes and took a long awaited and much needed shower. She stood still under the steaming hot water, allowing it to run over her fully developed body, which had more curves than a winding road. She then turned around and tilted her head so the water flowed through her hair. She swished her hands through it and felt refreshed but not quite clean, so she reached for her Mizani shampoo to cleanse her mane.

Once her hair was dirt free, she lathered her washcloth with some Missoni body wash. As the shower water was rinsing her body, she decided she wanted to light some candles and relax in a soothing hot bath. She turned off the shower, stepped out of the tub, pulled the curtain back, then wrapped a fluffy oversized towel around her body just long enough to get her bath water started. She lit three scented candles, set her water temperature, filled the tub with Missoni bath oil, stepped inside, and let the warm water engulf her body as she rested her head back on to the form-fitting neck roll.

After relaxing for a few minutes, Elise removed the soft wash cloth from its resting place, lathered it with body wash and began to caress herself. Her own sensations combined with the warm fragrances and water seemed to bring her body alive as it responded to her touches.

Her hands moved slowly across her nipples, causing them to become erect. A soft moan escaped her lips as she closed her eyes and saw Que's face behind her eye-

Sherrie Walker

lids. Elise's body became warmer while she reminisced about the man she was to marry and how he used to set her soul on fire. Her body temperature rose as one hand glided down to her private area. She began to massage her clit with her forefinger, rubbing it in a circular motion. Then she penetrated herself and stroked her vaginal area feverishly. Her breathing began to increase as she rolled a nipple between her fingers with her left hand. She couldn't stop thinking about Que and the last time they made love. With that thought in mind, she exploded in ecstasy.

Elise's breathing restored to normalcy and her body went limp as she slightly slumped down into the warm water. "I love you, Que," she whispered.

She got out the tub and looked at the alarm clock only to realize she didn't have much time to get as fresh as she wanted before meeting Trey. She properly groomed and decided that she wanted to rock Escada from head to toe, so she put on black underwear, a two-piece white miniskirt suit and a pair of strappy sandals. She blow-dried and combed her hair back in a ponytail, which reached the middle of her back. She checked herself in the mirror and liked what she saw. She completed her look with her medium-sized diamond cut hoops, her chic Y necklace and the ring Que had given her the night he was murdered.

Elise glanced at the clock and realized it was time for her to meet Trey in the lobby. She slid her watch onto her wrist, grabbed her sunglasses and headed toward the door. The phone rang as she turned the doorknob so she ran over and snatched it up.

"You about ready?" Trey asked.

"I was just heading out the door. I'll see you in the

Sherrie Walker

hallway."

"I'll be right out." They hung up and Elise exited the room. Within two seconds, Trey appeared wearing a silk Versace shirt, opened down to the middle of his chest, with matching pants and Mauri alligator sandals.

Elise could smell him before he came within two feet of her. Bvlgari for Men was his signature cologne and he wore it well, she thought, recalling that he smelled good all the time. *When he smiles, with those pretty white teeth, he can melt any woman's heart. Except mine! Mine is already taken. It belongs to Que.*

"You looking good." Trey smiled.

"Thanks, you do, too," Elise replied. "So, let's do this."

The two walked down the corridor and entered the elevator and Elise raved on about the pretty hotel and room. Trey watched her and smiled. He had never seen her that animated or excited about anything. It was like the little kid was coming out of her. They stood in front of hotel's main entrance looking for a taxi. Moments later, two appeared.

Trey told the driver to go to Disney World once they settled into the car. Elise continued to laugh and talk the entire ride. They only had time to see a little bit of the park, so they went to Downtown Disney and walked around until they found somewhere to eat before finally heading back to the hotel.

On the ride back to the hotel, Elise became quiet and sullen. Trey tried to comfort her by holding her hand, but Elise was reluctant to give in to him.

"You worried?" he asked.

"Lightweight," she said, staring out the window as they travel through the city. They pulled up to the hotel's

Sherrie Walker

entrance and Trey paid the driver. As they approached the desk, the clerk looked up and called Elise.

"Ms. Green, you have visitors waiting on you in the dining area. They've been here over an hour."

"For me? Are you sure?" Elise questioned.

"Yes, ma'am. They left instructions to inform you to join them in the dining room upon your arrival.

Elise looked at Trey, who shrugged his shoulders then escorted Elise to her fate. No one was in the room except for two distinguished-looking gentlemen.

Sago was an extremely handsome Italian. His skin was the color of olive oil without a blemish on his face. His hair was black and wavy until it looked unreal. It made Elise want to touch it. He had the most piercing blue eyes that appeared to have the twinkle of the ocean in them. He had a neatly trimmed mustache and pretty white teeth.

Cruz was probably one of the prettiest men Elise had ever seen. His hair was long, thick and black. It hung down to his shoulders. He was the color of sand – a deep, brown color that made him look like he stayed in the sun. He lips were full and juicy, and he had a natural habit of licking them often. Elise thought, *this man is prettier than some women I've seen.* They were sitting in a corner and one of them held up his glass.

"Are you strapped?" Trey asked.

"You know it," Elise responded.

They both walked over to the table. The larger, older man indicted for them to sit while the younger held up a bottle of wine for Elise and Trey.

"No, thank you," said Elise. Trey shook his head 'no' as well.

"I apologize for the change of plans," the older man

Sherrie Walker

explained. "But I was a bit anxious to meet the infamous Elise. Que told me many good things about you, so it is indeed my pleasure to finally meet his mistress. I am Sago." He held out his hand and Elise extended hers but had a puzzled look on her face. Sago gently held onto her.

"I apologize, maybe you misunderstood. I wasn't his mistress. I was his wife."

Sago laughed then kissed the back of her left hand. "Silly kids. A mistress is a man's wife, hence the abbreviation Mrs. Especially when she's an influential man's first lady." He released her hand. "Again, I apologize for my inconsiderateness. As I said, I am Sago and this is my brother, Cruz." Cruz tipped his head.

"Elise, of course, and my partner, Trey."

Everyone shook hands.

"Trey, I've heard good things about you as well. Que tried several times to introduce you to us but unfortunately we have to turn down a lot of people. It's just hard to trust people now-a-days. Que was different. A good man, he was. You were Que's best friend, were you not?" Sago asked.

"Yes, he was like a brother to me," Trey stated matter-of-factly. "I'm curious to know something, Sago. If Que couldn't get me to meet you, what changed your mind?"

Sago looked at Elise and smiled. "Let's just say … Elise can be very persuasive," answered Sago with humor and a twinkle in his eyes. Sago turned serious with his next sentence.

"Good. It's good knowing you were like brothers. It saddened me to hear about what happened to Que. He was a good, honest man," said Sago. "You take care of the problem. Yes?"

Sherrie Walker

"Part of it. The other half is in process. But, it will be handled, you can bet on that," Elise answered.

"Unfortunately, I'm not a betting man, but should you need my assistance, please don't hesitate to let me know. I liked Que."

"Thank you." Elise smiled. Sago looked at Trey.

"So, Elise, you think you want fifty keys a week?" Sago inquired.

"No."

"No?" Sago turned to Cruz, puzzled.

"I don't think I want fifty a week, I know I want fifty," Elise articulated.

"I can do that. I can give it to you for, say, eight per kilogram and deliver them to you."

"Seventy-five and I will pick them up myself, so you're making three seventy-five a week, Sago, plus you don't have to worry about transportation," she articulated, negotiating like the CEO of a Fortune 500 company. Poker-faced, she continued. "And, might I add, I will be paying for my packages up front so you don't have to give me nothing. Let's put it like this. I will give you three seventy-five for my first fifty, then I'll be back for the second the following week and we'll go from there. You'll always be ahead and I'll never be in the rear. That's what I can do." Elise sat back and watched her words permeate Sago's mind. She could see he was doing the mathematics and could almost hear him counting the money. "Do we have a deal?"

"I see why Que was crazy about you. For a woman, you have balls. I think we will be in business for a long time, Elise," Sago answered. "Madam, with the way you're talking about doing business, you're a *mistress* in your own right." Sago smiled.

"I guess I am," Elise said, smiling back but not allowing his compliment to stroke her ego for too long. "Now, no one will ever contact or come to you but Trey or myself. If someone else does, it's a set-up, I'm on lock down or dead. I will never come without Trey and he will never come without me, under no circumstances. These rules will never change."

"If anyone else was to contact me, let's just say, they would come up missing. But I hope it never comes to that," Sago disclosed.

"Hopefully, it won't," Elise replied. "I am a woman of my word and I would die before I break it."

Sago looked at Elise for a few seconds. "Mademoiselle, I get a good vibe from you," he declared. He kissed the back of her hand again, but this time she smiled.

"We'll call you when we get back to Cleveland and set up a time for next week. Until then, stay safe." Elise, proud of herself for sealing the deal, stood, as did Sago.

"Would you care to join us for a night out on the town? Both of you?" Sago asked. "I'm VIP at the hottest nightclubs. Wherever you want to go."

"Not this time. We have to catch an early flight, but we'll take you up on that on the next trip," Elise responded. Trey shook Sago and Cruz's hands.

"Good doing business with you," Trey said.

"Take care of her," Cruz ordered.

"I will."

Elise and Trey were about to leave when Sago called her back. "Elise, just out of curiosity, how do you plan on getting fifty kilos across state lines? There will be several police checkpoints with dogs between here and Cleveland."

Sherrie Walker

"I'll answer that if you will answer a question for me," Elise replied.

"Fair enough."

"How did you get this dining room emptied out and have no one bother us the whole time?"

"Easy enough … I own it," he answered. "Now your turn."

"The key word was police. I intend to drive it back to Ohio in a police car. Who's going to stop the police? The police? You gentlemen have a nice night."

Trey and Elise exited the restaurant and could hear Sago and Cruz laughing on their way to the elevator.

"She has big balls. Big balls," Sago repeated loudly.

~ ~ ~

They pulled up to a factory in a police cruiser and made the exchange. Sago was impressed with the police car and uniforms Elise and Trey wore. It was the beginning of what each thought would be a lovely relationship. After Elise and Trey packed all four of the doors of the police car and paid Sago, they headed back to Cleveland. For the most part it was a silent ride with brief intermissions of conversation.

Each was absorbed in thought as they made one of the longest, intense drives of their lives. The fifteen hour trip went without incident and once Trey started seeing familiar landmarks, he began to relax.

"You are brilliant, Elise," said Trey as they were traveling north on I-71 approaching the Inner Belt Bridge. "How in the hell did you come up with the whole police car idea?"

Elise laughed before answering. "Believe it or not, I saw it on cops one time. The rest was easy. The police always have an auction once a year where they sell all of their old cars. I bought one, had my boy on Carnegie paint it and hook it up and the rest is how they say … History!" Trey laughed a hearty laugh as he approached the inner belt bridge.

Seeing the Jacobs Field, Tower City and Hard Rock Café signage after being on the road so long was a relief, since the landmarks indicated they were very close to being home free. Trey took Dead Man's Curve at an easy 40 MPH and continued east so he could drop Elise off at home before putting the dope away. "No one would have the nerve to drive a police car full of dope from Florida to Ohio."

"That's exactly why it worked. No one would ever expect it," she replied. "Don't tell anyone how we got it back. For all they'll know, it was delivered to us. That way we don't have to worry about no one telling nobody nothing."

"Cool, I'm ready to get out of this funky-ass uniform though. I feel real corny looking like the police. How can they wear these things all day?"

"I think you would make a cute police officer," Elise joked as Trey pulled up to the entrance of her condo, the one she once shared with Que.

"Yeah, ok. I'm going to unload this package and put the car away. I'll meet you at the spot in an hour," he replied.

"Be careful." Elise walked to her lobby door, opened it and went inside. Trey watched her until she was out of his sight then drove off.

Sherrie Walker

eighteen

Six months after meeting with Sago and Cruz, Elise called a meeting with the crew. As she stood at the head of the table she couldn't help but smile inside.

Que, you would be proud of me baby. Everything we talked about before your death, I'm executing and am happily achieving. I feel confident about that the money coming in will fulfill my need to invest in our phenomenal idea to locate properties and build enterprises. If everyone just stays focused and sticks to the plan, I guarantee all parties involved will benefit from the royalties. My personal mission is to put us all on the legit plan to success. The sky's the limit! And in spirit I'm taking you with me. I miss and love you baby.

"I call this meeting to order," Elise announced and courteously thanked everyone for coming. "This has indeed been a good year for us."

Trey and California sat down at the small table. Tony and Aparis chose to sit against the wall, smiling and stealing glances at one another.

"First, can we all give ourselves a round of applause? I want to thank everyone for bringing something to the table." They clapped and Elise allowed the sound to descend before she continued to speak. "We are halfway to our mark. However, this is where it gets rough. We're in deep now. From this day forward, we must always be on top of our game.

"Now, I now y'all got a couple dollars and your pockets are on fire, but I am *stressing* to you to be mature, be responsible and remain low key. We are *still* on the grind! No fancy cars, houses, jewelry … *none* of that shit. I mean it," she stated, glancing at Tony. "We have to live below our means. Anything other than that will have the Feds taking our pictures, or the stick up boys lurking around every corner in Cleveland. We have to be alert and remain low key."

Elise noticed a couple of her team members were acting uneasy, but she continued. "Like I said before, we can't get caught slipping. So again, nothing fancy. And I mean nothing."

Elise stood back and watched everyone's reaction. Tony played with his locks, twisting them around as he watched everyone else like he was trying to see who was going to respond first. Cali cleared his throat several times and poured himself a glass of water as Dre stood and walked over to the window. There was an uncomfortable silence for several seconds. Elise knew that they wouldn't receive the information too well. She took a few minutes to reflect on her plot and decisions. It was time to let them know the rest of her plans. Tony interrupted her thoughts.

"What's the purpose of us hustling so hard if we can't enjoy the perks and benefits? I've been driving this raggedy car for the longest," he complained.

"Look, a raggedy ride beats a well dressed walk any day. At least you're driving. Get it fixed and keep driving it," Elise retorted. "We will not do as the ones before us

Sherrie Walker

have done. We will wait until we go legit before we start buying expensive cars and houses. I must have account-ability."

"When will that be?" California questioned.

"I'll let LaKiesha take the floor."

LaKiesha set up an easel and placed a chart on it which featured a map of Cleveland, Ohio. With a chart stick she began pointing at various areas.

"We're looking at property downtown in the Playhouse Square area, as well as other locations. I have already purchased two buildings in Shaker Heights and one in Bedford. Once we close the deal downtown, we will simultaneously open all six stores. That should happen by the beginning of the year.

"We've signed the contracts with software distributors and hired thirty-two employees for these stores. All are young, smart and fresh out of college. Also, Tony has been in the studio getting his debut CD together and samples of his songs have been sent to several record labels. We've gotten good feedback on it so it's scheduled to drop in August. I will keep you posted as things develop."

"Thank you, Kiesh," Elise said. "Also, Aparis has been accepted into a program at school in which she will learn to develop video games. And y'all know this is right up her alley. So eventually, we'll be featuring games designed by our very own Aparis Nixon."

Aparis walked over to the large 30' color television and plugged the PlayStation up to it. She popped in a CD and vivid, clear, colorful, images came across the screen. The song "*Hail Mary*" by 2Pac began to play as a black, beautiful woman began fighting different villains and slaying each and everyone as she went through dif-

Sherrie Walker

ferent levels of battle. The red blood that splashed across the screen was so real that at one point Cali sat back as he inhaled his breath. The heroine conquering the different villains had on a black, one piece leather outfit. Her belt was loaded with diamonds. Her body was curvaceous. And her hair was long. She had a black leather hat on turned backwards and a pair of black glasses that completed her attire. After five levels of excitement, action, fighting and victory, Aparis turned the entertainment set off.

Everyone clapped and Tony stared at Aparis, impressed.

"I expect we could open up our stores and branch out within the next year, providing we remain low-key and professional. Each of you will have your own store. You'll be president of that operation and take care of it as if it's your own child.

"We'll all be taking crash courses in business management. The drug dealing will stop and we will leave the streets behind us. We're going legit and staying legit! If we can pull this off, you all will be worth millions."

Finally Elise had their full attention. For the next few hours, she laid out her business plan in greater detail. It was clear to the crew Elise's plan was a genius.

"Now, if there's nothing else, Trey has some issues to address," she finished.

Trey stood and cleared his throat. "For the last year, we have been trying to obtain information on Ghost. He seems to have disappeared off the face of the earth. But we've increased the price on his head to a ticket that will undoubtedly get some mouths to open and tongues to flap."

"Keep your ears open, and it doesn't matter how

Sherrie Walker

small it may be, report any information to LaKiesha," Elise instructed.

"If there's nothing else that needs to be brought to the table, this meeting is adjourned. I'll see y'all later," Trey replied. "Elise, are you ready?"

"Yeah, but wait a minute. Aparis, LaKiesha, I'll see y'all back my house tonight. Tony, you need to get down to the studio. Cali, don't forget to ride past the house on Unwin Street and see what the problem is with them young boys that came up short." Everyone nodded and exited the meeting. Trey and Elise were the only two remaining.

"You ready to do this?" Trey asked. His boy, Roger, finally came through for him in locating Simone. It took almost nine months, but the previous night Roger called stating that he'd located Simone, but he wouldn't like the information he had for him. After a grueling nine month search, a lot of money, bribes and a few busted heads, Roger was able to find out the last known address on Simone and went there.

Her foster mother, Erma, better know as Gram, was an attractive, graceful, pleasant, warm-spirited woman who didn't mind sharing her love. She was truly a child of God. When Roger chimed her door bell, she welcomed him into her beautifully furnished Colonial home located on Cleveland's upper east side. Gram informed Roger that she tried to be encouraging, uplifting, and mentally, emotionally and spiritually nurturing to Simone and how she genuinely loved her as if she was her very own.

But Simone was very troubled and ran away three times despite her efforts. She also expressed that her door and heart were always open should Simone decide to return. She shared photos of Simone with Roger and provided him one to leave with.

Roger had looked at the photo and shook his head sadly. Simone was fourteen in the picture wearing a cute yellow sundress, and her black fine hair was pulled back in a long ponytail. She was the spitting image of Elise. She was gorgeous. Even though she was smiling, he recognized the sadness in her eyes.

Gram told Roger that Simone was known for running from one bad situation to another and it was rumored she met a pimp named Pretty Ricky who turned her out to the streets. It wasn't difficult for Roger to find her after that. He would sit in his car until the time was right and approach the prostitutes working. After a few thousand had been spent he was pointed in the right direction. One night he spotted Simone. He followed her for about a week and discovered where she and Pretty Ricky lived. He contacted Trey with the information and his job was done.

Trey didn't want to tell Elise that Simone was a prostitute, but he knew he had to. Surprisingly, she was calm about the whole situation. Now it was time to get Simone and he could tell that she nervous.

"As ready as I'm going to get," Elise responded.

"Let's roll."

Trey held the door open for Elise and she walked out with him on her heels. They approached the elevator in silence and Trey could feel the tension in the air. He sensed that Elise was in deep thought about what lay ahead.

They exited the building and as they approached his car he opened the door for Elise, climbed in the driver seat and drove. He jumped on the freeway and headed

Sherrie Walker

toward the west side.

Trey exited the freeway near Metro Hospital, made a left on West 25th and followed the street until he pulled in front of a strip club. He parked and turned off the ignition. They were surrounded by run-down buildings. The streets were littered with trash, bottles and all sorts of filthy debris. Even though it was 10:30 at night, the streets were lively and people were out and about.

Elise watched a young boy serve dope from a stoop directly across from where they parked. Customers were rolling in and out to buy his product. Prostitutes were stopping cars and walking up and down the block. She watched as one prostitute stepped off into a cubby way and dropped to her knees giving a trick a blow job as if they were invisible, couldn't be seen and no one else was around. Obviously they didn't care. A blond-headed black woman walked up to the car and knocked on the window. Trey rolled it down.

"What, y'all, Five-O or what?" she asked.

"Nah, we not po po," Trey replied. "We just waiting on someone if that's all right with you."

"It's cool! You sure you don't want to have a little fun with me, baby? We can have a threesome." The prostitute licked her big, red lips while eyeballing Elise.

"We cool. Maybe another time, slim," Trey responded. The prostitute continued to look at Elise, seductively rolling her tongue before walking away.

"I feel like putting her out of her trifling misery," Elise replied.

Trey laughed.

"What's so funny?"

"She was looking as if she wanted to sop you up like biscuits and gravy." Trey smirked.

Sherrie Walker

"Disgusting! She probably got diseases that's never ever been heard of and can't be cured. I don't know how they do it!" Elise cringed.

As they sat, waited and talked, a tricked-out Escalade pulled up in front of them and two young prostitutes stepped out. Elise stopped in mid-sentence as she watched the one in a cheap black spandex mini-dress and Payless stilettos adjust her clothes. She had a caramel complexion with long, thick hair that flowed down to the center of her back. Elise felt like she was looking into a mirror. Without reservation, anyone seeing the two for the first time would have said there was a strong family resemblance.

Elise opened the door and stepped out of the car. She wore a black, two-piece St. John pantsuit, a pair of black Christian Louboutin sleek sling-backs and a pair of transitional tinted Chanel shades. Her hair was pulled back into a ponytail that swung from side to side whenever she moved. Trey stepped out and leaned against the car, praying that all turned out well.

"Simone!" Elise yelled.

The young woman turned around to see who had called her name. She gazed at Elise for several seconds with a confused look on her face. Elise couldn't believe that this was Simone standing before her. The last time she saw Simone she was seven years old. That was eight years ago.

As Elise stood face to face with her, she looked older beyond her years. She was beautiful though – she had long pretty hair and the prettiest complexion, and her eyes were a light brown. Her lips were full and had a pouty look. She was 5 feet 4 inches with a body to die for.

She studied Elise and her eyes revealed that she rec-

Sherrie Walker

ognized her, but had trouble placing her. She swung her hair back and stood up as if to challenge Elise.

"Yeah, who's dat?" Simone asked.

"It's me, Simone ... Elise!"

"What, I dated you before? You came back for seconds, huh, ma?"

Simone and her friend laughed then gave each other a high-five. Elise walked up to Simone and looked her in the eyes.

"It's me, your sister. I've been looking for you. I've found you and I've come to take you home where you belong," said Elise. Simone looked at Elise as if she were crazy and started laughing. Even though she laughed she felt like she was in a twilight zone. She couldn't believe that Elise was standing before her.

For years she cried for Elise to come save her. She held on to the words that Elise told her before they were separated, "I'll come back for you, Simone. I'll come back for you." Every day of their separation she prayed Elise would come for her. Then one day she stopped believing, she stopped caring. Now here stood Elise claiming she's been looking for her and wanted to take her home. *As far as I'm concerned, it's too late. I don't need her.*

"Sweetie, I don't know what you're are high on, but either you're here for business or get to stepping. My time is money. I don't have time to waste. Besides, I don't have a sister, brother or nothing. My family is dead."

Simone looked Elise in her eyes, and for several seconds, Elise stared at her baby sister with hurt in her eyes. Simone looked back at her until the door of the Escalade opened and out stepped a man wearing a pink double-breasted suit with a white shirt and some pink and white big block alligator shoes.

Sherrie Walker

A thick, gold chain with a diamond encrusted cross hung around his neck and he gripped an alligator man-purse in his manicured hand. His hair was hard pressed into a ponytail at the base of his neck. He looked Elise up and down.

As Elise recognized and watched Pretty Ricky, she felt her anger begin to boil like never before. *This tired-ass, old, antiquated, pink pad, washed up still-wanna-be-a pimp is using my sister for his own selfish gain. This is the same sorry, sucker I used to sell my clothes to when I was boosting. If knew then what I know now I would've put him out of his misery long time ago.* As she stared at him she visualized putting a gun to his head and pulling the trigger. She wanted to satisfy the death wish that she knew he had, but he didn't. Elise knew that before it was all said and done…that's exactly what she was going to do.

"What the fuck? You may have thought you had the right idea, but you got the wrong one this time, Ricky. You won't be pimping on my little sister anymore."

"Whazzup's up, Ma? Damn! Girl, you fine. I see you done moved up in the world, huh. Make a brotha wanna leave the game and square up." He flicked his nose with his thumb a couple of times and turned his lips up while slightly hunching his shoulders.

Meantime, Simone caught an instant attitude and frowned while Pretty Ricky looked at her then back at Elise, as if trying to find a missing puzzle piece. He held out his hand to Elise. She cut her eyes so deep into him that he flinched. She sarcastically laughed.

"Ricky, my former hot boy," Elise said.

"Hot Boy?"

"Yeah, nigga, hot boy … fence, whatever you calling yourself today. You know what I mean."

Sherrie Walker

"Pretty Ricky will work just fine."

"Whatever. I'm not gonna lip wrestle with you about a name. But I am gonna say this. Guess what Ricky … that's my flesh and blood, so she's coming with me." She turned to Simone. "Let's go."

"Go? You the one betta get to steppin'. Kick stones, lady," Simone replied. Trey walked over and stood near Elise.

"Hold on. What you talking about, let's go?" Pretty Ricky asked, looking bamboozled. "Go where, Spice? Where she talkin' 'bout takin' you, hoe? Bitch, you bet not be tryin' to run off again. Don't make me get like AT&T and reach out and *knock* yo' ass."

"She on some type of drugs or something. Talking about she my sister and she came to take me home," Simone rattled.

"Nall, nall, Nall. I remember you now. You can't take da bitch without making a pimp rich," he announced. "Yo' money haf to really make a pimp's day if dat hoe dere walking away. So, if you aint tryin' to fulfill Pretty Ricky's needs, you and your little boyfriend can get gone, indeed."

"And, if we don't?" Elise questioned. Elise turned to look at Trey and smiled wickedly. She turned back to face Pretty Ricky and repositioned her hat backwards. She stood back on the balls of her heels and rocked forward twice before spreading her feet apart with her hands on her hips.

Pretty Ricky walked closer to Elise and stood within inches of her face.

"If you don't, you're gonna feel the wrath of a pimp named Pretty Ricky," he said. "Bitch, you need to be divided and guided."

Sherrie Walker

"Oh, is that right?" Elise challenged.

"What part of dis pimpin' don't you understand?" Pretty Ricky questioned. Elise laughed, put her sunglasses on and stuck her hands in her coat pocket. She swiveled to turn away from Pretty Ricky as if she was walking away but turned back quickly with her gun out and pointed at Ricky's head.

"Understand this, mothafucka. Simone is my little sister and you are exploiting her. She's only fifteen. You ain't shit, you fucking pedophile, good-for-nothing bum. I'll take your life and not think twice about it. Do I make myself clear?"

Pretty Ricky trembled like a mouse in a room full of cats as his face broke out in beads of perspiration. He raised his hands in the air looking like he had seen a ghost.

Ricky began to beg like a dopefiend begging for dope. "Please ... I ... I don't want to die ... I'm sorry fo' real..." Simone cut him off.

"You need to raise up, and raise up with the quickness, Elise," said Simone, holding a gun to Trey's chest. "Shoot Ricky and I'll shoot him."

Elise saw that Simone had a .38 Beretta pointed at Trey.

"So, it comes down to this, huh?" Elise asked.

"He's my family. Not you!"

Elise gazed at Simone and then at Pretty Ricky who stood still, looking like the first trembling coward. She looked back at Simone and had to fight the urge to smile. She paused for a moment and considered the situation. Simone was so much like her it was uncanny. Standing there with guns pointed, it seemed like Elise was standing in front of a mirror that reflected her eyes, hair, skin

Sherrie Walker

tone, build and even her attitude.

Furthermore, she sensed Simone wasn't bluffing. They were at a stalemate and Elise didn't want this to end ugly or with Simone getting hurt. All the time, money and years it took to locate her, she wasn't willing to risk losing Simone forever. She glanced at Pretty Ricky and smiled.

"You win … for now, anyway. Come on, Trey." Elise smiled wickedly then backed away, keeping the gun pointed at Pretty Ricky until they reached their car. When she got in, Pretty Ricky yelled some words that made her want to blow a hole in his head larger than a sewer drain.

"I teach da bitches to protect da pimp."

Elise, fuming, closed her eyes. "Oh, I can't wait till I see his maggot ass again. And I will see him again. Believe that," Elise said.

"You all right?" Trey asked.

"Yeah, I'm cool." Elise was silent for a few seconds.

She stared out of the window thinking as Trey drove. "Does he really think that's it?"

"We'll get her, Elise. She'll come around. Just give it some time."

"That cocksucker must have a death wish. Well, I'm going to take him out of his misery, I promise. He's fuckin' exploiting my little sister, Trey."

"I know, Elise, but try to stay calm. Do you want me to take care of this?" he asked.

"No! When the time is right I'm going to personally take care of this one. I'm going to wait it out. And when I roll up on his ass, he'll learn the meaning of the word wrath."

Trey pulled into the parking lot entrance of Elise's

Sherrie Walker

condo. They stepped out the champagne-colored Taurus and walked through the lobby to her door.

"Are you going to be ok?" Trey inquired. Elise looked away and was silent. Trey turned her face toward him. "Hey, we're going to get through this. I will take him out the game. Just say the word."

Elise smiled at him. "You are so good to me, Trey. I can't thank you enough. You need some time off to relax, go out and meet some girls. You don't have to be with me 24/7. How will you ever meet Ms. Right?"

Trey looked her in the eyes. "I already have." Trey ran his hands through Elise's hair and pulled back the few loose strands that had fallen in her eyes. He softly caressed her eyebrows. He loved her naturally perfect eyebrows. He slowly ran his finger down her face. Elise closed her eyes, caught up in his gentle touch. Trey replaced his finger with his lips and planted wet kisses down her face. He kissed her eyes, nose and was working his way to her mouth when Elise opened her eyes and pulled away. She placed her hand on Trey's chest and pushed him away, while trying to catch her breath.

"We can't, Trey."

"Why? You feel it Elise, I know you do."

"It's not right…you're Que's best friend. Trey…I" Before she could complete her sentence, he slowly brought his lips close to Elise's, but before he could kiss her she pulled away and fumbled for her keys.

"Trey … I … please …"

"I know, I know. I'm sorry, Elise."

"No, it's just … I … I can't."

"I understand, I do."

They both stood awkwardly still.

"Well, I better be getting on, it's late," Trey mumbled,

Sherrie Walker

hanging his head.

"Ok, call me tomorrow around nine. I want any and all the information you can find on Pretty Ricky."

"That's an easy task, but I'll get right on that. Good night."

"Good night," Elise responded as she closed the door. She leaned against it holding her chest as Trey leaned against it on the opposite side, holding his as his heart beat wildly.

"Why does he have to be so damn fine? I can't do that to Que. I can't," she reasoned.

"God, I was stupid, stupid, stupid. I know I can't have her, but I want her badder than old folk need soft shoes," Trey said as he walked away from the door.

nineteen

IT HAD BEEN two weeks since Elise located Simone. Two very frustrating weeks, because nothing she did or said would make Simone leave her sorry-ass pimp. She was trying to do it he right way because she knew that if she forced Simone, she'd rebel and run away. She wanted her to willingly come home.

Her next step would be to try and bribe Pretty Ricky. She didn't want to but she may have to in order to get Simone home and safe. As bad as she wanted to be out there that night trying to get Simone back home, she knew she couldn't miss Tony's first concert. He'd worked hard to achieve this and she wouldn't miss it for nothing. All the lights went out as the announcer began his introductions.

"Ladies and gentlemen, welcome to WENZ 107.9 The Big Station's anniversary bash. Oh! We got some major talent in the building. And, we gone shut C-Town down tonight ... and to getting it jumping off ... coming to the stage ... is the hottest youngblood rapper in the OH!"

The crowd roared with excitement. "Tony, we love you!" two excited young girls on the front row yelled. A guy with his hands to his mouth as if he was holding a bull horn hollered out, "Yo' Tonnna, my cats Mook, Jordan, Tyshawn, Jay Shawn and Lil' Russel said hold 'em down…rock the house…break 'em off a lit' somethin' somethin'. Stay down."

"Put yo' hands together and show some hometown love for ya boy … the one … the only, Akron's own Tony Montana!" the MC screamed.

The audience went crazy as Tony entered the stage with his hype men and began to rock the microphone. He opened with his single, "Straight from the Cooker."

The concert was being held at the Odeon in the Flats. The crowd was composed of teenagers and young adults, who rapped along with him, waving their hands in the air from side to side.

Everyone knew the words to the song because Elise's label pushed the CD like dope, selling nearly ten thousand units on the streets the first two weeks. It was played in all the nightclubs and neighborhood bars, and finally it was featured on the radio. Then people started requesting it, forcing the station to keep it in heavy rotation. He ripped the stage and had the audience going non-stop from beginning to end, prepping the crowd for the major artists who followed. Elise felt like a proud parent as she watched Tony perform.

"We are doing it, Elise." Trey looked on in approval.

"Yes, we are." Elise nodded her head.

"Three new companies and a record label with the hottest new Indie rapper on our team. I have to say, we've come up," Trey continued. Elise had to exhale as she smiled. She had to admit that things were looking real good for everyone. She had bought a condo on the North East side of Cleveland that she loved and a beautiful home in Bratenahl.

LaKiesha bought a split level home in Willowick, Ohio that was absolutely breathtaking with its large picture windows, four bedrooms, and two and half baths, that were in addition to the bright and airy sunroom and master suite complete with a large walk-in closet and private bath and balcony off the master suite.

Aparis chose a luxury three bedroom condo in Shaker Heights so she could be close to where she grew up. It featured an L-shaped formal living room and formal dining room area, and a deluxe island style kitchen. Her bedrooms were spacious with an expansive deck and a large garden tub in the master bath.

Trey snapped Elise out of her thoughts. "Where are you, Elise?"

She looked toward Trey and smiled. "I'm happy that we're almost there."

"Did you shut down the last two houses?"

"Just one more to go and all of them will be officially closed for business."

"Did you take care of Sago and Cruz?" she questioned.

"I wired the money to an offshore account yesterday, as requested."

"Plus their bonus?"

"Plus their bonus!"

"They tried everything to keep this going," Elise said. "They even lowered the ticket, offered to bring it to us, everything."

"What did you expect? You were making them richer than they already were. We were moving anywhere from fifty to a sixty birds a week, baby. Of course they don't want to lose you," Trey rationalized.

Sherrie Walker

"Have I misled them? It was good while it lasted, but it's time to move on," Elise replied.

"I feel you. I just don't want no war with them right now," Trey stated.

"Neither do they!"

"Let's get backstage. The show is almost over," Trey suggested.

Trey and Elise weaved through the overwhelmingly hyped crowd and showed security their backstage passes. There were major females standing outside of Tony's dressing room, eagerly awaiting the opportunity to see him. When Trey and Elise entered, Tony was spinning his little sister and Aparis around in the air and they were laughing. They were clearly celebrating. Cali was sitting at the bar drinking a bottled water and Dre was talking on his cell phone. Trey showed them both some love and Elise hugged Tony, smiling like a proud mother. She handed him a large glass vase with a beautiful fresh arrangements of roses, carnations, lilies, daisy palms, delphinium, and hydrangeas.

"You did it, baby boy." Elise hugged and congratulated him.

"They love me, Elise. You hear 'em screaming and singing the words to my song? A 'stud' is born," he kidded.

"Yes, I did," she replied.

"You're selling like crazy, too," Aparis commented.

"That makes me rich, don't it?" Tony asked. "I'm fucking twenty years old and I'm a millionaire. Can I finally buy what I want?"

Tiffany ran over to Tony and jumped in his arms. "Can I get a new car too, Tony?" Tony kissed her on the side of her cheek and looked toward Elise, awaiting her reply.

"Now we can all buy what we want." Elise picked up a glass, poured some champagne then raised it. "To the success of So Real Productions, Tony Montana and his new CD, '*Straight from the Cooker*.'"

Everyone toasted Dom Perignon.

"We couldn't have done any of this without you, Elise," Aparis said. "You had a plan and executed it well. You masterminded this whole thing. You kept us together and in check. We owe all our success and good fortune to you. Toast again to Elise and her strategic mind." Just then, LaKiesha walked into the room.

"You missed it, LaKiesha. It was off the chain for real."

Tony grinned with a gleam in his eyes and excitement in his voice. Pumping his hands up and down in the air, like, "Yes, I did this."

"I know, I got caught up in a situation." LaKiesha's voice sounded as dry as sandpaper.

"Is everything all right, LaKiesha?" Elise asked.

"I need to speak with you, Elise." LaKiesha had a sullen look on her face. Elise walked out of the room and LaKiesha followed with Aparis on her heels.

"Don't look too good, whatever it is," California said.

"I hope it's not no drama. Not when everything is going so good right now," Tony replied.

When Elise walked back into the room, he asked "Is everything cool?"

"Everything is fine. Tony, Aparis, y'all need to take Tiffany home and head over to the after party."

Tiffany pouted and put her hands across her chest while stomping her feet. "I don't want to go home. Why can't I go with y'all?"

Sherrie Walker

"Because you can't and don't argue with us, Tiffany."

"LaKiesha, take care of everything here and meet me at the hospital."

"Hospital!" Exploded Cali with alarm. "What's going on Elise?"

Elise looked at Tiffany and smiled, trying not to alarm her. She turned to Tony and Aparis. When she made eye contact with Aparis, she began to gather her things. "Let's go, baby, so we can get Tiffany home."

Tony looked from Elise to LaKiesha, shook his head and headed out the door.

After Aparis and Tiffany leave Trey is the first one to speak. "What the hell is going on, Elise?"

"We're going to University Hospital," Elise ordered. Elise walked to the door, opened it and turned back around. "Let's go. I'll fill y'all in as we walk to the car." Elise walked out leaving Cali, Dre and Trey standing there. Cali shrugged his shoulders and followed Elise. By the time they caught up to her, she was almost out the door, heading toward the parking lot and her car. Just as she reached her car, Trey caught up with her, almost out of breath.

"Who's at University?" Trey inquired. Elise opened her car door and slid inside. Trey slid into the passenger seat while Cali and Dre jumped in the back.

"Simone was beaten badly and is in critical condition. There's no way I'm going to let her die, but someone is going to be put to eternal sleep." Elise's voice was solemn, deadly. She laid her head on the steering while for a second, then raised up, started the car and pulled out the parking lot driving like a woman in search of her no good, cheating man.

"Do you know who did it?" California asked.

Sherrie Walker

"*Pretty* good idea." Elise's words were clipped. Her face was drawn tight.

"Let's go handle this then," said California.

"Oh, trust and believe, he'll get his," she said, flying down Euclid Avenue in her Honda Accord. "First, I'm going to see about my sister and make sure she's all right."

Elise pulled up to the emergency room entrance and jumped out of the car. Trey drove off to find a parking space.

"I'm here for Simone Green," said Elise when she reached the front desk.

"And you are?" the receptionist asked.

"Elise Green, her sister," she responded. The receptionist typed something into the computer and then picked up the phone.

"Paging Doctor Sung to the main desk. Dr. Sung to the main desk."

"If you'll have a seat in the waiting area, her doctor will be right with you."

Elise walked into the waiting room and sat down just as California and Trey entered.

"How's she doing?" Trey asked.

"I'm waiting on her doctor now," Elise responded.

"Do they know who did this to her?" California questioned.

As if in reply, Pretty Ricky walked in with a dozen roses before Elise could respond. He strolled up to the receptionist desk and Elise just stared at him. Both Trey and California followed her eyes then looked at each other.

"I know exactly who did it. Trey, you strapped?" Elise asked, never taking her eyes off the pimp.

Sherrie Walker

"You know I am, Elise, but what are you thinking? We're in a hospital." Trey lifted an eyebrow.

Elise didn't answer Trey. She turned to Cali. "Cali, you strapped?"

California looked around furtively. "This is not the time or the place, boss. We'll take care of the nigga. I promise you that." California deposited an image of Pretty Ricky into his memory bank.

A doctor then entered the reception area. "Simone Green. I'm here for the family of Simone Green," he said.

"I'm her sister." Elise walked over to him. "How is she?"

The doctor looked at Elise for a few minutes then cleared his throat. "Hi. I'm Dr. Sung," he said with an Arabic accent. He ran his hand across the back of his neck and sighed. "Your sister has a fractured rib and a hairline fracture in her jawbone, so she's on some heavy painkillers right now." The doctor hung his head. "It seems she was repeatedly kicked her in the stomach, because she's experiencing some internal bleeding in her abdomen. This was definitely an attack," Dr. Sung explained. "However, the good news is, with plenty of rest, she should be fine."

"Can I see her?" Elise cried. Just as she looked up, Pretty Ricky entered and approached the doctor with flowers in his hand.

"Doc, I'm here about Simone Green," he said.

The doctor looked him up and down.

"And you are?"

"I'm her fiancé. How is she? Can I go see her?"

"Ms. Green is heavily sedated right now. Do you have any idea who did this to her? Mr—? I didn't get your name," Dr. Sung continued.

"Ricky Barnes."

"Mr. Barnes, do you have any idea as to who might have done this to her?"

Pretty Ricky looked away and started fidgeting with the flowers. "Nall, I don't know. When I came home she was lying in a pool of blood and I called 911." He tuned up and *tried* to cry.

"You spineless piece of shit," Elise snapped. "Doc, let me really introduce you to this pathetic excuse for a man. His street name is Pretty Ricky and he's my sister's pimp. He beat her like a dog, and now he thinks he can waltz up in here with some off-the-street roses, sweet talk Simone into forgiving him and walk away with his number one hooker draped across his arm and they live happily ever after!" Elise shouted. "I don't think so."

"You know what …you talk too much! Playa, you bets to check yo' broad," said Pretty Ricky while looking at Trey. He turned toward Elise. "You need a man to teach you how to be a woman."

"Is that right? Who would that man be, you?" she scoffed, laughing in his face. "I'd sleep with a rabid dog before I'd *ever* entertain the thought of you." Pretty Ricky raised his hand as if he were going to pimp slap Elise, but the doctor grabbed his arm as California and Trey rushed over.

"I suggest you leave right now," Dr. Sung advised, releasing his arm.

"I'm not going nowhere until I see my fiancée," Pretty Ricky stammered.

"Fine … next on my agenda is to call the police and report my suspicions to them, anyway. So, you can stick around as long as you desire," Dr. Sung said.

Sherrie Walker

Pretty Ricky stepped back and bumped into California.

"I'll be your huckleberry," said California.

"I don't have time for this. I'll be back with my attorney. I'm going to sue you and this hospital, Doc." Pretty Ricky looked at Elise, smiled and winked. "I'll see you again, tiger ... that's a promise."

"That's a promise I look forward to seeing fulfilled." Elise shot him a chilling glare.

Pretty Ricky loped away, looked back and smiled as he left the hospital as if he didn't have a care in the world.

"Why do women let those type of men exploit them? I will never understand," Dr. Sung said. Then he led Elise, Trey and California to Simone's room. Elise gasped and held her hands to her face the moment she saw her sister. Her pretty face was swollen black and blue and she had bandages everywhere. Simone was out cold, totally unconscious of her visitors being there, looking down upon her with sympathy and compassion. As Elise stood over her, tears streaming down her face, a disappointed feeling overwhelmed her spirit.

After Trey, Cali and Dre left, Elise sat up all night by Simone's side. Rubbing her hands, talking to her. Praying. "Simone, it's me baby ... Elise ... your sister. I'm right here and I ain't going nowhere. You're going to be fine. I'm going to take care of you ... you're coming home with me. Simone, I love you," she whispered in her ear and kissed her on the cheek. She didn't know if Simone could hear her or not. It didn't matter. She talked to her like she could.

Elise cried for a long time and eventually fell asleep with her head lying on Simone's bed. The first thing in the morning, Elise called her attorney to start the process of adopting Simone.

Again, she felt as if she had failed to protect her baby sister. She thought of all the things she should have done, instead of leaving Simone in the streets with Pretty Ricky that night. Elise thought back to that night she confronted Pretty Ricky. She should've killed him then. She knew she could've forced Simone to come home with her because she was fifteen and a minor. Elise could force her, but she knew that Simone would just run away and keep running. She wanted her to come home and be happy to be there. Now because of her stupidity, her baby sister was lying in a hospital room all broken up. Elise knew what had to be done and this time she would do it right. By the time LaKiesha and Aparis arrived, she began to mentally calculate a plan.

Sherrie Walker

twenty

IT HAD BEEN three weeks since Simone had been hospitalized as a result of the beating Pretty Ricky put on her. He didn't mean to go as far as he did, but she'd really pissed him off when she kept talking about going to visit Elise. He forbade Simone to see or even talk about her. Yet, she continued to do so. So he commenced to kicking her ass. He had to stomp a mud hole in that ass to show her that he meant business. For a minute, he felt lost without his number one ho' on the stroll. She brought in good dough. But as luck would have it, he knocked off a fine little young piece name Alexis.

It was a good payday for Pretty Ricky since he had made a couple thousand. He decided to treat himself to a little nose candy and turn in early. He picked up his latest addition to the family and gave her some of his pimp juice. She was the chosen one for the night since she had brought in the money. Alexis was fifteen and Pretty Ricky knew he would make big money with her on his team. He also knew he needed Simone, his bottom, to turn Alexis completely out. As she lay in the bed, naked as the day she was born, Pretty Ricky felt like he couldn't be told jack and was full of himself.

Sherrie Walker

After all I did for her, this is how she treats me? I know her bitch sister is poisoning her mind. If I ever get the chance, I'ma break dat bitch neck, after I fuck the shit out of her. That's all she need is some good java. I still may find her and put dis pimpin' on her. That's what I'm going to do. Give her some of this magic stick.

He got an immediate erection, then leaned over and pinched Alexis' nipple. She cried out in pain but he pushed her head down toward his penis. She slowly took him into her mouth. Pretty Ricky gasped for air as she slid her tongue up and down his shaft. Then he flinched. "Watch the teeth, bitch." Alexis started to lick his testicles. "Nawl, suck it." She did.

Pretty Rick closed his eyes and started fantasizing about Elise. "Ah … yeah … suck it, baby." He was really getting into it when she all of a sudden stopped. "Don't stop, baby, please don't …" Ricky opened his eyes and was staring down the barrel of a shotgun. "What the … what do you want?" he cried.

Three gunmen wearing all black with ski masks and gloves stood before him with their weapons drawn. One gunman was holding a pistol to Alexis' head while the second was standing over Pretty Ricky. He motioned for the one with Alexis to leave. "Take care of her. We can handle this," said gunman number two, as gunman number one exited the room with Alexis.

"Take the money and leave," Pretty Ricky said. "I got about five hundred dollars on the dresser and some jewelry. That ought to do."

"We don't want your money, *pretty boy*," the third gunman said. Much to his surprise, it was the voice of a woman.

"Well, what do you want?" Pretty Ricky asked. The

Sherrie Walker

gunman standing over him swung the gun and knocked him unconscious. Pretty Ricky woke up to cold water being splashed in his face. He tried to move and realized that he was tied to the bed, spread eagle and butt naked. His head was throbbing where he had been struck. His mouth was dry as cotton. It felt like his tongue was glued to the roof of his mouth.

"What … is going on? What do you want?" he mumbled.

The third gunman walked straight up to Pretty Ricky and stood over him.

"Your life." Elise snatched off her mask and shook her hair loose. "Told you I would see you again, baby boy. And guess what … I always keep my promises."

"Look, I didn't mean nothin' by that."

"I did." Elise smiled.

"That little girl you had in the bed with you is fifteen years old. That's disgusting." California shook his head in disgust.

"You don't care where you stick that thang, do you?" Elise remarked.

"You know, in some countries they castrate men who rape little girls," California declared.

"Slice it right off," said Elise.

"I think those rules should apply in the great old USA. Don't you, Elise?"

"I would have to agree with you there."

Pretty Ricky looked from one to the other to see if they were just joking. As he turned back to Elise, she pulled out a switchblade and released the knife in one swift motion. Pretty Ricky tried to get up but remembered he was tied down to the bed. He began to scream and beg. "Please don't. I'll do anything. I promise. I'll leave town. I won't ever bother your sister again. Please!"

"Uh-uh, too late for all that. My sister will be released from the hospital soon and you'll be ... dead." Pretty Ricky started crying loud sobs while snot ran from his nose.

Elise looked down at him and felt nothing but contempt. She placed the knife next to his penis and slid it back and forth, making Pretty Ricky cry out more. Aaaaaggghh ... oh God..."

"Don't call on God now." Elise grabbed his dick and stretched it like a rubber band. Pretty Ricky began to squirm around on the bed trying to get away from her. Elise turned to Cali. "Hold this little bitch still."

Cali held Pretty Ricky's left and right thigh while applying pressure. Elise gripped his penis again and began to slice it slowly like she was cutting a piece of sausage. Then, in one quick move, she sliced it completely off and blood splattered everywhere. She turned her head as Pretty Ricky screamed and cried. Holding it up in front of her, she looked at his penis before throwing it on Pretty Ricky's chest. Pretty Ricky slowly looked down at his chest and then at the gaping hole where his penis used to be and fainted.

"Let's finish this and get the hell out of here. I'm starving."

Dre and Cali both looked at Elise and then each other, shaking their heads.

Sherrie Walker

twenty-one

ELISE GOT UP from the couch and walked over to the picture window to watch the waves roll across Lake Erie. Her condo was the one place she could relax and get away from the hustle and bustle of the games she played.

Things had been going extremely well, but like always, when things were looking promising, drama surfaced. She managed to maneuver her way through the dope game without enduring any major turbulence, used it as a stepping stone to come up, and now it was time to quit, get out the game, go legit and have a real life. She had reached her mark and refused to go beyond her destination. She understood it was a power move, but Sago and Cruz weren't making her exit strategy easy. They didn't want to lose the revenue Elise generated.

Sago lowered the price, agreed to deliver it and threatened Elise with the promise of a very ugly war—a war that she could not afford, especially since Simone was to live with her once she was discharged from the hospital next week. She reached a revelation, understanding that greed wasn't always the reason some players didn't quit.

Sago wasn't accustomed to being told "no," especially

Sherrie Walker

when the word was coming out the mouth of one of his top buyers. Elise had made Sago more millions than he could count, but the more she generated the more he desired—more money, more problems, right? It was never ending with him.

Elise thought back to the last meeting she had with Sago six months ago...and shuddered. He requested her and Trey's presence in Miami at his hotel, The Clazzi, so they could discuss their "situation" as Sago referred to it. There weren't too many things that made Elise nervous, however, this sudden meeting didn't sit to well with her.

Reluctantly, Elise and Trey flew into Miami on a late Friday night. They met with Sago and Cruz in the dining room to discuss business. Sago occupied his usual spot at the head of the table, and Cruz sat on his right side.

The air was thick and filled with tension. She knew meeting Sago on his time and turf was dangerous, and to decline his offer of a sit-down was even more dangerous. She felt damned if she did and damned if she didn't.

Elise was fashionably attired in her signature color – black. No matter what the occasion, she was stunning, classy and elegant in black. Her two piece St. John knit pants suit had a cut on it that complimented her shapely figure. Her Chanel sunglasses and a pair of Gucci ostrich pumps put the final touches on her exquisite look. Trey sported a crème colored Versace suit. He wore his jacket open, exposing a fitting brown silk shirt and a pair brown Fennix gators.

Offering gentlemanly service, Sago stood and pulled out Elise's chair out so she could be seated. Trey shook hands with Sago and Cruz and took his seat next to Elise.

"I hope you had a pleasant flight. Yes?" Sago smiled.

Elise returned the smiled. "Yes, it was first class all the

Sherrie Walker

way."

"Would you like something to drink? A cocktail maybe. Or a hot or cold beverage?"

"No thanks," they replied simultaneously.

Sago smiled and raised his drink in the air and tossed it down his throat. In a hard gesture, he placed the glass on the table.

"I was hoping we could all come to some type of mutual agreement. Prior to your arrival, I was telling Cruz that maybe I don't make you happy with the prices. You are one of my favorites, Elise. I want you to be happy and satisfied always. So what I've decided to do is lower the ticket for you. You were being supplied a key at seventy-five hundred a pop. I'm willing to reduce that ticket to six thousand a piece. Does that make you happy?" Elise looked at Trey and then Sago before she spoke.

"That's very generous of you, Sago. It's almost tempting, isn't it, Trey?"

"Very."

"As tempting as it may be, I'm going to have to decline, Sago. I just want out of the drug game. I've reached my quota and I don't want to be greedy. Greed is what sunk a lot of dealers and I don't want to be part of that statistic. We're going to have to say thanks, but no thanks." Elise watched Sago's reaction. His jaws clenched and his hand wrapped tightly around the glass he was holding. However, it was Cruz who spoke.

"You can't fucking quit us. It doesn't work that way. We gave you a fucking chance when no one else would. We enabled you to open all those fucking companies you have and you just want to shit on us? It's not going to happen. Those little companies you have can be demolished just like that..." Cruz snapped his finger while locking eyes with Elise.

Elise never broke her eye contact as she spoke. "Are you threatening me, Cruz?" Cruz smiled and sat back in his chair as he locked his hands behind his head. "I never threaten my partners."

"I'm not your partner, Cruz."

"Exactly."

"Fifty-five hundred, and we'll have them delivered, " Sago blurted out. Elise stared at Sago for a few moments.

"Sago, it has been good doing business with you, but that's it for us. We're out. Bottom line. I don't mean to end this meeting so abruptly, but with that being said, we have a flight to catch." Elise began to stand when Cruz stopped her with his next words.

"How's Simone doing, Elise? She's still in the hospital. Yes?" A wicked smile possessed his face. "It would be a shame if something were to happen to your little sister especially after all the time you took to find her. We know everything."

Elise was fuming on the inside. She looked back and forth from Sago to Cruz for several seconds and began speaking through clenched teeth.

"If anything, and I do mean anything, happens to my sister, I will personally cut your balls off and shove them so far up your ass until the medical examiner won't be able to pull them out. I know you don't want a war with me because I'm confident that you'll lose. Let's go, Trey." Trey stood and began to walk out with Elise.

As they reached the door, Sago yelled to them, "Think about what we talked about, Elise. This doesn't have to get unpleasant."

Elise turned back around and smiled innocently. "Fuck you, Sago."

Sherrie Walker

As they exited the dining room, Sago picked up his drink and smiled as he turned to Cruz. "Let's hit her where it hurts."

One week later, Elise's computer company, Que-Essentials, located on Chagrin in Beachwood, had gone up in smoke and arson was suspected. It had Sago written all over it. As badly as Elise wanted to avoid a war, it was inevitable. She couldn't, and wouldn't, stand by and watch him destroy everything she had built from nothing.

Elise had the manpower – some of her old soldiers who now worked for her legitimately – but would do what she needed them to do. They knew she had the capital and the artillery but also knew the Feds would come sniffing if too much blood was shed. Sago was backing her into a corner and only one of them would come out of it. Elise realized that a war meant a lot of causalities, so she tried to think of a way to make it a win-win situation. *If they want war, then that's what I'll give them, and I'll hit 'em where it hurts.*

The doorbell rang and she pressed the button on the remote to see who was in the lobby. It was Trey, so she released the lock and watched him approach the elevator on her sixty-inch flat screen plasma television. Elise went to the entry door, unlocked it, and left it open. She then made a dry Belvedere Martini with an olive. By the time he entered, it was ready and Elise handed it to him.

"This is what I call service. Thanks." He sipped. "And my favorite at that."

"No problem."

"How you been?"

"Thinking."

"That's scary," he said. "Dis good." He set the glass on

the bar.

"I came up with a plan, but I have to warn you, it's dangerous."

"Shoot." Trey sat on the couch and waited for Elise to begin.

"I don't want to go to war with them. However, Sago seems to be forcing our hand. I've got to arrange a meeting and hope we can come to some type of mutual agreement."

"If you ain't telling Sago that business will continue, he ain't trying to hear nothing else."

"I know!"

"Then, why meet?'

"'Cause, this meeting will go down in history, Trey." Elise walked toward the window. "If they want war, then that's what they'll get. No one is going to force me to do something I'm not interested in doing. So we'll hit Sago where it hurts the most."

"His pockets?"

"No, we can't dent his pockets, boy. I'm talking 'bout his family!"

"Family? Sago? How do you know he has family, Elise?"

"It's my business to know things like that. I have my resources, baby. They keep me will informed on any matter I bring to 'em. I've always suspected something strange about Sago. All my researching has paid off. Sago has a son who's his pride and joy."

"He has a son?" Trey appeared puzzled. "He said he didn't have children."

"He's supposed to say that. Sago's a billionaire, one of the top drug lords in the country, if not *the* top. He has property and businesses all over the United States and an

206

Sherrie Walker

army that makes the government's look like boy scouts. He manufactures weapons, legally!"

"And you want to go to war with that soldier?" Trey shook his head in disbelief.

"It's no longer a choice, Trey. We'll sit down with Sago and see what happens. If he forces me, I'll do what I gotta do." Elise put her hands to her head then massaged her temples. "I'll make Sago a proposition he can't refuse, and if all goes well, he'll accept my terms. Are you in?"

Trey gazed at Elise before answering then got up and walked toward her. He rubbed her face with the back of his hand and looked in her eyes. "Never ask me again if I'm in wit' you. I'd die for you and wit' you, girl. You never have to question that." He looked at Elise for several moments, held her hands, then slowly brought his mouth to hers. For a second, Trey felt the resistance. Then, slowly, she began to yield and lean in to him.

Elise closed her eyes and a vivid picture of Que came to her mind. She began to pull away from Trey as a feeling of guilt swooped upon her like a giant tidal wave. Her emotions were running rampant as her body betrayed her and began to respond. He pushed her soft, full lips apart with his tongue and kissed her passionately. A soft moan escaped Elise as she found herself caught up in the moment, and being pulled into a whirlwind of emotions, sensations, desires and needs – a need to let go and allow her body to experience all the pleasures she denied herself since Que's death.

He eased her to him and easily slipped his arm around her waist. Elise could feel his heartbeat against her breasts. As his hands traced her back, she felt a tingle at each spot they touched. She put her hand under his shirt to feel his chest and could feel his muscles spasm. His body was hard but smooth.

He started kissing and sucking the side of her neck, which drove Elise wild. No one but Que had ever touched her this way or made her feel the sensational pleasures that she was feeling. Elise's vagina was dripping wet and every nerve in her body kindled as Trey's penis pressed against her pelvis. Elise pushed Trey down on the couch, lifted her skirt, and could see his mounted bulge through his pants as she straddled on top of him. Then she started to suck his right earlobe, unbuttoned his shirt, and run her hand across his rib cage.

"Elise … I … I … want you so bad," said Trey, trying to catch some oxygen.

"I want you, too," Elise whispered.

"I have an appetite to feel you, to taste you, to make mad, crazy love to you…Let's go to your bed and…"

Without warning, the front door opened and LaKiesha entered with Aparis. They stood in the doorway, their mouths hanging open as Trey and Elise separated. Elise quickly dismounted Trey like a jockey getting off a race horse.

"Ooops, my bad, we'll just … um … we'll come back," Aparis said.

"No, no, Trey was just leaving," Elise responded as she tried to straighten her clothes.

"Gurll, didn't look like he was just leaving to me, and if he was he was making a hell'va exit. It's all good tho'… no biggie. We can holla at you later." LaKiesha smiled as she read the embarrassment written all over Trey's face.

"Yo, I got a some business to tend to and a few pit stops to make along the way, so I'm gonna go on and cut out," Trey stuttered, looking away. "Uh, Elise I'll get back

Sherrie Walker

to you on that one thing."

"Ok. That's cool. Call me later."

"One." Trey walked toward the door quickly, trying to avoid making eye contact with Aparis and LaKiesha as he passed, but he bumped into a bag draped over Aparis' shoulder. "Damn, girl, what's in dat big-ass purse?" he asked rhetorically while closing the door.

Elise tried to play things off by not looking at them. "Yeah, we were just going over some last minute details," she said.

"When! Look like y'all were detailing all right, detailing to get y'all a little bit," Aparis retorted. "You secretive dog, you could've told us." Aparis set her bag to the side of an oversized chair near the sliding balcony door. LaKiesha sat down on the couch next to Elise.

"Told y'all what?" Elise's eyes widened in a look of innocence.

"Oh, so we keeping secrets now, wench?" LaKiesha asked.

"Ain't no secret. *Shit*. That was not supposed to happen. In fact, it won't happen again. I just got a little caught up."

"Why are you being like that, Elise?" Aparis lifted her eyebrow and gave Elise an inquisitive look. "Trey's head over heels for you. And, he's fine. He ain't trying to leech off you, and you already know the brother is loyal as well as patient. So what's the hang up?"

"I can't. It's just not right. He was …" Elise's words were trapped in her mouth so she stared at the ceiling.

"He was what? Que's boy? Elise, Que has been dead for three years now. You're twenty-two, and I don't want you to waste another moment. Life is too short. You know that, we all know that."

Sherrie Walker

LaKiesha interjected as she shifted to get comfortable on the couch. She turned to look Elise straight in the eyes. "Girl, please. It is time for you to move on. Que was my brother and I know he would not want you to be alone. I think he would approve of Trey, Elise."

Elise crossed her legs Indian style as she repositioned herself next to LaKiesha .

"Gurll, why you sitting on that Mz. Kitty anyway? I bet that kitty cat is full of purrrrr," Aparis joked. "Ain't it?"

"I just don't think it's right. He was Que's best friend."

"That's why I know he would approve. Let go! It doesn't mean you don't or never loved Que. But he's gone and you ain't getting any younger," said LaKiesha.

"Don't let that man get away. I got to get mine, naimean?" Aparis interrupted.

"From what I hear, you're getting yours, Ms. Pussy," Elise snapped her manicured nails in a two circular motion.

"What you talking 'bout?"

"From what I hear, you and *Lil'* Tony Montana are tearing it up," Elise replied. "Yo, you a groupie now," she giggled.

"I see, you got jokie-jokes, but ..." Aparis paused. "Baby, little don't hardly describe what *Tony Mon-tana, ok,* is *workin' wit'*. I'll tell you this, he's so explosive that he has stroked up on a stack of redeemable coochie coupons in this spot for life," Aparis responded theatrically, rolling her neck. "If you only *knew*." She fell back onto the chair like she was exasperated and fanned her face with both hands.

"Oh, it's like that?" LaKiesha asked.

Sherrie Walker

Aparis regained composure. "Let me put it to you like this. I'm gone break it down for you ."

"Break it down then, baby girl, please break it down for us," Elise egged her on. "'Cause Mz. Kitty needs to know." Elise allowed her lower extremities to relax as she slouched to the side.

"Well, let me put it like this," Aparis continued. She moved to the edge of the couch and leaned forward with her arms resting on her legs. "The boy puts it on me so good, I speak in another language."

"Daaaannnnnng," said LaKiesha dreamily.

Aparis continued. "Mr. Mega Dick puts it on me so good that my pussy starts to overflow like a bathtub with too much water. Mmhmm, um hmm, vulgar, but true." Aparis relaxed while Elise and LaKiesha simultaneously turned toward each other, stopped and stared, then quickly looked back at Aparis.

"I haven't felt the need to see anyone else in three months and you know how I go for mine."

"Oh, no, girl, not you, the female player." LaKiesha crossed her legs, interlocked her fingers and placed her hands in lap. "So, does this mean you're tearing up your player card?"

"Nah, I wouldn't go as far as to say all that, but you know I am going to see where this leads." Aparis curled her glossed, perky lips.

"So." LaKiesha allowed her body to relax. "That young gun got you sprung?"

"Now, I ain't said all that either, 'cause for real, I lay it on him, too," Aparis pronounced.

"Do I hear wedding bells and whining babies?" LaKiesha asked, sounding less jovial. She suddenly stood and approached the window and looked down at the slightly disturbed waters. They were troubled by a mix of rain and sleet. She looked down into The Great Lake as if she could see beneath its surface. "We all deserve happiness, for real."

"It's true," Elise said. "So, Kiesh, what's up with you?"

"Yeah, I'm doing me, for real. And, I mean literally doing me! Yes gurrlie poo's, when I want that wonderful feeling, I get with Mr. Vibrator and we have a sensational date. Gurll, we take care of bizzzness. I've ran him so hot at times until I've had to throw him out my hands. Hell yeah." Elise and Aparis laughed. "Yeah, so in a word, I'm solo by choice and plan to stay that way for awhile." LaKiesha finally laughed and rejoined her friends.

"Ok, let's get down to business. Our game has to step up." Elise shuddered and goose bumps rose on her arms. "I'm having a little problem with Sago and Cruz. Our meeting last week didn't go as smoothly as I hoped, so we have to prepare for the worst. It looks like we're going to have to execute plan B. Aparis, did you find anything?"

"Do Muslims hate pork? Hell yeah I found something and y'all gonna love this shit."

LaKiesha gets excited, "Gurll, what."

"Here's the information you requested." Aparis reached into her Louis Vuitton bag and handed Elise a thick manila envelope. Elise opened it and examined the contents. She removed some pictures, looked at them and her mouth dropped open. LaKiesha snatched a few pictures and her mouth hit the floor right next to Elise's.

"Oh ... My God. This is disgusting," LaKiesha said.

"I hope I won't have to resort to this, but if I do, I will."

"Let's get busy then," said LaKiesha as she rose from

Sherrie Walker

the sofa. She headed to the bar and fixed drinks for everyone. "We're going to have a long night."

"How's Simone?"

"A little better. She's coming around pretty good. Hopefully, in another week or so, I can bring her home."

"Pretty Ricky didn't make the news or the paper."

"He wasn't worth the ink," Aparis chortled.

"How did Simone take it?"

"She's angry, but I think she'll be all right. She asked me if I had anything to do with it."

"What did you say?" Aparis sounded concerned.

"Of course not!" Elise slightly raised her voice. "I'm not a gangsta or murderer. I'm not! I'm a business woman."

"Did she believe you?" LaKiesha shrank back.

"Why wouldn't she? She doesn't know that part of me, and I don't want her to know. That part of me she will never see."

"She's bound to find out, Elise. This is Cleveland. You don't think it should come from you?"

"Hell no!"

"Hey, hey ... calm down." Aparis threw her hands up. "Don't jump all over me. I gotcha. You know that. I'm trying to look out for you because if she finds out, it could cause bad vibes between you two. Even though he was a dog and a good for nothing simp of a pimp, she loved him. I just want to make sure you are all right."

For a few minutes, no one said anything.

"I know, I'm sorry about that, Paris. I just ... I never want Simone to be exposed to that side of me, or what I used to do. That's all. I want to get her back on track in school and into some counseling sessions. That's why this plan has got to work or we'll be in an all out war. And I can't let anything happen to Simone, I can't."

"It won't!" La Kiesha solemnly shook her head. "This is going to work, baby girl. If he don't want to listen, we'll just smoke his Italian spaghetti-and-meatball-eating ass."

"Don't sweat it. We always come out on top, don't we?"

"Yeah, we do." Elise nodded. "And we will this time, too. So let's go over the plans one more time."

Sherrie Walker

twenty-two

FOUR DAYS LATER, the meeting with Sago and Cruz had arrived. Elise rented the split-level penthouse suite at the Marriott on Public Square. It was equipped with a full bar and kitchen, a Jacuzzi, a sauna, a spacious living room, a formal dining area and a luxurious bedroom. Its sky-lighted view of Cleveland was illuminating. Sago and Cruz arrived and sat on the sofa. They took the champagne Elise offered but didn't drink it. Both placed their glasses on the cocktail table. Elise sat across from them, next to Trey. The tension was as thick as the smoke in a car full of crack heads.

"So," Sago said, looking around the suite. "I like this." He nodded his head in approval. "This is nice."

"Thank you. I want you and Cruz to enjoy it for the next couple days. We have a nice weekend lined up for you. I want to show you a real good time while you're here."

"Such great hospitality, yes, Cruz?"

"Yes," Cruz responded.

"I've thought about your proposition, Sago and I must admit, it is quite attractive. I just don't think I want to get back into that game. The risk is too great. I have

Sherrie Walker

businesses to lose and I choose to discontinue playing this game. The negative consequences far outweigh the positive ones, so at this point, I must call it quits. I'm done."

"I have enterprises as well. I know the risk. But when you are good at what you do, you don't worry about those things, you just protect yourself ... you make it impossible for anyone to infiltrate your set-up. I've been in business twenty-two years, Elise," Sago paused, "because I'm wise. You have to be smart in this business. You are smart? No?"

"Thank you for the compliment, Sago," Elise replied. "However, my intelligence is the reason why I'm quitting. I must not go past the mark I aimed for. In victory, one must learn when to stop. Your luck is good, Sago, there's no doubt about that. I don't want to chance mine ..."

"Four thousand," Sago said.

"Four thousand ... that sounds too good to be true," Trey butted in. "What's your profit?"

"Believe me, Trey. At the rate you get rid of them, I profit." Sago smiled, exuding confidence. "We all get rich."

"We're already rich," Elise said.

"I'm afraid we are not going to be able to continue this arrangement, Sago," Trey replied.

"Where are your balls? Who exactly is the man here?" said Cruz. He quickly rose and stalked to the window. Trey looked down at himself, then back up to Cruz.

"Last time I checked, I still had both of mine attached." Trey laughed.

"I can make other arrangements for them," Cruz responded with his back to Trey.

"Is that a threat?" Trey asked.

Sherrie Walker

"Never," said Cruz.

"You do not want to play around with me, Elise," Sago pronounced.

"I dropped out of school because I didn't like recess. I don't play, Sago." Elise's voice was low. Everyone was silent for several seconds. Elise got up and walked over to the bar and fixed another drink. She sat back down and slowly crossed her legs. "One of my companies was bombed last week. That cost me a lot of money."

"Things like that have a way of happening, don't they?" Sago smiled, although there was an icy look in his dark eyes.

"Yes, they do. In that case, I guess I should say I'm sorry about your losses as well," Elise responded. Sago realized what Elise was saying and stopped smiling.

"Losses ... what losses?" Cruz turned away from the window.

"Oh, my bad, you wouldn't know, would you? You were on the plane when it happened." Elise looked at Trey. "Trey, why didn't you remind me to let Sago know about his accidents?"

"I'm sorry, boo. It just slipped my mind." Trey looked at his watch. "Your multi-million dollar Clazzi hotel, and I might add it *was* beautiful, blew up about ten minutes ago."

"And your bank," said Elise as she looked at her exotic timepiece. "Stone Key Bank blew up about two minutes ago." Sago and Cruz looked at each other and laughed.

"You're nuts, both of you. You wouldn't have the balls to mess with me," said Sago. Sago and Cruz's BlackBerrys went off. Sago continued to chuckle as he answered it. He stopped laughing and the smile slowly departed his face. He began speaking quickly in Italian.

Cruz stood there listening, glaring at Elise and Trey, murder in his eyes. Sago continued to scream into the phone before angrily hanging up. He stepped toward Elise and Trey. "You don't know what you have started. Have you forgotten who I am?"

"You started it, but I intend to end it." Elise stood and walked over to the bar and pulled out a manila envelope. "You want to play ugly, we'll play ugly."

"I am personally going to take the last breath out of your body. You fucked with the wrong one," Cruz growled menacingly.

"Do you want to see whose balls are bigger, Cruz? From the looks of it, you've seen all kinds of balls." Elise stared sternly into his eyes. "Sago, I wonder what would happen if some of your business partners learned they're in business with a homosexual?"

All the color drained out of Sago's face.

"Does your wife know? Does your son?"

Sago didn't say anything. He continued to sit still and glare at Elise, the shock apparent beneath the anger. Cruz walked over to the couch and sat down next to him.

Elise maintained a staunch stance. "Brothers, huh? I knew the first time I saw you two together that something was wrong. I just didn't know what. So I did a little investigation of my own."

She pulled out six 8x10 black and white photos with Cruz and Sago in various sexual positions and slid them across the table. Sago slowly picked them up as Cruz looked out of the corner of his eye.

"Sago, I hope you don't think you were his *only* piece. Oh, no, dear, seems as if Cruz got around, and he likes much younger boys." Elise pulled out more pictures of

Cruz and young boys in sexual positions.

Cruz averted his gaze. "This bitch is lying, Sago."

"Pictures don't lie, Sago. This little secret doesn't have to go any further than this room. It can all end here," Elise negotiated. "But, keep in mind, there are copies of those images located in several different places. So if anything happens to me or Trey, they will immediately be distributed to your wife, son and the heads of the seven families."

Dazed, Sago sat as if he had been knocked back.

"Yes, I know all about the seven families, Sago. I know about your ties to the Colombians and I even know about your offshore accounts. I know where all twenty-seven of your businesses are located." She pulled out some more papers and slid them across the table to him. He saw they contained information about his companies' values and locations. "I even know where you keep your son. A very nice island, indeed." She handed him a picture of Sago and his son posing on a beach. The photograph fell out of Sago's hand. "So, if so much as a brick falls off one of my buildings, I will destroy you piece by piece, business by business, until you're standing in the welfare line."

Elise got up and Trey helped her into her black gamma mink, with the words *Mistress of the Game* embroidered in the lining. She slid her arms into it. Once the coat was on, she flicked her naturally flowing mane over the back of it.

"This will be the last time we meet, Sago. Enjoy the room. It's yours for the weekend." She headed for the door but stopped in her tracks and turned around. "Oh, one more thing. I told you that Cruz liked young boys. Well, there's another photo in the envelope for you."

Sago looked at the envelope in his hand like it was a

Sherrie Walker

plague. He stared at it long and the silence was smothering as no one spoke or moved for what felt like hours. Elise watched Cruz and fought the urge to smile as one attempted to creep upon her face. Gone was the smugness, the big ego and the cockiness that Cruz always possessed. In its place was … fear. Sago looked as if he'd aged ten years in five minutes. He looked like a small man, as if he were trying to sink further into the plush chair and just disappear. She turned to face Trey.

After what seemed like hours, but was only minutes, Trey opened the door and they walked out. As Elise and Trey approached the elevator, Sago pulled the photo slowly out of the envelope. Tears streamed down his face as the picture fell out of his hands. His mind snapped and he pulled out his gun then emptied the clip into Cruz. Elise and Trey heard the gunshots just as the elevator door was closing.

Sago looked down at Cruz's dead body and next to him was the image of Cruz in a compromising position with Sago's eleven-year-old son. Both were naked.

Elise smiled as the elevator descended. "It's amazing what Aparis can do with two photos today. Digital is the new truth," Elise slightly shook her head, "projecting and portraying things that never even happened."

Sherrie Walker

twenty-three

TWO WEEKS PASSED without incident since Elise had shared the photos with Sago and Cruz. There was no news report on the death of Cruz or anything in the newspaper, so Elise assumed Sago must have called his people in to clean up. Elise doubted if she would ever hear from him again, but just in case she did, she was ready. A lot of money had gone into obtaining that information on Sago and Cruz, but in Elise's mind, it was worth every single dime. Business was going well. Tony's CD continued to sell.

So Real signed two new groups, a male R&B foursome called Dream Life and a very young rapper out of the Glenville area called Lil' Cee, who had the streets chanting.

The computer stores were booming, and the latest software was an instant success. Because it was the Black man's version of "*Lara Croft*", appealing to horny boys and men, "*Mistress of the Game*" was a number one seller. Even bootleggers posted at the entrances of check-cashing locations couldn't keep it in supply.

In the game, the heroine, Mistress Pearl, resembling Cleopatra Jones with hair like Elise's, progressed

Sherrie Walker

through various levels of difficulty by overcoming obstacles with her strategic mind and the use of subtle violence. Her signature outfit was a pair of black, perfectly tailored leather pants and matching five-inch, calf-high stiletto boots. Her MP initialed belt buckle, with 22 carats of encrusted green diamonds, stored some of her most imperative secret powers. Aparis figured antagonists would be blinded by the bling-bling. More times than not, it worked.

A leather Kangol hat turned to the back sat atop her head and kept her perfectly combed inward French braid in place. She never took her hat off, even though she could sometimes change clothes. She complemented her domineering appearance with black leather gloves and dark shades that looked like a pair of Chanels, but had diamond encrusted MP initials on each side.

The game even had settings that allowed the players to download their favorite Hip-Hop songs for the heroine's black Lamborghini or iPod. Players could even create an army of loyal "ride or die soldiers" that reacted on the point of a finger. Mistress Pearl, named after LaKiesha and Que's mother, sometimes had to rescue abused children as well as battered or drug-addicted women who were at wits end. She especially enjoyed beating down pimps, perverts and pedophiles.

Once Mistress Pearl successfully completed her mission, she took off her glasses and tossed them to the side; then, she removed her hat. And like a convict dropping the winning card in a drawn-out, intense game of Pinochle, she slammed the hat to the ground then loosened her braid.

At that point, Mistress Pearl shook her hair before

Sherrie Walker

throwing her hands up to the sky and falling to her knees, submitting to a force greater than herself. Once she stood back up, an emerald-colored, brand-spanking-new convertible Bentley Continental GT, with big, shiny socks and shoes, pulled up. Her lover, the Master of the Game, dressed to the nines as well, stepped out. They took each other by the hand, and together, they walked into the horizon then disappeared. The words, *NOW, SHE'S ONE WITH THE UNIVERSE* scrolled across the screen.

~ ~ ~

To celebrate her successes, Elise bought a brand new home in the old money community of Bratenahl. Nestled in Cleveland, her neighborhood was nearly ten miles east of downtown. She loved her home but wished she could have purchased one on the other side of Lakeshore Boulevard because Lake Erie served as the backdrop to those backyard landscapes.

Elise's 6,500 square foot, brand new home sat on almost two acres of land adjacent to I-90. Boasting a sunken living room and a finished basement, which she had transformed into an entertainment room with plenty of recreation, the house was her dream home. She had six bedrooms, three-and-a-half baths and a three-car garage. She loved the exclusiveness of the old established community, so she hired a designer to landscape her land. She practically lived at Petitti's Garden Center, selecting flora that would shape her dream front lawn. She didn't want her neighbors to think she didn't fit in. Somewhat to her surprise, she fit in fine, and was satisfied to know that she could "stump with da big dawgs."

Elise walked to the kitchen to grab a snack and another *"Martin"* DVD from her collection, remembering how he had made her laugh during some depressing times. She snickered while sashaying down the steps wearing a fitted baby doll T with her company's insignia across her breast and a pair of capri sweatpants displaying the same logo. She entered the kitchen in search of a granola bar. The box was empty and three crumbs lay on the countertop. As bad as she wanted to have a fit, she brushed it off, and then the crumbs. Elise stood still and took a deep breath hoping things would work out for the best.

Simone had only been discharged from the hospital a week ago and things were slightly hectic. Elise had grown comfortable with her exclusive living arrangement, and Simone had yet to come around, especially since she'd learned about Pretty Ricky's death and was upset that she couldn't pay her last respects. She voiced her opinion in the car on the way home from the hospital then refused to speak unless Elise spoke to her. And even then, she kept it straight like a shot of Rémy Martin.

"Would you like for me to make you something to eat?" Elise asked as Simone entered the kitchen and opened the Sub-Zero refrigerator, which was camouflaged within the mahogany cabinetry. She removed a half-gallon carton of orange juice and set it down next to a cookbook then looked for a glass.

"Nah, I'm cool." She slammed a cabinet shut.

"You sure? We got to start putting some weight back on you." Elise examined Simone as she searched the kitchen and kept coming up short.

"Quit acting like you my mama, 'cause you ain't, all right! As soon as I get back on my feet, I'm outta here. Fo' real."

Sherrie Walker

"You don't have to leave, Simone. This is your home, too. I want to help you."

"I don't need yo' help, Elise. I can take care of myself, all right? I been doing it all this time. And I don't need you now!" Simone sat down heavily in the contemporary styled high chair in front of the mauve-colored marble countertop. She flipped through Mo'Nique's *Skinny Cooks Can't Be Trusted* with disinterest. Simone stopped and read: *Hey Elise, baby girl – you doing yo' thang. Enjoy all, your sista, Mo'Nique.*

"I tried to find you as soon as I got out, Simone, but it took a minute." Elise spoke in a quiet, even tone. She leaned onto the counter, close to Simone. "We're sisters and I love you."

"Would you chill wit' all this Brady Bunch drama, already? I can fend for myself. I'm not a little girl."

Elise opened a cabinet near the refrigerator and removed a glass. "You're only fifteen, Simone, and whether you like it or not, I'm going to be here for you. You can't fend for yourself or else you wouldn't have …" Elise caught herself and set the tumbler down.

"I wouldn't have what? Become a hoe? Go 'head, say it. So what are you—Captain Save-a-Hoe?" Simone scoffed.

Elise moved over to her and sat down. She hesitated before speaking. "You were seven years old the last time I saw you. You were so little and terribly adorable. I used to change your diapers, feed you, dress you—all of that. Mama was caught up in her disease, she was never there so I took care of you."

"I didn't ask you to!" Simone snapped.

"At first … well … at first I thought it was so unfair. Mama had you, but I raised you. I was only six when

Sherrie Walker

you were born! What did a six-year-old know about being a mother? I learned, though." Elise paused. "It was instinct. You would look up at me with those big, brown, pretty eyes and smile and my heart would just melt. I loved you and had to protect you at any cost. All we had was each other. I taught you to walk, talk, I even taught you to color, and I loved every second of it. After awhile, it wasn't an obligation. It was a pleasure. So I became very protective of you because you were my little sister.

"One night, I noticed your bed was empty. It was awfully late and I thought you went to the bathroom by yourself. I got alarmed because the house we lived in was too dangerous. Too many perverts lived there." Elise sat next to Simone and rubbed her hand.

"I was asleep and woke up to find that you were out of the bed. I thought maybe you had wandered to the bathroom, which I forbade you to go to alone. Before I could get out of bed to find you, I heard you cry out, and I took off running. I ran to the bathroom and you weren't there. Then I heard you cry out again, I followed the direction of your voice, and it came from the living room." Elise stopped. The emotion became overwhelming as the nightmare stealthily crept back into her mind. She attempted to hold back her tears.

"I saw Walter ..." Elise nearly choked, "Mama's third husband ... he was standing over you naked with his penis in his hand about to force it in your mouth." The tears streamed down Elise's face as she struggled to continue. "You were so scared and helpless. Everything seemed to go in slow motion as I picked up the gun. Everything went red, I was so livid.

"All I know is he was molesting you. I quickly curled

Sherrie Walker

my index finger back against that metal and I couldn't stop firing. I emptied the gun and kept pulling the trigger even after I released all of the bullets. I killed him and still wasn't able to protect you." Elise broke down sobbing.

Simone looked away as Elise cried.

Simone allowed the mental voices of the "what ifs" to take over her thoughts. She was struggling on the inside. She loved Elise and wanted to accept her with open arms but she was scared. "What if" she allowed Elise in and she was to leave her? "What if" after a while, Elise decided that she didn't want her to stay there any more?

Simone allowed her sister's words to slowly sink into her brain. Finally, she reached for Elise. They embraced, both crying and consoling each other.

"I'm sorry, Elise."

"It's not your fault, baby. I just can't let anything else bad happen to you. Nothing! Don't you see? I have to protect you. I have to." They comforted each other. Elise got up and left the room. She returned, carrying a wet washcloth and wiped Simone's face.

"I'm not a baby anymore." Simone laughed, pushing Elise's hand away.

"You're still my baby, stinker," Elise joked.

"For years, I blocked it out of my mind. Or, at least, I tried. And deep down inside, I blamed myself. I thought I was a bad baby." Simone looked away from Elise.

"Listen to me," said Elise, turning Simone's head so she could look into her teary eyes. "It wasn't your fault. You were the perfect baby. Sometimes, I imagined having delivered you. You didn't deserve any of those things that happened to you, Simone. We just had a disturbed mother."

"Where is she?" Simone questioned.

"Mama?" Elise gathered herself before answering. "Agnes died of a drug overdose two years after we were separated. One day a social worker called me into an office in the orphanage and informed me that our mother died and I would have to remain in the orphanage until I was eighteen. You know what, Simone? Elise paused before continuing.

"No, what."

"I felt numb. I couldn't cry. I didn't shed not as much as one tear."

"What happened to our father, Elise?"

"He died of a heart attack at the age of thirty-five while mama was still pregnant with you. He was the best, too, Simone. Things were so good when daddy was alive. We were a close knit, happy, loving family. It wasn't until he passed that times got bad. Mama was never the same after he died.

A hush fell between the two women.

Finally, Simone spoke up. "Elise."

"Yes, baby?"

"Did you kill Ricky or have him killed?"

Elise thought for a minute, realizing that the answer would change everything she had just accomplished with Simone if she didn't respond correctly. She looked her in the face. "As much as I hated him for what he was doing to you, Simone, I could've killed him with my bare hands. But to answer your question, no, I had nothing to do with his death. At the same time, I can't say I shed a tear when I found out. He exploited and degraded you, Simone."

Sherrie Walker

"But, he loved me." She slightly lowered her head. "In his own way. He bought me nice things, and stuff, and gave me a place to stay when I ran away from the home."

"He bought you stuff with *your* money. You laid on your back or …" Elise caught her words again. "He saw you as a meal ticket, Simone. He didn't love you. He loved what you could give him. If he loved you, he wouldn't have had you out there selling your body."

Elise rubbed her sister's hair in a motherly fashion. "One day, you'll meet a man and you'll know that he's the one for you. He'll treat you like the queen you are. So, never settle for anything less than that, Simone. You hear me?"

Simone's head tilted. "Like," Simone smiled, "somebody like Trey."

"Trey?" Elise was taken aback. "Trey and I are just friends. He was my man's best friend, his right hand man."

"I may only be fifteen, but I'm not stupid. He loves you and you love him. I can tell by the way he looks and acts around you. You change, too, when he's around."

"Girl, please! Trey just my nigga, for real."

"Yeah, ok," Simone teased. Elise looked at her everyday watch, a diamond-studded Benny & Co. with an ivory face and an emerald-colored band. "It's time to be getting to bed. We'll finish talking tomorrow."

"Ok."

Elise bent down and kissed Simone on the cheek. "Good night, lil' sis. I love you."

"Good night, I love you, too."

As Elise ascended the stairs, Simone called her name. Elise stopped and turned around, halfway up the staircase. "Thanks," she whispered.

Elise smiled. For the first time since Simone was taken away from her, she felt at peace. She walked into her bedroom, then rested on the California King-sized bed. Feeling content, she looked up at the dark sky, then pulled back the emerald-colored, richly textured comforter and the ivory Egyptian cotton sheets. *Life is grand.*

She removed her watch and placed it on the nightstand. Scanning the room, she admired and adored the plethora of complementary pillows, but decided moving them would be a lightweight chore, so she simply positioned the neck roll for her personal comfort. She relaxed, picked up her remote control and pushed a button. Within seconds, the ceiling opened.

As Elise gazed into the night sky, with the exception of one star, positioned slightly above the others, the constellations above her house were perfectly aligned. She wiggled her foot as she remembered leaving that crack house in the police car wearing only one shoe. It seemed unreal to think of how far she had come. Far away from that shabby bedroom she and Simone used to sleep in. *I'll never forget the paint chipping walls, the floor with the mouse holes, the raggedy base boards, and the coldness. I'll never forget that bedroom, or the event that separated me and Simone.*

She thought about her life and how it had come together. At the age of twenty-two, she had accomplished more than most people achieved in a lifetime. She had money making money, *and* she was a legitimate businesswoman. The only unfulfilled desire that remained with her was to find and bury whoever was responsible for Que's death. So far, the trail had gone cold and lately she began to wonder if she would ever

Sherrie Walker

find his killer. It left her feeling incomplete. There was a void, which she knew would remain within her as long as Que's killer was still out there.

She would begin planning Simone's birthday party the next day and prayed that it would take her out of the hole she found herself in.

twenty-four

FOR THREE MONTHS, Elise planned and prepared for Simone's sixteenth birthday party. She went all out and spared nothing when it came to cost. She wanted it to be extremely nice.

When the day came, Simone was under the impression that she was going to one of Elise's company parties. As Elise and Simone walked into the Mirage On the Water, a nightclub located in the Flats, an area situated along the banks of the Cuyahoga River. Everyone screamed, "SURPRISE!"

Simone threw her hands up to both sides of her cheeks looking around, very surprised. She had the biggest Kool-Aid smile on her face as she looked at her guests dressed in their chic, trendy, Juicy Couture from head to toe. "Oh my God, Elise this is for me?"

"Yes all for you. Enjoy. Happy Birthday, lil' sis."

They exchanged a quick embrace as Simone began to feel like a celebrity as several guests approached her to exchange their Happy Birthday wishes. Elise managed to shut down the club for Simone's exclusive, private sixteenth birthday party. She wanted it to be special for her.

The guests were mostly Elise's friends since Simone

Sherrie Walker

only had a few, but before the night was over she had made many because Elise's guests who had sisters and brothers around Simone's age were invited to attend. They interacted, mingled, came for a party and they partied. Wasn't nobody on no hatin' or stuck-up acting trips.

The entire club was beautifully decorated in red, silver and white streamers and balloons. Elise guided Simone toward the back of the club to the area by the window overlooking the river. DJ Bim had 'em bouncing to the sounds of Dr. Dre, Scarface, Notorious B.I.G., Missy Elliott, 2Pac, Mariah Carey, Lil' Kim, Too Short, 8Ball & MJG and UGK. The crowd was staring at Simone who was wearing a Coogi mini dress with hints of burgundy, black and deep grayish-blue hues and a pair of thigh-high boots, as she followed Elise to the cake table. Her silver bangles jingled and her matching earrings dangled as she hugged Elise with excitement. "Wow, this is awesome. I am blown away. My very first birthday party and you've laid me out." Elise smiled with pride.

Everything was perfect, even the "cut out" cake shaped in the numbers 1 and 6. It had Italian Meringue Butter Crème icing and edible glitter on top of a cluster of flowers and lace.

Elise knew it had been a gruesome six months for Simone, especially since she had her going through therapy and counseling sessions.

It wasn't easy at first, but after several sessions, Simone started to show improvement. Although the physical scars from Pretty Ricky's beating healed nicely it was the inner ones that most concerned Elise. However, she sensed a resilience and strength in Simone and prayed that with the right guidance, nurturing, counseling and lots of love, Simone would mend inside out and

Sherrie Walker

be fine in time. She stood back, watching Simone look around at her party guest, and saw the gleam in her eyes as Tony entered.

Once Simone saw him coming through the crowd, nothing else mattered. She ran up to him and wrapped her arms around his neck. He embraced her in a big-brother, friendly way, then stepped back to look at her.

"Happy birthday, girl."

"Thanks. Yo, you, performing, right?" She put her hands on her hips to demand a response but Tony appeared a little spacey-eyed.

"Fo' sho, fo' sho. Wouldn't be a party if I didn't," he spat.

Trey swaggered in, sporting a black Zegna suit with a lime-green cashmere sweater and a pair of black Mezlan gators. His attire complemented his mocha complexion and the fresh fade he'd received from Herbie at the popular Glenville Sports Barber Shop.

Damn, Elise thought. He smiled at her and her heart melted. Sexy was an understatement when considering Trey. *He's so enchanting. Oh God, trying to fight this urge is getting harder and harder. Que baby, what would you have me to do?*

"Where's the birthday girl?" Trey smiled and Elise felt the wetness between her legs spread.

"On the dance floor." Tony was on stage performing, and Simone was dancing with the others, yet in a world of her own.

"You look breathtaking tonight," Trey said.

Elise had on a cat suit that looked as if she had been poured into it. It fit like a second layer of skin and complemented the smooth fit of her over-the-knee Christian Louboutin boots. She was truly feeling herself. Her girl,

Sherrie Walker

Meechie, the proprietor of Headlines by De'Franco Salons, made sure her crown of curls was elegant and flawless for the party.

"Thanks." She smiled.

"When's Simone opening her gifts?"

Elise checked her Piaget. "At twelve. The party's over at one," she answered.

"I'm going to go put mine with the rest of her gifts. I'll be right back."

Elise watched him as he strolled across the dance floor. "Lord … have … mercy. I can't hold out another day," she said to herself.

When the time came, Elise gave the DJ the cue and he announced Simone was about to open her gifts in the lounge area. Everyone filed over as she sat at the table and began to unwrap her presents. LaKiesha gave her a Louis Vuitton luggage set with four different sized pocketbooks to match. Aparis surprised her with a 2 carat, princess-cut solitary diamond in a custom platinum setting and a 2 carat tennis bracelet. Trey gave her a mahogany mink bomber jacket with a matching hat and muff that was off the chain.

Elise was the last one to give her a present. She handed Simone a little black box. Simone thought it was more jewelry until she opened it and pulled out a car key. She glanced at Elise who pointed to the exit. Simone raced out of the club and the first car she saw was a Toyota Tercel so she looked disappointed. Elise, standing in the door of the club, pointed to the correct car, which was sitting near the edge of the lot. It was a candy- apple red BMW 645Ci with chrome rims. Simone screamed and ran around the car before she opened the door and hopped inside.

Sherrie Walker

"Can I drive it?" she asked, jumping from foot to foot like a little kid in a candy store.

"Not until you get your temps, sista girl." Elise shook her head. She was adamant.

"Please, please, pretty please, Elise. I just want to drive it home," she begged.

"You don't have license or a permit, Simone."

"Look, I'll ride with her, Elise, make sure she comes right home," Trey interrupted, winking at Simone. Elise didn't see him. "Nothing will happen. It will be my pleasure to escort her to the crib." He smiled. Elise thought about it for a minute.

Aparis and Tony interjected. "Aw, let her drive, Elise. It's her birthday. We'll be right behind them," said Aparis.

"Right home, no pit stops," said Elise reluctantly.

Simone screamed and got in the car and Trey entered on the passenger side.

"I'm going to pay everybody and head in that direction," said Elise.

She hugged LaKiesha, Aparis and Tony before she went back into the club to finalize payments and make sure everything was in tact.

By the time Elise arrived at her house, the effects of planning and getting everything together had taken its toll on her. All she wanted to do was take a nice, long bath then crawl into her bed and fall asleep. She glanced at the clock on her bathroom wall wondering what was taking Simone and Trey so long.

Elise stepped into the bathroom and ran her bath water. She sprinkled bath beads in the tub and lit scented candles. She turned on her surround sound system and Mary J. Blige started singing, "I can remember

Sherrie Walker

when … we had … we had it all … you and I … you and I." She closed her eyes to relax and the next thing she knew, she dozed off.

She opened one eye as Simone knocked on the door while entering. She was still excited and full of energy. "I'm back. That car is sweet to death." She kissed her fingertips and threw kisses as Elise. "Thank you so much, Elise. I can't wait to get my permit and license so I can drive to school."

"I made an appointment for you to start your driving classes tomorrow."

"Cool. Trey's bringing in my bags of gifts. This was my best birthday ever!" Simone gushed. "I gotta go tell Trey thanks and bye. He is so fly, Elise."

"Tell him I'll be out in a minute," Elise responded.

"Ok," Simone said as she ran out the door.

Elise got out the tub and dried off. Then she put on some body oil and a touch of Romance by Ralph Lauren behind her ears. She slipped on a black silk nightgown and the matching robe and let her hair loose. She walked down the stairs and Trey was standing in front the fireplace with his jacket off. *He is so sexy.* "Thank you for bringing Simone home."

"That's my baby girl. It was my pleasure. And she loves that car. Good choice."

"With your help, it was the perfect gift. Would you like a drink?"

"Yes, thank you," Trey answered. Elise walked over to the bar and made a drink for Trey and herself. She handed Trey his glass then sashayed over to the entertainment center. Jamie Foxx's soulful voice crooned through the speakers. Elise was standing in front of the huge glass armoire, searching musical selections, when Trey walked up behind her and started kissing the back of her neck. He smelled so good that Elise was stuck. Trey took her drink out of her hand and turned her around. "May I have this dance?" He smiled.

"Of course," she replied.

They began to dance slowly and Elise placed her head on Trey's shoulder. He lifted it and began to kiss her passionately, driving her crazy. Elise could feel all of her inhibitions melting as she swayed from Trey's inebriating kiss. Her body began to respond in ways that betrayed her thoughts. She become lost in his embrace and felt like she never wanted to stop. Trey kissed her passionately as his tongue explored her mouth. He began to run his hands through her hair and pulled it lightly, which excited Elise more.

Trey picked Elise up and carried her up the spiral staircase to the bedroom. He laid her across the bed and she reached for the remote and opened the skylight to reveal the moon and stars. Then she gave her undivided attention to Trey.

Trey undressed and peered at her. He then removed his clothing. Elise's eyes were stuck as she took in the sight of his twelve-inch long penis with a plump head. He smiled when he noticed her looking at his manhood. He lay next to her and began to slowly and tenderly plant kisses all over her body. Very gently and easily, he took off her robe then kissed her up and down her arms.

His tongue was long, hot and wet as it massaged and traveled across her skin. He eased her negligee over her head and passionately began to suck her protruding nipples, slightly biting them with his teeth and licking her areolas. He stopped then quickly ran his tongue across her firm C-cup breasts. He softly licked them and his

Sherrie Walker

tongue stroked underneath the folds.

He began to slither his extraordinarily long tongue down her stomach, leaving wet spots as he journeyed between her legs. Elise started to moan and steadily thrust her body upward to meet his mouth. He reached her mound and parted it with his tounge until he made contact with the body part that's designed for the purpose of deriving pleasure. He flicked his tongue in a fleeting motion over her clitoris, then suddenly lunged deep inside her vagina.

"EEEEEE!" Elise squealed, then moaned as his tongue penetrated her succulently ripe love canal over and over. The more she moaned, the deeper inside he explored. His tongue started to move like an ocean wave, back and forth, motioning from deep inside to the top of her clitoris, until Elise exploded in ecstasy.

While she panted, Trey lifted her legs over her head and began to lick up and down her backside. Elise begged him to stop. "I want to feel you inside me, baby … please …Trey."

He positioned himself on top of her. At first, it seemed as if his penis would not fit, but Trey took his time allowing his firm tip to tenderly penetrate, inch by inch, Elise's warm, wet love tunnel until it was entirely filled with his pulsating python.

They became one. He glided smoothly in and out of Elise, bringing his head to the top of her opening, pausing then slithering like a nocturnal snake while his long fingers occasionally massaged her clitoris. He leaned forward and sucked on her nipples while never breaking the rhythm of his lower body. He started to pick up speed. Elise was thrusting her body upward in rhythm with his in order to give to him what he was giving to her—complete sexual satisfaction.

"Look at me!" Trey demanded. Elise opened her eyes. "I want to please you in every way possible. I ... love ... you, Elise."

"I love you, too," she said as her body trembled, starting with her thighs. Elise felt like a volcano had erupted inside her as her body began to shake and the heat coming from between her legs was a mixture of pleasure and sensuous pain. She felt Trey's penis get harder as he increased his pace and slid in and out of her, stroking the inside walls of her vagina and the center of her core. "Treeeeyyyy, don't ... stop ... harder, longer, deeper, I want it ... I want all of you."

Elise screamed as began to climax. Trey gripped her thighs and plunged deeper into her. Once he knew Elise was satisfied, Trey began to build his rhythm to a wild speed until he deposited his semen into her soul as they became one.

He rested on top of her, trying to catch his breath. After doing so, he lay beside her and took her into his masculine arms. They embraced and cuddled for hours, talking. Then, they made love again. She climaxed and fell asleep with a smile on her face and, for the first time in a long time, she felt complete.

Sherrie Walker

twenty-five

FOR A YEAR and a half, everything ran smoothly. Business was booming and the two new singing and rap groups were tearing the charts up. Additionally, they had seven computer software companies—two in Cleveland, two in New York, two in California, and one in Atlanta. Aparis was designing software for every console and operating system on the market. The games were popular because Aparis' graphics made the images look as if they were real life, especially in her athletic games.

Elise spent more time at home with Simone and Trey, allowing the presidents to oversee the day-to-day operations. Simone was in a private high school in the eleventh grade and appeared to be adjusting well. Elise had sought a private therapist to work with Simone as well. At the same time, Aparis and Tony were a hot item. She was pregnant.

There was still no information regarding Ghost. It looked as if everything leading to him came to a dead end.

Elise's twenty-fourth birthday was in two days and Trey had promised her a surprise. She thought about selling her share of all the companies and moving to an island to settle down.

I don't want to end up like a lot of these old millionaires, too busy to take pleasure in what I've worked hard to achieve. I want to travel the world, enjoy mine while I'm still young, settle down, and take care of Simone and Trey. Trey—umph, umph, umph— he is the best thing to come along since bottled water. An excellent lover, attentive, loyal and fine.

Her pleasant thoughts were suddenly interrupted by an intense wave of nausea. Elise jumped up and ran to the bathroom. She puked until there was nothing left in her stomach then sat on the floor feeling dizzy and light-headed. *Must have been something I ate.* She rested for a while than got up and ran some bath water and finished packing. *Wherever Trey is taking me, I want to have everything I need.*

"There's my favorite girl," Trey said as he tried to sneak up behind her.

"I better be your only girl."

"Well, I hate to tell you this, ma, but another girl has my heart, too," said Trey.

"Where is she? 'Cause I'm gonna kill the heifer."

"Her name is Simone."

"Ok, I can get with that, but we better be the only two who have your heart."

"Trust me, my hands are full with the two of you. You almost packed?"

"Yep, I'm ready. How did everything go at the studio?"

"Tony never showed up."

"Never showed up?" Elise looked puzzled.

"Did you try his cell phone?"

"Yeah, it keeps going to voicemail."

"What about Aparis?"

Sherrie Walker

"She said she hasn't seen or heard from him in three days. She's pissed!" Trey explained.

Elise instantly became annoyed. "This is beginning to be a regular thing with him, and I don't like it."

"Well, we'll schedule a meeting with everyone when we get back."

"That sounds like a good idea," Elise said. "What is wrong with him?"

"Cali said he been smoking wet. Those wacky cigarettes dipped in embalming fluid, and been on some other stuff."

"He still doing that? I thought he got enough of that when his ass took off his clothes on stage and they arrested him," Elise commented. Elise reflected back to that night and had to chuckle a little. Tony was standing on stage rapping and the crowd was going crazy. All of the sudden, he dropped the mic, unbuckled his pants and let them fall to his knees, exposing boxers and a peep of his black ass. He stood there with his penis erect and a wide grin on his face. Security stormed the stage along with a thousand screaming, hot and wet women. Tony was carted off to jail for indecent exposure. They bonded him out that night and Tony was remorseful claiming that he would never touch another drug again.

Elise guessed he was up to his old tricks. Trey's words snapped her back to reality.

"All that did was send his record sales straight to the top, so I think his P.R. guy made him feel like it was ok. You know going to jail increases record sales these days," Trey commented.

"What!" Elise continued. "Oh, he should've been fired."

"I did fire him, but Tony rehired him."

Sherrie Walker

"I take off for two months and things go crazy."

"Look. We'll address it when we get back. We'll be on track," Trey responded.

"You right! Tony is either going to get it together or we'll have to renegotiate his contract."

Trey walked up to Elise and took her in his arms. "Sexy, I don't want you worrying about nothing for the next couple of days. We are getting ready to go away and have a good time. Let me handle everything else." He kissed her forehead then her lips.

"Ok, Daddy," she chanted.

"Damn, baby, you get me so horny when you say that."

"Ok, Daddy," she repeated. "Ok, Daddy."

Elise dropped to her knees and unzipped Trey's pants. She stroked his erection and opened her mouth. "Ok, Daddy."

~ ~ ~

The next morning, a stretch limo pulled up to the house and the chauffer got out to put their luggage in the trunk after he opened the door for Elise. She slid inside and saw Trey wearing a white Akedemiks jogging suit and some crisp Air Force 1's. His hair was freshly cut, the waves swirling like those big rainbow-colored lollipops. He was holding a bouquet of red and white roses while *"Be Without You,"* played at moderate volume. He had two glasses of champagne ready as well but Elise leaned over and gave him a wet, lingering, passionate kiss that left his lips parched and lusting for more.

"Don't start nothing you can't finish, woman."

"Who said I can't finish? Don't you know I'm the starter, finisher, and Mistress of all games?" She smiled her naughty girl grin. "This is so nice, baby."

Sherrie Walker

"You haven't seen nothing yet, slim," Trey said. He and Elise cuddled all the way to the airport. When they arrived, the car pulled right up to a small plane.

"A private jet?" Elise shrieked with excitement. The chauffer opened the door for her and held out his hand. He escorted her to the Hawker 800 and up the steps. The interior was plush, with cream-colored leather seats, television monitors on the back of the seats, a Bose entertainment system, a large wet bar and a long chaise in the back. Its seating capacity was for eight, but for a special evening as such, it was seating only two ... Trey and Elise.

A stewardess appeared out of the back carrying a large tray of food including caviar, hors d'oeuvres, a shrimp pasta, crab legs and lobster—a feast of the finest cuisines. Trey escorted Elise to a small table with a burning candle and a red rose in the center. Elise took a seat then looked around with a smile.

So, girl, get comfortable
We about to do something
We've never done before...

"You know I love Jamie Foxx," Elise said. "Baby, this is so special."

"You're special. Nothing but the best for the best." The attendant set the table and served them. Elise stared at Trey the entire time. *I'm the luckiest woman in the world.*

They finished eating then lay in the chaise together watching *"Hustle and Flow"* until they arrived at their destination. Trey covered Elise's eyes with a white satin night mask so she couldn't see where they were landing. After the plane touched down, he lifted her body and carried her down the steps. Once they reached the bottom, he set her down and removed the mask.

She noticed a sign that read: Welcome to Paris. Elise

Sherrie Walker

screamed. "Paris! Oh, my God. I've always wanted to visit Paris. How did you know?"

"It's my job to know your every wish and desire," Trey replied, diving deeper into the chambers of her heart.

The limousine drove into the heart of the city and stopped in front of the majestic Hotel Ritz, which was famous for accommodating some of the world's wealthiest, from F. Scott Fitzgerald to Coco Chanel. The chauffeur helped Elise out of the car. She stood on the sidewalk and took a deep breath before Trey escorted her to the entrance.

The lobby was stunning, like something out of a movie with exquisite paintings from renowned artists, luxurious chandeliers and a vintage grand piano that was indeed a conversation piece. Elise noticed security cameras as they approached the registration desk and while walking to their suite. But all she thought about was being in the city of love with Trey.

Their room, with Louis XVI furniture and a marble fireplace, overlooked the famous garden. Elise felt as if she were in paradise. "It's simply beautiful," she said. She stood back and observed the exquisite and unique décor.

"I ... Trey ... I ... I don't even know what to say. This is the best birthday I've ever had."

"You deserve it and so much more." Trey pushed a button on the remote and Mariah Carey's "*We Belong Together*" began to play. He took Elise in his arms and kissed her hungrily. They tore off one another's clothes until they were nude. They stared at each other before Trey picked her up.

"Don't ever go getting fat on me 'cause I won't be able to do this, girl," Trey joked. He carried her into the bed-

Sherrie Walker

room and laid her on the bed. It was covered with rose petals that felt so good against her skin. Trey leaned toward the nightstand and picked up a bottle of body oil. He poured it onto her body then rubbed the warm liquid into her soft skin. He massaged between her legs, down her thighs and traveled to her feet. Taking her toes into his mouth, one by one, he licked and sucked between them. Elise felt like she was about to explode.

She turned over and took the oil from Trey then poured it onto his muscular body. She started at his chest then massaged downward to his manhood. She oiled and stroked it while he started to moan. She felt him get harder and harder as she increased her pace.

Elise stopped and he gave her the evil eye. She smiled, stood on the bed and straddled him. Elise then lowered her pelvis onto his Johnson and slowly eased all the way down. Her juices were dripping onto his manhood as she rode it. He grabbed her hips and moved her faster and faster. *"Joy Ride"* by Mariah Carey started to play and she began to gyrate to the rhythm of the beat. She felt a tingling sensation throughout her body as she and Trey experienced a volcanic orgasm together.

With her head on Trey's chest, Elise started to cry softly. He lifted it and was alarmed.

"What's wrong? Did I hurt you?"

"No ... I just never thought I would find love and happiness, ever again. You have given me both."

"Elise, I live to make you happy. I love you."

"I love you, too." They kissed, and Trey pulled Elise into his strong masculine arms and held her tightly. She felt secure and happy in his embrace.

Sherrie Walker

twenty-six

THE MORNING SUN was bright and beautiful and a tantalizing smell stirred Elise from her sleep. She opened her eyes to see Trey standing over her with a breakfast fit for a queen. They both knew she wouldn't eat half of it. Plus, Trey couldn't stop kissing her long enough to get food in her mouth anyway. He rushed her to get dressed because he was anxious to provide her with the best birthday experience of her life.

First, he took her to the Eiffel Tower and snapped pictures of her as if she were a supermodel. After the photo shoot, she shopped, hitting the finer boutiques and specialty shops. Her favorite store was Hermes. She loved the intricate and brilliant design of their scarves. In addition to purchasing other accessories, she bought a couple scarves for herself and one for Simone, LaKiesha and Aparis. They continued to shop until *she* begged him to take her in. That tickled him.

"It's not funny, Trey," she said as she took her shoes off and started walking with a slight limp.

After she got a second wind, they walked the shores of the Seine River, took in more sightseeing and then returned to their room to change for dinner. Elise

Sherrie Walker

entered the suite.

"Trey?"

"Yes, baby?"

"What will I wear?" she asked.

"I'm sure you'll find something in one of those many garment bags and boxes that you have." He scooted some things off the bed and reclined backwards to stare at Elise. "Come here, girl, Daddy will help you figure it out." Seductively, she approached him with an insatiable desire to provide him with absolute pleasure.

~ ~ ~

That evening, Elise stepped out wearing a sleek-fitted white Chanel dress with a pair of multi-ankleband stilettos. They dined at the hotel's restaurant while a live band played Van Morrison's "*Moondance*."

The maître d' escorted them to their table. Shortly after they were seated, Trey excused himself to go to the restroom. She sat at the table bobbing her head and humming the words. "It's a marvelous night for a moon dance … a fantabulous night to make romance." She stopped humming as she sensed someone watching her.

She turned and saw a man sitting at the bar. He smiled and lifted his drink to salute her but she turned her back around and wondered what was taking Trey so long. The stranger walked over to Elise and sat down.

"Excuse me, I just want to tell you that … you are so stunning," the gentleman complimented as he took her hand and kissed the back of it.

"Look, I'm here with my boyfriend," she replied, snatching her arm back. "And I don't think he would appreciate you sitting at our table, let alone putting your lips on me."

"Oh? No offense. You're not married, huh?" he said.

Sherrie Walker

"What? That's none of your business."

"Please, don't get mad. I'm just saying, a woman as fine as you should have a ring on your finger."

"Look, you got five seconds to get ghost."

Trey walked back to the table. "What's going on, baby? Who is this?"

"I don't know, but he's getting on my nerves, for real," she replied with an attitude as strong as an alcoholic's urine.

"Look, no disrespect, man. I was just telling your lady friend here that a woman as beautiful as she is needs to have a ring on that finger," the mystery man explained. Trey looked at the stranger, looked at Elise and then took off his jacket. Elise became alarmed.

"Trey, he's not worth it." Trey turned his back to Elise and faced the man. The man reached in his pocket and pulled out a small package and handed it to Trey. Trey took it then turned around and dropped to his knee in front of Elise.

"He's right." Trey presented the blue velvet box and opened it. "Would you please do me the honor of being my wife?" he asked, smiling since he was sure she'd say yes. Elise looked around the room and noticed everyone watching them. The band stopped playing and the stranger, still smiling, seemed as anxious for her answer as Trey. She looked at her man and tears slowly streamed down her cheeks.

"Yes," she whispered. "Yes," she said louder. "Yes, Trey, I will marry you!" she shouted. The people in the restaurant applauded and Trey took Elise into his arms and planted a juicy kiss on her luscious Mac glossed lips. He released Elise and she walked over to the table and went inside her Chanel clutch. "Now I have something

Sherrie Walker

for you, daddy." She pulled out a baby T-shirt that read, "I Love My Daddy." Trey stood dumfounded as he stared at the shirt. "This is going to be the first shirt *our* baby wears." Elise flashed a bright smile.

"I'm having a shorty?" Trey questioned and Elise nodded her head up and down. Trey picked Elise up and swung her around, then immediately remembered she was pregnant. He helped her into the chair then turned to the couple sitting at the next table.

"We're pregnant!"

~ ~ ~

Elise lay next to Trey with her head on his chest as they watched TV. Her thoughts were of how things were finally looking up and how everything was so perfect. In fact, they seemed almost too perfect. *Usually, when something appears too good to be true it is*, she thought.

"Penny for your thoughts," Trey said.

"I don't know … I was just thinking how wonderful everything seems to be," she revealed and ran her hand across his face, "almost too good to be true."

"There you go, worrying. Relax and just enjoy yourself, baby." Trey began to shower her with kisses, but was interrupted by his BlackBerry. Elise and Trey looked at it before he answered the call. Elise knew it was something important because everyone was instructed not to bother them unless it was an emergency.

Trey picked up his phone and read the message. He looked at Elise and immediately, she knew it was serious.

"What? Simone?" asked Elise. "What's wrong?"

"There's been a murder. Let's go, we've got to get back to Cleveland," Trey commanded.

Sherrie Walker

twenty-seven

IT WAS 5:10 P.M. when they arrived at Burke Lakefront Airport from Paris. They left the airport in such a hurry to see what was going on that they made arrangements for their luggage to be delivered to their house.

Elise and Trey drove through Cleveland and headed to the studio where everyone was told to meet at 5:30 p.m. During the ride through the city, both were quiet and deep in thought. Elise replayed the last conversation she had with Tony. She began to question herself and was wondering if she had been slipping lately. Had she been neglecting her duties and the people she cared about and loved? She tried to remember the last serious conversation she had with LaKiesha and Aparis and couldn't. The guilt began to pull on the strings of her heart as she realized her dilemma. Trey took Elise's hand and squeezed it.

By the time they arrived at the studio, it was 5:29. The ride in the elevator was quiet and strained. Neither one spoke. Elise and Trey entered into the room and were greeted by Aparis, LaKiesha, Dre, California, Tony's lawyer and Tony's P.R. agent, Pinch. The welcomes were out of the way and Elise proceeded to get

Sherrie Walker

straight to business. "What the hell happened?" she asked.

Tony's lawyer, Mr. Dinuchi, cleared his throat. "Tony was arrested this morning on one count of aggravated murder, aggravated robbery and fleeing the scene of a crime."

"Aggravated robbery?" Elise yelled. "Tony don't need to rob anyone—he has millions." A look of disbelief appeared on her face.

Aparis and Pinch looked at each other, then looked away, but not before Elise caught their exchange. Aparis couldn't look Elise in the eyes.

"Look at me, Aparis," Elise demanded, "What's going on? Spit it out." Elise watched Pinch as Aparis opened her mouth to speak.

"Tony is broke." Aparis was short and to the point.

"How in the hell is he broke?" Elise sat in the chair at the head of the table and leaned back. "His CDs are still selling. He's doing BET and MTV shows and making cameo appearances with various artists and also has stock in this label. So tell me, how the fuck is he broke?"

"What happened to his money, Pinch?" Trey asked as he approached and stood next to Pinch.

Pinch began to stutter. "I ... I ... he ... the advertisement and P.R. is expensive. Plus, Tony has a bad drug problem," Pinch blurted. "I didn't know that for a long time."

"By the time I found out, Tony was way out there. He'd been missing in action for awhile," Aparis said sadly, rubbing her belly, which was big as a basketball.

"It appeared Tony was in the wrong neighborhood last night when two guys tried to take his jewelry and car," Tony's attorney explained. "He started shooting and hit one in the back and the other in the head. The second guy died on the scene. Tony then emptied the man's pockets and took his drugs and money. Even though Ohio doesn't have a self-defense law, I could've fought hard for it because Tony was trying to protect himself. However, Tony removed items off the victim after he was dead and left the scene, so self-defense went out the window.

"There are two witnesses who said they saw the whole thing, except their story is a little different. They claim Tony pulled up, started an argument with the vic and shot him in the back when he went to walk away, and then robbed him."

"Who are these two witnesses?" Elise asked.

Tony's lawyer shuffled through his papers and pulled out a sheet. "Some two-bit hustlers. Both have records, so I would have a field day with them."

"So what we looking at?" Elise inquired.

"Without the two witnesses, the State will have a hard time proving that it was cold-blooded murder and robbery. Tony has no prior convictions. He's a musician and businessman, but they don't know he's broke. So we have to work on the two witnesses first," he explained, staring directly at Elise. There was an undertone to his statement and Elise sensed it. Elise turned to Cali and Dre, "Take care of that please." Cali and Dre nodded. They knew what she meant.

"What about his bond?" Trey questioned.

"That's being worked on. I'm meeting with the judge in his chambers at 9:00 a.m. I'll be pushing for bond then. He may grant one, he may not. This is a big publicity case, so it's going to cost."

"We'll take care of any and all expenses. Stop at the

Sherrie Walker

reception area and pick up your money. Keep me posted on everything. Do you need one of us to attend the hearing?" Elise asked.

"That would be nice," he answered.

"I'll be there," said Pinch.

"No, you won't," Elise pronounced. "Aparis, you and LaKiesha go and take a company checkbook so y'all have the money to post after the hearing, in the event a bond is set."

"Well, I'll talk to you tomorrow, Elise," Dinuchi said as he handed her a piece of paper.

"Thank you." Elise passed the note to Trey, but never took her eyes off Pinch. He began to squirm in his chair under her steady gaze. The tension in the room was as thick as a white cloud in a pipe stem. Trey looked at the addresses of the witnesses and passed the piece of paper to Cali.

After a long silence, Elise spoke, each word sounding threatening. "How long have you known Tony was hooked on drugs, Pinch?"

"Uh ... I ... um, not long," he stuttered. "Naah, not that long."

Elise walked over and sat on the table in front of him with her legs crossed, then gazed downward. Immediately, Pinch broke out in a sweat.

"You had your grimy little claws in his pockets didn't you, Pinch?" Bracing herself with one hand flat on the table, Elise leaned inward and gently patted his face with the other.

"No ... No ... I never took anything from Tony," Pinch stuttered.

"I think you're lying." The receptionist walked in and handed Elise some documents. She examined them then looked Pinch dead in his beady eyes.

"As a matter of fact, I know you're lying," Elise stated. "How does a public relations agent have more money in his account than the man he's working for? You got almost a quarter of a million in one bank account, and I haven't even looked at your other accounts, Pinch. That's a lot of money for a punk-ass P.R. person—especially when you're just starting out and have only one client."

"I've been saving all my money ... I never took nothing from nobody," he cried.

"You're fired, Pinch. And I promise, you won't ever find work in Ohio again," she growled. "You've got five minutes to get your things together and be out of this building."

Looking indignant, Pinch glared at everybody, stood up, fixed his clothes and cleared his throat. "Uhmm , you will not get away with this," he uttered.

"That's probably the same thought the IRS would have if they see how much tax- free money you have in this account. Even if you attempted to move it now, these statements show that it existed. Now, GET OUT!"

Elise turned her back to him and he walked out, slamming the door. She looked around the table at everyone before she spoke. "What happened? How did everyone not know what was going on with Tony? We are a family and it is our job to have one another's back. How did we not know what was going on with him?" Elise stared at everyone in the room.

"Elise, no disrespect, baby girl, but when was the last time we all got together to see about each other?" Cali asked. "Or when was the last time we had a meeting or attended one of Tony's concerts? No one went to see him on his birthday but Aparis. No one knew because we

Sherrie Walker

were all caught up in our own affairs, including myself. My work has kept me busy. Plus me and my girl just had a baby. Nevertheless, none of these are valid reasons. The bottom line is, we've all been slipping," he finished sheepishly.

"I tried to handle it on my own, but Tony ..." Aparis coughed, tears welling up in her eyes, then regained her composure. "He's changed. How you think I'm supposed to deal with that?"

Elise stood then approached the wet bar to pour a glass of water. "You're right, Cali. I know I've been busy with Simone and my personal affairs," she murmured as she reconsidered the entire situation.

"Ok, so we got caught slipping, but now it's time to pull together and get Tony out of this," Trey said. "Cali, Dre and I are going to go check out those two witnesses and see what we can find. Aparis, you go see Tony to gauge how he's holding up. Kiesh, you and Elise try to find out as much as you can about the victim—his family, finances and all that good stuff. We need to know if he has kids, his baby mama's name, what his family likes to eat, the whole nine yards."

Everyone looked at Trey then at Elise to see if she approved. Elise looked at Trey and smiled, relieved to know that someone other than herself was thinking, planning and taking charge of the situation. She hadn't felt this way since she was with Que, and it was comforting.

"You heard what he said, let's get busy," Elise advised.

Trey kissed Elise on his way out. California and Dre followed. LaKiesha and Elise went to Aparis and hugged her.

"Why did he have to go and do something stupid like

this?" Aparis asked. "I don't want to raise this baby without a daddy. I want my baby to have a mother and a father like I did." Aparis broke down crying in her friends' embrace.

"I know, Paris, I know." LaKiesha hugged her even harder.

"We're on top of this, ok? I assure you we're going to do all we can. Please don't start worrying. I'm sorry I wasn't there for you, Paris," said Elise.

"I understand. Sorry you and Trey had to come back so soon." Aparis wiped her eyes.

"Girl, we can always go back, anytime. Tony is family and it's important that we take care of this," Elise consoled her. "How is his sister holding up?"

"She's worried of course," Aparis said, "but she's been staying with their grandparents so she should have some stability."

"Oh!" LaKiesha said as she snapped her fingers to get her friends' attention. "I may have some information about Ghost. I'm supposed to meet with this chicken head next week to see what she's talking about."

"Who is she?" Elise questioned.

LaKiesha paused before she answered. "Some crack head who supposedly worked for Ghost. I don't know how true it is, but that dude, Po Boy, been putting the work out gathering all kinds of info about this lame. Everybody tryin' to get that dough for real."

"Why next week? Where she at now?" Elise probed.

"In rehab, she don't get out until next week," LaKiesha responded.

"Why don't you let Cali or Dre handle it?" Elise questioned.

"I don't want anyone to handle it but me. It was my

Sherrie Walker

parents and brother who were killed by this mothafucka and I'm going to find him if it's the last thing I do," she snapped.

"I was just trying to make sure you're all right. I want to find this Ghost just as bad as you do, Kiesha." Elise's tone of voice was conspiratorial.

"Do you?" LaKiesha challenged.

Elise looked at her as if she had lost her mind. "What … did you say?" Elise questioned. "Are you challenging my loyalty?

LaKiesha looked at Elise and Elise stared back at her until finally LaKiesha averted her gaze. "You know what? I'm going to leave before I say something I may regret because I'm pissed."

Elise looked from Aparis to LaKiesha. "I'll see you in an hour at your place," Elise said as she walked out the door.

Aparis looked at LaKiesha and rolled her eyes. "I should bitch slap you into next week. You can be so stupid sometimes, Kiesha. Elise has always looked out for us. Always! She's the reason why we're on top," she scolded.

"I'm sorry," LaKiesha replied. "I just want to find this dude and put him to rest so I can move on with my life. Although I've never seen him, this dude haunts me daily. All I'm saying is, sometimes it seems as if I'm the only one who continues to care about finding him."

"I'm the wrong one to be telling that to. I got to go try and get my man out of jail, so I'll holla." Aparis picked up her purse and wobbled out the door. LaKiesha flopped down into the chair and dropped her head in her hands. She began to think about where she was and how she arrived. She felt as if no one was really trying to find Que's killer anymore. In the beginning everyone was all gung-ho about finding Ghost, but after awhile that mission seem to have tapered off; no one even mentioned Ghost anymore. Everyone was so wrapped up in their own lives, including Elise.

She loved Elise and was happy that she was finally happy but somewhere along the line, Elise lost focus on the big picture. LaKiesha felt like she had to find Ghost. He was responsible for killing her parents and brother. He caused her so much pain. LaKiesha couldn't even begin to find love with a man because her every thought was consumed with finding Ghost. Elise used to be just as determined as she was, and Aparis used to be consumed with finding Que's killer, but neither one had mentioned Ghost or anything about him in at least two months. She had no choice but to continue the search by herself now.

LaKiesha tried to understand that both Elise and Aparis had a life now. Elise had Simone to think about, Trey and the baby she was about to have. She really didn't have bad feelings about Trey and Elise. Did she? At times she felt like all Elise cared about was Simone and Trey and she didn't want to feel that way. Elise and Aparis were the only family she had and she knew that there was mass love between them. After she found Ghost, maybe things would go back to normal. Until then, nothing else mattered.

Sherrie Walker

twenty-eight

THE NEXT MORNING at 8:30, Aparis and LaKiesha were sitting in the courtroom waiting for the hearing to be begin.

Aparis glanced at the State of Ohio seal planted on the wall behind the Honorable Judge Calvin Stearnes' bench when the correction officers brought the prisoners into the courtroom. Tony was dressed in an orange jumpsuit, socks and flip-flops. His hands and ankles were bound in shackles. The dozen prisoners filed in one by one and were directed to their designated seating area.

Aparis took a long look at Tony who looked as if he had lost a lot of weight and hadn't slept in days. The last time she'd seen him was weeks ago. They had been trying to be intimate, but his penis wouldn't stay hard. It was like mission impossible. Sweaty and annoyed, Tony had blamed Aparis for his inability to stay erect. After nearly forty-minutes of more pulling, then pulsating, he put on his clothes and left to go get some Viagra.

Aparis suspected Tony was using drugs heavily when he stopped caring about his music. But she was sure in her fourth month when he seemed to have lost interest in the baby. He was so excited when she first told him she was pregnant, he didn't leave her side for an entire month.

During that time, they went shopping for the baby's room, buying furniture, bottles, diapers, clothes and toys. Aparis knew that Tony was going to be a good father. This was one of the reasons she was determined to stick it out with him. *We will get through this. Once Tony is released I'll talk to him about getting some help.*

Aparis felt bad for Tiffany, since his behavior had changed toward her as well. She was the one who first brought it to Aparis' attention. *I know it's got to be killing her, too. It has to work out.*

Two days ago, she'd gone to the doctor to have an ultrasound. Even though they talked about waiting to see what they were having, Aparis had to know. She wanted to give Tony a son since that's what he wanted. The ultrasound revealed that she was carrying a boy, so she was bursting to tell her man the good news.

She hoped the Judge would grant bond. She believed the charges were weak and Dinuchi could surely beat the case. She planned to get him into a treatment center as soon as he was released.

Tony looked around the courtroom until he saw Aparis. She smiled to let him know it was going to be all right but his grin was halfhearted.

The Honorable Judge Stearnes entered and everyone rose only to sit right back down. Judge Stearnes was one of the hardest judges on the bench. Since he'd been on the bench, he had sent away hundreds of people, including first time offenders. He even convicted a seventy-two-year-old woman who stole a box of Efferdent from CVS, sentencing her to six months in the Ohio

Sherrie Walker

Reformatory for Women but granted her shock probation after thirty days. Stearnes said, despite her age, her behavior was unacceptable and he had to teach her a lesson. According to the arresting officer's report, when she was taken into custody, she had over eight hundred dollars in her pocketbook since she had just cashed her social security check. Judge Stearnes didn't believe it was her first time stealing, just her first time getting caught.

Aparis was attentive as the sharpest solider in a drill team line, peering at the judge who called several cases before reaching Tony's. She was worried and sensed Tony was also. No one had been given bond since the hearings began and she could see the anxiety and sweat all over Tony's face. Finally, he called Tony's case and Mr. Dinuchi stood next to Tony shuffling through some papers.

"Anthony Boone," the short, pot-bellied, bald head bailiff called. He shuffled to the podium facing the state seal.

"Mr. Boone, The State of Ohio has indicted you on one count of aggravated murder, one count of aggravated robbery and two counts of felonious assault in addition to fleeing and eluding the scene of a crime. How do you plead?" Judge Stearnes said.

"My client pleads not guilty, Your Honor."

"Not guilty has been entered," the adjudicator Johnny Phillips responded.

"Your Honor, at this time, I would like to request bond for my client."

"Your Honor, The State objects," prosecuting attorney Derrick Taylor interjected as he jumped up from his seat. "Your Honor, the prosecution considers the defendant a flight risk. Sir, he's being charged with murder and if released, he could very well leave the United States," he rationalized.

"Your Honor, my client is a very successful recording artist. He needs time to arrange his financial matters. Sir, he is also an active member in the community with a fiancée who is pregnant. I assure you my client will not abscond."

"Your Honor!" the prosecutor Taylor exclaimed. "We request the defendant be remanded to the county jail until the trial date to assure our citizens and the victim due justice."

"You seem to have forgotten, Mr. Taylor ," Judge Stearnes began, "Mr. Boone is innocent until proven guilty in a court of law. Bond hearing set for June 16th at 9:00 a.m. Call the next case." Judge Stearnes pounded the gavel.

Everyone was stunned because it was a true first for Judge Stearnes. Aparis and LaKiesha watched everyone file out. Tony kept looking back at Aparis. She smiled and winked at her man who was led out of the courtroom by a big black corrections officer. After the courtroom was completely empty, Aparis took out a thick white envelope and taped it under her chair. Aparis and LaKiesha sat for a few more minutes then left.

~   ~   ~

Judge Stearnes trudged back into the courtroom and approached the third to last row of chairs. He sat down in one and reached under it and pulled the envelope loose then stuffed it into the inside pocket of his suit jacket. With despair, he reclined back into the chair. He always wondered what the seats on the other side felt like but thought it was bad luck to sit in them. As he

Sherrie Walker

sat there, Stearnes remembered how he'd first gotten caught up in such a tangled web of deception, with the very criminals he vowed to put away. He'd been a judge for over thirty-seven years and never entertained the thought of accepting a bribe that is, until two years ago when his son became addicted to gambling and was caught up in gambling debts. Up until then, he'd been offered plenty, but never considered accepting until now.

Hamp was his only son. Stearnes' wife had their son spoiled as rotten as three-day-old milk. For that matter, they both did, as he was the center of their world. Hamp had gotten into plenty of small scrapes before, but this time he was in over his head. He owed the bookies over a hundred thousand dollars.

Two years ago, two distinguished looking Italian men came to Judge Stearnes' home late one night and woke him and his wife from their sleep. They only threatened them, as they wanted to deliver a message. It was a simple message: Pay or Hamp dies!

As they were leaving, one stopped and turned around. "Oh, by the way, Hamp wanted us to give you a little something to let you know we mean business." The goon took out a little black box and set it on the table. "If you call the police, we'll mail you Hamp's hand next. We'll be back in forty-eight hours to pick up the money."

With that said, they left. There were only two of them and Judge Stearnes knew he could describe the criminals to the police, but after his wife opened the box, they knew calling the police was not an option. Inside was Hamp's middle finger with his high school ring attached. Mrs. Stearnes fainted. Beyond a doubt,

Sherrie Walker

the judge knew he had to get the money if he planned to save his son. He called a colleague whom he knew accepted bribes. The other judge came right over and Stearnes and his wife explained the situation to him. The next day he gave the bookies a hundred grand and the corruption began.

Sherrie Walker

twenty-nine

THREE HOURS LATER Aparis sat in the visiting booth, waiting for the officers to bring Tony out. The cubicle was a 2 x 4 unit with one hard, gray plastic chair and a thick piece of glass that separated the visitors from the inmates. They were to communicate through a telephone attached to the wall. She picked up the phone several times as she anxiously awaited Tony. Sitting and waiting depressed Aparis.

I'll be so glad when this is all over. Tony will be out in three days and we won't look back. The guards finally brought Tony to where she was seated and she smiled, but he didn't. He sat down then waited until the guard left before he picked up the phone.

"Hi, baby," she said with excitement.

"Why am I still here?" he responded.

"Baby, we're on it. You'll be out of here soon, I promise."

"On it? I can't tell! I want out of here!" he yelled. "I can't take it. I'm going fuckin' crazy."

"Baby, calm down, please. Just trust me …"

"Trust!" he yelled. "I should've been out of here yesterday! Elise can make it happen, Aparis! Don't insult me! Elise owes me! Y'all all owe me! I made y'all … ME! If it wasn't for me there would be no companies. I'm the star!"

Aparis clenched her teeth and spoke in a low, chilling tone. "Nigga, you got one minute to lower your voice talking to me like you're crazy. Have you lost your mind? Now, like I was saying before you rudely interrupted me with your frail, dusty, skinny ass, I am on it! I'm not going to let you sit in here no longer than it takes to sign my name and pay them what they ask. We have—"

"We? Who the hell is we? Whose side are you on, b*oo*?" Tony callously interrupted.

"Whose side? You know what, Tony? Those drugs have fried your brain, for real, if you have to ask whose side I'm on. You're the father of my baby."

"Am I?" he asked, looking her dead in the eyes. Aparis sat back as if the wind had been knocked out of her body.

"Wha … what did you say to me?"

"I said, am I your baby's daddy? I mean, how do I know it's mine? It's not like I was the only one you was sleeping wit'. You wit' them, ain't you? Y'all trying to set me up?"

Aparis looked at Tony and his eyes appeared perplexed. His face morphed into a demon's mask.

At that moment, she knew it was over between them, and that Tony obviously wasn't the same man she had fallen in love with. The drugs had definitely changed him into a complete stranger.

"I'm glad I found out about you now. Never, and I mean *never*, think that my baby and I need you for a thing. I buy tricks like you and throw them away when I'm done. You ain't nothing but a crack head. A star?

Sherrie Walker

Please. Nigga, you a rock cocaine star!"

"Yeah, ok. But give Elise a message for me. Tell her that she don't want to play with me."

"Oh, what's that supposed to mean?"

"I know where at least twelve bodies are buried. If I go down, everybody goes down. I want out of here. If I'm not out—"

"Sucka, I'm getting ready to roll up out of here, for real. So you think long and hard about what you just said to me. Once Elise finds out about your snitching threat, you can count your ass as being grass! You're hit! We have arms to reach inside these walls, playa. Before you can even fix your mouth to tell anything, your tongue will be shoved so far up your narrow ass the medical examiner won't be able to pull it out. Have an average life, chump." Aparis hung up the phone and turned away.

Tony called to her, "Aparis, you'll be sorry!" then banged the receiver on the glass. Aparis kept walking and never looked back.

Tony slammed his chair against the glass, screaming for her. He was foaming at the mouth by the time the two corrections officers, one white, one black, rushed in to restrain him. He fought them back and what started out as a simple restraining procedure turned into a melee.

The white officer who accompanied the black officer had a huge grin on his face as he watched Tony, licking his lips anticipating cracking him upside the head with his club. His partner on the other hand didn't like to use force or beat on the inmates. He glanced over to his partner Roy and saw the evil smirk plastered on his face. "Roy, let me handle this," Lance suggested.

Roy broke his stare at Tony and looked toward Lance.

Sherrie Walker

"You got five seconds to talk to this scumbag, Lance."

"Scumbag? You white redneck, hillbilly, corn fed bitch!" exploded Tony.

Roy moved in closer to Tony with his club and raised it above his head. "Time's up, Lance," said Roy as he swung the club, connecting with Tony's elbow.

The cracking sound was loud as Tony grabbed his elbow and doubled over from the pain that shot through his arm. Roy came down with the club across Tony's back and he fell to his knees. As Roy lifted the club to bring it down over Tony's head, Lance stopped him with his voice.

"That's enough Roy. Raise up. I mean it. Don't swing that club another time." Roy froze with the club raised and looked toward Lance. In the few seconds that he took to look at Lance, Tony seized the moment and elbowed Roy with his good arm right in his nuts.

Roy screamed and fell to his knees, grabbing his nuts. "Aaaaggggh...oh shit...oh shit....aaagggh." As Roy rolled around the floor in excruciating pain, Lance moved in and as he tried to lift his club, Tony snatched it from him and began to swing wildly and with force. Each blow connected with a loud thud and after hitting Lance a few good times across his arms, back and head, he was to the point of dizziness. Tony spun around and began hitting Roy as he tried to stand. The first blow caught Roy across his back and the second connected with his jaw.

After several minutes, a third officer approached the scene and hit Tony with a Taser gun. He was instantly weakened and they carried him to the solitary hole, tossing him onto a cot.

~ ~ ~

Aparis made it all the way to her car before she broke

Sherrie Walker

down and cried. She sobbed until she started hiccupping. She hurt for her baby who wouldn't have a father. She cried for Tony, because after it was all said and done, she knew that she'd have to meet him at the crossroads.

Aparis hit the steering wheel with her hands out of frustration and laid her head against the steering wheel. *Damn*.

She knew that Tony was going to have to go. No matter how much she loved him or the fact that he was the father of her unborn child, he wouldn't be forgiven if he snitched, nor suggesting that he would. Aparis' heart was heavy. She couldn't believe that it all came down to this. She tried to love Tony and wanted so baldy to get married, have a baby and give her child what was stolen from her at a young age. She wanted her child to have a happy home with two loving parents. As she leaned back against her seat, she knew that wasn't going to happen.

Her heart felt as if it had been torn out of her chest as the tears flowed down her cheeks. No matter how much it hurt, Aparis knew what she had to do. She picked up her cell phone and called Judge Stearnes on his private line.

"Hello."

"Hello Judge Stearnes this is Aparis. I'm calling to inform you that all bets are off. Keep what we gave you for your troubles." Aparis closed her cell phone and turned the ignition to her Escalade truck. She wiped the tears from her eyes, put on her sunglasses and pulled off feeling like a broken woman.

Sherrie Walker

thirty

As LaKiesha looked around her plush, finished basement, equipped with a full bar, pool table, 50" plasma television, cream-colored leather furniture, she shook her head in sadness. None of it meant anything to her until she could avenge her mother, father and brother's death. Nothing would satisfy her until she found Ghost and killed him. She removed her cordless phone from its cradle and dialed Aparis. After two rings, Aparis answered.

"Hello," Aparis answered sounding strained. She'd been up crying most of the night.

"What's wrong, Paris?" LaKiesha could hear Aparis sniffling and waited while she blew her nose.

"We're going to have to 187 Tony."

LaKiesha took the phone away from her ear and looked at it before placing it back against her.

"What the hell is wrong with you? Kill Tony. What are you talking about? What happened?"

"That crack head nigga had the nerve to tell me that he was going to sing like Anthony Hamilton live and in concert if we didn't get him out like yesterday. He was talking real crazy, Kiesha."

LaKiesha sat silently holding the phone for a few

Sherrie Walker

minutes trying to process the information before responding.

"That nigga done lost his mind. Paris, baby, I'm not being insensitive to what's going on with you, but can we talk more about this later? 'Cause I'm about to roll out to meet that chick who has that information about Ghost. Soon as I leave her, I'm coming through to your house. In fact, I need to hang up 'cause it's almost time to meet her. Just sit tight and I'll be right over. Let me handle this first though, ok?"

"Please let me go with you, Kiesh," Aparis begged.

"You have enough to deal with right now, Paris," LaKiesha responded. "I can't believe Tony played you like that. Then he gone threaten to tell on us. You know what's going to go down once Elise finds out, right?"

"Yeah, I know. Why did it have to be like this? I loved him so much."

"Well, baby girl, don't seem like he's loving you," LaKiesha responded. "Fuck 'em, you don't need that lousy sperm donor for shit. And your lil' shorty will be raised up fine. He'll have two godmothers who's going to spoil him rotten."

"Kiesh, I got a bad vibe about you going to meet this mystery person. How do you know it's not a set-up?"

"I don't." Her chin set, LaKiesha was adamant. "But I'm prepared. Believe that. I have to do this, Aparis. I'm going to find out who killed my parents and my brother to settle this once and for all. I can finally avenge their deaths," she said. She was sitting on the edge of her bed, loading her weapon. "Don't worry. I'll be all right. You need to keep trying to make contact with Elise and tell her what's going on. She drove Simone up to that private school this morning, but they should be back by now. It's time for me to go. I'll hit you up when I'm done."

"Kiesh, let me meet you. I'll just stay in the background."

"Girl, please! Not with your stomach sticking out everywhere. How are you going to stay in the background? I'm cool, Paris. I'll call you when I'm done. But keep trying to get in touch with Elise. One!"

LaKiesha hung up, hurried out the door and got into her BMW. She didn't bother to turn her cell phone on because she knew Aparis would call and try to talk her into allowing her to participate. She didn't like keeping secrets from Aparis and Elise, but this was something she had to do alone. It was up to her to seek, find and destroy Ghost. He'd destroyed everyone in her family. She had mixed feelings about not wanting Elise to help her with this. She knew Elise loved her and loved her brother Que. But lately Elise had been too consumed with her own life and it left questions and doubts. LaKiesha felt it would be only right that she handle this.

LaKiesha pulled up to an old four-story greenish-colored condemned apartment building on Eddy Road and parked in the front of it. Every window was boarded up and the grass was tall as weeds. She swallowed hard and turned off the ignition.

Damn, I don't know. This building looks like a death trap waiting to happen. Maybe I should call Aparis back and let someone go inside with me. She removed her key from the ring and placed it in her Mary J. Blige CD case.

If something happened to her, they would know where to look for her key. It was a code Aparis, Elise and LaKiesha had come up with a long time ago to signal if there was something wrong. Plus, she didn't want to make it easy on the person or people that snatched her if

Sherrie Walker

she got caught slipping.

LaKiesha pulled out her 9 mm Glock. *Clack, Clack,* the gun sounded as she checked it, then stepped out of the car.

She hit the remote to lock her car, *Chirp, Chirp.* The lights on her car flashed, signaling that her alarm was set. She walked stealthily up the filthy path that led to the building's entrance. The door was locked so she went to the back of the building and found one that was wide open. She squeezed her pistol and entered.

~ ~ ~

Simone and Elise pulled off the highway somewhere between Akron and Cleveland on Interstate 77 South. They were returning from enrolling Simone in a private school in Akron, Ohio.

Elise could've kicked herself for leaving her cell phone at home. The service engine light was on and smoke billowed from underneath the hood of her black Jaguar. She popped the hood and got out to take a look even though she was clueless as to what the problem could be. It smelled like something was burning.

"Damn!" Elise yelled.

"What is it?"

"I don't know. I just bought it. Nothing should be wrong with a sixty thousand dollar Jag after only two months. Something ain't right with this picture."

"That's why you should go American," Simone said, getting out of the car.

"Simone, please be quiet while I try to figure this out."

"Figure it out? Sis, you ain't going to figure this out. It's a Jaguar. Even the dealership can't figure out what's wrong with these cars half the time. We better start trying to hitchhike a ride. Now that's my specialty." She smiled and winked.

"Don't say another word. I mean it."

"So what are we getting ready to do? Sit out here and wait for someone to pull over? Sis, we are living in a crazy world. People don't just stop no more out of the kindness of their hearts. We are going to roast out here. Why did you leave your cell phone? That was stupid. You're never supposed to go nowhere without your cell phone. You took mine from me so I don't have one either. Why did you take my horn, anyway?"

Elise looked at Simone as if she was crazy so she stopped talking and drew a zipper across her lips. "If you say one more thing, I promise I'm going to shoot you in the foot and let you bleed to death on the side of the road."

"I believe you're crazy enough to do it, too." Simone stomped back to the passenger side, got in and slammed the door. Elise looked at the sky. "How did I forget my cell phone? I never forget to put my cell phone in my purse."

The baby kicked and Elise realized that she had not eaten lunch. She knew she had to figure something out quickly. Simone was right about one thing. A lot of cars had zoomed by and not one stopped to assist them.

~ ~ ~

The building smelled like stale urine and trash, and LaKiesha stood still to let her eyes adjust to the darkness before moving any farther. After her eyes focused, she proceeded up the loose, raggedy wooden stairs to the third floor as instructed. She reached the landing and her heart skipped a beat as she came across two rats tearing into a dead cat's flesh. She felt the pancakes and eggs

Sherrie Walker

she had eaten rise to her throat but she fought to keep it down. The rats felt her presence and ran in different directions, leaving their half-eaten meal. The odor from the feline nearly made LaKiesha regurgitate again; however, she covered her mouth and nose with her shirt and stepped over what was left of the cat to enter the corridor leading to the units.

The eerie silence almost made LaKiesha want to turn around and call Elise and Aparis. But she was so close and didn't want to blow the opportunity of finding Ghost. She firmly decided to continue her solo mission.

She turned left and looked at the numbers on the doors until she came upon 313. With her heart pounding rapidly, palms sweaty and clammy, LaKiesha looked around the hallway once again. She had a sour taste in her mouth like she'd eaten something spoiled. She tried to swallow and couldn't without forcing it. Again, the thought came to mind to turn around and call Elise. Or, at least call Cali and let him know her whereabouts. As she reached for the door, she noticed her hand was shaking badly.

She pulled her hand back quickly and said a silent prayer – something she hadn't done in a long time. Standing there praying with her eyes squinted, but not completely closed, she felt something scurry across her foot and almost screamed as she opened her eyes wide and saw a mouse run into the apartment in front of her. *Shit!*

She grabbed her chest and tried to slow her breathing down to a normal pace. It felt like she was hyperventilating. Emotionally she was a wreck as she stood in front of the door. LaKiesha took several deep breaths before reaching for the door again.

The door was slightly ajar so she pushed it open with her foot and brought her gun up as she stepped into the apartment, scanning the four corners of the room. Her heart was beating fast and LaKiesha felt as if it could be heard like the snare in a drum line. Her mouth was dry and she was breathing out her nose in short gasps. She realized she was in a living room with an old, brown, beat up sofa to the right of her and a table with three legs turned upside down to the left.

Beer cans, cigarette butts and matches were strewn across the floor and a stained wool blanket was folded and sitting on top of a broken down La-Z-Boy chair. LaKiesha inched her way into the living room, being careful not to step on anything foreign in her path. Then she eased down the hallway and came upon the bathroom without a toilet or tub.

LaKiesha noticed two buckets in the corner, and the smell that reeked from them let her know that they served as commodes. This time, she couldn't hold it in. She bent over to gag and released her breakfast. She wiped her mouth with her shirt because she refused to use anything in the so-called bathroom. She exited cautiously.

She came to a door that was closed. Sweat was trickling down the sides of her face as she placed her hand on the knob and started to turn it slowly. *I should stop and call for help.* She turned the handle and opened the door. To LaKiesha's surprise, a young girl was strapped to a chair in the middle of the room. Her hands, feet and mouth were covered with duct tape.

Sherrie Walker

thirty-one

ELISE AND SIMONE were sweating profusely. The car wouldn't turn over so they couldn't roll the windows down. They had the car doors open but there was no breeze to cool them off. As Elise sat in her seat she thought, *something isn't right. I can't remember a time when I've forgotten my cell phone. I never leave out without it.*

"Any bright ideas yet, Elise?"

Elise rolled her eyes at Simone and leaned her head back against the seat. Simone looked at Elise and concluded that something had to be done. She pulled her shirt off, exposing a red sports bra, then tied her hair up on top of her head. She rolled her pant legs up and put on some lipstick.

"Simone. What are you doing?"

"Getting us the hell out of this stifling heat. If nothing else, think about the baby."

Simone got out of the car before Elise could respond and started walking seductively toward the road while holding up her thumb. Elise had only placed one foot out of the car when she heard screeching tires and saw two cars pulling over. Simone walked up to one and began talking and laughing. The first man stepped out of

Sherrie Walker

his Ford pickup and walked toward the Jag. The guy Simone was talking to got out and walked over to Elise as well. The first man was a big white guy with wide shoulders.

He spoke with a southern accent. "Howdy, ma'am. Let me take a look fer you." He peered under the hood as the second guy talked to Simone. "Well, I don't know how it happened but this bad boy is outta oil. Good thing you pulled over when ya did causing ya woulda blew yer engine. I'll take ya up yonder and grab a quart of oil and put it in for ya and y'all will be all set." He smiled. "Oh, sorry for my manners. My name's Jed. I'm from Alabama. Visiting my brother in Akron. Would shake yer hand, but on account of all the grease and oil, I can't do it right now."

"My name is Elise and that's Simone." Simone was smiling at the fine black dude in the second car. He was young, fly, draped in gold and flashing a sugary sweet smile, so Elise immediately knew what he was about. He was driving a tricked-out Cadillac and you could hear his music from inside even though the doors were closed and the windows up. He had dope boy written all over him.

Simone walked back over. "Uh, Diamond said he'll take us home, Elise."

"Thank you, but no, thank you. Jed here has offered to take us to get the stuff we need. Come on, let's go." Simone looked back at Diamond a minute too long. "Now, Simone! We'll be right with you Jed. Thank you so much."

"No problem, ma'am. I'll be waiting on you. Be sure to lock up." Jed walked back over to his car as Elise grabbed her purse.

Sherrie Walker

Simone pouted. "What was wrong with Diamond? He would've done the same thing. How do you know Jethro ain't going to try and kidnap us or something?"

"Two reasons." Elise held up her gun. "Smith and Wesson. Let's go."

~ ~ ~

LaKiesha stared at the young girl. She had a light mocha complexion and thick, jet-black, medium-length hair that looked as if it hadn't been combed in several days. As LaKiesha's eyes moved away from the damsel and around the room, she noticed a mouse quickly exiting a hole in the hardwood floor. Roaches scrambled for food crumbs left on a small, cheap, round dinette set that sat in front of an old, raggedy couch. The stench was overwhelming.

Strapped to the chair, the girl began to wiggle her body to the point where the chair moved with her every motion. She also labored to mumble through the duct tape. LaKiesha put her finger to her mouth, signaling her to be quiet and sit still. Then she motioned to the girl, asking if anyone else was around. The girl shook her head from side to side. LaKiesha eased her way over to the girl, stooped down and pulled the tape off her mouth.

"Who did this to you?"

"Dis man. Gotta get out here before he comes back. Please get me out of here," the girl pleaded. LaKiesha set her gun down and began pulling the tape off. She freed her hands then her feet. Then, LaKiesha heard a sound and turned around. She was overcome with shock as she saw who was standing before her with a mean expression and icy cold demeanor. Her mouth dropped open and her eyes bucked. For several seconds she couldn't speak.

Sherrie Walker

"You … it can't be … why?" LaKiesha asked. She remembered she laid her gun on the floor and wondered if she could make a move for it when all of a sudden she felt the barrel of it pressed against her back as she noticed it was no longer on the floor. At that moment, she realized she'd been set up.

She looked straight ahead and prepared herself for death. Pap…pap… LaKiesha succumbed to darkness.

Sherrie Walker

thirty-two

THREE HOURS LATER, after Jed helped Elise and Simone get back on the road, Elise pulled up to the house exhausted and hungry. When she saw Trey standing at the door, she knew something was wrong by his facial expression.

"What's wrong Trey?" Elise and Simone walked up to the door and Trey held it open for them to enter.

"We haven't seen or heard from LaKiesha."

"What the hell you mean no one's seen or heard from her?" Elise's face took on a fierce, protective look.

"Elise, I spoke with Aparis and she said about a few hours ago LaKiesha went to meet the female who had some information about Ghost. She'd being trying to call her ever since and she hasn't answered either of her phones. It seems as if LaKiesha is missing, baby."

Elise stood there looking at Trey, trying to ingest his words. Before she could respond, the phone rang and Elise ran and snatched it up. "Hello...hello? What ... she hasn't shown up at none of the companies?" She listened intensely. "Contact everybody we have available and have them hit the streets. No one sleeps until we find LaKiesha. Somebody has seen her or knows something.

Get on this and stay on top of it." Elise slammed the phone shut, and then pounded her fist on the table in the great room of her house.

Where the hell is Aparis? She then dialed Aparis' cell phone. It went directly to voicemail and her house phone went to her answering machine. Elise slammed the phone down again, frustrated. She grabbed her temples and massaged them.

"Baby, calm down," Trey said. "You can't go getting upset like this. Our baby is due in three months and you don't need to make yourself sick." He patted Elise's stomach, reminding her of her pregnancy.

"How long has she been missing?" Simone asked.

"Since this morning," Trey responded. "I have a feeling Ghost is behind this. If he so much as displaces a hair on her head, I swear I will hunt his ass down and kill him with my bare hands."

Elise plopped down on the couch with her face in her hands. For years she'd been haunted by Ghost and it seemed like he kept causing pain in her life. If something happened to LaKiesha, it would kill her. She loved LaKiesha and Aparis like sisters.

They'd been through hell and back, built a successful empire together and Elise felt like she had to protect them both. She should have forced LaKiesha to tell her more about this mystery person she was meeting. Had she become so self-absorbed now that she found Simone and was engaged to marry Trey? Had she been slipping?

Had she let LaKiesha down? She felt as if her world was tumbling down around her and it was nothing she could do about it. She became paranoid and began to guilt trip with the thought of her friend being in danger, or even worse...dead. The guilt she felt was overpower-

Sherrie Walker

ing.

Simone sat down beside her and held Elise tightly.

"We're going to find her, sis. Don't worry."

Trey watched the woman he loved and it tore at his heart that she was hurting. He knew how close Elise was to LaKiesha. He was afraid that all this stress wouldn't be good for the baby.

"I feel like it's my fault. I don't feel like I've been there for LaKiesha. I should've made her tell me who she was going to meet. I should've done more…" Trey was on his knees in a matter of seconds reaching for Elise's hands.

"No, you are not going to blame yourself for this, Elise. I won't let you. None of this is your fault, you hear me? You are a good friend to LaKiesha and Aparis. You're dedicated, loyal and supportive. We are going to find her and Ghost, baby. I promise." Trey took Elise in his arms and hugged her tightly to his chest. He reached around and pulled Simone into the hug as Elise broke down and cried.

She cried for the pain they all had suffered. Aparis, LaKiesha, Simone and herself. *Sometimes life is so unfair.* They'd been dealt some ugly hands in life and all she wanted to do was make everything right for those she loved.

Aparis and Cali rushed in and found Simone, Elise and Trey huddled together on the couch. One look and Aparis was running to embrace Elise. She sat beside her as Trey and Simone moved aside and Aparis and Elise held each other crying and rocking. Cali batted his eyes to keep the tears from falling as he watched. Simone ran to the bathroom to get tissues for everyone. When she returned, she handed them to Aparis as she blew her nose and wiped her eyes. Trey and Cali had a side bar going as they stood to the side talking and planning. Elise blew her nose into the tissue and looked at Aparis with red, swollen eyes.

"We've been trying to get in touch with you for hours." Aparis' eyed widened.

"I took Simone to Akron to enroll her in school. Somehow I left my cell phone and my car stalled on the road, and we were without a phone. That was ususal because I never leave home without my phone."

"What? What's wrong with the Jag? How did that happen? That's a brand new car," Cali asked.

"Good question, Cali. I have no idea, it seemed to have run out of oil. But never mind that. What is going on with LaKiesha. Did she give any type indication where she was meeting this person?"

Aparis filled them in on the conversation she had with Lakiesha and how she left in search of Ghost's information. "She wouldn't tell me anything, Elise. I tried to talk her out of it, but she wouldn't listen. I even begged to go with her but she insisted that she would be ok and wanted to do this by herself. You know how stubborn LaKiesha can be once she sets her mind to do something. I'm scared, Elise."

"So am I, Paris. So am I."

"She should've never gone by herself. She knows better, Aparis." Elise got up and began to pace back and forth.

"Doesn't she have that tracking system in her car? And if she has her cell phone with her, she can be tracked that way. I know a girl who is a pretty good hacker. I could give her a call and let her do a trace," Simone suggested. Everyone was baffled for a few moments, just

Sherrie Walker

staring at Simone. "We're wasting time here." Simone placed her hands on her hips, rolled her eyes, rolled her neck and patted her foot impatiently.

Aparis spoke up first. "I've already tried her cell phone and it keeps going to voicemail but only after it rings about eight times."

"Which means her phone is turned on but for some reason she's not answering," added Cali.

"Uh huh… yeah, I'll call the girl. I'll need my cell, can't call her from a landline." She pointed upstairs. "It's upstairs in my first drawer." Simone and Aparis went upstairs while California, Trey and Elise waited.

"It's more to her than meets the eye." Elise looked a little amused, in spite of how upset she was.

California shook his head. "She's your little sister. What did you expect?"

Elise didn't answer California's remark. She changed the subject. "I can't believe Kiesha did this."

Trey walked up behind Elise and wrapped his arms around her. "We all know that once she makes her mind up to do something, no one can stop her, kind of reminds me of someone else I know." Trey squeezed her tighter and smirked. Elise laid her head back against Trey's chest, basking in his comfortable embrace.

"I just wish she would've told somebody where she was going." Elise continued to pace the floor and Aparis and Simone returned to the great room.

"My people's on it. We should be hearing something soon," Simone reported.

Elise removed Trey's arm from around her and took an authoritative stance in front of Simone. "Your people?" Elise raised an eyebrow.

"Don't start, Elise." Simone rolled her eyes, sucked

her teeth and snapped defiantly.

Aparis' phone rang and she immediately snatched it open. "Hello." She listened for a minute. "Fine, Mr. Dinuchi. What can I do for you? No, he hasn't. When was he released?"

Aparis felt queasy as she listened. "Who bonded him out?" She grabbed the bottom of her stomach and sat down in the oversized chair. "No! If … if I hear anything I'll let you know. Thank you, Mr. Dinuchi." Aparis closed the phone.

"What's wrong? Elise asked.

"What was that about?"

"Mr. Dinuchi said Tony was released this morning, and he didn't show up for his one o'clock hearing. Pinch bonded him out."

"Pinch?" Elise inquired. "When did Tony and Pinch become so close? And why are you so upset about it, Aparis?"

"Yeah, you should be happy," Trey said.

"I would be if I didn't know what I know." Aparis rubbed her stomach harder and faster.

Aparis told them the entire conversation, nearly verbatim, that she had with Tony on their visit.

"I smell a rat," Trey commented.

"Oh … my … God," Elise exclaimed, hardly believing the words that were coming out of her own mouth. "Do you think Tony is in with Ghost?" Elise walked over to the window and looked out before she went on. "No, he can't be Ghost. He's too young."

"Doesn't mean he isn't working for Ghost," said Cali.

"He was in with Canine, and Canine was in with Ghost. After his sister was safe, he could have double-crossed us, just like he did them." Trey was thinking

Sherrie Walker

aloud. "He might have Lakiesha. She would have trusted him."

Aparis jumped up and ran to the bathroom to vomit. She was holding on to the toilet, dry heaving when Elise and Simone entered. Elise wet a towel and wiped Aparis' face.

"He … can't be a traitor, Elise. He can't." Aparis' eyes filled with tears. She covered her ears as if this was too much truth to comprehend.

"I don't know what to think, baby, but you have to get yourself together. You can't go making yourself sick. You are pregnant and nothing is more important than our babies right now. Finding LaKiesha and protecting our babies are first. We have to stay strong them." Aparis went to the sink and rinsed her mouth out and smoothed her hair down.

"Come on and let me get you a cold drink and try to figure out what we're going to do. I need you to calm down." They all walked back into the living room and Simone's phone rang. She opened it and they stood listening.

"Yo!" Simone listened and averted her eyes when she saw Elise studying her.

"Damn … ok … thanks." Simone closed her phone and Elise could tell from the dismayed look on her face that the news wasn't good. "They found her car on Eddy Road. She's been shot twice."

Aparis was dizzy. The entire room was spinning as she fell. Before California or Trey could react, Aparis' body made contact with the glass cocktail table, shattering it. Elise screamed and ran over to Aparis as California and Trey lifted her off the glass and noticed a laceration across her stomach.

Sherrie Walker

"Nooooo!" Elise screamed. Trey grabbed his phone and called the paramedics.

"Hurry … grab some towels, Trey. Hurry up," Simone ordered. "We have to apply pressure to keep her from bleeding out." Trey and Cali stood frozen while looking down at Aparis.

Simone screamed out again. "Please, move! Get some towels!" Simone grabbed a pillow off the couch and propped it underneath Aparis' head. The whole time, Elise watched in a state of awe, confusion and panic. *Where did Simone learn to do that?* Trey ran into the room with towels and handed them to Simone. She immediately began padding Aparis' wound and applying pressure as Aparis winced from the pain.

"I have to stop the bleeding, Paris."

"My baby … what about my … baby. Oh God, Elise." Elise grabbed Aparis' hand and squeezed tightly. "I'm right here sis. Just hold on." Cali leaned over and grabbed her free hand. "Aparis, the ambulance is on the way." Aparis smiled weakly and Elise squeezed her hand again. Aparis looked at Elise and the fear reflected in both of their eyes.

"Why? Why, Elise?" Elise's eyes begin to fill with tears, but she blinked them away quickly so she could appear strong for Aparis.

Dre burst through the door yelling, "Have they found LaKiesha—" He stopped dead in his tracks the moment he saw Aparis lying on the floor with blood oozing from her abdomen. "What happened? What the fuck has happened?"

"Aparis became faint and fell on glass table when we received the news about LaKiesha," explained Cali. "The damn ambulance is taking too long, man."

Sherrie Walker

Dre turned back to the door.

"Fuck the ambulance...if it ain't here by the time I swing the car closer to the door...we're the hell out of here."

Simone looked up suddenly. "I don't think it's a good idea to move her, y'all. I know it seems like an eternity, but it hasn't been but a couple minutes...give them a few more before we panic and kill her and the baby for sho."

Dre opened the door and looked back toward them. "We ain't waiting no longer. I'll be right back."

He left out the door before Simone could object. Elise looked at Simone skeptically. "Where did you learn all these medical techniques?"

Simone shrugged her shoulders nonchalantly. "Just picked it up from being in the streets. It's a lot I know, Elise. Maybe one day I'll tell you about it." Simone's cell phone rang, and she looked up at Trey.

"Here, keep applying pressure while I answer this."

Trey knelt down and pressed the towel while Simone wiped her hands on another towel before answering the cell phone.

"Yeah, yeah...hello," she answered frantically. She had an intense look on her face before dropping her head. Elise sensed its bad news.

"You sure...ok...thanks. I owe you big time."

Simone closed the phone and kept her back to them before she turned around to deliver her news. Elise let go of Aparis' hand and rose from the floor. "What is it Simone? Is it Kiesha?"

Simone spoke slowly. "Yes, it's LaKiesha. They found her in an abandoned apartment building. It doesn't look good." Elise reached out for the arm of the chair to support her wobbly legs, and fell into the oversized chair.

Sherrie Walker

"Damn!" yelled Cali.

Simone walked over to Elise. "LaKiesha is at University Hospital. We have to get going. How are we going to do this?"

"Elise, are you staying here or going to see about LaKiesha?" Trey asked.

Elise stood frozen, and for the first time in a long time, she didn't know what to do. She was trying to determine if she should go to LaKiesha or stay with Aparis and it was one of the hardest decisions she'd ever had to make. Aparis reached up to Elise.

"Go ... go ... to Kiesh," Aparis whispered.

"I don't want to leave you, though. I don't want to have to choose between you two. I love you both. Y'all are my sisters."

"You don't have to choose. I'm telling you to go. I'll ... be ... Ok. Now —"

The whole house shook from the sounds of an AK-47 being fired from the street.

"Dre!" California shouted as he took off toward the door and pulled out his gun. Trey was right behind him and Elise followed.

While rushing to his car, Dre never saw Tony approaching with the weapon in his hands. By the time Dre realized what was occurring, he had been shot and was falling to the ground. Tony jumped back in his car and sped off, laughing maniacally.

Cali glared down the street to his left and didn't see anything. Then he looked to his right and saw Dre trying to drag himself back toward the house. He was on his stomach and his blood left a trail behind him.

"Dre!" California screamed as he ran to Dre, dropping down to his knees when he reached him. Dre was

Sherrie Walker

fighting to breathe. California lifted him up, propping Dre's body against his. Tears streamed down his face as he held and rocked his dear friend. He'd been hit three times in the stomach and blood was gushing out of him.

Through his blurred vision, Dre was trying to focus on Cali. He tried to mouth words but was choking on his blood.

"You're going to be all right, dawg. Just hold on. Think about your little shorty. He needs you. Hold on, the ambulance is on the way."

Elise and Trey ran up to them. "Ah, man," said Trey as he looked up and down the street.

"Who was it, Dre?" Elise questioned.

"T … To … Tony," Dre said as blood burbled out his mouth.

"I got you, dawg. Stop talking." Dre gurgled up more blood and started to spasm. He inhaled sharply, but never released his breath. "Dre? Dre?" California gently shook Dre then realized that he had taken his last breath.

Trey bent down and picked up California's gun. "We have to get out of here, Cali. You staying to take care of this?"

California nodded his head as tears slid down his face. "Go ahead. I'm staying with Dre."

"We'll call you as soon as we find out what's what. We're going to deal with Tony," said Elise. They heard the ambulance and sirens approaching.

"Come on, Elise. We have to go," said Trey. They got into the car and pulled off.

California continued to hold onto Dre. "I promise you, dawg, he is going to get his. I promise!"

thirty-three

THE EMERGENCY ROOM of University Hospital was packed and Elise and Trey had been sitting around waiting for three hours before a doctor came to talk to them about LaKiesha's condition. Elise kept stepping out, using the phone to check on Aparis. She was at The Cleveland Clinic Hospital and they had to perform an emergency C-section because she lost too much blood.

Her son was placed in NICU immediately after delivery. He only weighed 2 pounds, 3 ounces and the doctors didn't expect him to survive through the night.

Finally, Dr. Termerski entered the waiting room and pulled Trey and Elise to the side to discuss LaKiesha's injuries. A befuddled look crossed his face. "There's no easy way to say this, but LaKiesha lost a lot of blood. She was shot in the neck and stomach. The bullet to her neck passed clean through without causing any damage. But the wound to her stomach is what we're most concerned about.

"We have to reconstruct her intestines to stop the internal bleeding. The oxygen to her brain has been reduced and she's in a coma. How long she will be that way, we don't know. She could wake up tonight, tomor-

Sherrie Walker

row, next week, or next year. Only time will tell. The next seventy-two hours are going to be critical."

"Can we see her now?" Elise inquired.

"I'm afraid not. She's in the ICU and is heavily sedated," the doctor explained. "I'm sorry, I think it would be best if she was to rest undisturbed, at least tonight. I'll allow you to visit with her in the morning." The doctor patted them on their shoulders and left. Elise felt like screaming, attacking and killing someone, anyone. She felt a sense of loss and guilt. Her dearest friends were laid up in the hospital fighting for their lives and she was furious. She wanted someone to feel the pain she was feeling. Hurt the way she was hurting. She felt so powerless.

"Let's go check in on Aparis and the baby," Trey said, soothingly. "Another thing, Elise, from here on out we're to wear our Kevlar vests everywhere we go. Until we catch up to Tony and Ghost, we won't be taking any unnecessary risks." Elise looked as if she was about to protest but Trey stopped her. "This is not a request, neither is it debatable, Elise. Everyone is to be suited up. Now let's go see Aparis." He led Elise to the car.

Elise complied. She was physically, mentally and emotionally exhausted. She felt as if her world was crumbling. LaKiesha and Aparis were her family. They'd been friends for what seemed like an eternity, and to think that she almost lost them both in one day made her feel so helpless. *One thing I know for sure, blood is going to be shed.*

~ ~ ~

Tony pulled up to his secret hideaway located on West 25th. The spot was a little hole-in-the-wall project. But for Tony it was his second home, where he did his dirt and could lay his head.

The one bedroom apartment was cheap and sparsely

Sherrie Walker

furnished with four chairs surrounding a round table in the kitchen, a microwave set on the counter and an empty refrigerator took up corner space on the left side of the room.

What he liked about his spot was the fact that no one knew about it. Tony sat at his favorite spot, the kitchen table, and inhaled the thick, white smoke that exited the glass pipe through a charred, black tip. Sweat ran down his face, his underarms were saturated and the funk permeating from his body was disgusting. He was unshaved and his hair was wild and unkempt.

With each hit, he grew angrier and angrier. Money had been missing from his account for a while now. He thought about all the money he made for So Real Productions. In the last year he'd sold over 15 million units alone, plus he had share and stock invested in the computer stores.

About six months ago he'd noticed his account balances were dwindling, so he confronted Pinch about it and was informed that someone was dipping into his accounts, stealing money. Pinch assured him that he would get to the bottom of things and get back to him later.

In Tony's drug-induced mind, he believed that Elise and LaKiesha put Aparis up to stealing his money. Aside from Pinch, she was the only other person that had access to his accounts. *Bitches! I should've never trusted her. Now she wants me to believe that I'm the father of her baby. I'll make them all pay.*

His voice was slurred. "Who they think they fuckin wit'? They don't want to fuck wit' me."

Tony picked up his AK-47 and loaded it. He placed it back on the table and inserted the clip into his nine mil-

Sherrie Walker

limeter. He put the 9mm in his waistband and his AK under his coat, took another hit off his crack pipe, popped an Ecstasy pill and left his home.

Once in the car, he turned his radio up and drove toward So Real Productions. He pulled up and there were several people standing around smoking cigarettes. He took another hit, then stepped out of the car and proceeded to So Real's building.

"Devils," Tony whispered.

The security guard at the desk looked up and smiled as Tony entered. "Mr. Boone, how are you today, son?"

"Fine. How are you, Smitty?" Tony nodded his head cordially as he walked to the elevator. The door opened and the elevator was empty. Tony pushed the button for the nineteenth floor and rode to the top, where the executive offices were located. He pulled out his crack pipe, already packed with dope, blazed then took the longest hit he could inhale. Once Tony reached his destination, he placed a silencer on his nine millimeter and kept it ready for automatic fire. When the door opened, he stepped into the hallway and started walking.

He came to the Assistant to the CEO's office first. He was sitting behind his desk talking on the telephone. Tony removed the nine millimeter and pointed it at the man. His eyes widened and he dropped the receiver as soon as he looked up.

"Devil!" Tony screamed, shooting the man directly between the eyes. He closed the door and kept walking down the hall. The second door he came to was Elise's Personal Assistant. He opened it and entered.

She was busy on the computer and wasn't aware that someone had entered the room until several seconds later. "Hi, Tony. I didn't know you had an appointment

Sherrie Walker

today. What can I do for you?" she said flirtatiously.

"Where's everybody?" he slurred.

"In a meeting in the conference room. Some big wigs in today."

"Thank you." He shot her in the chest and walked out. He continued to the end of the hall, put his nine millimeter away then pulled out the big gun. He opened the door and two executives and a couple investors were sitting around a long, cherry-finished conference table.

Before anyone could react, he sprayed the room with bullets. People scrambled and tried to run for cover, but he picked them off one by one. Tony stepped into another room and peeked under the table. He saw two men trying to hide so he turned the slab over and opened fire, shooting them both. Thinking he heard laughter, he looked around only to realize that the laughter was his own.

"Damn! I'm high," he gurgled as he walked back to the elevator. The door opened and Smitty was inside.

"Someone called and said there were gunshots," said Smitty as he looked over Tony's shoulder, trying to see what was going on.

Tony smiled, drew the gun and pointed it at Smitty. "There were," he said simply. Smitty eyes practically bulged out of his sockets. "Wha...what's going on?" Smitty trembled.

Tony eyes became small as slits as he cocked his head sideways, glaring at Smitty. He had one of the most demonic smiles on his face. "What's going on, Smitty? I'll tell you what the fuck is going on, you fat doughnut-eating mothafucka. They stole all my damn money and now them fools gon' pay. When you get to hell, tell the devil that Elise is right behind you." Pap.

Sherrie Walker

Tony pulled the trigger and Smitty took a bullet in the head. Tony dragged his body out of the elevator and left it in the hallway. He rode it down to the first floor. He started rapping the lyrics to one of his most famous songs, "Murder Mission."

"I'm on a motha fuckin' mission, niggas come up missin,' shots to frame, true to the game. Killa what they call me, blood bath freezing bodies…" When the elevator reached the ground level, Tony exited the elevator and calmly walked out of the building rapping his song.

"Run, nigga, run…here I come, blasting these fools to king…dom…come…" He reached the ground level, exited the building and whistled as he walked to his car.

Sherrie Walker

thirty-four

THREE HOURS AFTER Aparis was admitted into Cleveland Clinic Hospital, she lay in her bed with a sense of loss and hopelessness. She wanted her baby to survive more than she wanted anything in life. Her baby was a new beginning for her and she would protect her son from this cruel and unjust world.

Aparis prayed to God to spare her son, and hoped that her parents were looking down on her and would protect her son. Elise and Simone had been by her side ever since she came out of the recovery room, but even Elise couldn't bring her any comfort or security like she normally did.

After an hour of silence, Aparis turned to Elise. "So, Tony killed Dre?" Aparis asked, looking up from her hospital bed.

"Yeah. Shot him like a dog in the street," Elise replied.

"Don't no one know where he is?" Aparis questioned.

"He's a coward. He's hiding. I'm telling you, if you let me make a phone call, my people can handle it for you," Simone responded.

"What people, Simone? Who did you get to find

Sherrie Walker

LaKiesha's car? What kind of people have you gotten yourself tied up with?" Elise inquired.

"It don't matter."

"It does matter. I don't want you caught up in the streets, Simone. It only ends one or two ways."

"It didn't end that way for you."

"Because I got out. Even in doing so, look what's happened." She pointed to Aparis. Elise looked down at her body and tried to adjust the Kevlar vest. "This damn vest is so uncomfortable."

"Look, I'm not getting ready to argue with you about this. Those are my peeps and I'm not saying word about 'em. We need to be worrying about Tony before he strikes again." She stood and stared at Elise.

"All I ever wanted was to be happy," Aparis cried. "My career, a good man, family … you know, give my kids the security I never had after my parents died. A home with two parents. I thought I found all that in Tony but I guess I was wrong." She allowed the tears to fall as she rested her head on the pillow. "He wasn't always like this."

"But he is now and you know what needs to be done," Elise said.

"I know."

"Oh, my God!" Shocked, Simone pointed at the TV. "Ain't that the building where your label at?"

Elise and Aparis looked up to the television and a newscaster was standing in front of her building. Police were running in and out and yellow tape was everywhere. "Turn it up, Aparis." Aparis took the remote and increased the volume.

"This is Ruth Barnes reporting. I'm standing in front of So Real Productions, a record company owned by

Elise Green, Aparis Nixon and LaKiesha Hayes. Forty-five minutes ago, a rapper named Anthony "Tony Montana" Boone, once on the company's record label, entered the building and opened fire, killing five people and critically wounding four.

"If anyone sees this man, please call the police immediately. Do not try to apprehend him. He is armed and extremely dangerous." The picture of Tony remained on the screen as Aparis turned the volume down.

"Oh ... my ... God." Elise held her hand over her heart. "I can't—"

"Ms. Nixon," the doctor said as he entered the room, bowing his head. "I am so, so sorry. I regret to inform you that your son has passed. There was nothing more we could do. We tried to save him but his heart just wasn't strong enough." Standing over her bed, the doctor gently squeezed her hand as he tried to comfort Aparis.

"If you would like for us to contact the hospital's Chaplain for you, we will," he continued. "I know you will need to make the necessary arrangements for your son, so if we can be of any assistance, please do not hesitate to let us know. Our staff is willing to assist. I'm so sorry, ma'am."

The doctor looked at Simone and Elise then nodded toward Aparis. Elise assured him that they would take care of her and the doctor squeezed Aparis' hand again.

Aparis lay there numb and in shock as she stared straight ahead at nothing. At twenty-four she had lost her baby, her baby's father and at this point she didn't care if she lost her life –after she found Tony and buried him six feet under.

"Nooooo…God nooooo…Why…Why my baby…God noooo!" she wailed. Her cries tore Elise's heart in two as

Sherrie Walker

she clutched Aparis and held onto her like her life depended on it.

"Oh, God Elise … why my baby? My little baby … my son. His name was Iman. Daddy, why didn't you protect him?" Aparis looked upward and sobbed uncontrollably as Elise held and rocked her. Simone sat back, not really knowing what to do.

After forty-five minutes of crying Aparis dried her eyes and stood up. She spoke up in a hoarse, bitter voice. "I'm going to bury my son and then I'm going to find that lousy motherfucka and bury his ass, too."

"I know you're hurting, but what you're feeling you're not feeling alone, Aparis. I'm here with you and for you. You know I am, but first things first. You only have a day or two before you're to be discharged. Give yourself that time and in the meantime we will take care of Iman's funeral arrangements. You have staples in your stomach. Give yourself time to heal, Aparis."

Aparis turned and looked at Elise with anger in her eyes. "I know what I need to do and that's what I'm going to do. That was my baby who just died, Elise. I won't stop until his father is dead and buried, too. Would you make arrangements with the doctor for me to see my baby? No, better yet, I will."

Aparis slowly walked out of the room as Elise and Simone watched. Elise knew it was nothing she could say or do that would change Aparis' mind.

Simone turned to look at Elise. "I think it's time we discussed getting me a gun and Kevlar vest, too. An Uzi fits me just fine." Elise shook her head at Simone as she left to catch up to Aparis.

Sherrie Walker

thirty-five

FOR TWO DAYS the reporters and newspapers dubbed Tony's killing rampage as the "So Real Massacre." No one had seen nor heard anything from Tony. It was as if dropped off the face of the earth.

Against doctors' orders, Aparis signed herself out of the hospital and Elise insisted that she at least stay with her while they had people looking for Tony.

Elise and Trey had his house staked out because they knew that sooner or later he would resurface if for no other reason, to see his little sister Tiffany, who'd been worried sick about Tony. LaKiesha was still in a coma and everyone took turns staying by her bedside at the hospital.

Elise called a meeting in her home and present was Trey, Aparis, Cali and Simone. They discussed business in the sitting room.

"We have to be extra careful," Elise said. "The police questioned me for two-and-a-half hours about the shootings. They are all over this. When we find Tony, he has to disappear, totally. We don't want the police to find his nothing, not a tooth," said Elise. "Cali, we know that Pinch bonded Tony out. I need you and Trey to pay him a little visit. If he knows something, make him tell it."

"I'm going with you." Aparis stood before them, looking tired but determined.

"I don't think that's a good idea, Paris," Trey responded.

"I didn't ask you what you thought, Trey. I'm going." She gave him a challenging look until he turned and headed in another direction.

"Can I go, too?" Simone asked, excitedly.

"NO!" Trey and Elise said simultaneously.

"Simone, I want you to go with me to the hospital to see LaKiesha," Elise directed. "Every soldier on our squad is looking for him. It's only a matter of time before we find the lame. All right. Time to roll. Call me on my cell phone if you hear anything. After we leave the hospital, we're going to stop at So Real so I can make some arrangements for everybody. That's where I'll be until I'm done," she continued. "Be careful and alert."

Aparis slowly walked up the stairs, as each step took effort. "I'll be right back!" she hollered.

"I really don't think she's fit for this, Elise. She still got stitches in her stomach. Can't you talk some sense into her?" Trey asked.

"Yeah, right! She's not going to stop until we get Tony. Just watch her back," Elise commanded as Aparis came back down the stairs carrying a long Louis Vuitton duffel bag.

"Let's roll. I even put on my vest, Trey, so you should feel better," Aparis said as she hobbled out the door.

"I'm afraid to ask what's in the bag," California laughed.

"Me too," Trey added. He kissed Elise. "I love you, baby. Trust me. We'll handle this. You got my word on it."

"I love you, too. Be careful."

"I will. Take care of my wife and seed, Simone," Trey instructed as he left with California.

"I got you, boo," Simone winked. "Have you given any more thought to getting me that gun, sis? Shit is getting hectic. You feel me?" Elise looked at Simone like she was crazy, turned and headed for the stairs with Simone following her like a shadow.

Sherrie Walker

thirty-six

PINCH WAS LYING in bed, watching TV and eating a supreme pizza in his large brick ranch-style house in Cleveland Heights. He released a loud, voracious laugh, causing his 256 pounds to jiggle like Jell-O. Suddenly his doorbell rang and he looked over at his clock. It read 10:45 p.m.

"Who the hell could it be at this time of night?" Pinch wondered aloud. He growled and grumbled as he swung his feet around then pulled himself up with the support of a chair by the bed. He shuffled to the door and was out of breath when he swung it open. Immediately, he was looking down the eyes of a double barrel shotgun.

"Hello, Pinch," Trey said as he marched in, forcing him to step backwards. Aparis and California entered behind Trey. Aparis had her pearl-handled .38 caliber pistol ready, and California's 9 mm was drawn as well.

"Wha ...What is going on?" Pinch stuttered.

"We have a few questions for you, Pinch," Aparis answered.

"Questions? What kind of questions?"

"Why don't you have a seat, Pinch?" Trey commanded as he pushed Pinch into a chair.

Sherrie Walker

"Why did you bond Tony out of jail?" Aparis asked.

At first Pinch didn't answer. Then he spoke up. "I didn't!" Pinch lied. Aparis shook her head and slowly walked up to Pinch. She lifted her shirt to reveal her bandage and ripped it off in one quick motion. Cali and Trey turned away as the long red, inflamed incision is revealed. Pinch grasped each arm of the recliner he was sitting in tightly and turned away.

Aparis smiled. "I don't have time for your lies, Pinch. Wrong answer." She shot him in his left hand. Pinch screamed and grabbed his wounded palm while trying to rise out of the reclining chair in fear. Cali leaned over and shoved him back into the chair.

"Now I'm going to ask you one more time. Why did you bond Tony out?" Aparis probed as if she were the police.

"He … he said, if I didn't … he would get out and kill me. He's crazy. Oh God … please …" Pinch whined as he held his hand.

"Where is he?" Aparis asked.

"I swear …" Pinch began, but Aparis walked over to the other side of the chair and pointed her gun at his temple.

"Nine-nine-zero-one West 25th, Apartment D. Please … I need, some, some help … please," he cried.

"All right, we're getting ready to go. Now that wasn't hard, was it?" Aparis mocked. She started to walk away, then pivoted and shot Pinch in the head. "Let's go get this piece of shit," Aparis pronounced.

Trey and California looked at Pinch then each other. "Damn!" They looked around to make sure they didn't leave anything to link them to the murder then left as quickly as they had come.

Sherrie Walker

~ ~ ~

Trey, California and Aparis pulled up to the raggedy apartment building, where they immediately spotted Tony's SUV.

The street was infested with dope fiends and small-time dealers. A group of young dealers stood in front of a building playing a game of dice and drinking forty ounces, talking shit to one another. Several kids were running around kicking a ball, playing their street version of soccer. Two baseheads were leaning up against Tony's SUV.

"How stupid can dis nigga be?" Trey criticized. "Every cop in Ohio is looking for him and he has his truck parked at one of the hottest drug spots in Cleveland."

"The truck's not in his name. It's in his uncle's so he thinks he's safe," Aparis explained. "Plus, those drugs have fried his brain. Come on, let's roll."

"Look, wait here while we go check it out. When we give you the signal, you come," said California, trying to slow her down. California and Trey got out and walked up to the crack heads.

"What's up, yo?" California broke the ice.

"Where he at?" Trey asked, peeling off five one hundred dollar bills, then holding them in front of the men.

One-eye Willie looked like walking death with his nappy, matted, lint-filled hair. Then he had the nerve to constantly smile as if that one brown, rotten tooth hanging in the center of his mouth was invisible. He licked his chapped pink lips, staring at the money. His partner Marble was a few inches taller than One-eye Willie. He was high yellow and had so many red pimples on his face that he looked like a busted open pomegranate. He weighed every bit of ninety five pounds. There was no mistaking that his diet consisted of "Stem Fast."

Willie smiled to reveal his wretched mouth. "That all us?" he greedily asked with green in that one eye.

"Every dollar," Trey replied.

"He's in apartment D, but that nigga strapped like Fort Knox, nai'mean? Told us to watch the truck until he get back."

"How many he rolling with?" Trey inquired.

"Solo, without the artillery. Got two chicken heads up in there, though. Nothing but some ole round the way hoes."

"How long he been here?" Trey continued to interrogate.

"'Bout three hours. His time up fo' real. He gave us a fifty for two hours so we was 'bout to move out anyway. His meter is up."

"Who he copping from?" Trey asked but both dope fiends froze up and started looking nervous.

"You po po or what?" they sang at the same time.

"We look like po po, fool?" He lifted his shirt to reveal his gun. "This here is personal. Look, this what I want you to do, homey." Trey gave One-eye Williethe five hundred dollars he was holding. "I need you to knock on the door and get dude to open up." Trey reached into his pants pocket and pulled out another knot of money and counted off five more one hundred dollar bills and held them out.

"What I gotta do once he opens the door?"

"Run and keep yo' mouth shut," Trey instructed as he handed the man the money.

"It's on! I don't like the nigga no how." He took the money from Trey's hand and tucked it in his pocket and

Sherrie Walker

began to walk toward the apartment building. California signaled Aparis, who slowly climbed out of the truck and walked up to them. They fell in step with the guy, who led them into the building and up two flights of stairs. They reached the second landing and music was blaring loudly. As they approached the apartment, Trey and California got on one side of the door and Aparis posted up on the other. Aparis inserted her clip as California and Trey followed suit. The drug addict knocked on the door and movement could be heard from inside the apartment.

"Who is it?" Tony screamed.

"It's me, money! Yo, dawg, we 'bout to dip."

"I told you two hours, nigga!" Tony screamed.

"It's been three and unless you give us a little something more, we ghost."

Tony snatched the door wide open and was standing in the threshold butt naked with a glass stem in one hand and a long, red lighter in the other.

"I said, I'll be out, nigga! Damn—" Before Tony could finish his sentence, Trey pushed the pawn out the way and pointed his gun against Tony's forehead.

"Breathe wrong and the next time you blink, you'll see black." One-eye Willie restored his balance and took off running down the hall. Trey shoved Tony back into the apartment. California stepped through the door behind him.

"Get out!" Trey yelled to the two women, who looked like junkies.

"Take all that nigga's money and dope while you're at it," California added. Happily accepting the invitation, one woman snatched the dope off the table while the other removed the knot of cash from Tony's pockets,

Sherrie Walker

leaving him with nothing but lint.

"Get his jewelry, too," Trey said. They took a plat-inum chain with a rainbow-colored iced-out So Real emblem, two invisible set diamond pinky rings, his Jacob and Co. watch, a pair of 6 carat diamond stud earrings and his Paul Wall custom grill.

"Forget all about this here," California instructed the women, pointing his gun.

"Forget what? I don't know what you're talking about," one woman responded. They both ran out of the apartment.

"Whores! I should've smoked them harlots. Women are whores," Tony laughed. Aparis stepped into the apartment carrying the duffel bag. Tony's laughter ceased. "Caught me with my pants down, huh?" He start-ed laughing again.

"You've been a very naughty boy, *Tony Montana*." Aparis smiled.

"Y'all never saw me coming!"

"No, we didn't. You had us fooled. You were in with Ghost the whole time."

Tony's smile wavered slightly but then he began to laugh as Aparis bent down and unzipped the bag. Aparis pulled out another long, black, thick duffel bag and shook it loose. After she unzipped that one she went back into the first bag and pulled out a long, dart gun and screwed a hypodermic needle to the dart gun.

"You think you so smart. You ain't that smart. Elise thinks she has the world in the palm of her hand. I'm the man! Not her, ME!" Tony arrogantly ranted. When Aparis straightened up, she had what appeared to be a gun in her hand. Tony looked at her like she was crazy and so did Trey and California.

Sherrie Walker

"What you supposed to do with that?" Tony asked.

"This…" Aparis held the dart gun up. "…should be the least of your concerns, trick. I have a whole night of fun and games lined up for you, Tony baby. You see this?" Aparis lifted her shirt, revealing her stitches. "Because of your simple, crack smoking, ignorant ass, I loss my baby."

Tony smiled and opens his arms in an I-don't-care gesture. "Yeah, you right…*your baby*….cause the bastard wasn't mine anyway." Aparis pointed and fired the dart gun, hitting Tony in the chest.

Tony looked down at the needle sticking out of his chest. With a shocked look on his face, he looked back up at Trey, Cali and Aparis. He gasped, then fell to the floor, unconscious three seconds later.

"Hell hath no fury like a woman scorned," Aparis said, smiling sinisterly as she placed the dart gun back into the bag and pulled out a pair of gloves. She grabbed two more pairs and tossed them to Trey and Cali.

"Time to get busy, fellas. I have a long night ahead of me."

thirty-seven

THE PHONE SOUNDED and Elise snatched it up on the first ring. "Hello!"

"May I speak to Ms. Green, please?"

"Speaking."

"This is Dr. Termerski over at University Hospital. We need you to get over here as soon as possible, ma'am."

Elise's heart dropped to her stomach. "Wh … what happened, Dr. Termerski?"

"Nothing's wrong. Your sister has awakened from her coma, and she's asking for you and her other sister."

"Oh … ok. We're on the way now! Thank you, Doctor!"

~ ~ ~

Tony regained consciousness only to find himself duct taped to a chair with a strip across his mouth. He felt woozy, but he tried to collect himself and figure out his surroundings. Because of the damp, mildew smell, he realized he was in a basement and his feet were on a cement floor.

Aparis appeared and stood in front of him. With the exception of a pair of meat-cutter style, long orange, rubber gloves and the plastic cap on her head, Aparis was

Sherrie Walker

butt naked. "Hey, big daddy." Aparis smiled as she looked down at Tony's genital area.

He stared at Aparis in disbelief, as he couldn't avoid seeing the stitches across her belly. Tony looked from her stomach to her face and Aparis could tell he was smiling internally by the gleam in his eyes.

"Oh, that's funny? I want to see how long you're going to be laughing in a little while. All I ever wanted to do was love your simple ass. Give you kids and take care of your home and be a good wife to you. I didn't sweat you when you wouldn't come home until the wee hours of the morning, or find traces of lipstick and scents of perfume on your clothes, Tony. You know why? Because I've learned that men will be men. It's just your asshole nature.

"As long as you respected and loved me and your child, that was all that was important. Then you gon' turn your simple ass around and deny your baby. Just like a little bitch."

Tony labored in an effort to speak but the tape across his mouth prohibited that attempt.

"Oh you have something you want to say?" Aparis roughly snatched the tape from Tony's mouth.

"Aaaagh, shit…" Tony bellowed as he stretched his mouth trying to loosen up. He turned to look Aparis in the eyes.

"Bitch…save the sob story from someone who gives a fuck. I trusted your ass and you and your people are going to steal *my* mothafuckin' money."

Aparis stepped back from Tony and placed her hands on her hips. "Your money? Do you hear how simple you sound? What the fuck we gon' steal yo' money for? Nigga that little chump change ain't and wasn't shit compared

Sherrie Walker

to what I have in my accounts. Stupid ass nigga, Pinch was the one taking yo' money. When you was in jail, Elise discovered that Pinch had millions, not only in his account, but in several other accounts as well."

Tony started to wiggle in the chair.

"You lying, yo'. Pinch wouldn't steal from me. That's some creative bullshit on your part. I know what time it is fo' real though."

"Is it Tony?" Aparis stood watching him as he continuously fidgeted to loosen the tape that obviously had him bound to the chair.

"I would call Pinch for you, baby. But seeming that's he's buried six feet under, you'll have to ask him once you join him in hell." Aparis reached down and massaged his dick and as badly as he didn't want it to rise, it did. He tried to scoot back but the chair was welded to the floor.

Before walking away, Aparis reached down and gently stroked his dick again and again. She took that same hand and rubbed Tony's face while looking him square in the eyes. She lowered her eyes from his and walked away only to return carrying a large, serrated knife. Tony began to wiggle frantically and whimper. His face was a contorted mask of perspiration, panic and fear.

"Yo...what the fuck...what you doin'...get the fuck away..."

In one fluid motion, Aparis grabbed Tony's penis and cut it off. She held it in front of him and then tossed it over her back. It hit the floor with a thud. Tony fainted.

~ ~ ~

Elise and Simone burst into LaKiesha's room. LaKiesha was propped up in the bed drinking from a cup of water with the nurse's assistance. Tears welled up

Sherrie Walker

in LaKiesha's eyes and Elise's were watery as well. She ran over to the bed and hugged LaKiesha then stood back. Their eyes locked, then LaKiesha looked toward Simone. "I need to talk to you, Elise."

"I know what that means. I'll be in the cafeteria. I don't know why y'all think I don't know what's up. But before I leave, can I at least see the bullet wound?" Simone asked. LaKiesha turned her head slowly. "Girl, give yourself a high-five, that's a battle scar, you're wearing the tattoo of a real soldier now! You know that, right?" Simone tried to move the covers but LaKiesha and Elise both gave her a crazy look so she threw her hands up in the air, surrendering.

"I'm out." Simone walked out the door and the nurse followed.

Elise turned to look at LaKiesha and could tell that it was bad.

"Sit down, Elise ... please." LaKiesha reached for Elise's hand. "I don't know how to tell you this, Elise, because I know it's going to hurt you just as much as it hurt me." LaKiesha tightened her grip on Elise's hand. "Never in my wildest dreams would I..." LaKiesha became choked up and her eyes fills with tears.

"LaKiesha, what's wrong? You're scaring me."

"When I turned to see who was standing behind me...it's like the whole world began to spin out of control. I couldn't make sense of nothing. It still doesn't make sense, Elise. I keep asking myself, why?"

"LaKiesha. ... please tell me what the hell you are talking about. Please."

LaKiesha turned and looked Elise in her eyes. Elise could see the pain, confusion and turmoil as she looked back. LaKiesha gripped both of Elise's hands tightly.

Sherrie Walker

"Elise, it's Trey." Elise released LaKiesha hands and jumped up from her chair, slowly backing away from LaKiesha.

"What? Kiesha, what are you talking about? What do you mean? How is that possible? It doesn't make any sense."

"Elise, Trey tried to kill me. He's the one who shot me." LaKiesha flinched, then held her side before continuing.

For a moment, Elise's mouth remained open. Then she sat back in the chair, dazed, while rubbing her stomach. She was still sitting there twenty minutes later when Aparis entered. Aparis ran over to the bed excited. She hugged LaKiesha.

"Girl, I came as soon as I got the message. Look at you, tramp. Girl, you're too thin to fry. We got to put some meat on them bones."

"How you doin', boo?" LaKiesha's voice sounded weak.

"How am I doing? I got a little present for both of y'all." Aparis opened up her purse and took out a black bottle with a lid on it. She gave it to Elise.

"What is this?"

"More like *who* is this would be a better question. It's Tony!!! Heey, Boo. Those are his ashes. What's left of them anyway."

"You crazy as hell," LaKiesha said.

"Hey, I did what I had to do. Thought y'all would be happy. What's wrong?"

"Tony didn't shoot me, Paris," LaKiesha explained.

"What? What the hell you talking about? He killed Dre, went to the label and shot up a bunch of people. He was working for Ghost, right?" Aparis questioned.

Sherrie Walker

"I'm not saying he wasn't supposed to die, because he was. But we are saying that he didn't shoot LaKiesha," Elise explained.

"Well, who is Ghost? Who shot you?" Aparis wondered aloud as LaKiesha and Elise looked at each other, trying to determine who would reveal the shooter's identity to Aparis.

thirty-eight

ABSORBED IN DEEP THOUGHT, Elise sat in her living room facing the lake, staring out the French doors. She'd witnessed too many deaths and was tired of all the violence. She had come to understand why it was called "blood money" as well as why the cycle never stopped once it started. She was determined to make it stop with Ghost and Trey.

Why? she continued to ask herself. *What would drive a person to that kind of hatred?*

A pair of headlights briefly flashed in her face as a car pulled into the driveway. She heard the garage door retracting and waited patiently for it to close. A few minutes passed and Elise heard keys turning the lock on the door.

"Elise!" Trey yelled.

"I'm in the living room," she responded.

Trey turned on a light. "Why are you sitting in the dark, baby?"

"Thinking. You know I do some of my best thinking in the dark."

Trey walked over to the bar and poured a drink then sat across from Elise.

Sherrie Walker

"What's wrong, baby? You look stressed."

"Of course, you know that Tony is dead." Elise spoke softly.

"Yeah." Trey sipped his drink. "I'm afraid Aparis took a little too much pleasure in that one. But can you blame her? Look what all he did to her, hell to us and the company."

"I guess you're right. Payback is a bitch."

"I've heard that before," Trey said, standing then walking over to refill his drink. Elise continued when he was just about to put the glass to his lips. "LaKiesha woke up." Trey almost choked on his drink. Elise watched him closely.

"Did she?"

"Yep!" She continued to study him. "She had a very disturbing story to tell me."

"I bet she did," he responded as he finished his drink then poured another. "Everybody has a story to tell."

"Do you?" she asked.

"Of course!"

"I'm listening." Elise folded her arms.

Trey walked over to the chair and sat down across from her, crossed his legs, and drained his drink. "My dad and Que's father used to hustle together and they pretty much had Ohio sewed up. But, as always, greed reared its ugly head and Que's father set my dad up. He was busted with ten kilos of cocaine hidden in the doors of his car. No one knew where they kept the dope but my dad and Mr. Hayes." Trey stood to fix another drink. "Once the indictment was served, he saw Mr. Hayes' name was on it, and speculation was put to rest. My dad was sentenced to twenty-two years and wasn't gone two months before Marcus' sorry ass started sniffing around my mother like a dog in heat." He sipped some more and leaned on the bar. "Marcus Hayes started coming by our house every day because he and our mother was having a hot, steamy affair. And, still made us refer to him as Uncle Marcus. Ain't that some shit! I grew to hate him with everything in me, Elise.

"At night, I would lay awake and hear my mother cry herself to sleep. In the beginning he used to give her money. He kept her living the way she was accustomed to living before all the madness began. Then after he became bored with my mother, he tried to dump her like she was a bucket of shit. Do you know how many times I wanted to throw up when I heard my mother on the phone begging that sorry motherfucka to come over, or to help her with the bills, or just for some money to feed us?"

Elise thought, *who is us?*

"I came home early from school one day and caught her in bed with him. I hated that nigga with a passion." He set the glass on the table then gazed into Elise's eyes. She had not moved since he started talking. "Then lo and behold, the bitch comes up pregnant." Trey exploded and began to yell each word. "SHE LET THE ENEMY GET HER PREGNANT." Trey paused and straightened his jacket.

Elise watched as he flexed his jaws and began to clench his teeth. Trey noticed Elise watching him and he smiled.

"My mother didn't know that I was telling my father every little thing she and that snake were doing. He would call me when she wasn't around and I would tell him everything. We began planning at that point. I was my father's little soldier. He knew he could count on me.

Sherrie Walker

Then, on a technicality, my dad won his appeal and unexpectedly walked into the house one day. My mother almost had a heart attack.

"I told my father that she was pregnant by Uncle Marcus Hayes," he said sarcastically. He tried to beat the baby out of her, and in a way, he did. She went into labor and had a baby girl. Afterward, he made her drop it off at Mr. Hayes' house. They took her in as their own. You didn't know Que's mother only had one child, did you?" Trey asked.

Elise sat there stunned by the revelation. *"Kiesh?"*

Trey nodded, smiled and sipped as Elise peered upward into his eyes.

"Yes, Elise. LaKiesha is my half-sister."

"So you tried to kill your own flesh and blood?"

He set the glass back down. "She's nothing to me. My dad put that hit out on Marcus. My father was Ghost. Que and LaKiesha would've died that night, too, but he had some type of panic room built into his wall that saved them. That was the plan." Trey hung his head.

"My father was never able to get back like he was before doing time. He started committing robberies to put food on the table while Mr. Hayes was living in the lap of luxury. My dad caught another case for some shit he didn't even do but was convicted by that bitch-ass Stearnes due to his priors. Mr. Hayes stole his fucking joy.

"My father died," Trey's voice cracked but he continued, "six weeks after the last time I visited him. On our last visit, my father told me that Que came to see him, asking about Ghost, and that it was finally time to put him to rest. So I vowed that I would and I did." His voice grew squeaky and scary.

Elise steadily absorbed Trey's words.

"At that point, I started operating under the name Ghost, to carry on my father's legacy. I arranged to have Que killed that night. Plus, I was tired of seeing the nigga pushed up in yo' grill, pretending like he loved you. So, I had to snatch his joy like his father robbed me of mine. I loved my dad, Elise. My ol' man was the world to me, and I to him. But we rarely got the chance to spend time with each other because of ..." Trey extended his arms, unfolded Elise's arms then took her by the hand. Her eyes enlarged but she played along, watching and listening, patiently waiting for him to drop his hold card so she could finish the game.

"See, he didn't deserve you and I wasn't going to let him take you away from me like his father took my mother from my dad. YOU BELONG TO ME!" Elise listened intensely. "Que didn't want you until he saw us together, Elise. That day when I was with you on the porch and he came over, he had the audacity to tell me to back off, that you was his woman. YEAH RIGHT, MOTHAFUCKA!" Trey screamed.

Elise didn't flinch. However, she did withdraw her hands.

"Where is your mother Trey? After she had Kiesha what happened to her?"

"My mother had a nervous breakdown and was never able to recover. She was committed and has been ever since."

"I love you, Elise. I loved you from day one when you used to come down the way to see Que." Trey sat quietly, allowing himself to calm down then started back up. "I had to remove LaKiesha, she was getting too close to the truth."

Sherrie Walker

"But you didn't, Trey. LaKiesha is alive."

"I know. That's a problem we have to take care of, she's a loose end."

Like a Pentium processor, Elise sat back filing information into her memory bank. "You are one sick son-of-a bitch," she said in a low tone.

"Now, there's no need for name calling, Elise," Trey said softly. "Don't you see that I love you and I want to make you happy? After we take care of LaKiesha, we'll get married, go on our honeymoon and forget they ever existed."

"I wouldn't be with you if my life depended on it."

"Oh, but your life does depend on it, Elise. I know too much, and did you forget, you're carrying my seed! We're stuck like Siamese twins. You'll never be able to leave me, baby girl."

Elise never took her eyes off Trey. She was silent for a moment. Finally she spoke. "Maybe not. But you'll be leaving me."

Without warning, Elise drew the mother-of-pearl handled Derringer, which was hidden in the crease of the couch cushions, and pointed it at Trey's chest. He smiled.

"So, it comes down to this huh? You think you can kill me, Elise. I'm the father of your child. Do you really want to kill the father of your child?" Trey recognized hesitation as he stared into her eyes. "I love you, baby. Everything I did, I did for us. So we could be together. No one has ever loved you the way I do, Elise. You have to know that. We can get through this..."

"Shut up! Just shut the fuck up, Trey!" Elise's hands trembled and her stomach churned, feeling as if she was going to regurgitate at any given moment.

Everything that Trey said was running through her

Sherrie Walker

mind and she knew she should've pulled the trigger a long time ago. Even though he was the father of her child, she couldn't excuse the fact that he killed Que and tried to kill LaKiesha.

He'd betrayed her. So many emotions were going through her mind. The contents of her stomach kept rising to the tip of her throat.

Trey continued to smile and uncrossed his legs. He leaned forward in his chair and stood. "Put the gun away, Elise, you don't want to do this." He could see the gun shaking as she pointed it at his chest. He took a step toward her.

Elise gripped the gun tighter. "Stop right there, Trey." Her voice had a tremor in it. She sounded unsure. Trey put his hands in the air as if he was surrendering.

"I love you, baby. I love my seed you're carrying. Put the gun away, Elise." He took another step toward her. A few more steps and he would be right up on her.

Elise gripped the gun with both hands. "I'm not going to tell you again, Trey. Don't come any closer." Trey stopped and placed his hands in his pockets. He smiled and lunged forward.

Pap...Pap. Two shots rang out as Trey was thrown back from the impact of the bullets. He fell on his back and Elise jumped up and ran to the bathroom. She fell to her knees over the toilet placing the gun beside her, her dinner erupting from her stomach until there was nothing left but yellow liquid, her throat on fire.

She slowly lifted herself from the floor and shuffled over to the sink where she rinsed her mouth with water and splashed some across her face. Elise looked in the mirror and the tears began to flow. She cried for all the lives that had been lost. She cried for Que, his parents

Sherrie Walker

and LaKiesha. She cried for Trey. She knew that underneath the surface, Trey was a good man that was infected with his father's handfed deceit, revenge and hatred. In a sad, twisted way, Trey was a victim also.

She took a deep breath. There was still plenty of work to do. She removed the gun from the floor that lay beside the toilet and headed for the living room. Her heart skipped a beat as she entered the living room. After closing and reopening her eyes, she scanned the living room, looking for what she knew was there before she left. Slowly she walked further into the room as if in a trance. She stood where Trey's body went down. He was gone.

Sherrie Walker

327

thirty-nine

ONE HOUR LATER, Cali and Aparis sat in Elise's living room, trying to calm her down. Elise had been frantic when she called Cali. He couldn't even understand what she was saying at first. He jumped in his car and flew over.

"You have to calm down, Elise. All this worrying isn't going to help the baby." Aparis embraced Elise and tried to comfort her. "We're going to find him, I promise." Cali hung up the phone and walked over to Elise and grabbed her hand.

"Everything is going to be all right. We have people on LaKiesha and I sent a couple of our best guys to pick up Simone from computer class. We got you, Elise."

Elise stood up and walked over to the window, trying to see the waves as they rolled in from the lake. The only thing she could see was the darkness which matched her mood.

"How did I not know he would have on his bullet-proof vest? I should've known and aimed at his head." Aparis flipped open her cell phone and dials.

Elise began to massage her temples, which felt like someone was pounding against her head with a hammer.

Sherrie Walker

Aparis closed her phone. "It's still going to voicemail." She tried not to show her fear but something didn't feel right.

Elise said what Aparis was feeling. "Something isn't right, Cali. Simone never turns off her cell phone. Not even in school. I think Trey … I think …" Elise broke down before she could finish her sentence. Aparis ran over to her and hugged Elise tightly. "I'll die if anything happens to Simone … I'll die."

Cali began to pace back and forth thinking. "He won't hurt her, Elise."

"He's twisted, Cali. There's no telling what he'll do. He's not the person you think he is. I was put in touch with the demented side of Trey. He's sick. Oh God, why didn't I shoot him in the head when I had the chance? Oh God."

"We don't even know if he has her, Elise. Maybe Simone's battery is low. I think we're jumping the gun."

As soon as the words left his mouth, the house phone rang. Everyone froze and looked at the phone. Aparis looked at Elise.

"You better answer it. It could be Simone." Elise felt as if she was having an out-of-body experience as she walked over to the phone. It felt like her feet had a hundred pounds of lead in them as she walked. Her heart pounded in her chest and she couldn't inhale or exhale calmly.

The phone seemed to be ringing loudly like a bell and it felt like death was on the other side of the receiver. Elise removed the phone from its cradle and could barely find words. In a hoarse whisper she said, "Hel…hello."

"It didn't have to come to this, my love. All I wanted was to love and protect you. And this is the thanks I get?

Sherrie Walker

329

I don't think so." Trey began to scream into the phone. "YOU FUCKING SHOT ME, BITCH. AFTER ALL I'VE DONE FOR YOU! Now you'll have to pay for that, Elise." He paused before continuing. "I want you to come to me. The address is 542 East 97th Street. The door will open. Tell Cali and Aparis if they come with you...I'll...I'll kill Simone. And, you know I will...don't you, baby?"

On that note he hung up, leaving Elise immobilized and lost in thought as she held the phone against her ear, listening to the dial tone.

Finally, she lowered the phone from her ear and in a dazed state, placed the receiver back into its cradle. *My worst fear has come true. All I wanted to do was protect Simone. I went through all of what I've gone through and Simone fell into harm's way anyway.* Aparis snapped her out of her thoughts.

"Who was that, Elise?" she asked, even though in her heart she already knew the answer.

"He has Simone and I have to go get her."

Cali grabbed his coat. "Come on. Let's go."

"NO! I have to go alone. He will kill her if I don't." Elise grabbed her purse off the table and headed for the door.

"Elise? Wait, you can't go by yourself. How do you know he won't kill the both of you?"

Elise stood thinking about the question. "He won't, not as long as he thinks he has me. I'm going to make him think whatever he needs to think and whatever will put me closer to killing him. And this time I won't miss."

Elise took her nine out of her purse and put it in the small of her back. "I'll be back."

Aparis ran over to Elise and hugged her. "Promise me

Sherrie Walker

you'll be back."

Elise looked her in the eye. "I promise." She turned and walked out the door, letting it close quietly behind her. Aparis hadn't been that scared since the night of her parents' death. Cali wrapped his arms around Aparis and said a silent prayer.

~ ~ ~

Even though it was only a fifteen minute drive to the address Trey gave her, it felt like it took an eternity to arrive. The whole time Elise was driving, vivid images of Simone lying dead haunted her mind.

It was a wonder she didn't have an accident before she pulled up to the small, gray house that reminded her of one of those haunted houses she'd seen on TV a thousand times. Leading up to the porch of the old two story home were three concrete steps. The lawn was well kept and there were several white rocks neatly lined up starting from the end of the driveway to the path leading to the steps.

The porch furniture was a soft gray and white with an old fashioned swing that rocked back and forth with the light breeze. On the interior, there was only one light on in the entire house. Elise looked around the street and there wasn't a single person walking or sitting on a porch.

Elise stepped out the car putting her keys in the Mary J. Blige CD and placing it in the console between the seats. There was no need to lock the doors as she proceeded toward the house on shaky limbs. She walked up the three steps and stopped in front of the black steel screen door and rang the bell. After a few seconds passed with no answer, she rang it two more times before trying the screen doorknob. It creaked open.

Sherrie Walker

Reluctantly, she stepped inside and had to wait a second for her eyes to adjust to the darkness. Elise found herself standing in what appeared to be a modestly furnished living room with a fruity smell. There was a white leather sofa with two matching chairs on each end, and a long glass table in the middle of the room. A few pictures adorned the walls.

There wasn't a sound coming from within the house. She remembered the light that was on upstairs and proceeded to ascend the cream-color carpeted stairs. As she reached the top of the stairs, she noticed a light coming from an open doorway. Elise made her way toward the light. When she stepped in front of the door and looked inside, she covered her mouth to stifle a scream that threatened to erupt.

Sherrie Walker

forty

"CALI, WE SHOULDN'T have let her leave. It's been an hour and we still haven't heard anything. I'm scared, Cali."

"We have to have faith right now, Paris. Elise is tough and if anyone can pull this off, it's her. How in the hell did we not know that it was Trey? Haven't y'all been knowing each other forever?"

"Since junior high school. Trey and Que went back further than that. If Que didn't know nothing, there was no way in hell we could know anything. That nigga was good at hiding that shit."

"That nigga is dead, yo. We gots to bury his ass. Let me call the hospital and check on Kiesh." Cali opened his cell phone and dialed LaKiesha's hospital room. Aparis walked to the bar and poured a drink for her and Cali and hands Cali his. "Kiesha wants to speak with you." He handed Aparis the phone.

"What's up, sis?"

LaKiesha still sound a little weak. "Anything yet?"

"Nah, Cali and I are worried sick. But Elise will come out on top, she always does."

"I want to sign myself out so I can be there."

"Hell no. Stay yo' ass right there. We'll keep you

updated. Get some rest, sis. I love you."

"I love you too."

Aparis hung up the phone. "Come on, Elise." She prayed.

Sherrie Walker

forty-one

SIMON WAS LYING on a four poster bed and Trey had a hypodermic needle pressed against her neck. Simone's eyes were closed and she wasn't moving. "What have you done to my sister?"

Trey stroked Simone's hair with his free hand while looking at her lovingly. "She'll be all right, for now that is." He looks down at Simone. "We could've all been a family, Elise. You, me, our baby and Simone. I could've made you happy, had you given me a chance…"

"What the fuck have you done to my sister you sick mothafucka?!"

Trey jerked his head up to look at Elise.

"Watch your voice. Now I said she'll be all right. I just gave her a little shot of Valium to make her sleep, but if you keep disrespecting me I'm going to ram this needle filled with pure heroin in her veins. Need I mention the effect it will cause? What the fuck you mad about anyway? You the one that shot me. I should be the one mad."

Trey pointed the needle at Elise with his next words. "You better show me some respect. I'm getting tired of this shit, Elise. I've worked too damn hard for this shit,

Sherrie Walker

you UNAPPRECIATIVE BITCH!"

Trey pointed the needle in the direction of Simone's neck and, at that moment, Elise knew how she had to play her hand.

"You're right, Trey." Trey looked at her skeptically, like he didn't believe what he heard.

"What?"

Elise stepped farther into the room and dropped her hands to her side. "I said, you're right. I guess I was just trying to sort through all of this. It is a lot for me to absorb. I mean it's not like you didn't keep secrets from me. How do I know I can trust you, Trey?"

Trey cocked his head sideways, looking at her strangely. "Trust me! You're the one who shot me."

"I know … I just panicked, Trey. I didn't know what to believe. I love you." Trey smiled and slowly brought the needle down. He stood and walked up to Elise and stopped within inches of her.

"Everything I did, I did for you, for us. I've never loved anyone the way I love you. I'll never let you go." He gently stroked the side of her face. "I love you, Elise."

"If you love me, throw the needle away, Trey. We have to start trusting each other. If you really love me, get rid of it now."

Trey looked at her for a few minutes and threw the needle across the floor and pulled Elise into his arms and started caressing her arm and kissing her. His hands began to travel the length of her back and Elise tried to pull away before his hands reach her gun. Trey pressed his body even closer and pinned one of her hands behind her back, while his hand reached the gun. Smiling, he pulled the gun out and pushed Elise.

"I know all your tricks. So, I guess this means we can't

Sherrie Walker

work things out, huh. Oh well, I tried." He slowly brought her gun up and pointed it at her. Elise stepped back with a heavy sense of failure. She'd failed Simone and knew that Trey was going to kill Simone next.

Truthfully, she didn't think she could live with Simone dead so she closed her eyes and prepared herself for what she felt her future had in store for her. It seemed like forever as she stood with her eyes closed. Suddenly, she heard the loud shot that shattered the silence in the house. After a few seconds, she realized she was still standing and felt no pain.

Slowly, Elise opened her eyes as Trey's body crumbled to the floor. Simone was sitting up on the bed with Trey's gun in her hands. Elise stared down at Trey. His eyes were wide open and a bright red flow of blood was seeping from the back of his head. She ran over to Simone and held her tightly. They both were crying as they held each other.

"Are you all right? I'm so sorry, baby...I'm sorry." Elise repeated over and over as she rocked Simone in her arms

"I'm ok. I'm just so groggy feeling."

"You were injected with Valium. But it will wear off." After a long embrace, Elise reached into her purse and called Cali and Aparis. She briefly explained what happened gave them the address and instructed Cali to bring a clean up crew.

After hanging up the phone she helped Simone out of the bed and down the stairs. Simone stopped, "Sis, stop blaming yourself. It wasn't your fault.

"I can't help it, though. I feel so responsible for your well-being and you being put in position to kill someone is not what I feel you should have been subjected to. You

Sherrie Walker

should've never had to kill nobody. I tried to protect you from things like that. I killed a man when I was thirteen Simone and..." Simone cut her off with her next words.

"And so did I, Elise. I have killed before. One day I'll tell you the story."

The two sisters stood looking in each other's eyes for awhile. What passed between them that night was something that would never be forgotten ... an understanding that they both had skeletons in their closets and they dually possessed secrets. Secrets that in an unspoken way bonded them together with an unbreakable pact that nothing or no one would ever be able to touch.

~ ~ ~

Cali and his crew arrived at the address Elise provided and cleaned up the house. After they were done the house looked like it hadn't been lived in for a long time. They carried Trey's body to the crematorium and burned his body scattering his ashes in Lake Erie. His name was forbidden from their mouths and it was like he never existed.

Sherrie Walker

epilogue

FOR SEVERAL WEEKS AFTER, the police searched for Tony, who became one of America's most wanted criminals. His face was plastered in Post Offices, Sheriff's Departments and even on TV. The police questioned everyone at So Real Productions and visited Elise on several occasions. When Trey came up missing, investigators automatically suspected Tony for the disappearance. Elise played the role of a grieving fiancée superbly, and other than Elise, no one knew what really happened to Trey but California, LaKiesha and Aparis, and the two soldiers who destroyed Trey's body. They vowed to keep the secret sealed with the spirit of Ghost.

LaKiesha was devastated when she found out Trey was her brother. She remembered times when her mother Pearl and Marcus argued, and for some odd reason, she felt the disputes were about her since they would stop as soon as she entered the room. But they had never treated her any differently than Que. So, in her heart, the Hayes family was the only family she ever knew and loved, aside from Aparis and Elise.

Three months after the day Simone killed Trey, Elise rested in a hospital bed, having delivered her baby. Elise felt no remorse about Trey's death, though she did feel a grave sense of loss as she turned and stared out of her hospital bedroom window.

She wondered if it was really over. She turned and stared at her newborn and her face was filled with joy. She saw the baby as a sign from God that everything was going to be ok.

Elise sensed something that she had not felt in a long time. Hope! She prayed. She prayed for violence and death to end, for happiness for everyone and forgiveness for all the sins she had committed.

As Aparis, Simone and LaKiesha oohed and ahhed all over Lil' Que, Elise couldn't help but smile. She looked from Aparis to LaKiesha to Simone and felt such an over-powering urge to embrace them.

LaKiesha noticed the intense expression on Elise's face and grew alarmed. "What's wrong, sis?"

Elise took a few minutes before she responded, not wanting to sound crazy, yet wanting them to understand where she was coming from.

"Destiny...we are all a part of destiny. From the very first moment of our making one another's acquaintance, a friendship was established and an unbreakable bond was developed as we became connected and remained that way. Everything was designed for this exact moment and time.

"We have survived many obstacles and maintained a helluva relationship in the process. We are the true essence and epitome of what a true, genuine friendship is about." Aparis and Simone exchange weird glances at one another as LaKiesha began to nod her head in agreement. Simone touched Elise's forehead with the back of her hand feeling for a temperature.

Sherrie Walker

"I think they gave you too much pain medication, Elise." Simone laughed.

"No." LaKiesha nodded her head in agreement. "I feel where you coming from and where you're going with this, Elise. Because one night as I was laying in bed thinking, it tripped me the hell out how some things were tied together, and how family isn't necessarily those who you share blood with.

"After all, Trey was my brother, come to find out, and he tried to kill me. His father had my parents killed. Then Trey had Que killed.

"Elise, you end up falling in love with my brother Que, and if it wasn't for the hatred in Trey's heart, there was no doubt that you would've been married by now. It's like we came full circle to arrive where we're at today."

Aparis blurted excitely, "Hell yeah. Just like out of all the orphanages for you two to end up at, you both went to St. Agnes where my Aunt Garnett worked."

"And we met you," added Elise.

"That was *destiny*," said LaKiesha.

Elise looked at Simone. "Finding you again Simone was destiny."

"Through all the pain and heartache I've endured in my life as a result of losing both my parents, Aunt Garnet, Tony and my baby, the one thing that kept me sane is the friendship, sistership that we…you LaKiesha, you Elise…have maintained. We have been through a lot and survived and weathered many storms. Not to mention the obstacles that tried to get in our way. And, in case I haven't told y'all in a while… I am ever so grateful to have you both in my life. I love you both."

LaKiesha's tears began to flow as she choked up on

Sherrie Walker

her words, "I feel…I feel…like all the drama we've been through has been through only brought and made us closer. Those were challenges. And, guess what, the challenges of life made us champs."

"I don't need you and y'alls blood running through my veins to validate our sisterhood. Our tears, sweat, loyalty and love have bonded us," Elise added.

Aparis blew her nose. "You know what the most ironic thing is, y'all? My dad is probably doing flips in his grave about hard-nosed Judge Stearnes. Who would've ever thought that the same judge my father was preparing a case to present to on the eve of his death would be the same judge that would accept bribes from me years later?"

Elise snapped her finger in the air and said, "And here we have him in our hip pocket."

"Boy, the traffic of life." Aparis laughed.

"Even though we have lost a lot, we gained even more. One for all…" Elise and LaKiesha placed their fists next to Aparis.

They all said together…"And all for one."

Several moments of silence pass as each reflected on her journey.

Simone shattered the silence with her next comment. "Well what the hell am I, a potted plant?"

Elise, LaKiesha and Aparis turned to look at Simone who was standing with her hands on her hips, tapping her foot, with her lips turned up. They all bust out laughing. Elise held her hands out to Simone who pouted and walked over to them. Elise, LaKiesha, and Aparis embraced Simone laughing.

Lil' Que began crying and Aparis turned to look down in the baby bed next to Elise's bed.

Sherrie Walker

"He is so adorable," Aparis said, looking down at the 9 pound, 8 ounce, healthy newborn with light brown eyes and a head full of jet-black hair. He yawned, stretched, puckered his lips and smiled, displaying his dimples. Aparis appeared as if she wanted to hold him but something was holding her back. "Lil' Que is too cute."

"I can't believe he has the nerve to favor my brother," LaKiesha added. Simone reached down and picked Lil' Que up.

"I'm going to spoil him rotten," Simone said. She cooed while kissing Que's fat little cheeks.

"Look at his eyes. They just sparkle." LaKiesha laughed.

"Hand me my nephew," California said as he entered the room carrying a bouquet of roses. "Da lil' playa aint tryin' to hear all that girly jibber-jabber." He handed the roses to Elise as he reached over and removed the baby from Simone's arms.

"What's up, playa? Dis your Uncle Cali, here. I'm going to teach you how to spit, hawk and scare the lil' girls with worms, boy," California cuddled and cajoled.

"That's gross." Aparis scrunched her face with the other girls. When her face was restored to its natural structure, she appeared sullen. "Just think ... if my Iman would've lived, he and Lil' Que would've grown up together."

"Bae, you are going to have more kids, and until you do, we'll share Que." Elise reached out her arm and patted Aparis in an attempt to comfort her.

A nurse entered and smiled. "It's time for the little one to get changed now," she announced as she took Que out of California's hands. "Say bye-bye to Mommy." She turned the baby around so he was facing Elise.

"See you later, Mommy's lil' man," Elise replied as she threw her son a kiss. The nurse slightly lifted Lil' Que's arm to wave goodbye and then quickly exited the room. Elise smiled and paused.

LaKiesha stood there stuck for a few seconds, staring at the door. Elise noticed her standing there and called out to her. "LaKiesha...Kiesh," She didn't answer the first two times.

It wasn't until Simone tapped her shoulder that she snapped out of her moment.

"I need y'all to gather around and hold hands." Elise looked at each of her friends. "We're going to do something we should've been doing a long time ago. But, from here on out we're going to do this every time we get together. You know how the saying goes...a family that prays together, stays together."

They looked at each other, wondering if she was joking, but the look on her face said she was dead serious, so as always, they obliged her.

"I have a very special prayer in mind that my father taught me and I have remembered verbatim. Psalm 143. This is an opportunity we shall take advantage of and go to God in prayer. Let's pray. "

As instructed, they gathered around the bed, lowered their heads and joined hands as Elise led them in prayer.

"Most gracious heavenly Father, we come to you with bowed heads and humble hearts thanking you for this day and for the birth, death and resurrection of your son, our Lord and Savior, Jesus Christ. For had not died on the cross of Mt. Calvary for our sins, we would not have hope for eternal Salvation. Thank you, Lord. Thank you for His grace and mercy.

Sherrie Walker

"Hear my prayer, O LORD. Give ear to my supplications: in thy faithfulness answer me, *and* in thy righteousness. And enter not into judgment with thy servant: for in thy sight shall no man living be justified. For the enemy hath persecuted my soul; he hath smitten my life down to the ground; he hath made me to dwell in darkness, as those that have been long dead.

"Therefore is my spirit overwhelmed within me; my heart within me is desolate. I remember the days of old; I meditate on all thy works; I muse on the work of thy hands. I stretch forth my hands unto thee: my soul *thirsteth* after thee, as a thirsty land. Selah.

"Hear me speedily, O LORD: my spirit faileth: hide not thy face from me, lest I be like unto them that go down into the pit. Cause me to hear thy loving kindness in the morning; for in thee do I trust: cause me to know the way wherein I should walk; for I lift up my soul unto thee.

"Deliver me, O LORD, from mine enemies: I flee unto thee to hide me. Teach me to do thy will; for thou art my God: thy spirit is good; lead me into the land of uprightness.

"Quicken me, O LORD, for thy name's sake: for thy righteousness' sake bring my soul out of trouble. And of thy mercy cut off mine enemies, and destroy all them that afflict my soul: for I *am* thy servant. I ask this prayer in faith in your darling son, Jesus Christ name. Amen."

When she finished praying, a sense of peace covered Elise, and for the first time in a long time, she felt like it was over and everything was going to be all right. She looked around the room at her friends, smiled, then closed her eyes.

Sherrie Walker